The SOUL RETRIEVAL

I love you very much!
Cathy
April 2015

The SOUL RETRIEVAL

A Novel
By
Ann W. Jarvie

JazzComm Publishing

Copyright © 2015 by Ann W. Jarvie. All rights reserved.
www.annwjarvie.com

Cover design and illustrations by Maureen Pasley.

ISBN-13: 978-0692368206

For Paul, Dane and Luke

And for my mother

Chapter 1

July 3, 1959

Something in the air shifted when Joe Loco limped into the doctor's cottage. Maybe because the sun shot through the window just as he opened the door, and light was now spilling over the kitchen table like a radiant tablecloth. Or maybe it was because of the way Joe was dressed. Today, he wore a trendy sport coat, colorful striped shirt and baggy black pants—all over blue-suede moccasins. He had coaxed his black bangs into a soaring pompadour, higher than Henrietta had ever seen. Granted it was all the craze for fashionable young men that year. Everything Elvis— people just couldn't get enough of the hot young singer. But Joe wore his puffed-up hair with a shoulder-length braid on each side of his light-brown face.

"Henrietta, you remember Joe, right?" her husband said.

"Yes, Jeff, of course," she replied. *How could I possibly forget someone so … so strange?* she thought. "We met on your first mission here. How've you been, Joe?"

Joe shifted a full brown paper bag into his left arm. "Never been better, thanks for asking, Mrs. Clayborn. And you?" He reached for her hand.

Joe's baritone voice was exactly as Henrietta remembered it: surprisingly accent-free, though he occasionally sprinkled his speech with a few Apache words. His smile was as sweet as melted milk chocolate and, unlike most Apaches she'd met, his face held delicate features. Some might say he was downright pretty. He moved with a childlike enthusiasm despite a limp. His clothes were usually colorful and fashion-forward, but always with a native twist. He was an attractive oddball and a happy curiosity—Henrietta was glad to see him again.

But when their hands touched, his brow furrowed and his eyes narrowed.

"Wait. You're the same, but different, *ha'aa,* yes?" Joe said. His hand lingered on hers. He cocked his head to the left then right, studying Henrietta's eyes and the area around her perfectly coiffed blond hair.

"Well, um, I suppose," she said. She pulled her hand away and looked down. *Dear God, what's that nut looking at?* Henrietta thought.

Out of the corner of her eye, she peeked over at her husband, who'd thankfully returned to his seat at the table and was reading the newspaper.

"You're still off today, I presume?" Jeff asked, eyes on his paper. He either didn't hear Joe's question to Henrietta or had chosen to ignore it.

"*Ha'aa*, yes. I'm needed at the Sunrise Ceremonies most of the week," Joe said. "I hope that's still okay, Doc." He smiled, returning to his previous upbeat manner.

Henrietta let out the breath she was holding.

"Yes, of course," Jeff answered as he looked up. "So, what brings you by this morning?"

"Well, I had a meeting with the elders earlier today and wanted to see Altie before going to—" Joe was interrupted by a knock on the door. "Ah, here she is now."

Altie, Joe's petite wife, glided in like a graceful Apache ballerina. She wore a simple blue and green cotton dress with matching jacket, but also a stunning large turquoise-stone necklace. "*Yati' dahbidá'*, good morning," she said, speaking in the stilted, almost inflectionless way so common among Apache Indians. "The stars and sun are in agreeable positions for the ceremonies." Although she had learned English words and grammar perfectly—albeit a bit formally—at the Agency school on the reservation, Altie, like most Apaches, pronounced her "th" sounds with a "da" giving her speech a distinctive accent.

"Henrietta tells me you offered to take the kids to the Sunrise Ceremonies," Jeff said, after they all greeted her. "That's an incredible honor for them, Altie."

"*Ha'aa*, the honor is mine. I should get the little one ready," Altie said, but Henrietta knew it was meant as a question. Altie never seemed to ask anything in a direct way.

"Thanks, Altie," Henrietta said, "but if you don't mind, I'll keep him here until he wakes up from his morning nap." She was referring to Jefferson Junior, her eighteen-month-old son. "We'll join up with you and the girls down at the ceremonies in a little while." Unexpectedly, tears stung Henrietta's eyes, but she discreetly rubbed them with a handkerchief from her pocket.

When Henrietta looked up, Joe was staring at her while whispering something to Altie in Athabascan, their native Apache language. When his eyes turned away from hers and met Altie's, Henrietta sensed some invisible communication passing between them. Her stomach churned.

In the uncomfortable silence that followed, Henrietta walked out of the kitchen toward the staircase. "Girls," she called out, "Miss Altie's here; let's make it snappy."

"We'll be down in a minute, Mama," one of the twins yelled.

"Sorry for the wait, Altie," Henrietta said. She fanned her face, feeling a rush of heat on her neck and perspiration forming between her breasts despite the summer morning's cool breeze.

"On the way over, I picked up my costume for tonight's ceremonies," Joe said, turning to Jeff. "Do you mind if I try it on here?"

"Not at all," Jeff said, taking a sip of coffee. "There's a bathroom around that wall; help yourself."

Joe limped out as Henrietta and Altie chatted about the Sunrise festivities. After a few minutes, Henrietta paused.

"Whew, I don't know why I'm so hot this morning." She pulled her hair up off her shoulders before searching the refrigerator for ice tea. Shutting it as she straightened, she stopped abruptly, stunned by what she saw: Joe Loco was standing in the middle of their kitchen wearing nothing more than old work boots and what appeared to be a giant flannel diaper.

"Looks good, *ha'aa*?" Joe said with an impish grin.

For a moment, everyone was speechless.

Joe's skin was a shade lighter than most Indians living in Medichero. Henrietta thought of it as being more like the tawny color of sunbaked straw. On the skinny side, with that piled-up hair, and in the ridiculous diaper, Joe looked like he might have been an escapee from a mental institution for half-naked scarecrows, rather than a Medichero Apache Indian. He was also sockless and Henrietta saw for the first time why he limped: most of his left calf muscle was missing.

"That's your costume?" Henrietta said with eyes still wide. She had expected Joe to come out of the bathroom wearing the typical fringed buckskin and a headdress made of eagle feathers. She covered her mouth with her hands as she looked over at Jeff, who was snickering like a schoolboy and shaking his head.

"Not quite," Joe Loco said, donning a mask with the face and long ears of a donkey.

Jeff was laughing out loud now.

"Joe is dancing the part of the sacred *Libayé* this year," Altie said, as though that explained everything.

"I thought the Sunrise Ceremonies were a rite of passage for your tribe's teenage girls, not, um, incontinent donkeys," Henrietta said. She laughed, unable to resist being pulled into Joe's indigenous comedy.

"The *Libayé* teaches many lessons," Joe said. He removed his mask.

Jeff smiled and gave Henrietta a wink.

"The *Libayé* is a clown-like character who is supposed to look contrary to four beautiful and powerful Mountain Spirit dancers," Altie said. "They will perform together for the maidens and an audience at sunset tonight around a great bonfire."

"I see. Then why are you dressing so early?" Henrietta asked. She looked down at his heavy work boots. They were oversized and had no shoelaces; their tongues arched out grotesquely like some rotting, leathered form of aloe vera leaves.

"I wanted to make sure my diaper and boots fit well enough for this evening's dance now because I'll be tied up for most of the afternoon as one of the singers." He headed back toward the bathroom to change.

After he left, Frannie ran into the kitchen, breathless. "I'm here, Miss Altie!"

"Me, too," Annie seconded.

The nine-year-old twins with blond braids were dressed identically in blue dungarees, pink plaid blouses tied at the waist, and white sneakers. They sat next to their dad and started eating the egg biscuits Henrietta had laid out earlier.

Joe returned fully dressed, but he had replaced his sport coat with a white, fringed buckskin overshirt. His pompadour had been re-combed and pomaded into a noticeably higher crest.

"Altie, I forgot to ask, do you or Joe want anything to drink, or how about some breakfast?" Henrietta asked. She tried not to stare at Joe's big hair. "I've got coffee and plenty of eggs and bacon left. Have y'all ever had grits?"

"Sweet hero. If you feed me …" Joe said and struck the pose made famous by Elvis Presley. He began strumming an invisible guitar, bobbing his shoulders and singing a slightly altered version of a hit song: "I'll be your teddy bear, put a chain around my neck, and lead me anywhere … oh just let me eat … and I'll be your teddy bear."

The girls squealed and applauded.

"Thank you, thank you very much," Joe said, taking a dramatic bow.

Altie rolled her eyes. Jeff was laughing again.

"Okay, Joe, I get it. You'd like some breakfast. How about you, Altie?" Henrietta said, smiling.

"No, thank you. We ate earlier, but it is hard for Joe to say no to food. The girls and I can go now," Altie said. They were kissed and out the door just as the telephone rang.

"I'll get it; it's probably Dr. Belzer," Jeff said.

Henrietta watched her husband as he left the kitchen, and kept staring long after he had disappeared from the room. When she turned back to Joe, he was giving her that intense look once again.

"It's just as Bear foretold," the Apache said. He closed his eyes and moved his hands in small circles with palms out. "The fire's burning, but no one's home in your teepee."

"Excuse me?"

"You don't feel like yourself, you're feeling vacant and disconnected, like something's missing." Joe spoke as he opened his eyes.

She gaped at him in stunned silence before whispering: "How ... why would you say something like that?" Henrietta's heart thumped in her chest as she nervously glanced toward the living room. Jeff was still talking on the phone.

"Your soul speaks volumes through your eyes."

"You see something in my eyes?" And she rubbed them again with her handkerchief.

"I see what was there, what should be there, but is not now."

"Don't be silly. I'm fine. My eyes were just watering, that's all." She winced, knowing that it wasn't true, hating that she'd become such a liar.

"It's okay, I'm here to help," he said. He placed his folded hands on the table after sitting down.

His smile and disarming empathy surprised Henrietta, but she wasn't going to be moved by what seemed like a sweet and insightful gesture. Joe Loco was absolutely the last person in the world she'd choose to confide in.

"Thanks, but there's really nothing to help with. I'm fine." She was determined to maintain her fiction, though her stomach tightened and jumped as if trying to digest rocks. Mechanically, she started to reheat some cooked bacon in the fry pan, stirred the grits she'd kept warm and cracked open a few fresh eggs next to the bacon. "Your breakfast will be ready in a few minutes." She diverted her eyes to avoid his continued scrutiny but could not help stealing a look back at him. *What is it with that Indian? Doesn't he know it's rude to stare?* she thought.

Joe continued to look fixedly at her as he hummed and tapped an accompanying tune on the table. He quieted for a moment without shifting his gaze. "It's okay, I'm here to help," he repeated.

No! Henrietta didn't want to be charmed or disturbed into divulging any sordid details of her past. She had simply wanted to be friendly to this man, and only in a neighborly sort of way because he worked with Jeff at the hospital and was Altie's husband. *But, dadgummit, he is pushing all kinds of buttons!*

Still hearing Jeff talking on the phone, she exhaled dramatically and turned to face Joe. Before she could stop herself Henrietta blurted out in a strained whisper: "Okay, I don't know how you know it, but you're right. Something awful's happened to me since our first mission here. And now, I feel like I'm not all here. Something is missing. And I don't know what." *Oh dear God! What am I doing? What am I saying?* She blushed, feeling exposed and vulnerable by her sudden candor. She jerked her hands up and covered her mouth.

"Don't worry. It's obvious your soul has fragmented and is in need of repair," Joe said with a calm certainty, as if it was an everyday matter to be dealt with.

"What?" Henrietta put her hands down and stared into space, bewildered by his words. In the quietude, the sizzle of the frying eggs and bacon filled the room like a choir of rattlers. *My soul has what?* When she looked again at Joe, planning to demand exactly what he meant, his eyes were closed, and he was whispering and holding his palms up as though in prayer.

So she placed the cooked food on a plate, poured a glass of milk and put both down in front of him. He opened his eyes and smiled up at her.

"That's one of the strangest things I've ever heard—a soul fragmenting," she said. "How would something like that even be possible?"

"It can happen when we believe or experience something bad we don't want to face." He took a bite of eggs and grits, closing his eyes again to savor the combination. "Oh, this is yum-yum," he said.

When he looked up, it was Henrietta who was staring.

"The good news is that lost soul fragments can be recovered and healed. It's not hard, if you know how, if you know the secret," Joe said.

"Are you saying you know how to do that? That you know the secret?"

"The Great Spirit works hitherto and I work."

She crossed her arms. "So what are you, some kind of soul repairman?"

"Ho, ha!" He laughed out loud. "In truth, I'm a practitioner of the Great Spirit's bear medicine, which in your case, would start with a ritual called the soul retrieval. It's something that could really help you." Joe took a sip of milk while nodding to himself.

"Bear medicine? Soul retrieval? I was raised in a church where just saying that kind of stuff could get you tarred and feathered." Henrietta tried to say it like a devil's advocate and a joke, but she wasn't kidding.

"I wasn't aware your people use feathers in rituals," Joe responded with no overt sarcasm, wiping his mouth with a napkin.

"Ha! That's not exactly it." She gave a false laugh, shaking her head. "I'm from a place where saying or even thinking things like that is considered blasphemous and will get you into a lot of trouble with Baptist ministers. Do you know what I'm saying?"

"Apaches consider asking questions to be so rude, it's like a sacrilege," he said, his voice uncharacteristically stern.

"Oh!" Henrietta blushed again as she realized she was still ignorant of many of the life-ways and traditions governing Medichero Apache Indians. "I'm sorry, I didn't know."

"Please, there's no need to apologize. I was just trying to make a point: sometimes it makes sense to discard old rules that no longer serve. I actually believe asking questions is a great way to learn and grow. Do some of our elders consider me a heretic for thinking that?" He shrugged his shoulders. "Probably."

"And that doesn't bother you?" She'd never met someone so audacious or unconcerned about what others thought. Especially about what religious leaders thought.

"Religious dogma that's become too rigid is like a hound dog with rigor mortis—not good for much." He squeezed his nose between his fingers. "Smells bad, too."

It didn't exactly answer her question. Still she couldn't help but smile.

"We must not fear questioning anything, even outdated rules of etiquette or what some consider forbidden," the Apache continued. "We must not let dead dogs dictate our paths. We must follow the Great Spirit's Truth wherever it may lead us."

For several seconds, Henrietta stared out of the window at nothing, trying to assimilate all that he'd said, wondering if she should just dismiss it as nonsense. But she had to admit, given the horrible things she'd experienced, there was something undeniably intriguing, comforting and perhaps even tempting about his concept of retrieving and healing lost soul fragments. She realized she wanted to know more. *Could something like the soul retrieval really be possible? And could it help me?* Henrietta shook her head to clear it of this foolishness.

"Please keep eating before it gets cold," she said, turning back to face him. It was all she could think of to say.

After finishing, Joe tidied up where he'd eaten, limped over to the sink with his dishes and rinsed them off. "That was a delightful breakfast—many thanks," he said, bowing. "And those grits, they were terrific."

"I'm glad you liked them. I brought them with us, all the way from South Carolina."

"Please allow me to return the favor," he said.

"Oh, you want to cook something for me?"

He shook his head, grinning. "If you want to experience the soul retrieval and more, please come to our teepee tomorrow; it's right behind our house. At about noon would be good; my singing's not required at the ceremonies then."

Me? Take part in a soul retrieval? Her stomach fluttered, and Henrietta wasn't sure if that meant the idea was appealing or if it just plain scared her.

"Um, thanks …" she started. But the thought of letting a crazy Indian tinker around in her soul gave her more than pause. "I'll have to think about your offer."

"Altie can tell you more about it," Joe said. "And, because we've already agreed, she won't mind if you ask her any rude questions about it." He smiled as he picked up the paper bag that contained his diaper costume, sport coat, work boots and, apparently, some hair supplies.

"What do you mean, you've already agreed?" she asked, once again taken aback.

Joe had no time to respond since Jeff returned and changed the subject. "Sorry, but Dr. Belzer wanted to fill me in on Billy Santana's condition."

"You were on the phone quite a while. Is everything okay?" Henrietta frowned, knowing that this favored child within the tribe had been in the hospital for about a week and his condition was critical, as he was among those affected by the influenza epidemic that had recently swept through the reservation.

"Let's just say the boy's stable for now," Jeff said. He glanced at Joe with a frown, as if to belie his statement.

"I can go with you now and help," Joe offered.

Jeff held up his palms. "You've got the ceremonies today, and I think we can handle it."

"If you change your mind or if the situation changes, you know where I'll be," Joe said before turning back to Henrietta. "Again, thank you for a most delicious breakfast. *Ka-dish-day*, farewell, for now."

"Ka-dish-day," Henrietta and Jeff said at the same time as Joe limped out the door.

Her husband looked down at his watch. "I'm relieving Dr. Belzer in about forty-five minutes. Why don't we go into the living room until I have to go?" He walked over and nibbled on her neck. His voice was both warm and animated as he added, "I've so much to tell you about my research."

"Um," she started. "There's something I need to tell you, too." *Maybe I can get it out this time.* She pushed back the wilting blond curls falling over her stinging eyes; her hands trembled.

"Well first, how about a little concerto? Just for you, Peaches," he said, calling her his favorite pet name. He pulled her toward the living room piano.

Chapter 2

Henrietta shifted restlessly in her seat on the living room sofa as she tried to give her undivided attention to Jeff as he played Chopin's *Nocturnes No. 9.* She usually loved listening to him as much as he enjoyed playing for her; his fingers on the keys were fine instruments that created soothing sounds, something that could and often had eased her mind.

After finishing the second nocturne, he looked up at her. "You know that I've been researching the high incidence of spontaneous healings here, right?" Jeff was both a lead physician and medical researcher at the Medichero Indian Hospital. He reached for a pack of cigarettes from the pocket of his short-sleeved white shirt.

"Uh-huh," Henrietta said. She barely heard what he said. *How am I going to get into it? How am I going to tell him?* She had asked herself these questions at least a million times. She picked up a pen and notebook from the coffee table, trying to keep her hands busy.

Jeff smoked in silence a moment before continuing. "There's more to it than even I imagined."

"More to what?" she asked. She absently doodled on the page without looking up. *How am I going to tell him?*

Jeff blew smoke. "The spontaneous healings that I'm so interested in ... the medicine men here seem to be doing something *real* to affect the recoveries."

Now he had her attention. "They are?" She looked at him. "Like what?"

Instead of answering, Jeff got up and turned toward the bay windows that cradled the piano in a small alcove off the living room. His silhouette against the bright morning light was a man-shaped eclipse, his muscled edges luminous and blurred by the smoldering tobacco. It gave him an unworldly appearance, and Henrietta was reminded about how often she felt like an outsider here, and even back home.

"Henrietta, would you mind if we stayed here a while longer this time?" Jeff stepped out of the blinding light. He had a grin on his face, but nervously rubbed his fingers through his light-brown hair.

"How much time are we talking about?" His first medical mission in Medichero five years ago had lasted six months; the second mission two years ago was cut short after only two weeks.

"I could really use another year, at least. Maybe two."

"But we agreed to six months at a time, and your father …" Henrietta's heart began racing and her head throbbed.

"Listen, there's been an increase in spontaneous remissions since the last time we were here, and this gives me an incredible opportunity. For research purposes, these live case studies are like gifts from heaven. But I won't feel right about staying longer and pursuing them unless you're okay with it." He extinguished his cigarette, sat down next to her and gently rubbed the small of her back. "Please tell me you're with me on this."

Here, there. Would it really matter? She didn't want to think about the consequences of either choice. "Why do you think you're seeing more healings now than before?"

"Truthfully? I think it's because Medichero's most extraordinary medicine man has joined the hospital staff. And he's around more now than before." Jeff paused, then added: "They say he's gifted." His eyes moved to meet hers, making a silent understated exclamation.

"And who would that be?" Henrietta asked, but had a sick feeling that she already knew what he was going to say.

"Bears Repeating."

"Jeff," she said. She exhaled and leaned back away from her husband. "You don't mean that crazy Indian who just made a spectacle in our kitchen? You can't be serious. Joe Loco is your gifted healer?" She had heard many times before that Joe's native name was Bears Repeating. She also knew that he worked at the hospital with Jeff as some sort of aide, but at the moment, couldn't remember exactly how Jeff had described his function.

"Yep," Jeff said. He smiled.

"Jeff, you know I love you. And I love Altie. But I have to be honest. That guy's not exactly credible. He says the most outlandish things. He talks about dead dogs and wounded souls that have fragmented. And he's funny even when he's not trying to be. He's got some kind of Elvis fetish, I think. He wears blue-suede moccasins and a pompadour, for heaven's sakes."

"Joe's more than he appears," Jeff said. He stood and walked back to the piano.

"I've also seen him sitting like a Buddhist on the hill over there for hours," she said, pointing out the window. "And wearing Catholic rosary beads like a necklace."

Jeff's smile broadened, but he wasn't laughing. "Since Joe started working at the hospital, there have been comprehensive healings of patients that I considered beyond hope."

"You're kidding." *Could this really be true? Could this Joe Loco and his strange bear medicine actually help me?*

"Despite, let's say, a few idiosyncrasies, all of the medicine men, including the elders, respect him and consider him a great healer ... and so do I."

"What's different about him? No, scratch that. It's obvious there's something different about him," she said. "What I meant to ask was this: What exactly is Joe doing to influence these miraculous healings?" It surprised her that her old writer's curiosity resurfaced; it had lain dormant far too long. She really wanted to know what Joe was doing.

"It won't make sense unless you understand the basis for their medicine, which is also their religion."

"So explain it."

Jeff grinned. "I'm not sure I can, without sounding like a raving heretic." He lit another cigarette.

"Just give it a shot," she said. "I promise not to tell Father O'Reilly." Father O'Reilly was a Roman Catholic priest at St. Paul's Mission, the only church on the reservation. "Or anyone back home," she added in a whisper.

"Well, okay. Let's see." Jeff paused as if considering how to begin his answer. He pushed the piano keys softly, playing a few light chords. As government housing went on Indian reservations, pianos were not standard issue. So Jeff and Henrietta had been surprised to find one already there, as well as the unexpected Victorian-style doctor's cottage, which had been built in the early 1900s. They considered the large furnished house and the piano good omens for the missions in Medichero.

"Joe says it's got something to do with tapping into this … this thing the Medichero call…" Jeff paused before speaking slowly and with reverence, *"Bik'ehgo'ihi'dań binádidzołi."*

"Bick ah … what?"

"Bik'ehgo'ihi'dań binádidzołi. It's Apache that translates into something like God's breath. The Medichero describe it as a kind of loving and creative presence that's in and around everything, including us, nature and even inanimate objects. But sometimes they just call it all the Great Mystery."

"That's certainly easier to pronounce." Henrietta smiled and leaned forward.

"My colleagues would call it animism. No, sorry, they'd say it was radical nonsense and treat me like the hemorrhoids of the medical community," Jeff said.

"What does that mean?"

"A pain in the ass that's fairly easy to cut out."

She smiled. "I know what hemorrhoids are, silly. I meant what does animism mean?"

"Of course." He grinned. "Animism is the belief that animals and objects, like rocks and such, as well as natural phenomena, like wind, fire and water, all possess a certain level of consciousness with the ability to communicate. Of course, there's more to it, and I'm just starting to understand. But I'm trying."

She looked at her husband and frowned. "Geez, Jeff, I'm surprised you're taking their beliefs so seriously. You've always been so … so science-oriented. And besides that, you were raised a Baptist!"

"Yeah, I know," he said and smiled. "But right now, I'm just trying to understand what *they* believe they're doing to make these healings happen. And don't forget I've actually witnessed a few things I can't yet explain with medical science. Then there's the lab. I'm really excited about what I'm starting to see there."

"Like what?"

"I've been running tests with cells and bacteria in petri dishes while Joe and some of the other medicine men are in ritual meditation. And both the cells and bacteria are somehow being positively affected."

"I find it incredible that the medicine men are actually going along with your experiments."

He nodded. "It turns out that some of the younger ones are as curious about the test results as I am. I can hardly wait to hook them up to my new EEG."

Henrietta looked hard into her husband's blue eyes and realized there would be no chance of changing his mind. But she still feared getting further involved in what was definitely forbidden in their southern Christian world. And she worried about Jeff's daring to venture outside the lines and protocols of conventional medicine.

"You won't get into trouble for poking your nose in the Indians' medicine, will you?" she asked. "Remember the Department of the Interior's edict not to interfere with or encourage their spirit medicine, or whatever they call it."

"Nah. I don't think the government guys will find out, and I'm certainly not going to tell them right now." He gestured with his hand, causing ashes to fall to the carpet.

"Well, I wouldn't want you stirring up trouble with your employer, just when we've finally found a little peace ourselves." Henrietta pursed her lips, unable to ignore the ashes.

"I'm not worried, really," he said, putting the cigarette in an ashtray on the piano. "Besides, Ray Santana and his brothers are probably more concerned about my interest in their spirit medicine than the government guys would be."

"Is that supposed to make me feel better?"

"Oh, sorry, Peaches, I shouldn't have brought that up."

"Please tell me they're not dangerous?"

"I know Ray and particularly his brother Victor look a little intimidating, and they've startled me a time or two, showing up unexpectedly in dark corners or spying on me through my office window since we arrived on this mission. But I've gotten used to them being around—they seem pretty harmless." He shrugged his shoulders.

"Why are they watching you like that?"

"I'm not supposed to know this. But apparently they've recently been charged by the Medichero elders to safeguard their so-called old ways from, let's say, outsiders like us. But I really believe their bark is worse than their bite." He lit another cigarette, though the other still burned in the ashtray.

"Well, I've learned it's not smart to go around teasing dogs, especially ones that look like pit bulls," Henrietta said. She stood and put her hands on her hips.

"I'm not teasing dogs or Indians who might resemble pit bulls." Jeff chuckled. "Joe and I can handle the Santanas."

"Oh, right. That Joe's a really scary guy. What is he, about 145 pounds?"

"Would it make you feel better about Joe if I told you that he's well educated? And has an extensive home library?"

"Maybe. But only if he can throw books at those brothers to defend you."

"Very funny. But I bet you'd be surprised to learn that Joe has an undergraduate degree in psychology."

"You win the bet. I couldn't be more surprised."

"Well, get this: he also has a medical degree!"

"Okay, now I know you're just pulling my leg!"

"No, I'm dead serious," Jeff said.

"Holy cow, Jeff!"

"Joe's higher education does give him added credibility, even though he doesn't really use it in any official way. He hasn't filed for a residency program yet, even though I've told him many times I'm happy to supervise him," Jeff said. "He simply won't answer directly when I ask him about it. Maybe he's just not ready. But, in any event, what's important to remember is that he's smart and well respected within the tribe as a true healer, which means if he's participating in my research, everything's copacetic. So you don't have to worry about Ray Santana and his brothers."

"I'll try not to," Henrietta said. She sat next to him on the piano bench. "I just don't want you to cause a problem here. Okay?" She leaned her head on his shoulder.

"I won't, I promise. But honestly, I care more about not causing a problem for you." He caressed the back of her neck.

"Oh, Jeff." She sighed and kissed him tenderly on the lips, thinking about how much she loved him, despite everything that had happened to her and the secret she believed she had to hide from him.

"But seriously, Henrietta, you know me." He turned and took her in his arms. "If I didn't believe this spirit medicine had the potential to help modern medicine save lives, or if I thought it was too great a risk, I wouldn't be here and I wouldn't want you and the kids here either."

She nodded. "I know."

"But this research ... it's become almost like a sacred thing to me," he whispered. He placed Henrietta's right hand over his heart. "I've got to find out more about what they're doing that heals people. And I think I will."

"I understand. But I'm not sure what you want me to say."

"I just need you to say that you're on board with my work, even though there might be some slight opposition to it. I'd love to see you return to your writing and be happy with me, right here, or wherever we might choose to live for the rest of our lives."

Henrietta's eyes began to water. "Oh, Jeff. You know I'm happy to be with you, no matter what you're doing or where we are. And I've just hit a dry spell with my writing, that's all. Of course that happens to even the best of writers. But it doesn't mean I can't be excited about your work. And as strange as it all sounds, I think your research is noble. Besides, I don't want to go back to South Carolina right now, anyway." Her voice cracked and a tear ran down her cheek.

"Hey now, let's not get upset again." He pushed back her hair, sticky from the moisture on her face. "Your parents are going to be fine in Georgia."

It wasn't why she was crying. But, out of habit, she let him think that it was.

"Jeff, there's something I've been needing to tell you." Henrietta's voice turned to a whisper at the same time the grandfather clock in the foyer began to chime.

"Oh no, the time," Jeff interrupted. "I was so caught up in talking about Joe and my research, I completely forgot about relieving Dr. Belzer. Can it wait until tonight? I should run."

They both got up and walked quickly toward the kitchen, Jeff's forgotten cigarette ashes trailing behind him.

"I guess so," she said.

"Why don't you try getting back to your writing today? Love you," he said, not waiting for an answer. He pecked her on the cheek after grabbing his navy cardigan and brown medicine bag off the top of the washstand, then headed out the door.

She stood there alone, arms by her sides, feeling defeated again.

Chapter 3

Henrietta padded back to the living room, sat at her writing desk and stared at her Smith-Corona typewriter. She rolled in a fresh sheet of white paper and stared some more. Seconds, perhaps minutes, passed. Nothing. Exasperated, she finally typed: *Where have my words gone?*

But as soon as she typed, she answered herself: she had buried her words, her voice, along with her unspeakable secrets. In that same second, the horror of a hideous past came pressing back on her, scorching her mind like a red-hot iron on soft tissue.

As she remembered, tears poured down her face. Her arms had been pinned down, and she had been seized by a fear so great, she couldn't move anyway. She had tried to scream, but nothing came out. She remembered the ripping sensation. How the air had been sucked from her lungs. And the blackness.

No, stop! She coughed, straining to breathe. She shook her head, determined to force the memories back down into the subterranean cage of her mind, where they could be locked away once again from herself and the world.

She reached for the typewriter keys, desperate to return to something solid, something she loved, to keep her mind in the present. She typed: *My writing.* She paused, fingers in place, ready to continue. But as before, she couldn't think of anything else to write.

With a heavy sigh, she began straightening a small stack of papers containing an incomplete short story she'd titled *Peach People.* It was supposed to be the last in a collection of short dramas about the eccentric inhabitants of a southern peach plantation. For the last two years, she had worked on this anthology, trying to embed as much commercial potential into it as her first set of successfully published short stories, *Fields of Glories.* She had wanted to finish *Peach People* before moving on to something new. But the once-treasured tales inspired by her childhood home, located in the middle of a peach orchard, no longer mattered. As much as she tried, and even now, she couldn't muster the energy needed to get back to writing them.

Seeking something lighter, she let her thoughts wander back to Joe's earlier antics, which reminded her of something curious he had said, even for him. *Why had he and Altie made a pre-arranged agreement about me asking so-called rude questions? And how would they have known that such a pact would even be necessary?* Henrietta intended to find out. Until then, she wanted to just ponder what he had described as a fragmented soul.

She put her head in her hands, knowing something about the subject was pulling on her and drawing her in. What was it? And was she willing or brave enough to let an Indian poke around in her soul to find out?

She looked up and began fingering the typewriter keys again when a new writing idea hit her. *Of course!* Granted it would be a much different topic to address in her work, but that was just as well. This new storyline would require firsthand research. But she had plenty of spare time. It would be challenging, taking her out of her areas of provincial comfort. There was no question about that. Still it was accessible and maybe even had some potential. Well, maybe it didn't have potential in commercial literature, but she intended to use the subject privately anyway as a means of exploring and writing about something that was fascinating to her on a personal level, and as an exercise to help her break through her writer's block. But it was also a story of intrigue, tribal and mysterious. And, she thought playfully, she would be like an investigative reporter researching it.

Yes, that's it! Her new perspective and now racing thoughts provided an unexpected sense of courage and inspiration. She yanked out the paper from her typewriter, rolled in a clean sheet and typed three words at the top of the page: *The Soul Retrieval.* There. Her mind was set. Her heart was beating rapidly and she realized she was smiling.

Little Jeffie's cries cut into her thoughts. But she bounced up, feeling that nothing could dampen her renewed sense of confidence and direction. After changing his diaper, she brought her son into the kitchen, and placed him into the high chair.

"I thought we could go to the Sunrise celebrations in a little while," she said, giving him a bowl of eggs and grits. "Would you like that?"

"Yeah, Mama!" He clapped his hands. "Watch Roo Roo first."

While little Jeffie made a mess of breakfast, Henrietta pulled out the stroller from a closet and packed a diaper bag. Finished, she washed his face and hands with a clean damp dishrag. He promptly crawled out of his high chair and ran into the living room, turned on the TV and began watching *Captain Kangaroo*. Meanwhile, Henrietta was humming a happy tune as she started another load of wash and went out to the side yard to hang up some towels and diapers.

It was late afternoon by the time she and Jeffie set out to join Altie and the girls on the ceremonial mesa. She held the stroller tightly as they descended the steep incline on the cinnamon-colored path, slowly rolling and bumping along its rocky surface. Beyond the edges of the path was toughened vegetation that Mother Earth had wisely equipped with tiny arrows and spears: Spanish needle, prickly pear and hedgehog cactus were a few of those scattered among the scraggy tall grasses. A line of giant soaptree yucca plants stood ominously silent like tall armies with razor-sharp green swords. But Henrietta held no fear of her new environment as she traversed this dirt path alone. Over the course of their two mission trips, she had become a respectful observer in tune with the peaceful seasons and amiable rhythms of a once-warring Apache people. An inherent beauty and measured poetry permeated the spiritual clans who now lived among these knobby foothills, practiced sacred rituals and celebrated the fruitful cycles of girls blossoming into young women.

At the ceremonial grounds, she was met with a sweet confluence of cotton candy and fry bread. She navigated the stroller through the crowds, feeling a little conspicuous as her passing was given subtle but noticeable acknowledgement.

Henrietta spotted Altie and the girls sitting in the lower seats of the grandstands overlooking a ceremonial arena shaped like a half-acre horseshoe. On the open side, a gigantic white teepee stood nearly twenty feet tall. "Hey, y'all," she said, rolling up. She noticed that her voice sounded much lighter than before.

"Mama! The maidens blessed us with pollen, and Mr. Joe is one of the medicine men singing to them," Annie said. Standing up, she pointed toward the large teepee. Annie's and Frannie's foreheads were rubbed with yellow pollen, a sacred substance to the Medichero.

"How lovely!" Henrietta looked over at Joe singing to the Apache debutantes, who had been dancing or moving around in the arena nearly nonstop for fifteen hours. "They look tired, but what an interesting experience to be able to see," Henrietta said.

"Look at their costumes and jewelry," Annie added. "They're so beautiful." The Medichero maidens wore buckskin skirts and overblouses, heavily fringed and elaborately beaded. Some of the costumes were the traditional ocher color, while others were dyed white.

"Would you like to make some beaded jewelry, like theirs?" Henrietta asked her daughters.

"Oh, Mama, yes!" Both nodded their heads.

"I noticed some craft booths on the way over. Why don't we go visit them after the dancing?"

"The maidens will be moving inside the Holy Lodge soon," Altie said. They watched as Joe and seven other singing medicine men led the maidens toward the large ceremonial teepee, where they would continue their sacred rites inside and hopefully rest.

"Why doesn't Joe wear a full traditional costume like the other medicine men?" Henrietta asked. Before delving into her new writing idea, she figured she'd better first learn as much as she could about Bears Repeating.

"He likes to say we are more than the costumes and traditions we wear."

"Hmm." Henrietta was beginning to realize that many of Joe's statements were often messages hidden in metaphor.

"Joe considers himself a Quero Apache, Tlish Diyan medicine man, Catholic, Buddhist and more," Altie continued. "He is also half white."

Henrietta shook her head. "Well, bless his heart. Altie, I'd really like to know how all of that came about."

Altie nodded, and in her usual slow, stilted tone explained that Joe's mother, Bird, was a descendent of a long line of great Medichero Indian medicine men and women. Henrietta learned that Joe's biological father was a photographer passing through on an ornithological assignment for *National Geographic,* but apparently, found the exotic Bird Mancito more interesting. Although the unknown photographer spent a couple of months with Bird, he took off and never returned after she became pregnant. Bird was left with a half-breed baby, Joe. But she loved and nurtured him, and like most of their tribesmen, raised him as a Catholic at the reservation's St. Paul's Mission Church. When Joe was eleven, Bird married Sam Loco, a full-blooded Mescalero Apache, who adopted Joe and treated him like his own son.

"Bird is also more than a Catholic," Altie said. Then she paused, and Henrietta thought maybe Altie was embarrassed about having told too much of Joe's illegitimate birth. But she continued anyway, saying that Bird decided to teach Joe her own brand of spirit medicine, the Tlish Diyan philosophies of her Quero Apache ancestors. Later, because of Joe's obviously high intelligence and her practical nature, Bird encouraged her son to go to the white man's schools and then on to medical school where he also had an opportunity to explore other cultures and religions.

"Doesn't his, um, combining of religions and philosophies pose a problem here? Isn't his approach a bit confusing for the people here?" Henrietta wanted to ask a million questions, but remembered Apache etiquette. "My questions ... I don't mean to be rude." She covered her mouth with her hand.

Altie shrugged. "It is okay."

"It's just that Joe's such a fascinating man," Henrietta said honestly.

"I have found this to be true also," Altie said. Her face remained as expressionless as her voice.

"Mama, I'm hungry," Frannie said, pulling on Henrietta's sleeve.

"Can we get something to eat at the concessions?" Annie asked.

"Sure, let's go on our way to the craft booths," Henrietta said. "I love their tamales."

It was starting to get dark by the time they returned to the stands still full of tamales, piñon nuts and fry bread. By then, the girls were wearing colorful beaded necklaces they'd made, and Indian spectators were moving into the grandstands in faithful migrations.

"The Dance of the Mountain Spirits will begin soon. Let us get a seat," Altie said.

A great bonfire, probably eight-foot tall and just about as wide blazed in the middle of the earthen stage. Henrietta and the girls sat awestruck in quiet anticipation. Jeffie had fallen asleep in his stroller. Altie covered him with a blanket against the cool night air. She also pulled out four wool shawls from her backpack, handing one to each of them before putting the fourth over her shoulders.

Once the grandstands were filled with spectators, Henrietta's heartbeat accelerated as four colorfully garbed, athletic-looking Mountain Spirit performers entered from out of the shadows cast by the Holy Lodge teepee. They sang and danced, but not always in unison. They wore traditional ocher-colored buckskin kilts, sashes and mid-calf moccasins, all vibrantly beaded and encrusted with tiny cone-shaped tins that jingled as they moved. Unlike the feathered headdresses of powwow dancers, the Mountain Spirits wore fan-shaped head coverings that looked like tall wood planks tethered vertically. Black hoods made the four men faceless, unearthly and somewhat frightening. Their bare torsos were brush-painted with celestial symbols, while their muscular biceps were draped with red streamers and eagle feathers. At the end of each dancer's waist-sash hung a tin bell the size of a large apple, providing added rhythm to their singing and dancing calisthenics.

Behind the fourth Mountain Spirit dancer, a klutzy Joe Loco performed brilliantly his role of the sacred *Libayé*, said to be a living paradox, displaying implied power through weak and awkward movements. His purpose was to highlight the vivid eminence and divine imagery of the Mountain Spirit dancers by providing a necessary contrast. As he raised his knees and jerked his booted feet around in exaggerated circles, Joe intentionally moved out of step with the others.

But in the finale, all performed in synchronized choreography as the leader struck his thighs with sticks to establish order and set a dancing pace. For an encore, they ran all at once toward the great bonfire, hooting like deranged owls. Although she wasn't quite sure what it all meant, Henrietta knew they had just witnessed something sacred and secret.

After they were on the steep path home, Henrietta asked in a low, respectful voice about Joe's injury.

"He considers it the greatest blessing of his life," Altie said.

"You and Joe are perfect for one another. You both like to speak in riddles."

Altie offered a rare smile. "Joe was not always a gifted medicine man." She continued to explain that at age eighteen, Joe was attacked by a grizzly she-bear attending her cubs. She bit off part of Joe's rear end and

most of his left calf muscle. Afterward, she took her cubs
away, leaving Joe bleeding profusely and near death.

"Well, he obviously didn't die," Henrietta said.

"*Ha'aa*, but he did."

"Come on, Altie."

After Joe's physical body expired, he traveled to
what Altie described as the land of Spirit, where he met
some of his ancestors and talked with a number of
spiritual beings he would later call Ascended Masters.
They told Joe that it wasn't his time to leave this life yet
and he would be sent back. But while in Spirit, he
learned about his life's purpose and mission. If he was
willing, Joe would spend the rest of this life seeking out
the Great Spirit's true medicines as well as the universal
principles in all religions, including his own. He would
bear witness to the Great Spirit's truth and repeat
ancient healing secrets. And in the process, he'd be able
to help the sick and heal the soul-wounded. Joe agreed
to the plan wholeheartedly and was returned, carrying
healing gifts and spiritual knowledge he did not possess
before the bear incident. After he regained
consciousness, Joe dressed his wounds with bandages
that he made from his torn clothing. He used a pine
branch as a crutch to get home, where his mother, Bird,
nursed him back to health. Bears Repeating was his
native name from that point on.

"Wow, that's an amazing story," Henrietta said
with a new and genuine appreciation for Joe Loco. She
was beginning to think that maybe this man would be

able to help her. After a few minutes, she turned toward her friend. "Altie, would you mind if I asked you about the soul retrieval?"

Chapter 4

Earlier that day, Jeff had been in the hospital clinic, giving Rosa Thundercloud a final follow-up pelvic examination.

"You may feel a pinch or two, Rosa," Jeff said. He was hunched between her splayed legs, which were partially covered with a white sheet. Her bare feet were in metal stirrups. Taking an endometrial biopsy, he used a long and slender straw-like metal instrument to break off tiny pieces of cell tissue from her uterine and cervical walls and rub the specimens onto glass slides. Finishing, he rolled back on a wheeled stool and stood up, covering her again with the sheet. "Well, Rosa, I believe you were right." Jeff was smiling and shaking his head back and forth.

Rosa's lips held a sly grin as she raised her eyebrows. *"Ha'aa!"*

"Your uterus and cervix look perfectly healthy," Jeff said. "You can get up now."

"I told you, Dr. Clayborn," she said. She clutched the large cover sheet around her hospital gown and jumped off the examining table. Rosa was a compact, muscular and middle-aged Chiricahua Apache with large breasts, lustrous brown eyes and a teased mane of bronze-streaked black hair. "Told you, told you," she said, singing it. She started to skip and spin around. She looked like a little dancing Pekingese in a toga.

"You certainly did, Rosa," Jeff said. He chuckled. "Just to be sure, though, like before, I took some tissue samples to look at under the microscope. But I can already tell that everything will look positively normal there, too."

"Told you, told you," she repeated, obviously taking great delight in his incorrect and abysmal assessment of her once-cancerous condition. "I have more to do here in this life. You believe it now, too."

"Well, I couldn't be any happier about being wrong," Jeff said. He smiled and shook his head. "Quite honestly, when you walked into this clinic two years ago, I considered your prognosis rather grim, actually irreversible. Most women in your situation would've had their uterus, ovaries and fallopian tubes removed by now. They might've even died from it. But look at you: I'd say your uterine cancer is in complete remission." He paused, then added, "From a medical science perspective, your healing is ... well, it's quite inexplicable."

Rosa grinned and put her hand on her hip. "Doc, it's just like Joe said: 'the Great Spirit is the medical science that healed me.' I was hoping you'd caught onto that by now." She winked at him.

Jeff smiled. As Henrietta had noted, he had always considered himself a rational, science-oriented physician. But here he was agreeing with Rosa Thundercloud that the Great Spirit had healed her without surgery, pharmaceuticals or any of the white man's science, sending her into spontaneous remission.

Hearing the drumbeats and ritual singing from the ceremonial grounds below, they both turned toward the open windows.

"I'm free to go to the ceremonies, then," Rosa said. Her voice was as bouncy and fragrant as her untamed hair that smelled like the plumes of a thousand red rose hips. "You know, I only agreed to come in today for a follow-up because you've just arrived back into town. And I like you, Dr. Clayborn." She winked at him again.

"Thank you, Rosa. I like you, too. And let's just say I owe you one. By all means, go ahead and dance around with the Mountain Spirits, all you like. I'll be in the lab if you need me." He carried her biopsied specimens with him as he walked toward the door, leaving her to get dressed. "Oh, and have fun."

"You know I will," she said.

Jeff was still grinning when he walked into the hospital's laboratory and toward his desk. Aside from his family's peach orchards, the lab was his favorite place to be in the world. He loved how clean glass beakers, test tubes and assorted hand-labeled bottles glistened in the sunlight like fine crystal. They covered almost every available surface, including a center table and a row of cabinets that lined two walls. A white lab refrigerator as well as Jeff's prized mint-green centrifuge, the size of a good washing machine, sat against one wall. He used it for separating blood and colloidal particles in liquids. Two desks occupied the opposite wall next to a cabinet that included a stainless steel sink. A round table with four chairs for small conferences sat in front of the room's only set of windows. And next to the conference area was the rolling table that held Jeff's newest and most treasured research tool: an electroencephalograph, which he had purchased with his grant funds. He planned to use the EEG to detect and record changes in the brain waves of agreeable medicine men in meditation. Looking at it now, with all its beautiful electrodes, amplifiers and controls, his heart almost skipped a beat. He could hardly wait to use his EEG on some of the younger medicine men coming into the lab tomorrow.

But for now, Jeff again focused on using his optical microscope standing on a desk also cluttered with stacks of research papers and piles of file folders. He pushed them out of the way before adjusting the magnification knob of the microscope to examine Rosa's biopsied tissues. He was smiling again when he opened a large lab notebook, turned to Rosa's case and sketched out the normal-shaped cells he saw on the slides today next to the drawings of irregular-shaped diseased cells he'd taken from Rosa two years ago. He scribbled notes under both sets of illustrations and finally dated today's entries, substantiating the healing impact of Bears Repeating's improbable but definite cure.

He sat back and placed his right hand over his heart. *What an incredible day!* For Jeff, it wasn't just a pivotal moment. It was more than that. It was a validation that what he was doing was right and he was exactly where he was supposed to be. This was the third time he had personally witnessed and scientifically verified the result of what appeared to be a miracle healing of a terminal case. Awestruck and mystified, he had to know more about the how and why.

But he worried about what to do with such incredible results. Rosa's landmark case, the comprehensive healing of uterine cancer, should attract the attention and sponsorship of everyone in the medical community. But Jeff was a realist; he knew it would not. Even if he was able to compile the additional evidence needed through experimental study and an iterative process involving protocols for replication, he understood that this work, if published, would inevitably be subjected to huge doses of professional denunciation. The unorthodox methodology involved and the mystical language required to describe it would repulse and repel the scientific community as surely as if he'd presented a paper on the efficacy of voodoo.

Despite all that, it was the challenge as well as the deep mystery of these healings that ignited every research cell in his body, making him all the more determined to construct new and perhaps undreamed-of experiments and classifications to describe what had happened. He was plowing ahead because he had opened his mind to the possibility that spirit medicine was indeed a true science, even though he had not admitted it to Rosa. It was simply a case of not yet knowing how to prove it.

Nevertheless, he would begin by using the standard procedures that would be applied to any area of scientific research. This meant investigating the phenomena under a variety of criteria, controls and measures. But it could be that this *spirit science,* as he was now beginning to think of it, was beyond standard scientific approaches. It might instead be governed by an unknown set of higher natural laws, in need of his discovery, requiring new ways of proving it, using a new set of terms.

As he paused to let these random thoughts incubate in his mind, Jeff thought about how remarkable his research opportunity was, how profound his witness to the healings of Rosa and others was, and how utterly wrong his father had been to oppose his work. He remembered one of their early conversations about it.

"Did you just say you want to work on a goddamn Indian reservation, in goddamn New

Mexico?" His father, who was known as Dr. Colonel, had shouted this at him as they stood in the library of their massive home in Greenfield, South Carolina. "What in the hell is wrong with you? You must've lost your goddamn mind!" As he yelled, Dr. Colonel's face turned bloodred and his tightened fists revealed the knuckled whites of metacarpal bones under thin skin.

"Father, please calm down," Jeff tried. "It's only a temporary position through the U.S. Department of the Interior that'll enable me to function as a physician as well as to start some of the clinical research I'm interested in. Henrietta and I are both excited about seeing and experiencing new places—and Henrietta thinks it'll be a great setting for her writing."

"Now what makes you think I'd give a damn about what she thinks? How about what I think? How about what I want? How about what your mother wants?"

"Mother wants what I want."

"No, she doesn't."

"Look, I did what you asked of me: I became a doctor, like you," Jeff said reasonably. "But now, I want to try my hand at medical research even while I'm practicing medicine; specifically I want to learn more about how native healers affect spontaneous remissions. I've looked into it a little. Some people call the native healers shamans, and I'm interested in what they're—"

"Shamans are goddamn weirdos," his father interrupted. "Oh, yes, I know all about them. They go into trances, they have visions about dead people, they talk to animals, they sing to goddamn rocks."

"I think you're trivializing an ancient medicine that's apparently worked for centuries, not to mention the modern-day miracles that are reported to have occurred there," Jeff argued. "Anyway, it's important to me. I'm going to research native healings to determine if they have any scientific legitimacy. We're going to Medichero for six months."

"Medichero? Goddammit, boy," his father had said, shaking his head. "Let me tell you somethin' you might not have learned in medical school, even though I've spent thousands of dollars putting you through what I thought was a fine and accredited institution: the idea of trying to find a scientific basis for talking to rocks is goddamn preposterous!"

Jeff laughed at the memory of his father's words, but as he returned to his notes on Rosa's case, tears slid down his cheeks. He knew that his father would never understand or accept his interest in Indian medicine, and it cut him deeply.

But Jeff's pull toward researching it was just as intense. It was unshakable, a calling even. For the sake of saving lives and possibly to quiet an internal drive toward the unknown, Jeff was inspired and convinced that spirit science was deserving of his research, time and advocacy. It was even worth a rift with his father.

His reverie broke when he heard, "Doc Clayborn?"

Gladys Burke, the senior nurse on staff, poked in her head from behind the lab door.

"Yes? What is it, Nurse Burke?" Jeff quickly wiped the tears from his face.

"I don't aim to bother you none, but I'd think you'd want to check in on Billy Santana right about now. That young'un ain't doing so good." Nurse Burke was a tough mountain woman with a gaunt face, bony-looking limbs and leathery tanned skin, which made her look older than her forty-nine years. She had been widowed in her twenties, never remarried but earned a bachelor's degree in nursing and a reputation for being efficient, dependable and slightly curmudgeonly. "He's been complaining about a bad ache near his belly button," she added with a grimace.

"I'll be right there," Jeff said. He placed Rosa's slides back into a sterile stainless steel pan and hurried them over to the lab refrigerator for safe storage before following Nurse Burke out.

He rushed down a long hall and into the small patient room occupied by twelve-year-old Billy. He was the son of Ray Santana, also known as Big Eagle Feathers. Lily Santana, the boy's delicate-looking young mother, sat on the bed patting her son's forehead with a cool, wet cloth. Billy had not yet recovered from influenza when he had contracted a stubborn case of strep throat. After nearly a week of penicillin, fluid replacements and even the prayers of Bears Repeating, the boy's condition wasn't improving as much as Jeff would have liked or expected.

"Hello, Mrs. Santana; now let's see how our boy is doing."

"He is trying to be brave," she answered. "Maybe too brave."

After taking the boy's vitals, Jeff applied gentle pressure to the boy's abdomen, then released it quickly. "Does this hurt?"

The boy shook his head, but Jeff detected a wince.

"Son, you're a fine young brave. But right now, it's more important to be truthful than strong. If it hurts here, we need to know so we can help you." Jeff pressed again on the boy's right side.

Billy nodded and began to cry, "*Bimaa!* It hurts!"

"There, there," Jeff said, patting the boy's arms. "Now we can make a plan to help you feel better. I'm going to visit with your mother now."

Jeff motioned the two women into the hall with him. Shutting the door, Jeff turned to Nurse Burke. "A severely inflamed peritoneum is indicated. Please draw some blood immediately. I need to check his white-blood-cell count again and see how much it's elevated. While I'm doing that, it'd be helpful if you'd send someone to locate Mr. Santana at the ceremonial grounds and bring him here as soon as possible. Oh, and see if Joe can come in, too," he added, following his intuition that all forms of medicine would be needed to save the boy's life.

Speechless, Lily Santana's brown eyes were filling with a mother's worst fear.

"Mrs. Santana, you and your husband are both needed here. And you should prepare yourself: I'm afraid your son needs emergency surgery. It looks like acute appendicitis."

Chapter 5

The next day while the twins were in the Agency's summer school program and little Jeffie was taking an afternoon nap, Henrietta sat at her desk contemplating the potential of the soul retrieval process as a story. She wished she could go to the library or a bookstore, get a book and read all about it, as was her usual routine when exploring a new writing subject. But she realized it was futile to even check. The Indians she knew didn't write books about their spirit medicine. Nor would there be any volumes about the secrets of Bears Repeating.

At this point, all she knew about the soul retrieval was what she had gleaned from Altie last night. Some native healers attributed the emotional agony experienced after a trauma to something called soul loss, a state where pieces of the soul have broken off and left to escape the full and painful impact of some horrific event. Where these parts went was still a mystery to Henrietta. Sometimes, the lost soul pieces weren't able to return after a traumatic event—also a mystery. Nevertheless, the voids created by the soul fragmentation could fill up with negative thoughts or spirits, which according to Altie, could cause mental illness, physical sickness or both.

Henrietta put her head on the desk. As peculiar as it all sounded, the soul retrieval made sense to her. Probably because it did feel like something was missing from her being. And it had been this awful dark hole, coupled with a feeling of not being able to do anything about it, that was making her crazy! She sat up as a genuine feeling of hope began to take hold. Maybe, just maybe, healing from her soul-shattering experience was possible. *Dear God, please let it be true.*

Henrietta exhaled and looked at the typewriter on her desk. To its right sat an empty journal, ready to be filled with notes about her possible healing story. To its left was a framed picture of her father, Hampton Smyth, taken just before she and Jeff had moved to Medichero for their first mission. Henrietta had snapped it while her father, who was then the general manager of the Clayborns' massive peach orchards, was pouring seeds into a variety of birdfeeders hanging from trees at their home. Her childhood home was a modest farmhouse that everyone on the plantation called "the cabin." Before the Smyths moved in, the cabin had been renovated and painted a sunny yellow color, it stood in the middle of a two-acre secluded yard within the plantation's ten thousand acres like a small tropical island in the middle of a green sea of gently rolling farmland. Lush southern vegetation covered the property and included masses of bushy azaleas, wisteria vines climbing an arbor and flowering dogwoods as well as three large Spanish moss–covered live oaks planted before the Civil War. A hundred yards away from the birdfeeders sat a white barn and fence that encircled a riding ring for ponies and horses, also tended by her father. Past the horse enclosure and some of the plantation's vast peach orchards, toward the north end of the Clayborn estate, the red clay had given birth to a field of prolific pecan trees. In between, cotton grew so abundant and white it looked like the angels had sprinkled powdered sugar on fields of small green plants.

"Are you upset that we're moving way out to New Mexico for a while, Daddy?" Henrietta had asked before taking his photograph.

After a brief pose for her picture, the big man turned to his daughter and said, "I think of you, my only and dear child who is now a full-grown woman with chickadees of your own, like the cardinals, blue jays and finches I'm putting feed out for," he said. As he capped off the fifth birdfeeder, several pairs of cardinals flew into a nearby pine, lighting it up like a Christmas tree.

"How so, Daddy?"

"Now, you know, these beautiful birds are my pets," he said, motioning toward the cardinals. "I just love 'em to pieces, so much so that I'd like to put them all in cages so I can see and hold 'em whenever I want. But you know why I don't do that?"

She shook her head.

"Because they wouldn't be happy about being locked up." He turned to smile at her.

A rush of tears welled up in Henrietta's eyes as she remembered her daddy's love of songbirds and his care of the feeders that tragically no longer hung in that fragrant side yard. Just as the tears were falling, she heard a distinctive little tap at the kitchen door, since the screened-in porch door was usually left open.

Altie, she thought. Henrietta wiped her eyes and blew her nose in a handkerchief. "Come on in," she shouted.

"*Yati' hayaazhʔ*, good afternoon," Altie said. She sat on the sofa. "Oh, you are crying." She stood up. "Please allow me to help you."

"Thanks, but I was just thinking about my sweet daddy and remembering the cabin I grew up in."

"Ah, love tears," Altie said, sitting back down.

"Yes. And I've also been thinking more about the soul retrieval. I had some reservations earlier. But now I don't," Henrietta said, with her father's story of freedom fresh in her memory. "I want to fly with it. I'm ready to experience what it's like to have the soul retrieval."

"Ah, *nzhoo*, very good."

"Are we meeting Joe at the teepee?"

"Joe is up at the hospital."

"He isn't at the ceremonial grounds?"

"There was an emergency with Billy Santana last night."

"Oh, yes. I know," Henrietta said with concern in her voice. "His appendix burst, poor thing. His condition, it's very serious."

"*Ha'aa*, yes. The soul retrieval may need to wait until the boy is better. I will check with Joe. May I use your telephone?"

"Of course. But, Altie, you actually just asked a question. I'm surprised."

"I have learned a little about your people's etiquette."

"*Ha'aa*, you have," Henrietta said, grinning.

Altie dialed the hospital. After about five minutes, she put down the receiver. "Little Eagle Feathers is okay for now," she said, using Billy's native name.

"How about Jeff?" Henrietta asked because he had come home very late, sleeping only a couple of hours before dashing back to the hospital.

"He was able to rest in his office and is okay now, too."

"I'm so relieved." She knew that Jeff had a bed in his office for such occasions but worried he didn't use it enough.

"The staff and some of the medicine men also are relieved. So they were all celebrating in the lab, playing around with Jeff's new egg until they were interrupted."

"Are you talking about the E-E-G? That's Jeff's new research machine."

"Oh, *ha'aa*," Altie said without a hint of embarrassment. "Joe also said they had wrapped up their E-E-G tests for the day, and he will be able to meet us at our teepee at half past the hour. He said that there would be time for your soul retrieval before he is needed again at the ceremonial grounds. Come, let us gather up your little one and go. My mother will be able to babysit."

Chapter 6

Just when Jeff thought he was being revolutionary with his freshly minted theory of spirit science, Joe casually informed him that native healers had always known their spirit medicine operated with a higher set of natural laws. And like the three other young medicine men joining them shortly in the lab, Joe held the optimistic view that the white man's science would one day catch up with what the natives had known for centuries. This was one of the reasons why the younger medicine men were willing to participate in Jeff's research and risk provoking the tribe's elders.

"So, let me get this straight, Joe," Jeff said, "your remarkable healings are considered neither miraculous nor magical, but rather the by-product of some perfectly natural, orderly system of higher laws? And you've always believed that this is the way it works?"

"Ha'aa," Joe said, nodding.

Jeff's mouth dropped open.

"I think of the natural laws of science as the sub-tribe and the laws of spirit as the overall tribe," Joe said.

"Your analogy makes sense," Jeff said. He nodded his head, letting it sink in. After a few minutes, Jeff asked: "Isn't it surprising that I came up with a theory that uncannily parallels your understanding, but I did so on my own? You've never mentioned a higher set of natural laws to me, have you?"

"No. I have, however, mentioned the principle of the Great Spirit's oneness with and in everything, including the insights we occasionally tap into."

"I guess there really is nothing new under the sun," Jeff said.

"Ah, but there are many old but useful ideas in need of our *rediscovery*."

Jeff smiled. As an ongoing student of spirit medicine under the tutorage of Bears Repeating, Jeff was still amazed at how this relatively young man—Joe was only a few years older than himself—continued to baffle and inspire him all at once. Jeff was about to comment on that point when the three medicine men that had been visiting Billy filed into the room.

"Good afternoon, gentlemen," Jeff said. He was addressing Benny Shanta, George White Water and Charlie Mangus, three of the younger medicine men. They were still dressed in their ceremonial leathers from the early morning rituals. Not surprisingly, Joe had already changed his clothes, now wearing Elvis-style baggy trousers, a pink and white panel shirt, white socks and the ever-present blue-suede moccasins, all under a white knee-length lab coat, like the one Jeff wore.

"Afternoon, Doc, Joe," Benny said. The rest acknowledged Jeff and Joe with a slight nod toward each. "You were right about Little Eagle Feathers being better; he's resting peacefully now," Benny said. "It turns out we also have some time to start helping with your experiment before this evening's ceremonies."

The personalities and clan makeup of the three medicine men were as diverse yet harmoniously integrated as the sub-tribes of Apaches who had fused together on the Medichero Indian Reservation. Benny Shanta, a twenty-nine-year-old Mescalero Apache of average weight and height, loved and participated in sports of all kinds, including the rodeo events during the Sunrise Ceremonies. He had an athletic build, calloused but well-proportioned hands, and tan-brown skin the color of the dirt in a baseball diamond. He was the only one in the group with eyeglasses and short barber-cut hair.

The face of George White Water, a thirty-year-old Quero Apache, was sweet like Joe's. Although only five foot five, George was known for his powerful singing voice. He performed not only during the Sunrise Ceremonies, but also in Sunday Mass at the reservation's St. Paul's Mission Church, and always to awed crowds.

Charlie Mangus, a thirty-two-year-old Chiricahua Apache, was the tallest one of the three, at nearly six feet. He had shoulder-length thick black hair, a long flat nose, extremely thin wide-set lips, and small onyx beads for eyes, giving him a wild, almost coyote-like appearance.

To corroborate Rosa's case study and accumulate harder evidence, Jeff had convinced these younger medicine men, with Joe's help of course, to participate in a series of controlled laboratory experiments involving the EEG and a variety of biological test subjects. They'd start with cells in petri dishes, then move to chicken eggs and mice, and finally to human and control patients. The order of testing was designed to ensure his preliminary results would be free of bias and what was a phenomenon recently discovered and dubbed the placebo effect. One last advantage: cells, eggs and animals wouldn't be swayed by religious prejudices. Or fears of eternal damnation, for that matter.

"Excellent," Jeff said. "How about we roll that cot closer?"

"Sure," Benny said. He and the other two medicine men pulled the rolling bed from the corner and next to the EEG.

"Our objective for today is to measure the different states of your minds ... a medicine man's mind ... using the electroencephalograph here," Jeff said, patting the equipment.

"You mean like when we're awake, resting and in silence?" George said. He spoke softly and smiled.

"That's exactly right, George," Jeff replied, sitting in a chair behind the table with the EEG. "But first things first. Once we print out the basics on that"— Jeff pointed to the display device—"we can move on to the more exciting part of this experiment. That is, seeing what your brain waves look like during an actual healing event."

"Sounds good," George said. He looked at some of the sample printouts Jeff had shown them earlier.

"I'll be interested to see what the *Kopave* looks like, too," said Benny. He was referring to what Jeff understood as an Apache term that meant being in a deep meditative state with no thought for the purpose of receiving spiritual guidance.

"We'll probably make waves in the theta-delta frequencies," Joe said, holding a clipboard.

Everyone looked at him and stared.

"Hey, I used one in medical school," Joe said. He looked down at his clipboard while explaining. "Brain-wave patterns are named after Greek letters: alpha is for alert, beta for hard thinking, delta for deep sleep and theta for meditation," Joe said. He looked up and saw the puzzled faces of Benny, George and Charlie. "Well, maybe we could create our own names ... in Athabascan," he added.

"Good idea, Joe, we may need to," Jeff said.

"Ha'aa," the other medicine men agreed in unison.

"Now, who wants to go first?" Jeff asked. He raised his right hand like a grade-school kid in need of the restroom.

"I will."

"Thanks, Benny, have a seat. But before you lie down, I need to attach these electrodes to the top of your head," Jeff said. He was holding up a cap made only of wires and sensors.

"Dr. Clayborn?"

"Yes, Charlie?"

"You aren't going to scalp us with that thing, are you?" asked Charlie, the coyote-looking one. His black eyes opened wide.

All four of the medicine men snickered like teenage boys who'd just heard a hilarious joke.

"No, Charlie, there's no scalping involved," Jeff said. He was laughing along with them. "I realize this contraption looks a little strange, but these small round things are electrodes; they are sensors that capture the data we need. They're perfectly harmless, and you won't feel a thing, I promise."

"Just wanted to make sure," Charlie said. He held up his palms.

"We use gel to attach the electrodes to your skin." Jeff placed the all-wire cap over Benny's head and started digging through his hair with the nozzle end of a gel bottle. "Sometimes it's hard to get out of your hair, even your shorter style, Benny. Sorry in advance about that."

"What we sacrifice for the sake of the white man's science," Charlie said.

They were still chuckling when Ray Santana and his massive brother, Victor Two Feathers, barged into the lab, looking like highly annoyed Indian cops. At six foot four, Ray towered over most Medichero men and could fill up a room with his presence alone. But together with his stocky-built and nearly as tall brother, the lab seemed to grow tiny and claustrophobic.

Ray had been the lead Mountain Spirit dancer last night, and he still wore his ocher-colored leathers, although the paint and pollen had partially rubbed off his upper torso. Victor wasn't wearing ceremonial regalia, instead, he sported his usual blue jeans and a button-down plaid shirt. But he always wore two feathers in a dark-red headband, which added about twelve inches to his already six-foot height and made an unsettling brushing noise on the top of doorframes.

Jeff exhaled heavily with exasperation because he knew what was coming. Like everyone else in the room, Jeff was fully aware that the tribal leaders had charged these brothers with protecting sacred traditions from outside threats. And most likely the old guard would find his little science experiment, involving some of the tribe's best medicine men, to be a tad disrespectful.

"Well, Doc, it was nice seeing you," Benny said, pulling off the cap and jumping up from the cot. Before Jeff could respond, three of his test subjects darted away from the EEG, scattering like lab rats suddenly on the loose, before slipping out the door.

"That wasn't very helpful," Jeff muttered half to himself, half to Joe.

"My son sleeps too much," Ray Santana said. He sounded like a worried father, suggesting another reason altogether for their unexpected visit.

"Mr. Santana, I understand your concern," Jeff said, as he stood and looked up. *Good god, the man is a giant.* "But as I explained earlier, your son is recovering from very serious surgery, and although he's stable, it'll take a week or more before he's able to resume any normal activity. Sleep is good," Jeff said. He nodded his head for emphasis, trying to maintain a professional calm, but all he could think about was the grisly cracking noise that bones make when broken.

"You should do more to help," Ray said. He crossed his muscular arms and stiffened his broad back. His eyes narrowed.

"We check on him every half hour, around the clock," Jeff said a little defensively. "Medically speaking, we're following all of the standard protocols for his condition."

Victor stepped forward and stood only a foot away from Jeff, crooking a menacing smile with his slash of lips. "You say you're giving your white man's medicine to Little Eagle Feathers. But it doesn't look like you're doing that." Victor shook his head, his two feathers swishing menacingly above his furrowed brow. Victor's nose was long and broad, his complexion acne-scarred and his eyes bloodshot; he smelled of sweat and day-old whiskey. "In fact, it looks to me like you're meddling in our medicine and trying to confuse our medicine men," he said. He picked up the electrode cap between his fingers as though it were a dead fish gone bad. "It looks like you and the boys are getting distracted."

"Um, Joe?" Jeff swallowed hard, transfixed by Victor's hard black eyes.

"Dr. Clayborn is doing all he can for Little Eagle Feathers," Joe said. His voice was calm. He stepped in between Victor and Jeff, forcing them to back away from each other. He faced Victor. "We all are. Little Eagle Feathers is receiving all forms of the right medicine, including ours."

In the breathless silence that followed, the bulky Indians grunted before withdrawing and shuffling out.

"Excuse me, excuse me," Nurse Burke said. She was running and nearly bumped into Victor on the way in. "Joe, the operator's sending in a call to you from Altie. Dr. Clayborn, there's no change in Billy Santana, but ..."

Big Eagle Feathers and Victor Two Feathers halted and turned back.

"There ain't no emergency neither," she added for their benefit. "It's just time for a check, Doc."

"Gladly," Jeff said. He rushed past the feathered brothers like a bullet, while somewhere under a stack of papers, the lab's telephone began to ring.

Chapter 7

After carrying little Jeffie's stroller down the front-porch steps of the doctor's cottage, Henrietta and Altie headed toward the path that would lead them down to the Locos' ceremonial teepee. The scraggly grasses crunched as they rolled and walked over them toward a grouping of tall pines. Underneath the trees grew spindly shrubs the size of wagon wheels. Just behind the mass of vegetation was the path's entrance, blocked by a pair of Appaloosas. Big Eagle Feathers and Victor Two Feathers were riding them.

Looking up as though she were gazing at high-rise buildings, Henrietta saw the tired state of Ray Santana's day-old ceremonial costume. It was understandable, he'd obviously been up all night with his sick son. But as he dismounted his horse and approached them, Henrietta couldn't help noticing that he wasn't just an oversized Medichero man. He had the kind of imperial beauty and sure-footed gracefulness one might associate with a rare stallion. He moved with an almost unnerving sensuality that belied a powerful force underneath, which, Henrietta imagined, held both the splendor of the Sierra Blanca and its violent potential for avalanche.

Their sudden appearance reminded Henrietta of the conversation she'd had with Jeff just yesterday morning, when he'd admitted to having some trouble with these hulking brothers. They'd been spying on the doctor since he had arrived on this mission. And the brothers had expressed their disapproval of his research not only to Jeff, but also to Joe. So why would they want to approach her and Altie here and now? Did they mean to intimidate the wives as well?

Henrietta was too afraid to find out, but couldn't seem to move her legs or even slide her eyes to her right to see how Altie was responding. She was gripped by an absurd paralysis, an infuriating reaction she'd known all too well before.

The huge older brother stopped several feet away from them before speaking. "We have come from the hospital," Ray said.

"Oh, oh, yes. I'm sorry your son's been so sick," Henrietta said, snapping out of her mind-freeze by falling back on the ingrained etiquette of her southern roots. "But I'm told he's stabilized and recovering. I'm sure he'll be well soon." She tried to smile.

"We are hopeful, but concerned," he said. He paused before adding, "Your husband's research ... his interest in our spirit medicine ... it is distracting him from attending to my son." He aimed his focus at Henrietta.

"What? That … that doesn't sound like J-Jeff," Henrietta said. But it was, in fact, exactly what she herself had worried about. "Jeff would never put research before the care of your son—or any patient," Henrietta said. She would not admit her fears to this man.

Victor Two Feathers leaped off his horse and landed square in front of the stroller, causing Henrietta to jump backward with it. His hardened eyes raked over her, traveling from head to toe, then back up to her face in a way that made Henrietta's skin crawl. There was something almost reptilian in Victor's eyes, and she couldn't look at them. Turning and stepping away a few more feet, she was reminded, and in no uncertain terms, that she and Jeff were outsiders and should not be getting involved in things that did not concern them. *What if these brothers knew that I, too, have become interested in their spirit medicine? What if they find out I am going to Joe's teepee for the soul retrieval at this very minute?*

"I'm not sure what you expect me to say or do, Mr. Santana," Henrietta said, trying to ignore Victor's intimidating glare. "Jeff's a committed and talented physician, and I'm sure he'll do whatever's right for your son's condition."

"Maybe you could remind him of that, ma'am," the taller man said, almost politely.

That's why he's here? He wants me to help keep Jeff focused? Henrietta thought she saw a momentary softening in this father's eyes, perhaps even a touch of fear, the kind that came from knowing his son's situation was beyond the control of brute strength.

"Yeah," Victor said with a sneer. "And maybe you should remind him to stick to his own medicine from now on."

Henrietta cringed before looking back over to Ray Santana, seeking something more civil and less scary, but the frightening intensity had returned. He crossed his massive arms. His eyes darkened.

Holding up her right hand, the diminutive Altie walked in front of the brothers, meeting their piercing black stares without so much as a flinch. She then spoke in her native language in a calm, assertive tone. After a few seconds, the towering men parted like the heavy gates of an imposing fortress, granting them free passage.

Altie stepped on the path and Henrietta followed, pushing the stroller between the two men flanking the trail's entrance. That Jeffie had slept through the entire encounter was both a mystery and blessing.

Once the men rode away, Henrietta exclaimed in a loud whisper, "Wow, Altie! You were fearless ... and great. What in the world did you say to them?"

"An undeniable truth."

"And that was?"

"How does it harm a son for his doctor to become a true healer." It was a statement more than a question.

"Wow," Henrietta repeated. "You weren't even afraid of them!"

"The power to create peace is within us all. There is no fear in making peace."

With that, Henrietta moved down the path feeling safer and more aware of her petite friend's talents than ever before. That Henrietta had witnessed something authentic and intrinsic in Altie, there was no question. *But what is it? How does it translate?*

She now wondered: *If this little woman knows how to move mountain-sized men out of her way with only a look and a few mild words, perhaps she could also teach me how to … survive.*

Chapter 8

For the past twenty or so years, the Medichero people had gained a respectable and semi-independent financial freedom through businesses grown out of the Earth, becoming masters of forestry as well as sheep and cattle farming. Reservation and township commerce was generally based on supporting and servicing these farming businesses. Their community was organized into congregated clan groups with each containing a variety of structures from teepees and mobile homes to domed-thatched Apache wickiups and rows of small government-built tract homes. There were only a few larger homes dotting the landscape, with the unusual five-bedroom Victorian-style doctor's cottage being something of a standout as well as a misnomer: it was the only large, custom-style house.

Although she'd never been inside the Locos' home, Henrietta knew exactly where it was located. They lived about a five-minute walk down the hill from the doctor's cottage in one of the smaller split-level tract houses on a terraced row, which could have been in any

American neighborhood, except that Joe had erected a large teepee in their backyard. The tip of it could be seen from the street below.

For reasons Henrietta didn't know, Joe and Altie were childless and, from the appearance of their home's exterior, lived barely above the level of poverty even though Joe now had a well-paying job at the hospital. Their modest house was unremarkable and even dull with faded brown-wood siding and dried-up orange-red brick. The front lawn looked neglected, dominated by an unknown variety of low-growing vegetation that was marked by sporadic patches of bald dirt. There was an old rusted-out Rambler, without tires or windows, and on concrete risers in a small side yard.

Henrietta was still reeling from their run-in with the Santanas as she entered the chipped-up, tan-colored front door. But like the Locos themselves, their home's interior was colorful and full of useful information. The main living area could have passed for a small library with its overflowing bookshelves occupying every wall, floor to ceiling. The center of the room held twin reading chairs covered in bright green, red and royal blue fabrics, showcased like a pair of prized parrots. The walls looked freshly painted in a golden color, the trim a creamy white. A braided rug covered a shiny, clean wood floor. Between the two plush chairs sat a table that held a lamp and record player, while underneath a hundred or so record albums crouched on a shelf.

"Gee whiz, who's the collector, you or Joe?" Henrietta asked, amazed.

"Joe, mostly. But I usually like the books and music he chooses. Make yourself at home. I will get Jeffie settled with *Shimaa*." She picked up the sleepy-eyed boy.

"Thanks, Altie."

Altie carried him into the kitchen, where her mother, Naomi Songbird, was obviously making something sweet. The aromas of oatmeal and freshly baked cookies filled the entire house. Henrietta followed but stayed only briefly, just to express her appreciation to Naomi for babysitting. It was easier to get away by letting Altie divert her son's attention, and so Henrietta slipped out, heading back to the library room.

Henrietta could now understand why Jeff thought of Joe as something of a polymath. He had packed his home, and presumably his mind, with encyclopedias, textbooks, biographies and rows of great literature. Henrietta ran her fingers over the creased spines, tempted to forget the soul retrieval for the day and delve into the irresistible books. But how could she back out of her appointment with potential wholeness?

Even though she was nervous, she had a much stronger urge to experience what had become a daring attraction. It was perhaps the spiritual equivalent of that first roller-coaster ride.

Still, books remained important to her despite her damaged soul and writer's block. The Locos' library contained popular fiction and poetry as well as an entire bookshelf committed to classical literature and Shakespearean plays. Like Jeff, Joe seemed to be attracted to science books and the texts of Francis Bacon, Isaac Newton and Albert Einstein, as there were several shelves devoted to them. She might have thought the Locos resented America's founding fathers for their mistreatment of Indians, but here was a row dedicated to the lives and writings of George Washington, Benjamin Franklin and Thomas Jefferson, to name a few. Another wall attended to the exotic and esoteric with a series of books by psychic wonder Edgar Cayce, the positive-thinking minister Dr. Norman Vincent Peale and the famed psychologist Dr. Carl Jung. Then there was an emerald green collection of *I Am Discourses*, intriguing tomes of at least twelve volumes, brought forth by a theosophist—whatever that meant—named Godfré Ray King. After thumbing through *Unveiled Mysteries*, the first of King's volumes, Henrietta paused to consider if there might also be a book on the soul retrieval somewhere on these crowded shelves. She had just started looking for one when Joe walked in.

"Greetings," he said. He gave a smiling nod to Henrietta before limping straight over to Altie, who was coming back from the kitchen. He leaned over, wrapped his wife in his arms and kissed her on the lips.

As Apaches aren't typically demonstrative, Henrietta blushed, feeling like an intruder on their intimate moment. She turned back to the shelves, pretending to read the book in her hands as they conversed in native whispers.

After a few minutes, Joe faced Henrietta. "So, how do you like our little library?"

"I'd say it's quite comprehensive and really wonderful."

"Feel free to borrow anything that strikes your fancy."

"Thanks. Maybe after the, um, soul retrieval," she said, her voice cracking.

"Ah, so you're ready, then."

She nodded with a cough. She wondered again what mysteries she might learn and experience today. She realized excitement was welling up inside her.

"Come," Joe said, limping toward the back door. "You will be better soon." He stopped to address Altie who nodded when he said, "Please join us as soon as you can."

Henrietta's stomach jumped as she followed Joe into the backyard toward the tall ceremonial teepee. The bottom two-thirds consisted of a white-colored canvas, while the top-third and ground-level edges were dyed a sky blue. Joe opened a large flap, and they sidled in through a hole. Once her eyes adjusted to the triangle-shaped dimness, Henrietta could see the interior was bigger than she'd expected. Maybe two hundred square feet, a little bigger than most one-car garages. Joe lit some kindling and small logs in a centered fire-pit. Henrietta thought the fire was unneeded since it had turned out to be a warm July afternoon in the mountains. But as the flames hissed and cracked, Henrietta could only watch in silence as the smoke traveled up toward the hole in the roof as though it were inside an invisible chimney. The hot air's rise caused cooler air to come in from vent-like slits in the walls near the ground, transforming the stuffiness into something more comfortable. Still, she was glad she had chosen to wear a sleeveless blouse, shorts and sandals.

Joe wore his usual baggy pants, short-sleeved panel shirt and blue-suede moccasins. Altie entered, and Henrietta noticed that she had changed from the cotton dress she'd been wearing to a fringed leather one. It didn't match her and Joe's modern '50s style, but it did, Henrietta decided, fit in perfectly with this bizarre new experience.

Altie moved behind an Indian drum the size of a milk pail and began lighting beeswax candles placed on a bench-size wooden altar that held an odd variety of paraphernalia. Henrietta eyed, with some relief, a framed portrait of Jesus. The altar also held a foot-high statue of Mother Mary, draped with dozens of rosary beads, and Henrietta remembered that the Locos were Catholics as well as native healers. Next to the statue sat turquoise chunks, quartz crystal and amethyst rocks the

size of eggs; tiny carved stone figurines in various
animal shapes; an assortment of feathers and herbs
bundled with strings; and a Coca-Cola bottle filled with
a semi-transparent liquid.

"We're almost ready," Joe said.

Henrietta sat down on a blanket that functioned
as a rug covering the dirt floor. Like many of the textiles
created by Medichero women, the blanket-rug was
made of scratchy wool and embedded with patterns of
circles in deep red, orange and black.

"Also need this blanket," he added, spreading
out one with colors similar to the one she was sitting on,
except it was made of soft woven cotton and edged with
bear motifs. Joe sat near the head of it, designated by
two small pillows in white cases.

"Interesting blanket, Joe. Altie must've made it,"
Henrietta said, fingering it.

"Nope, I got it at Woolworth's. The bears
repeating caught my eye."

Henrietta chuckled, starting to relax. "An
Indian buying an Indian blanket at Woolworth's?"

"Looks good, don't you think? Lots of style.
Nice and soft to sit on, too. I've been trying to get Altie
to make one like it."

Altie rolled her eyes, but her expression reflected
a shaman's good sense of humor.

Continuing his preparation, Joe laid a strange
wood carving on the blanket. Curious, Henrietta picked
it up.

"I wonder what the purpose of this is," she said, trying not to ruin the flow of the ceremony with a question and breach of Medichero etiquette.

"It's a soul catcher," Joe said. "I made it."

Joe's hollow carving looked like an oversized wooden straw. It was about fifteen inches long by one inch wide, with bear heads engraved near each end. An abstract design was painted in its middle.

"I use it, in a symbolic sense, to carry back your soul parts before returning them to you. Some medicine men choose wolf or snake heads for their soul catchers. But I preferred one with bear heads on both ends."

"Let me guess," Henrietta said, putting it back on the blanket. "Because it looks like bears repeating?"

"You are most astute," Joe said. He gave her a smile before turning more serious. "Henrietta, this will be a deep healing. Through the process of establishing oneness with the Great Spirit within us and with the assistance of our power animals and spirit guides, your missing soul fragments will be returned."

Henrietta stared moon-eyed at him in the burning light, trying to grasp the meaning of his bewildering prescriptions. They were confusing to southern ears still unaccustomed to the terminology of medicine men with soul catchers. But she wanted to understand. She needed to understand.

Altie handed Joe a bundle of dried sage, crispy and fragile, and he lit it in the fire. After a second, he pulled the sage out and blew on its flame, creating incense that was both purifying and pungent before placing the smoldering herb into an ashtray-like shell, which had once housed a turtle.

"You can lie down on the bears repeating blanket now," Altie said, pointing to one of the pillows before carrying the drum to the foot of the blanket.

Trying to join in the cooperative harmony and way they worked seamlessly together, Henrietta complied, moving into position before looking back at Altie and then up at Joe. Questions were practically popping out of her eyeballs, but she decided to remain quiet.

Mercifully, Joe began to explain what was happening. "When Altie starts to drum, I'll use my rattle and sing my power song in Athabascan to call in the power of the four sacred directions. These tools and rituals help me to move into the light of Spirit, through my conscious and subconscious minds," Joe said.

Henrietta couldn't help it; she had to ask: "Your subconscious mind?"

" 'Our remedies oft in ourselves do lie.' "

"Is that some kind of Apache saying?"

"No, it's Shakespeare," Joe said without expression.

"Shakespeare?" Henrietta smiled, remembering the set of plays on one of Joe's bookshelves.

"It means the medicine we most often need lies in our innermost part, through what is now called the subconscious," Joe added.

"I get it. I just really didn't expect you to say something like that."

"We find the inner medicine by taking an inner journey in Spirit," he said, ignoring her astonishment. "Until you learn this skill for yourself, I'll be journeying on your behalf, appealing to your soul, subconscious mind, spirit guides and faith in the Great Spirit's power to heal you."

"My faith?" She propped herself up on one elbow.

"It's definitely needed."

"You mean I must believe in this healing for it to work?"

Joe nodded. "You must trust the Great Spirit within you and be willing to allow the healing to take place. But of course, it's up to you to make a free-will choice. Are you willing?"

"Yes, I am."

"Very good. When I blow on your head with my soul catcher, it'll mean I've found your missing soul parts and returned them to you."

"What should I do while you're, um, journeying?"

"It's best to give a prayer of thanks to the Great Spirit's healing presence within you, which will draw your missing soul parts back to you like a magnet, as well as to Jesus the Christ, our beloved Ascended Master of healing."

"Of course," she said, encouraged by his inclusion of Jesus.

"It also does a world of good to invoke the assistance of our beloved Mother Mary. She's the queen of the sacred soul retrieval," Joe said. He pointed to her statue on the altar table.

"I've never heard of such a thing."

"It is, nonetheless, a truth."

"But, Joe, I'm not Catholic."

"Don't worry. Mother Mary isn't prejudiced about your religion or anything else," he said. His smile sweetened.

"I guess I can use all the help I can get," Henrietta said.

"And it's better to stay awake to receive this good healing," Joe said.

"I'm too nervous to fall asleep," she mumbled, fidgeting to get comfortable.

"Once I feel myself moving into Spirit, I'll lie down next to you, and my journey will begin. Our shoulders and ankles will touch."

Henrietta felt awkward about Joe lying next to her in such an intimate way and looked over to his wife for reassurance.

"It is safe; it works better that way," Altie said. Her low voice was calming. "You can relax."

"Okay, I'll try." Henrietta took a deep breath and clasped her hands together over her stomach. She was eager to begin reconciling with the prodigal parts of her soul. In fact, she could hardly wait to feel like her old self again. *Was it really possible? Was this really going to happen?*

"You will feel better soon. Let us begin." Joe scooted his left palm under the back of Henrietta's head. With his right hand, he began to shake a bear-claw rattle in unison with Altie's drumming.

He was still singing when he moved next to Henrietta on the bears-repeating blanket. They were both lying supine, parallel to one another, and touching as described. Joe's eyes were closed, and his singing became more like a hum. Altie continued drumming steady and strong, like a heartbeat.

Henrietta closed her eyes and poured out a silent prayer: *Dear God, beloved Jesus and Mother Mary, I'm so grateful for the opportunity to have my soul healed and my lost soul fragments returned. I've missed them. Thank you for your assistance and the healing, which I believe is taking place now. In Christ's name, Amen.*

Finally relaxing into the nurturing rhythms and herbal smells, Henrietta tried not to go to sleep or think about the weight of her secret worries and the tragic cause of her misery. So, as Joe journeyed through the land of Spirit, she chose to portage through time and over geography, toward the part of her memory that held forever the fragrance of peach blossoms and the ripening of young love. She was traveling. She was going home.

Chapter 9

Henrietta's day of initiation into the privileged world of the Clayborns began with a broken wrist and ended with a bump into new love. She had been thirteen, the same age as the Medichero Indian maidens going through their ceremonial rites of passage. Like theirs, hers was during the most blessed of seasons. But it wasn't July. In Greenfield, South Carolina, the most hallowed time of life was springtime. And so it was in her thirteenth year: peach blossoms were perfumed and pregnant with the advent and hope of a healthy yield, and the honeybees were among the busiest workers on the Clayborn Plantation, spreading their sacred pollen. Her father had just been hired as general manager of the orchards, and the Smyths were newly installed in their sun-colored cabin on the Clayborns' lands.

Because the migrant workers wouldn't arrive until June's harvest, the springtime fields were generally clear of most other workers and would be for another two months, except for the foreman Carl Jenkins, known as Jenks and one of only four employees who worked on the plantation year-round. It was Jenks who had caught Henrietta red-handed that April afternoon as she was climbing in a peach tree, something absolutely forbidden on the Clayborn peach plantation at this crucial time, when the peaches were in their most vulnerable stage of development.

Jenks was ruddy-faced with piggish features and the bulk and body language of an elephant in musk. His job included maximizing production and managing the migrant workers, consisting of poor whites, Negroes and Mexicans, during the summer and fall. But, because of his volatile behavior, he wasn't very popular among the men. It was rumored that he had once come close to beating a Mexican worker to death, and the pickers seemed to both fear and loathe him. He also had an annoying habit of loitering behind the trees like a Peeping Tom, even when there was no work-related reason for him to be in the fields. He wore the same thing every day: a sweat-stained white T-shirt that barely covered a disgusting beer gut, cut-off blue jeans of varying lengths, muddy work boots and a ratty straw hat. The thought of Jenks, much less seeing him in person, was enough to give Henrietta a scare.

"What're you doing up there, girl? You get out of that tree, now!" His voice was like a vicious dog attack, coming out of nowhere. He started to grab at her, which caused her to jump back. Henrietta lost her balance and tumbled out of the tree, hitting the ground with a thud and a sickening crack.

Thankfully, her father wasn't too far away, and he came running when he heard her scream. Once she regained the breath that had been knocked out of her, she tried to get up and run, but she couldn't move very quickly. Her right wrist and hand were hurting something fierce and already puffing up like small purple pastries. She was crying and whimpering as her daddy arrived on the scene.

"Dr. Colonel don't allow this; there ain't no climbing in the flowering trees. I thought you both knew better than that," the repellent Jenks had the nerve to say.

"Back off," her father said as he elbowed the lower ranked Jenks out of the way.

Without a scold or even a disapproving look, her daddy scooped her up and placed her into one of the plantation trucks, speeding over to the warehouse for some ice. Afterward, as her throbbing wrist cooled, he rushed them over to collect her mother from the Clayborns' mansion where she worked as a secretary to Mrs. Clayborn, before breaking all speed limits to get them to the closest thing to an emergency room Greenfield had: Dr. Colonel's downtown medical office.

After checking in, a slender brunette with big brown eyes, a wide smile and flawless complexion came in and introduced herself as Nurse Harrington. She was dressed in a crisp white uniform and cap. "If you can, come with me, sugar," she drawled. "Your folks, too." She motioned for them to follow her into an examination room. There, Nurse Harrington took Henrietta's temperature and blood pressure, noting the results on a form. "Okay, sugar, everything's fine except, well obviously, that wrist of yours. Dr. Colonel will be in to see you shortly," she said. She left them behind a closed door and Henrietta winced.

But, at that moment, Henrietta was feeling more guilt than pain. "Gosh, I'm sorry, Daddy and Mama," she said, crying. "I shouldn't have been climbing in that tree. I hope Dr. Colonel won't be mad."

"Don't worry, Henrietta," her mother said. "I don't see much of him when I'm at work, but I'm told Dr. Colonel is one of the best doctors in our area. His real name is Dr. Jules Beaufort Clayborn. But everybody just calls him 'Dr. Colonel' because his name is so close to Miss Julia's and he was some kind of war hero," she said before whispering, "They say he's a genius."

"Good morning, my dear Smyths," Dr. Colonel said, coming in with a warm smile. "Now, whatever do we have here?"

Dr. Colonel looked stately in an impeccably tailored steel-gray suit, starched white shirt and navy silk tie. Overall, he was pleasant-looking with a light complexion, fine features and dark-blue eyes that softened when he smiled. His light-brown hairline was receding and silvering at the temples. But perhaps the most noticeable thing about him was that his posture was perfect. He looked to be standing at attention even when relaxed.

"Henrietta was climbing in one of the trees and fell—and I'm awful sorry about her doing that, sir," Hampton said. He had a sheepish expression. "Broke her wrist, I'm thinking."

"Don't give it another thought, my good man," Dr. Colonel said. He hung his jacket on a chair, revealing the fit lines of a disciplined military man. "Now, let's take a look," he said.

Although her wrist hurt terribly, Dr. Colonel's touch was gentle.

"If you don't mind, I'd like to use a machine to get an inside picture, dear," Dr. Colonel said. "Don't worry, it doesn't hurt."

"I'm told you built your own x-radiology machine, Dr. Colonel," Elizabeth said. "That's so impressive."

"Well, yes, I built one," Dr. Colonel said. "I've always been interested in photography, you see. At one time, I was going to make a career out of it and even worked freelance out West for a couple of magazines when I was younger, at the end of my army days." He paused as if remembering something. "But that's neither here nor there. Anyway, once you understand the mechanics of photography, building an x-radiology machine is rather easy."

"I find that hard to believe," Elizabeth said.

Dr. Colonel chuckled. "It's true. But, if I do say so myself, it sure is a thing of beauty." He offered a winsome smile and playful wink. "Well now, I'll be right back. Need to get it set up, okay?"

"Isn't he amazing?" Elizabeth gushed after Dr. Colonel left the room.

After about ten minutes, Nurse Harrington returned. "Dr. Colonel's ready for you, sugar," she said. "Y'all can come with me."

As they entered another room, Dr. Colonel was standing behind a camera-like cylinder, rubbing it with a cloth as though buffing a fine silver sculpture. "Have a seat here, child," he said as he patted the back of a chair. "Careful now. We'll just put your wrist on this table, like so." He helped her place her lower arm in the right position.

While Dr. Colonel developed the film, which took about an hour, they were given a stack of *Life* and *National Geographic* magazines, and the medication Henrietta had been given earlier finally started to ease her pain. Afterward, Dr. Colonel confirmed that she had indeed broken her wrist. He put a cast on it himself and dressed it with a sling, a gentle touch and a smile. And Henrietta saw how a doctor could possess both genius and a kind bedside manner.

"You'll be good as new in about six weeks, Henrietta," Dr. Colonel said, finishing. "Now, let me just walk you out." His hand was light on Henrietta's back.

"Dot, there's no charge to these fine folks today," he said to the receptionist after arriving at the front desk. "Mr. Smyth's our new general manager out at the plantation, and, of course, Mrs. Smyth has become indispensable to my dear wife; we're just going to overlook all of this with their daughter."

"That's not necessary, Dr. Colonel," Hampton said. "We're able to pay."

"You should know this about me, Hampton. I always take care of my own." He spoke with an exaggerated grin that showed perfectly white-capped teeth.

"Well, then, we're much obliged," Hampton said. He shook the doctor's hand. "Henrietta, what do you say?"

"Thank you, Dr. Colonel. And I'm so sorry about climbing in your peach tree. It won't happen again. I've learned my lesson."

"Well now, not to worry, my dear child," Dr. Colonel said. "We all make mistakes. But sometimes, we just have to learn the hard way, now don't we?"

They turned to exit as a young Jefferson Clayborn came walking in. When he saw Henrietta, he stopped and his face turned beet red. "Hey, Henrietta," Jeff said. His voice was a little shy. "I heard you had an accident. Are you all right?"

Henrietta smiled and looked down at her cast. "I broke my wrist, but I'm fine now, Jeff. Thanks for asking, though."

"How are you, Jefferson?" asked Elizabeth.

"I'm doing just fine, Mrs. Smyth, thank you," Jeff said. He turned his attention back to Henrietta. "Are you sure you're all right?"

"It didn't hurt too much. Your father was real nice," Henrietta said.

She looked over at Dr. Colonel, who was now staring straight at his son's face, still the color of rouge. But Dr. Colonel no longer looked happy. The friendly smile he had been giving her and her parents before was gone. In its place was an expression that made her shiver without knowing why.

Later, during the summers of their high school years, Jefferson Clayborn and Henrietta Smyth were more often than not in the peach fields, nibbling on ripened fruit and each other.

"Henrietta, catch," Jeff said one day after lunch, while throwing a couple of his picks down to her from the top rung of a ladder. It stood next to a tree heavy with blushing fuzzy fruit and waxy-looking lanceolate leaves.

"Got 'em!" She was wearing a sleeveless violet and white plaid dress that her mother had made. It featured a smart white collar, full skirt and matching belt. Jeff was in his work shorts, shirt and boots.

After jumping down, he cut one of the peaches in half with his pocketknife. "There, a peach for a peach," he whispered, placing a piece of the soft yellow flesh gently in front of her lips, which she opened for him. Face-to-face, they ate in smitten silence, captivated more by each other than the succulence on their tongues.

After their picnic, they held hands while Jeff carried the basket she'd brought in his free hand. Jeff walked her unhurriedly through rows of bulging trees toward an adjacent field, stopping somewhere in the middle, a spot hidden from the prying eyes of fathers and itinerant foremen. After Jeff spread out a red-and-white-checkered tablecloth, they kissed and shared something that was as sweet and alluring as the sensuous acreage in which they stood.

His arms were strong and tan from working in the orchards, but his hands touched her cheeks with a pure tenderness before moving to the violet ribbon holding her hair in a ponytail. He loosened the bow and it fell into his fingers as he guided her down onto the picnic cloth, where their mouths found each other, hungrily and urgently, in a fiery dance of young passion and desire.

Henrietta's head was reeling, her heart pounding. She was drunk with passion. Every nerve, every sense, was alive with a rapturous and fervent intensity for Jefferson Clayborn.

Pausing between the heat of wet kisses, Jeff cupped her face with his hands, and they gazed into each other's eyes. "Marry me, Henrietta," he whispered. "Please say you'll marry me after we graduate. Then we can escape to the West and live happily ever after."

Ever since Jeff learned his father had served in the army and was stationed for a while in Alamogordo, New Mexico, where he took the fascinating photos of the White Sands Desert which hung in his study, Jeff had wanted to go and explore the state. Jeff also had a bit of anthropologist in him, a curious gene that guided him toward researching ancient cultures and the medicines of indigenous peoples. A medical degree would only add fuel to that ambition.

"Oh, Jeff, of course!" Henrietta was about to burst with excitement. "It'll be hard to wait. But I'm so in love with you, and I don't care where we live once we're married," she said. She melted back to his irresistible mouth. "But we could stay here, too," she added between kisses.

"I kind of want to see and experience new places. But only with you at my side," Jeff said. He touched her nose with his finger before kissing it. "You're so beautiful, Henrietta. I want you to be wherever I am."

She smiled; her heart was soaring through the skies. "Me, too!"

The noise of migrant pickers moving toward them caused Jeff to pause and look at his wristwatch. "Come on, Peaches," he said. "We'd better go before one of the men catches us out here, and anyway, I need to get back to work. You want to get a cold drink before going home?"

"Sure," she said. She picked up her hair ribbon and smoothed out the creases in her dress.

As they were exiting the field next to the Clayborns' mansion, they overheard Dr. Colonel talking to Jenks.

"Goddammit, Jenks, I don't want to hear any more about the fucking brown rot growing in the orchards. That's what I hired a goddamn general manager for. Now you get over there and tell Hampton Smyth I said to get on it. Now!"

"Oh!" Henrietta said, sucking in air. "Is your father mad at my daddy?"

"Shh," Jeff said. He held a finger to his lips and backed them up behind a tree.

After Jenks left, Jeff led Henrietta out in the open.

"Hello, Father," Jeff said. He squeezed her hand, perhaps trying to shore up some courage for them both.

Dr. Colonel transfixed on their clasped hands before crossing his arms and blowing out his breath in a way that showed irritation. "What were y'all doing out there in the middle of the afternoon, son?"

Henrietta was now self-conscious about her wrinkled dress and loose hair, and she started to nervously smooth her skirt with her free hand.

"We were just having lunch on my break; is there a problem?" Jeff asked.

"How many times have I told you that brown rot can be easily controlled with proper sanitation and the right fungicides?" He was now wagging his finger at Jeff.

"About a million times," Jeff said. He crooked an uneasy smile at Henrietta and squeezed her hand again.

"Well, I've said it about twice that many times to my goddamn employees. Jefferson, I want you to start reinforcing that message. You're coming of age now, and you'll soon have managerial responsibilities on this plantation between semesters at college and medical school. It's no longer acceptable that you waste your time," he said. Dr. Colonel looked at Henrietta's face for the first time. "Especially, when there's serious business at hand."

She'd never seen Dr. Colonel angry or heard him cuss before and she could feel her hands getting sweaty, but Jeff was holding on tight.

"I've been working all morning, Father. In the warehouse. We were having lunch."

"Well, I want you to start working on the brown rot that's apparently threatening this year's crop. You'd better run home, Henrietta," Dr. Colonel said with a scowl. "Jefferson's got more important things to do this afternoon."

"Sorry, Hen. I'll just walk her back to the cabin."

"Well, all right. But no dallying!"

"Yes, sir," Jeff said. He and Henrietta ran back into the orchards, still holding hands. Jeff's father had never encouraged their romance, but for the first time, she had felt something threatening in Dr. Colonel's manner.

As the serenades of Bears Repeating continued, Henrietta's thoughts jumped again, landing in May of 1949, when Jeff had arrived back at Clayborn Plantation with his medical degree from the Medical College of Charleston. Having earned a B.A. in journalism from Augusta College four years earlier, Henrietta was already working at *The Greenfield Weekly* as a staff reporter.

Henrietta was anxiously anticipating Jeff's return later that evening and didn't expect him to pop over to the cabin this early. She was in her bedroom when she overheard Jeff laughing with her parents outside on the porch.

She jumped up and ran outside to embrace her long-awaited boyfriend. Turning back to her parents, she noticed her daddy's face held a curiously broad smile as he pretended to clean some pruning shears, and her mother was squealing with delight even after knocking over the paper bag of green beans she'd been snapping.

"Oh, Henrietta, Jeff's here to ask you something," Elizabeth said. She put her hand over her mouth.

With a lovesick grin, Jeff gently pulled on Henrietta's hand, and off they went, running and laughing into the forest of peach trees.

"Close your eyes," he said, before pinching off a spray of budding peach blossoms from a nearby tree. "Come on, don't peek."

"I'm trying not to!"

He pulled out a ring, carefully chosen from his mother's family jewels, and placed it on the flowers. Bending down on one knee, he held up the blooms that were now shiny and sparkly. "Now you can open them!"

"What on earth?" she said.

"A beautiful peach bouquet for my beautiful peach. Henrietta, will you marry me, for real this time?"

"Oh! Of course! Yes, yes! Finally, yes—for real this time," she said. She gently plucked the exquisite ring off a peach stem. She was crying happy tears as she embraced him tightly. "Oh, Jeff, how I love you so!"

"Here, let me help you with that," he said. He took the ring and placed it on her finger. "I wanted to make it official with this."

"This ring's so, so ..." Holding up her hand, she was rendered speechless by the huge oval-cut emerald surrounded by diamonds.

"The emerald's five carats. It was my great-grandmother Pridgen's ring," he said. "My mother wanted you to have it, too."

"Oh, that's so sweet, and I'm so honored. It's gorgeous! I'll wear it with pride, Jeff."

"You're my pride, Henrietta; I'm so happy we can finally be together."

"Me, too," she said. They kissed again.

Hand in hand and staring into each other's love-struck eyes, they returned to the cabin, where Elizabeth looked like she might explode with excitement.

"Come on in here—I've got a surprise," Elizabeth squealed, bringing out a bottle of inexpensive champagne she'd gotten on sale at the Winn-Dixie and was saving in the refrigerator for a special occasion. "This is just so wonderful!"

Hampton popped off the cork and poured the effervescing liquid into four mismatched wineglasses.

"Ooooh! That ring is something; may I see it?" Elizabeth asked.

"Of course, Mama. It's a Pridgen family heirloom. Isn't it the most beautiful and special thing you've ever seen?"

"No, you are, my sweetie," Elizabeth said. Tears welled up in her big blue eyes. She pulled out a handkerchief from her apron and blew her nose.

"Oh, Mama," Henrietta said. She was wiping away her own tears.

"Hey now, let's not get carried away with all of this boo-hooing. I want to make a toast," Hampton said. "Here's to the most beautiful and smartest daughter ever." They started to clink when Hampton added: "Not yet; I'm not done. Here's also to the best future son-in-law in the world and congratulations to him for graduating at the top of his medical class." Glasses finally clinked.

"We're so proud of you both," Elizabeth said. "We'll have so much fun planning your wedding. Have you set a date?" Elizabeth asked, talking rapidly.

"Not yet, Mama," Henrietta said. "We just got engaged!" She put her arm through Jeff's and squeezed it.

"Do you have any special requests for your wedding?" Elizabeth asked Jeff. "Or do you just want Henrietta and me to handle everything?"

"Well, now, I don't believe I've ever been asked for my opinion before," Jeff said. And they all laughed, knowing how bossy his father could be. "I just say the sooner the better. We've been waiting long enough— and it'll give Father less time to meddle. And, let me add, whatever Henrietta wants, I want the same."

"Aww," Elizabeth said. She was clapping her hands. "How about your parents? Do they have any preferences? I'm assuming you've told them."

"Um, not exactly. Of course, I talked to my mother about the ring but I thought Henrietta and I could announce it properly over dinner tomorrow, after my interview with Dr. Kepple at the Aiken County Hospital; I'm hoping he'll take me on as an intern."

"He'll snatch you right up," Elizabeth said. "That is, if he knows what's good for him."

"I hope you're right," Jeff said. "Well, I guess since I just got home, I should go spend some time with the folks. I'll be off now. Thanks again for letting your daughter marry me." Jeff kissed Elizabeth's cheek and reached out for his future father-in-law's right hand. But Hampton, a large, brawny man with a heart as considerable as the orchards he managed, ignored the hand and gave Jeff a bear hug instead.

"Thank you so much," Jeff said. He whispered it as a tear rolled down his cheek. He turned and walked out the door with Henrietta. They stopped a little way past the front porch.

"I just love your parents," Jeff said. "They're so easy to be with and genuinely loving." He rubbed his wet cheeks.

Henrietta couldn't speak. She was touched by his raw emotion.

"So, my beautiful peach," Jeff said. "How about I come by to get you tomorrow evening about six-thirty for an announcement dinner up at the main house? We'll spring our engagement on the old man after some wine. Lots of wine."

"For heaven's sake, Jeff, it's not like our plans have been a big secret. Your mother even let you give me her family's ring."

Jeff sighed. "I wish you didn't have to see what I mean." After kissing her good night, he walked off into the darkness, his voice drifting back to her. "No matter what they do, no matter what he says, just remember that I love you and we're going to have a happy life together."

"I love you, too, but ..." She didn't finish; Jeff had already disappeared. *Doesn't Dr. Colonel think I'm good enough for his son?*

The next evening, when they announced their engagement at the Clayborn mansion, there was no champagne brought out, only the usual dinner wine accompanying the customary formal dining experience.

At least Miss Julia, Jeff's mother, seemed happy about it. "I, for one, am thrilled," she said, her sightless eyes concealed behind her customary dark glasses. "Let me say congratulations, son, and best wishes to the beautiful bride-to-be." But as she raised a glass of wine, she knocked over her water goblet.

"Well, you've finally done it," Dr. Colonel said before Regina, the housemaid, ran in to clean up the spilled water. "Congratulations," he added. But he looked like a simmering stew of raw sewage, while Jeff acted as if he was holding his breath to avoid the stench.

Wishing she could run back to her parents' cabin, Henrietta looked around the room in an attempt to ignore the tension. She noted how the buffet and china cabinet were both beautiful and intimidating in their bulk, as was the twelve-seat mahogany dining table, which sat on massive carved legs. Lalique crystal vases with bird motifs stared out of the leaded glass shelves of a coordinating display cabinet with aged wood veneers polished to a high shine. Walls and windows were draped in light-green silk fabrics. Oil paintings of southern landscapes and bird dogs holding limp mallards wore ornately gilded frames, while in a corner there stood a large golden cage containing brightly hued parakeets. Despite the live birds, the room remained cold and stilted, as if it was trying too hard to be impressive. It reminded Henrietta of her visit to the state capitol's museum, which held the musty, acidic odor of Civil War relics.

Thankfully, after a peach cobbler for dessert, Dr. Colonel asked Jeff to join him in his study to smoke a cigar. That was when Miss Julia finally seemed to relax and regain her usual composure. Henrietta sighed with relief.

"Let's go to the living room, dear," Miss Julia said.

Miss Julia took Henrietta's hand and using her walking stick led them into the living room, navigating around the furniture in her lifelong home with the speed and precision of a bat flying through a dark narrow cave. Reaching the elegant Regency sofa, they sat down.

"You'll have to excuse the Colonel," Miss Julia said. She hugged Henrietta. "It's just that he wants to hang on to Jeff. He simply can't let go, and he can be so dang stubborn."

Henrietta didn't understand what Miss Julia was trying to say. The woman's expression was indecipherable as her eyes were hidden behind the black sunglasses. After Jeff had been born, Miss Julia had had complications with her diabetes, which caused her to become blind as well as deaf in one ear. The dark glasses covered what had once been a striking face with vibrant light-blue eyes framed by dark-brown curls. She now wore her hair pulled back in a severe bun at the nape of her neck, and her clothes were uniformly black in the fall and winter and all white in the spring and summer. "That way, I know I always match," she would say with her ever-present good humor.

"He doesn't want us to get married?" Henrietta asked. Although Miss Julia had one good ear left, it wasn't perfect. But Henrietta didn't want Dr. Colonel to overhear. So she was speaking softly into Miss Julia's good ear while using the tactile sign language she'd learned when she worked the summers at the Clayborn Orphanage & School for the Blind and Deaf, an organization founded, funded and run by Miss Julia. Henrietta had become skilled in regular as well as tactile sign language largely because of Brodie Thompson, a light-skinned colored kid and one of the deaf orphaned students who'd been there since he was a toddler. Truth be told, Brodie was Miss Julia's favorite—although she loved all the children there, whether they were white or a racial mix, like Brodie. Because she encouraged it, eight-year-old Brodie would often visit Miss Julia at the house or show up unexpectedly by Henrietta's side, wanting her to practice sign language and spend extra time with him. But Brodie had never been a bother; in fact, he was a sweet little guy who'd made learning sign language easy and fun. Henrietta genuinely liked him and understood Miss Julia's attachment.

"Now don't you worry about what the Colonel wants," Miss Julia said. "Leave him to me. I care more about what our Jefferson wants, and I can clearly see that he wants you, my darling girl. Yes, that's right. I can see it." She was smiling as Brodie came in and sat close to her. "You're perfect for one another, and I couldn't be happier with his choice." She patted Brodie's hands before reaching over for Henrietta's left one.

"Ah, look, Brodie, Henrietta's wearing the Pridgen ring," Miss Julia said, fingering the large gemstone with diamonds. "Isn't it beautiful? It was my grandmother's and I'm so pleased Jeff wanted you to have it."

"Yes, and thank you, Miss Julia. Jeff told me it was a family heirloom," Henrietta said. She was still leaning close to Miss Julia's good ear.

"That ring was bought by my grandfather, Arnold Pridgen, for his bride, Cynthia. She was a Cavanaugh from Charleston, and I reckon he had to entice her with something special to get her to move way out here to the country," Miss Julia said, chuckling. "Anyway, they're the ones who first expanded the original farmhouse to what we live in today."

"Why don't you wear it?"

"I have too many rings to wear, my child. This one was being saved for Maxwell. You may have heard me talk about my beloved brother. He was killed in the war. Oh, how I miss him; he was such a loving person … and funny, too. He surely was a special person." She sighed. "Anyway, since poor Max passed away before marrying, this ring's just been sitting in a safe deposit box. Such a shame and a waste."

"Yes, I suppose so."

"That's why when Jeff expressed an interest in it for you, I did indeed encourage him." Miss Julia smiled.

"I'm so honored that you and Jeff want me to wear it. But, Dr. Colonel—he doesn't?"

"Please, dear, don't fret about that."

"I don't understand … what's the problem?"

"He may not say so, but the Colonel knows as I do that you'll bring strength, beauty and character to this family. You'll have to forgive him."

"Forgive him for what? I still don't understand."

Miss Julia paused and pursed her lips. "He won't act like it. Now, tell us, I bet your mother is excited…" She patted Henrietta's hands again and smiled, effectively changing the subject.

A month later, Henrietta was sitting in the same spot, waiting for Jeff to come home from his internship with Dr. Kepple. She was tapping her fingers on the coffee table when Dr. Colonel came in. Without so much as a hello or a how are you, Dr. Colonel put his hands behind his back, began pacing and started speaking with a sharp tone.

"Given the circumstances, I've planned what will be a proper engagement party for Jefferson's station in our community," Dr. Colonel said. "It'll take place in three weeks, and I've taken care of everything. All you've got to do is show up," he said. He stopped walking and looked Henrietta up and down. "And for God's sake, buy a new dress, something fashionable, something of quality. Not that homemade stuff you usually wear."

Henrietta sat speechless.

"Go to Aiken, to Angelica's shop," he said, continuing almost without pause. "She'll know exactly what you need to look proper and nice for our Jefferson. Get your hair and nails done. Jesus Christ, stop biting your nails!"

Henrietta jerked her fingers out of her mouth.

"And try to act like a lady. Get a book on table manners. Then read it. We'll soon be hosting dignitaries and South Carolina's finest families. Here, use this for a new wardrobe," he said. He slapped two hundred dollars in cash on the table and walked briskly out of the room before Henrietta could comment.

She balled up her fists. *Table manners. Oh! That man is a complete jerk!* Henrietta's face turned red hot. In defiance, she left the money on the table and walked out of the house, slamming the door behind her. She couldn't remember why she had been waiting for Jeff. And at that moment, she didn't care.

The next day, she found the cash on her bedroom dresser and a handwritten list of fresh orders from Dr. Colonel, including a request that she come by that afternoon for a conference with him and Miss Julia. Not wanting to create any more problems and reassured by the inclusion of Jeff's mother, she went. But when she got there, only Dr. Colonel was present. It left him free to rant without the restraints of Miss Julia's calming influence.

Often, when his daily doses of condescension became too much to endure, Henrietta would sneak off to the library or hide in her quiet spot, a small one-room office-like structure her daddy had built for her under one of the live oaks near the cabin. Jeff found her there one day about a month before the wedding. She was sitting at a small desk, her left elbow on its surface and palm propping up her chin, absorbed in deep thought while her right hand moved a pen aggressively on a yellow pad of paper.

"Henrietta!" Jeff shouted. He sounded concerned.

"Oh, Jeff, you startled me." She hadn't heard his approach. Nor was she aware of being watched through the open-air window by the creepy foreman, Jenks. But Jeff was more observant.

"What are you doing here, Jenks? Get lost, man! Now!" Jeff shouted. He pointed toward the fields.

"Yessir, sorry, Mr. Jeff," the beefy man said. With an inexplicable glare at Henrietta, Jenks hulked away, slowly disappearing into the adjacent fruit trees.

"Dear Lord, Jeff, I'm so glad you're here!" She ran to her fiancé's arms. "I must've been too absorbed in my writing to notice that creep. Oh, Jeff, you're my hero," she said and kissed him on the lips.

"If that guy ever gives you trouble, you come straight to me," Jeff said.

"You know I will. Jeff, let's never hide anything from each other, deal?"

"Deal. I couldn't even if I wanted to. You're my everything, Henrietta." They kissed again.

"Hey, how come you're off work so early?" she said.

"I wanted to come home and make love to my beautiful fiancé," he whispered, pulling her toward an old loveseat that sat against the back wall.

She returned his kisses fervently as their bodies entwined awkwardly in the narrow space. But after a few minutes, she forced a pause. "Now, Dr. Clayborn, you're just going to have to wait until our honeymoon."

"Damn," he said. He sat up slowly. "Hey, I've been thinking about something. I don't want to live up at the main house after we're married. I want to move into our own place, maybe in Aiken where I can be closer to Dr. Kepple's office and the hospital. Would that be okay with you?"

"But your father wants . . ."

"I know Father wants us to live in the east wing under his thumb, but we have our own life to live and I want to be alone with you." He rolled her backward again. "What do you think, you want to?" He tickled her neck with kisses.

"I don't care where we live, as long as we're together," she said between giggles.

"Well, how would you feel about moving out West, like to New Mexico? Would you be open to that, Henrietta?" He sat up and looked at her, all seriousness.

"You still want to do that?"

"Henrietta, you know I've always wanted to explore New Mexico, but it's not just that. I'd like to be able to come and go without having to check in with a colonel. I'd like to know what it's like to be a real civilian and live at least part of my adult life outside of the army," Jeff said. He sighed.

"I know what you mean. Your father, he's so demanding and, at times, very unpleasant. It seems he wants to control you, me, us and everything connected with us. And if he doesn't get his way, watch out! How does your mother put up with him?"

"He's amazingly gentle and agreeable with her, as you know."

"Yeah, he doesn't want to kill his golden goose."

"What?"

"Oh, nothing. I was just kidding," Henrietta said, wishing she'd held her tongue. "Now, about moving to New Mexico, why don't you try to find something on a short-term basis, maybe after your residency, so we can see how we like it before doing anything permanent."

"What a great idea! I'll look into what's available," Jeff said.

"Surely even your father would be okay with something temporary," she added.

"Henrietta, you're a genius!" They kissed again.

A week before the wedding, Elizabeth was pacing in the cabin as Henrietta and her father watched.

"I don't care if they fire me; I don't care if they fire you." Elizabeth pointed her finger at Hampton. "I simply cannot take Dr. Colonel's insufferable bullying any longer."

"Lizzie," Hampton said, "honey, just calm down."

"I will not. The man's impossible. I don't care who he is or who he thinks he is. He butts into things that should be our decisions to make."

"Mama, we've only got one more week to endure," Henrietta said. "I just want to get through this as peacefully as possible."

"We plan one thing and he goes off and does another," Elizabeth said. "Makes his own arrangements, without even asking or talking it over. Oh, the nerve of that man. Do you know that he's changed the reception from the church to the Clayborn mansion? The man's beyond contempt."

"He did? But we've already sent out the invitations. He can't do that," Henrietta said.

"Well, he sure enough did, I'm telling you as I live and breathe." Elizabeth had one hand on her hip, the other over her heart. "Printed up the change in a special bulletin he intends to give out during the wedding, which, if you ask me, is rather tacky. He claims it's because he and many of *his* guests want to be able to toast with champagne, and the church won't allow it, of course. He also went and fired Lydia's Catering, just like that." She snapped her fingers. "For *his* reception, he's hired some fancy chef from Augusta, service staff and a live orchestra. He's having additional flowers, tented rooms ... the whole shebang. Can you believe the gall of that man?"

"Mama, as I said, we've only got to get through the next seven days. Then we can spend the rest of our lives avoiding him. Please, Mama. I can't take your anger, too. He's about all I can handle." Tears welled up in Henrietta's eyes.

"Oh, Henrietta, I'm so sorry, honey. You know I don't want to put any more pressure on you. He just makes me so doggone angry ... I mean ... he could make a saint go insane." She sat and returned to her work on the seam in Henrietta's bridal gown.

"I know, thank goodness Jeff rented an apartment in Aiken so at least we don't have to live with him after we're married."

"Don't be so sure, honey. While I was typing a letter for Miss Julia yesterday, I overheard him talking on the phone with one of his good-ole-boy buddies, Boyd Peterson, the man who rents most of the apartments in Aiken."

"Thanks for the warning," Henrietta said. She kissed her mother on the cheek. "But I need to dash to the newspaper before I'm late. Don't worry, Mama. All I know is Jeff makes all of this worth it."

Despite the interferences of Dr. Colonel, the wedding turned out better than Henrietta and her mother could have imagined. By evening, the summer sun dipped on the horizon just as a string of shiny limousines and expensive automobiles delivered beautiful guests and VIPs to the red-carpeted steps of the Greenfield Methodist Church, where Henrietta worshipped with her family every Sunday. Photographers mingled with guests, including one from *The State*, South Carolina's oldest and largest newspaper, sent all the way from Columbia to cover the wedding event of the year. The sanctuary was flawlessly ornamented and comfortably cooled, thanks to a generous gift of eight brand-new air-conditioning units from Dr. and Mrs. Jules Beaufort Clayborn.

"I don't understand all the pretense and fuss of southern bluebloods," Henrietta said to her mother as she dressed in the church's bridal parlor. "They get worked up over the silliest little things. Can you explain it?"

"Not me, it's like trying to understand higher math or the cause of mental retardation," Elizabeth said.

Henrietta laughed out loud. "You're right, but we'll just get through it together. Right, Mama?"

"Oh, my sweet girl, you bet. You're so beautiful right now, look at you. You're about to enter a whole new world with a wonderful young man. I couldn't be more proud. But, hey now…" Elizabeth sniffed as the maternal tears came. "You just remember who you are—a beautiful, brilliant, talented young woman who is loved and loving, and also you remember where you came from, and everything will work out just fine. Your father and I love you more than you could possibly know. And if you ever need us, we'll always be here for you."

In that sentimental moment, in that snapshot in her mind, everything in Henrietta's life was peaceful; everything in their wedding was picture perfect.

Her dress was a masterpiece, designed and created by her talented mother. Jeff in his tuxedo, and five handsome groomsmen, fellow medical graduate friends of Jeff's, were paired with her best friends, dressed like peach flowers tied in blue-velvet bows. Two little girls from Miss Julia's orphanage, aged five and seven, looked like Shirley Temple dolls in coordinating blue gowns with peach-colored bows as they meandered up the carpeted main aisle, tossing peach-colored rose petals. And, perhaps most importantly, for just that one day, Jeff and Henrietta had no worries about Dr. Colonel.

From experience, they knew Dr. Colonel would be on his best behavior in the public setting, morphing into the ultimate southern charmer, the proud papa and great benefactor of poor orphaned children. And they were right. His performance included a profusion of affection for Miss Julia as he guided and supported her down an aisle adorned with spectacular dendrobium orchids and scented candlesticks nesting in French giltwood torcheres. He projected pride and pleasure toward a model son and his beautiful golden-haired bride. His eyes held tears of joy as he provided great theater for his handpicked audience of southern aristocrats.

No expense was spared for the reception. In air-conditioned, tented rooms a sit-down dinner with an appropriate wine for each course was followed by a choice of cakes that looked like lavish high-rise buildings. Champagne flowed, and toasts were given amid an orchestra's waltzes. Giant ice sculptures topped strategically placed pedestals, gargoyles guarding the elaborate party-scape. Everything ran with a friendly precision and gracious style. Even Elizabeth stopped her feuding with Dr. Colonel and danced a foxtrot with him. When Henrietta thought her feet were about to give out, she and Jeff made a dash to change into their traveling clothes, though Jeff had kept their honeymoon plans a secret, even from Henrietta.

Jeff wanted to surprise his wife and prevent his father from meddling. And for once, he had been successful in keeping his plans private. No one knew the destination of their honeymoon was Santa Fe, New Mexico. Initially, Dr. Colonel had fumed about the secrecy, but eventually gave in to Jeff's desire for mystery, probably because she and Jeff had finally agreed to live in the east wing of the Clayborn mansion.

Dr. Colonel had won this war of wills. But, of course, as Henrietta was then only beginning to understand, he always did.

Chapter 10

Joe's soul retrieval journey ended, and he brought Henrietta back to the present with his soul catcher, blowing a spray of something wet over her face and chest. It wasn't spit that spewed over her. It was more like a silky mist that had a light cologne quality to it. *What was it?* The liquid from the Coke bottle came to mind, but she didn't dare ask about it at that moment.

"Welcome back, Henrietta," Joe said. His words were soft and warm.

Henrietta blinked her eyes, and as she started to arise, she felt a strange bubbling up sensation in her chest.

"You can get up whenever you're ready, and I'll tell you what I saw during my journey in Spirit," Joe said.

She suddenly let out a laugh almost like a sneeze. "Oh," she said. She put her hand over her mouth. "I don't know why I did that." She started to giggle.

"I'm delighted with your laughter. It's good medicine for your soul's return."

"Please, tell me what you saw," she said, trying to contain herself in front of her serious friends.

But like two birthday piñatas hit at the same time, a bright bounty of laughter spilled out of Joe and Altie, amazing Henrietta, who had never before imagined she would ever share in such a spontaneous explosion of joy with two Apache Indians, and certainly not while sitting with them in a grand-scale teepee.

When the three of them regained their composure, Joe said, "You should know that what I see is most often given to me in metaphor or symbols. We must interpret what we see. You can help with that."

"I'll try," Henrietta said.

"I saw in the Cave of the Wounded a young Indian maiden," Joe said. "Before she came to that cave, this Indian girl was known by all in her tribe to be full of passion for life, and she had many beautiful gifts. Everyone in the tribe adored this little girl, all except one man. He was jealous of her rich passion and love of life. His jealousy turned into rage. He wanted her power for himself, and one day, he began to stalk her. He chased her with trained swine into a cage of fire where there were pens, pokers, blazing princes and rotting flesh. Trapped and aching, she was cornered, but he tied her up with fleecy ropes anyway, near babes wrapped in blankets. He choked her with one hand and beat his fist on her heart, over and over. Because of her great light and power, the maiden did not die, but this attack caused parts of her soul, which contained most of her passion, to split off, run away and hide. After his assault, the man left her alone. But something was terribly wrong with the young maiden. She was still alive, yes, but she felt dead. She had become a member of the walking dead, for she was missing essential parts of her soul. Without wholeness, she was no longer able to let the Great Spirit's light shine through her and into the world of form."

Henrietta stared at Joe, her mouth agape. "Pens, swine, pokers, blazing princes, rotting flesh," she said, repeating some of the key words in his cryptic narrative. "Aching ... fleecy ropes ... near babes wrapped in blankets ... Oh dear Lord!"

"I took this symbolic story as yours, Henrietta," Joe said. "So I ventured into the Cave of the Wounded and found your missing soul parts, the passion and love of life, hiding there. I had to convince them to return to you here by assuring them it would be safe. I told them they were needed for you to awaken and fulfill your divine mission for the Great Spirit, that you wanted and needed them to live life fully and in wholeness, to work and raise your children in harmony, peace and love. They agreed and came with me after this negotiation, and I blew them into you."

"I don't know what to say." Henrietta spoke softly.

"You must see the reality of your healing," Joe said.

"I don't know what that means," she said.

"It means you must put the image of yourself being whole, without fragments, into your mind and trust in that. You must love and talk to your returned soul parts and tell them it's safe to stay. Don't let the dark spirits trick them into leaving. Love your whole self." He paused to interject: "Did you know that most people do not love themselves? This is a grave mistake. But that is a subject for another day." Joe then continued with instructions. "In any event and as I was saying, you must love your whole self. Pray to the Great Spirit for protection. Envision this spiritual protection as a bright-white light all around yourself, as in the shape of my soul catcher. To imagine and see with your mind's eye helps the healing process."

Henrietta was no longer trying to suppress any giggles. Her emotions had done a one-eighty. She started to cry, shaking her head back and forth. It was incredible: Joe had somehow become privy to the story she had been hiding. Joe had seen the cause of all her suffering.

"The man in the dream, the one who wanted to steal your passion, you know who he is," Joe said.

Henrietta nodded, but she didn't want to think about him. She wished her retrieved soul parts could also somehow push all remnants of him out of her memory banks forever.

"You also know what the symbols mean," he said. His voice was comforting as he offered her a handkerchief.

"As weird as your journey dream sounded, I think I know how all of it translates," she said.

"That's a good sign, Henrietta. We will now pray to seal you and express our infinite gratitude to the healing presence of the Great Spirit within us, to our spirit guides and to Jesus the Christ and Mother Mary for their loving assistance," Joe said. He placed some wild tobacco into the fire.

After they completed their songs of thanksgiving, Joe looked at Henrietta and smiled. "Now that your soul parts have been returned, healing from trauma is possible. Before it was not," he said.

"You cannot heal what is not there," Altie added.

"Hmm, I guess that makes sense," Henrietta said.

Altie got up from behind the drum and stood next to her husband. He put his arm around her waist and they looked at one another. Henrietta noticed that they made a striking couple with a kind of flawless mocha beauty that was captivating. Their raven hair was always shiny, but never appeared dirty. They smelled of sweet fry bread and mesquite, a rich earthiness and the essence of flowers. Their eyes twinkled and smiled, although their lips did not always do so. They lived and breathed each moment fully. They were aware of the power of their dreams.

"Talking will be good medicine now," Joe said.

"I'd love to. But first, I'd like to pay you." She stood up.

Joe held up his palms. "It's our pleasure to help."

"Well, please let me fix you something to eat, then, before you have to go to the ceremonies. It's the least I can do."

"Sweet karma. You know what that means," Joe said, releasing his wife to strike an Elvis singing pose.

"That's okay, Joe," Henrietta said. She was laughing. "As entertaining as your 'Teddy Bear' routine is, please, let me do something for you and Altie."

"I was going to sing something else. But perhaps 'Hound Dog' isn't appropriate right now." He was grinning. "I am, however, always happy to receive your good cooking."

"At this time, I must deliver some herbs to a friend in need," Altie said. "If it is agreeable, I will take Jeffie Junior with me on that errand and then sit with him so you can continue healing with the talking medicine. We can join you at the doctor's cottage later."

Humbled by the continual giving and helpful natures of these trusted friends, all Henrietta could do was embrace them. "Thank you," she tried to say, but she was overcome with emotion. Tears streamed down her face.

Chapter 11

After she exited the ceremonial teepee, Henrietta had to pause to adjust from the dizzying bright sunlight and regain her equilibrium.

"It may take a while to get reacquainted with your returned soul parts," Joe said, coming out behind her. "Sometimes it's right away. For others, it takes a day, a week or even up to six weeks. It's different for everyone."

"To hold on to the soul fragments returned to you, you must love all of yourself," Altie added. "Be kind to yourself, forgive yourself and the world. Feel good."

"I'll try." Henrietta was feeling slightly woozy as an irrepressible laughter began to bubble up once again.

"Ho, ha!" Joe said. "I can see our young brave's feeling the hug of wholeness already. Isn't our Great Spirit great?" He beamed at her before slipping on a pair of stylish sunglasses.

At that moment, it seemed that Joe's smile was brighter than it had been before. Or maybe Henrietta had never noticed it. His teeth were a dazzling white against his beautiful light-brown skin, like the bright facets of diamonds sparkling on a velvety dark backdrop. He almost looked like a tanned movie star.

"Oh, Joe, I do feel different. Very different. I feel ... wow ... everything's so alive and wonderful and colorful ... the trees, the mountains, the teepees. Look! There's someone in full regalia. Oh, his costume's magnificent," she said. She twirled around. "This is just so ... " She paused, feeling a bit tongue-tied. "I can't explain it, except it's like the joy I felt after having the twins."

"You choose a name first," Henrietta remembered saying to Jeff nearly a decade ago, after giving birth to their daughters in the Aiken County Hospital where her husband worked.

"Okay, I like the name Frannie, short for Frances. What do you think?" Jeff had said.

"Well, hello, Frannie," she said, addressing the tiny infant in her right arm. "Now for your sister. My turn," Henrietta said. She smiled up at Jeff.

"Of course, Peaches," he said.

"Let's see, what name goes with Frannie? How about Annie?"

"And so they shall be Frannie and Annie Clayborn, the most beautiful girls in all of Greenfield," Jeff said.

"They still need middle names, Jeff."

"How about Frances Julia and Ann Elizabeth?"

"I like those names, too, Jeff. They're perfect. Our two girls will be named for their grandmothers, the most important and wise women in our families," she said.

"No, you are, my darling. If they take after you, they'll be perfect."

Henrietta started to cry.

"What's wrong, Peaches?"

"Not a thing! Oh, Jeff, there's so much emotion in me. I'm so relieved they were born healthy. I'm so thankful for that and for you, Jeff. I couldn't be happier than I am at this moment," she had said. Her husband had embraced all three of them with tears in his eyes.

"And little Jeffie's birth, too?" Joe Loco said, breaking into her reverie about the twins. "Was it the same feeling with him?"

She heard him but didn't respond because she was still absorbed in the memory of her precious girls.

"Henrietta?"

"Oh, sorry, Joe," she said. She didn't want to stop the momentum of joy she felt. "You know what? I believe I'm going to be all right. That soul retrieval was so amazing; I already feel better in ways I can't really explain right now." She started walking toward the doctor's cottage. "Come on, let's get something to eat."

Once they were in the doctor's cottage kitchen, Henrietta half-whispered to Joe: "When you said 'talking medicine,' did you mean that I should talk about my secret? What I've been hiding from Jeff?"

Joe nodded. "Facing fears in a safe environment is helpful to the healing process."

"Hmm. That makes sense." Henrietta had never been to a psychologist, but she imagined the sessions to be similar to Joe's talking medicine. "Well okay, let me think about where to begin." As Henrietta gathered her thoughts, she began to cut up some raw chicken, onions and carrots.

Joe sat at the kitchen table, humming with his eyes closed.

"I should preface my story by saying that after Jeff and I fell in love in high school, we thought we would be able to share everything and be happy forever."

Joe opened his eyes. "I can see that."

"But as you correctly saw in your vision, an evil man in our tribe ruined everything. And since then, it's been a fight for me to make it through each day without cracking up even more."

"Ha'aa."

"I thought coming here would make telling Jeff easier," Henrietta said. "But it hasn't."

"The soul retrieval and talking medicine will help. They're the beginning of an ongoing inner journey we are meant to walk."

"Well, be that as it may, before I can get on with telling my awful secrets, I'll need to give you a little history," Henrietta said. She was planning to take Joe on another kind of journey. But in this expedition, there would be no metaphors or cryptic references to interpret. She would lay bare the cold and hard truth of a devastating past. And the cause of a soul's shattering.

Chapter 12

"Why, Dr. Colonel, this is a surprise," Henrietta had said as she opened the front door of the cabin. While Jeff was on his first visit to Medichero to interview for an opening there, Henrietta and her three-year-old girls were staying at her parents' cabin. They had been there for nearly a week when Dr. Colonel showed up.

"What brings you by this afternoon?" Henrietta said.

"I was wondering if you'd do me a favor, Henrietta," Dr. Colonel said, walking past her and into the small kitchen. "But first, where are those beautiful granddaughters of mine?"

"I just put them down for their nap, and I'd prefer not to wake them up, if you don't mind. What can I do for you, Dr. Colonel?" Henrietta said. Her tone was direct, business-like.

"Well now, I was thinking it sure would be nice if you'd come up and have supper with us tonight," Dr. Colonel said. "My Julia's not been feeling well since

Jeff's been gone, and she misses you, too. I think it'd do her a world of good if you'd come by."

"It's not like we've been gone that long. We can all have supper tomorrow night after Jeff gets back from Medichero," she said.

"I know, but really, we'd like a little time with just you before Jeff gets home. Besides, since you've been cooped up in the cabin all week, I'd think you'd want a break for yourself. Why don't you let your mama and daddy babysit? We'll have some fun. And I can't stand it when my Julia's not happy. Please, for our Miss Julia's sake."

"Well, I suppose …"

"Wonderful. We'll see you at seven o'clock." He walked out the door without waiting for her to finish.

Henrietta didn't want to disappoint her mother-in-law, so that evening she walked to the Clayborn mansion as instructed. She knew how Dr. Colonel abhorred tardiness and the last thing in the world she'd want to do is make him angry. Consequently, she arrived at the front door precisely at seven. She paused to consider whether she should walk in or knock and let the housemaid, Regina, answer the door. The thought of doing that was strange, she realized, because she obviously wasn't a guest. She had lived in the mansion for more than three years. Before she could decide, Dr. Colonel startled her by opening the door himself.

"Welcome back, Henrietta," Dr. Colonel said. "I'm so pleased you're here and right on time." He gave her a hug, holding her a little too long.

"Thanks," she said, backing up. *Great, now I'm going to smell like his overbearing cologne.*

Dr. Colonel led her into the dining room, where there were three place settings evenly spaced on one end of the long table. The dishes had silver-plated dome covers on them. *How odd that the food is already served,* Henrietta thought with a twinge of uneasiness.

"Looks like y'all are all ready to eat," Henrietta said. "I hope you haven't been waiting on me."

"Oh, no, but we can get started," he said. He pulled a chair out from the table. "Please, take a seat." Henrietta looked at him suspiciously, but acquiesced, sitting in the proffered chair.

Dr. Colonel walked over to a bottle of champagne that was chilling in a silver bucket and prepared to open it, all the while staring at her. Henrietta tried to ignore his steely glare by getting up to visit with the colorful little parakeets in the corner of the room, thinking how sad it was they were imprisoned in a cage, though it was gilded and rather large.

Bang! Henrietta nearly jumped out of her skin as the champagne cork whizzed past her head. It hit the birdcage like a miniature cannonball. The poor panicked birds were now flapping violently, hitting each other and the walls of the enclosure.

Fearing they would become injured, Henrietta palmed the cage to try to settle them down. "It's okay, it's okay."

"Don't worry about those damn birds; they'll be fine," Dr. Colonel said. "It's not like they've never heard a champagne cork being popped in here before." He chuckled. "Come back over here and try this." Dr. Colonel poured the bubbly liquid into two fine crystal champagne flutes.

Henrietta dutifully complied and sat back down. "Are we celebrating something? Where's Miss Julia?"

"Yes, I suppose we are. Jeff's coming home tomorrow and things are going to change for the better around here as soon as he does," he announced.

"I'm looking forward to that myself," Henrietta said. She wasn't sure why she hadn't noticed before, but Dr. Colonel was sporting a new hairpiece in what seemed a silly attempt to disguise his receding hairline. How it stayed in place was a mystery.

"You probably won't realize how special this champagne is. It's a Louis Roederer Blanc de Blancs, one of the very best in the world. I was saving it for Jeff's return, but I know that he's usually willing to settle for lesser quality than I am." Her father-in-law looked down at Henrietta and smiled like a Cheshire cat.

Ignoring his insult, she said, "Shouldn't we wait for Miss Julia?"

"Here's to a fine Clayborn homecoming," he said. He held his fluted crystal up in the air.

Okay, don't answer my question, Henrietta thought. She took a sip of the best champagne she had ever tasted.

"Brilliant, isn't it?" Dr. Colonel said. He twirled the golden liquid around in its glass before sticking his aquiline nose over the top. He sipped it slowly, savoring it. "Its aroma ... almonds, ripe fruit, yes, and a hint of warm brioche ... it's rich, sensual, fleshy."

Dear Lord, he looks orgasmic. Henrietta was disgusted.

"I'm so delighted that you accepted my dinner invitation, Henrietta," he said. He placed the glass down on the table. "It gives you and me a chance to agree on Jeff's future, don't you think?"

"I think *our* future is between Jeff and me," Henrietta said. She took another sip of the superb vintage.

"Now, Henrietta, don't you know who's in charge around here?" The older man spoke with buttery sweet sarcasm.

"Why, Miss Julia, of course," Henrietta said, mimicking his tone.

"Touché, my dear. I'll give you that. Everyone knows my Julia rules my heart."

"Yeah, sure. Speaking of Miss Julia, where is she? The food is probably getting cold, even under these ... um ... lids," Henrietta said. She lifted the silver-plated cover. On the platter was a full-bodied trout, lying on a bed of wild rice and mushrooms, its glassy eyes staring at nothing.

"Oh, didn't I tell you? She had a migraine so I had to give her a sedative."

Henrietta froze, every hair on her neck standing up. "What?" she said.

"It turns out it's just you and me tonight, my dear. And this gives us a nice opportunity to agree on a few things," he said. His eyes had turned to blue ice.

That was the moment she realized she was in the presence of a seasoned adversary, an enemy who was both unpredictable and battle-ready. And she was frightfully unprepared.

"I really think we should wait for Miss Julia," Henrietta started.

"Don't worry, she'll be all right. Just out for hours, the poor dear."

"But why the place setting?"

"As you know, our Regina is a midwife. She needed to go to her sister, who's having a baby tonight. I offered to help her, but you know how proud she is," Dr. Colonel said. "Anyway, I told Regina to just get everything on the table, then she could go. She did, seconds before you arrived."

"I see."

Dr. Colonel's facial expression had taken on a crazed, almost inhuman appearance as he raised his glass. "And now for another toast: to a perfectly fine-tuned Clayborn future," he said, quickly downing his second glass of champagne. "Now, let's eat," he barked.

How am I going to get out of this? Henrietta thought, and it was a phrase that kept repeating over and over in her mind. She looked doubtfully at the dead fish and then over at Dr. Colonel, who was viciously attacking a Caesar salad. It was sickening to see and hear. Her appetite had vanished when she saw the trout, but mechanically she put a fork full of rice in her mouth, chewing until it was gone.

"Now, let me tell you somethin'," the doctor said. He pointed at her with his knife as though he were lecturing a child. "This is how it's going to work: You're going to convince Jeff that moving to an Indian reservation in New Mexico right now after just completing his residency is a bad idea and insist that you refuse to leave your mama and daddy and friends. You got that straight?"

Henrietta considered thoughtfully before answering. Should she continue absorbing his condescending rudeness or should she stand her ground and risk dealing with an explosion of his ugliness? Neither option was good.

"Dr. Colonel, if Jeff and I decide to move to New Mexico, then we will," she said, choosing the latter and the right to act like the thirty-year-old adult that she was. She would have hated herself for bowing down to or running away from his obnoxious bullying, but she was struggling to remain calm and unperturbed.

"Besides, the medical missions in Medichero would be temporary, lasting only six months at a time. Why're you making such a fuss about it?"

"I don't think you heard me right."

"What?" She wasn't sure if the word actually came out of her mouth.

Dr. Colonel stood up and stepped over to Henrietta, roughly pulling her up and out of her chair, which fell backward. He thrust his face an inch from hers and tightened his grip. "You will tell Jeff that you don't want to go to New Mexico, and you will make sure Jeff does not leave his ancestral home. Is that clear?"

Henrietta was stunned, like a deer caught in the headlights.

"And let me tell you somethin' else ... If Jeff does go and work on that goddamn, filthy Indian reservation, for any time whatsoever, I'll hold you personally responsible." Dr. Colonel pressed his mouth over hers, his tongue probing, his arms pinning hers to her sides.

Oh my God! What is he doing? His breath was grotesque, a mixture of garlic and bile. Henrietta thought she might vomit. *This can't be happening.*

"You better not disappoint me, girly, or I promise, you will pay a very heavy price." After a last squeeze of her arms, he released her. "Now, get the hell out of my goddamn house."

Henrietta bolted out of the front door, Dr. Colonel's vehement laughter chasing her. She jumped off the front porch and stumbled before slamming straight into Jenks, who stood as unmovable as a wall of smelly pig flesh. He reached out to grab her, but she slipped out of his sweaty hands and ran into the rows of blaze prince peach trees directly adjacent to the Clayborn mansion. She stopped behind one to catch her breath and hide from Jenks. *What is this?* She realized she was standing in something mushy and sticky—it was a pile of rotting peaches ... rotting flesh.

"You better go find her," she overheard Dr. Colonel saying to Jenks. "And—"

Before she could hear another word or see Jenks move in her direction, Henrietta ran. She didn't stop running until she'd made it safely inside the cabin, locking the door behind her.

"Henrietta, what on earth?" Elizabeth said, rushing in from the bedroom.

Holding up one finger, Henrietta gasped for air. "It's ... Dr. ... Colonel. He's insane, Mama," she panted, still trying to regain her breath. "That was positively the worst experience of my life. That ... that ... man ... is ... oh, Mama, he threatened me. I'm afraid he might ... I think he might kill me."

"Don't be ridiculous, Henrietta. Dr. Colonel's irritating, pompous and even mean sometimes, but he's not going to kill you."

"Well, if he doesn't, he'll get that Jenks to do it for him."

"What do you mean? Your daddy would never let anyone hurt you!"

While she rinsed off her peach-slimed loafers in the sink, Henrietta filled in her mother about what Dr. Colonel had said, leaving out the part about how he had violated her mouth. She wasn't sure why. Perhaps she was ashamed or too vulnerable to admit Jeff's father had so assaulted her. Or maybe she wanted to protect her mother in some strange way.

"Where was Julia?"

"He claimed she had a migraine, so he'd given her a sedative. He said she'd be out for hours. Convenient, huh?"

"How dare he. Well, I'm going to speak to him tomorrow."

"I don't think that's such a good idea."

"Why not?"

"You didn't see what I saw in those eyes, Mama. I'm scared of what he might do to me—or get that Jenks to do to me. I think there's something terribly wrong with Dr. Colonel. And there's definitely something wrong with that disgusting Jenks; he was chasing me back here. I'm not sure what he would've done if he'd caught me."

"Oh dear Lord, Henrietta," her mother said. Her hand went over her mouth but she soon pulled it away. "I have a better idea, honey. I'm going to tell

Miss Julia about this. And your father will not tolerate that Jenks threatening you in any way. Don't you worry, we'll make sure Jenks gets what's coming to him."

But Henrietta had a terrible feeling about her mother's involvement and seriously regretted telling her. "Mama, I don't want you or Daddy to get hurt in this. Maybe you should just let me and Jeff handle it."

"I'm not sure I could bite my tongue that hard, Henrietta."

Chapter 13

The next morning, Elizabeth Smyth walked boldly toward the veranda, moving between the massive fifty-foot white columns of the Clayborns' antebellum mansion, where she worked nearly every day for Miss Julia.

Before she could ring the doorbell, Regina opened the front door. And there was Dr. Colonel standing on the bottom step in the foyer, apparently all ready for her.

"Why, hey, Elizabeth, don't you look lovely this fine morning in that beautiful blue dress," Dr. Colonel drawled.

He was wearing a burgundy smoking jacket, standing with his left hand in the silk-trimmed front pocket and his right holding a pipe as though posing for a men's magazine cover.

What a pompous ass, Elizabeth thought. "Don't hey me; I've got something to say," she replied icily. She walked into the expansive foyer. But before moving through toward her office, she acknowledged the uniformed housemaid who held the door open, softening her tone. "Good morning, Regina," she said.

"Morning Miz 'Lizabeth," Regina returned. There was a grin on her dark-brown face.

"That'll be all, Regina," Dr. Colonel said. The words came out crisp.

"Yessa, Dr. Colonel." Regina continued to smile at Elizabeth before scurrying back to her work upstairs.

"You know our Miss Julia was just telling me how much she appreciates your work here and also at the orphanage," Dr. Colonel said. His voice was almost too polite, further raising Elizabeth's hackles. He gestured with his pipe. "And so do I. You're simply indispensable to us, Elizabeth."

You can't con me, old man. "Jules," she said, using his real first name, "you and I both know why I'm at work early." She turned and walked into the grand living room.

He followed her in. "I'm not sure what you mean, Elizabeth, sweetheart."

She turned back toward him. "Don't you sweetheart me, either," she said. She removed her white gloves. "I want to talk about your little meeting with Henrietta last night. I'll have you know that I'll not stand by and let you threaten my daughter with such viciousness. I'm planning to tell Julia."

"Now, hold on, we were just having a little chat over a nice dinner, maybe Henrietta misunderstood something I said. Or maybe she's exaggerating. Have you ever thought about that? Even you'll admit that your daughter has a very creative mind, writing fictitious stories, and all," he said. The doctor smiled, his cold blue eyes mocking.

"That's fiction, Jules; Henrietta writes fiction, but she's no liar. And I'm quite sure Julia will see that. She won't tolerate how you're treating Henrietta."

"I rather think my wife will give me the benefit of the doubt." He smiled like a satiated lion and smoothed back the sides of his hair. "But I'm afraid she continues to feel poorly, and she's still sleeping."

Elizabeth's face turned red hot. "Well, when she wakes up she might not be as forgiving as you think, especially when she finds out about that little secret of yours. You know that little indiscretion? Or should I say that little bastard child of yours?"

In a flash, his smile was a scowl; his voice sharpened. "What the hell are you talking about, woman?"

"Oh, I've known about it for quite some time, now." She folded her arms. *I've got him now.*

His eyes narrowed, contempt written all over his face.

"You're wondering how I could possibly know such a deep, dark secret, aren't you? "I didn't go looking for it, but sometimes, Miss Julia has me do a bit of digging around through old files and papers, searching for things she stashed back when she had her eyesight. It's amazing what you can discover hidden in an old house like this. So, if you don't want me talking to Julia or anyone else about your bastard child, I'd suggest you be on your best behavior around Henrietta from now on."

His mouth was actually hanging open.

"And another thing: if that sidekick of yours, that disgusting Jenks, ever lays one finger on my Henrietta, or does anything to threaten or make her feel uncomfortable ever again, I'll not only go to Julia about everything, Hamp and I will also go straight to the police!"

Dr. Colonel puffed out his chest and stepped forward, his finger pointing. "Do you know who you're goddamn talking to?" he said. His voice was a growl between gritted teeth.

"I didn't always know, but now? Yes, I know exactly who you are, Dr. Colonel," Elizabeth said. She returned his stare in equal measure. "And I know who Julia Pridgen is, too," she added, before turning on her heel and walking past him into Julia's office and slamming the door.

Chapter 14

"Lord knows why, but my feisty mother felt justified confronting Dr. Colonel like that," Henrietta said to Joe, shaking her head. She was recounting the report her mother had given her about what she'd done and said on that ill-fated morning so long ago. "And though I appreciated her wanting to defend me with her 'secret weapon,' I was terrified of what it was going to stir up." She paused. "Unfortunately, I'd be right about that."

Joe raised his eyebrows as he finished up the chicken, vegetable and rice dish Henrietta had made for him.

"But still, even now I can't help wondering if what she'd said about Dr. Colonel having an illegitimate child is true or not. If it is, that means Jeff has a half-brother or—sister—and my kids have an aunt or uncle." She smiled at the possibility.

"Is it true?" Joe asked.

"I don't know." Her voice flattened and smile vanished.

"I find it rather surprising that you wouldn't have asked any follow-up questions about something like that," Joe said.

"To be honest, right after Mama did what she did, I was too afraid to go poking around in such dangerous territory. You have to realize that in the South, I mean the Southeast, this would be a shocking scandal that would have severe social implications: Mr. White Pillar of the Community siring an illegitimate child, probably with someone from the staff. And anyway, there's no way he would have left a trail, not after what my mama did. If there was a child, the mother was probably long gone, either on her own or with a lot of help from you-know-who. I do admit, however, to grappling with what to do with that information. Should I tell Jeff? Or not?" She shook her head. "In the end, because it could've been just a rumor and because of our likely move to Medichero, which was going to cause a whole other set of problems, I decided to keep it to myself, at least for the time being."

"Your first bad secret from Jeff," Joe noted.

Henrietta let her shoulders fall forward. "One of many, I'm afraid."

"Don't let it get you down now. Just get it out. Let it all go. Please, go on," Joe said.

"When Jeff finally got back home from his interview and visit in Medichero, it was late at night. No one was waiting for him. His mother was still sick in bed, his father was playing cards and getting drunk with his buddies and I wasn't even there to greet him. Given the circumstances with Dr. Colonel, I'd decided to stay at my parents' house until Jeff actually got home."

"That's understandable," Joe said.

"As soon as Jeff discovered we weren't at his parents' home, he sensed something wasn't right and immediately came looking for us."

Henrietta had waited for Jeff on the cabin's front porch swing, moving it impatiently back and forth with her feet. As she rocked, the rusty chains squeaked, mimicking the chatter rattling around in her mind. She hated waiting for Jeff, or anyone. And she dreaded having to tell him about his father's actions toward her. But she knew she might burst if she didn't tell him the second he arrived.

Hearing someone approach, she spoke nervously to the night's starry darkness: "Jeff? Is that you?"

"Hello, Peaches," Jeff yelled joyfully, running from the blackness into her arms. "I missed you so much."

"Me, too," she said. She returned his kisses, but knew she felt tense.

"Is everything all right?" Jeff asked.

"Let's sit down." She didn't know where to begin to explain about Dr. Colonel. But sitting on the swing with Jeff and holding his hand, she started to feel safe and calm for the first time since it had happened. "I didn't want to wait up there," Henrietta said, "because your father . . . "

Jeff sighed heavily before wrapping his right arm around her shoulders. "It's okay; I know how he is."

"No, you don't understand! Jeff, he ambushed me!" She straightened her spine. "He demanded I talk you out of going to Medichero, said if I didn't we'd be sorry, that we'd see his wrath." She was getting worked up again. "And that he'd hold me personally responsible." Henrietta crossed her hands over her heart. Tears were welling up in her eyes.

"I was afraid of something like this. That's why I was glad when you and the kids stayed here at the cabin for the week."

"He still found a very effective way of getting his ugly point of view across. Jeff, why does your interest in Medichero bother him so much? And why does he have to get so mean and nasty about it?"

"I guess he's not happy unless everyone's following orders—his. And he thinks wanting to work with Indians is an embarrassment."

"But your research would be about so much more—and anyway he spent some time out West himself when he was younger."

"Be that as it may and regardless of what he said, Henrietta, we need to get away from here ... from him ... at least for a while. Medichero is as good as any place to go and a great opportunity for my research.

Please say you'll come with me to the Sacramento Mountains in New Mexico."

"But your father . . . "

"It'll just be for six months, he'll have time to cool off and we'll have a great family adventure!" His face lit up.

Now she felt guilty. "I'm sorry, Jeff. I didn't mean to spoil your homecoming or your good news. From that look on your face, I take it you had a successful trip. Was Medichero everything you hoped it would be?"

"No, it was better. Just as I had been informed, the natives are friendly, and I was able to confirm that there's been an inordinate number of spontaneous healings there. The hospital is surprisingly new and modern; the lab's perfect for my research. The doctor's house is huge, fully furnished and surrounded by the most amazing natural beauty—although everyone insists on calling it a cottage. And get this: it also has a piano in it, a baby grand. I take that as a good sign, don't you?"

"Really? I wouldn't have expected something that nice."

"Did you think we'd have to live in teepees?" he teased.

"Yes." She giggled a little before getting serious again. "I'm still concerned about what your father might do."

"What can he do? Henrietta, we're adults with lives of our own to live."

"I know. It does seem silly to worry about him, but he can be so intimidating and downright scary," she said.

"True."

"Maybe the six months away will be enough time for your father to cool off about everything," she offered, disregarding her own common sense.

"We definitely need an escape. I've wanted one for a long time now, as you know."

"So you're banishing us to an Indian reservation?" she joked. "There's the great irony."

"Yeah." He chuckled before becoming serious. "But it's more about the research."

"I know, Jeff," she said, looking into his deep-blue eyes. Moving closer, she raised her hands and cupped his face. It felt so warm with excitement about New Mexico and his research that it touched her and thawed her fear of what the move would bring. "Well, it'll be difficult; there's no doubt about it. Your father will be impossible. But I love you so much," she said. Her eyes were watering. "Call me foolish, but I'm going to support you and this crazy heart's desire of yours."

Jeff had kissed her mouth fervently and deeply, and she had been able to ignore, at least temporarily, her worries, fears and the uncomfortable rumbling in the pit of her stomach.

"We came out here right after that," Henrietta said to Joe. "Do you remember our first six-month mission in Medichero, five years ago now?"

Joe nodded. "You were different back then. You were happier and raring to learn about everything in Medichero, with 'Why this? Why that?' Your questions … they were endless, a little annoying, but also endearing."

"Yes," Henrietta said. She tried to reconnect with the woman she'd been on their first mission. As she picked up the milk carton to refill Joe's glass, she began rummaging through the backstory of this chapter in her life. Her ability to now remember that time surprised her. Before the soul retrieval this morning, her former self seemed like someone she'd once loved, lost and now barely remembered, like a childhood best friend who'd moved away and never returned.

"I had no idea that asking questions would be considered rude by Apaches or anyone, really," Henrietta said, her face blushing. "I just thought Apaches were standoffish. You and Altie were the only ones who'd answer some of them or even talk with us initially."

"From Bear and a dream, I knew you'd be coming," Joe said. "I knew that we should talk with you." He got up and limped to the sink, carrying his dishes.

"Don't you mean Jeff? That you should talk with Jeff?" She took the plate, fork and glass from him, rinsed them off and put them into some sudsy water.

"Not just Jeff." His lame leg had saddled him with the swaying, uneven gait of a chimpanzee, but Joe also was as agile as one. He pivoted gracefully on his good leg and padded back to his chair.

"A bear told you this." Henrietta joined him at the table, wanting to hear more, even though it sounded ridiculous to her.

"*Ha'aa.* My bear guide from Spirit suggested that I would need to give you some medicine to help you recover from some bad trauma."

"Okeydokey." She was tempted to respond with a more sarcastic remark, but there was something noble and credible in Joe's injured manner.

"When we first met you, you seemed to be happy and stable, and I'll admit that I didn't understand the dream initially," Joe said. "Then just before you came out the second time two years ago, Bear repeated the dream for me even though I wasn't here at the time, so there was no apparent relevancy. He's been known to do this. But now, in hindsight, I think it showed some real style on his part, don't you?"

"Yes, I suppose it did," she said with a grin. She found herself accepting his bizarre explanation.

"Please allow me a moment to express my sincere gratitude for a most delicious meal," Joe said.

He got up and bowed. "Thank you, thank you very much," he added, Elvis-style.

"You're most welcome," she said, smiling. "Do we have time to continue in the living room?"

Instead of looking at the wall clock or a wristwatch he didn't wear, Joe peered out of the window to gauge the sun's position in the late-afternoon sky. "*Ha'aa*. About an hour."

"Oh good. Go ahead; I'll be right in with some dessert."

Joe was sitting on the living room carpet like a Buddha when Henrietta brought in a tray holding two glasses of ice tea and a plate full of gingerbread cookies.

Now used to his unconventional habits, she rested the tray on the floor beside him without comment, and as she did, Joe's eyes opened and lit up.

"Hey, I'm wondering about what you said about a bear," she began, continuing their previous conversation. "How could some sort of spirit bear, or you, have possibly known that I would be coming and in need of help? And why would he, or you, have cared?"

She realized how strange her questions sounded. It was as if she were inquiring about the true thoughts and feelings of a cartoon character.

"I wasn't planning to get into this now," he said. He sipped the tea. "But since you asked … " He paused to sample a cookie. "The tea and ginger man are yum-yum."

"I'm glad you like them, but please go on."

"There's a problem you may be able to help us with."

"And what could that possibly be?"

"Bear said that our people's knowledge of ancient wisdom and spirit medicine are in danger of becoming extinct."

"Maybe he's confused. I've read that because of poachers and big-game hunters, bears are the ones endangered and might become extinct one day."

"Perhaps Bear is more sensitive than others to the plights of medicine men and women."

"Perhaps," she said. "But what does that have to do with me?" She took a sip of ice tea.

"Bear said you have a special power that could help," he said. He got up and half-stumbled toward her writing desk. "And it looks like Bear was right, once again." He pointed to the typewriter.

"Oh, sure," she said. She was waving her hands in the air, wielding her glass like a wand. If she'd had any special power whatsoever, she'd have used it to return to an idyllic life with Jeff in South Carolina, without the nightmares, the fear or the need to keep dangerous secrets from him.

Leaning on the desk, he crossed his arms and tilted his head with a look of mock annoyance.

"Okay, what's my special power?" she said.

"Bear said you had the wordsmith power," Joe said.

"Well, it's true that I'm a writer, or at least I used to be one in South Carolina, and my maiden name is Smyth. Hey, wordsmith. That's a coincidence, Joe."

"Well, there you go. That should make it clear to you." He stretched his arms up before returning to sit cross-legged on the floor.

"A coincidence should make it clear? Make what clear?"

"Don't you know that coincidences are usually given by Spirit for a reason? They contain great power. Look and listen for what Spirit is trying to tell you."

"Now how would I know that? In my world, a coincidence is merely a fascinating concurrence of events. There's no hidden meaning. No secrets involved."

"Please know that a coincidence is most definitely a message from Spirit, but you must have eyes to see it and ears to hear it. In this case, it is your wordsmith power that will be useful and healing to you and maybe to us. You've been sent here. Do you not see this connection?"

"Sure, I see the amusing connection between the fact that I'm someone who has used words to make a living and my maiden name is Smyth. Oh, but it's spelled with a 'y' instead of an 'i.' " She laughed. " 'Y' … why."

"Never let it be said that Spirit does not have a divine sense of humor."

She laughed again. "Okay, I know you're kidding around. There's no way a traumatized, albeit often curious, white woman from South Carolina is going to be some kind of Apache wordsmith who'll save your people's medicine from becoming extinct."

"I said help save it. Geez, sometimes white people can be a little arrogant." He smiled again as if making another joke, but something had changed in his eyes.

"You're serious."

"Ha'aa."

"Come on, Joe. Even if I were willing to be your wordsmith, I'd be afraid of getting something wrong, of misrepresenting your people and their traditions somehow. The Apache people, they'd be greatly offended. And I wouldn't want to risk doing that. No, I'd be terrified of doing that."

Without warning or making a sound, an albino cat appeared on the ledge of the open bay window, stretching and scratching itself on the frame like a ghost with an itch.

Henrietta jumped as though she were seeing an apparition. "What in the world?"

Pausing, the red-eyed feline looked over at Joe before bounding to the floor and running over to him with a warm greeting, rubbing fur as pure and white as Ivory soap on the sleeve of his pink-and-white panel shirt.

"Don't worry, she's a friend," Joe said. He returned the cat's affection, scratching her head and spine. She moved in unison with his caresses, mirroring his strokes with sinuous grace. "You shouldn't worry about offending my people, either," he added.

"How can you say that?" she asked, still mesmerized by the cat.

"Because, if you're willing, you'll be writing about your experience with bear medicine, which is more universal than the one practiced by my beloved people. And don't misunderstand. What my Medichero brothers and sisters believe and how they live—many of their old ways are indeed effective in walking the sacred inner path. But there is more to know. From a personal perspective."

The cat curled up in the space between his folded legs and, purring loudly, closed her eyes.

"Bear medicine? From a personal perspective? I don't even know what bear medicine means."

"It means bearing witness to ancient divine truths and repeating them as well as healing secrets long forgotten, but preserved by natives, mystics and Ascended Masters for the benefit of all." He moved slightly, but the cat remained sleeping. "It's about achieving spiritual wholeness with the Great Spirit through the application of an inner science." He put his right hand over his heart and thumped it twice. "It's about waking up, becoming enlightened to that idea." As he continued, his tempo picked up. "It's what natives learn from entering the *Kopave*, or sacred silence. What Jesus the Christ described as the 'Kingdom of God within you.' What theosophists call becoming one with the 'Christ Consciousness' and the 'I AM Presence.' What psychologists might call 'mastering the power of the subconscious mind.' And it's what I call 'the ancient medicine and wisdom of the Great Spirit that bears repeating,' or simply 'bear medicine.' " He let out a breath and smiled.

"You're right." She made an exaggerated shrug with her shoulders. "Why should I worry about offending Apache Indians when I could offend the Pope, a world full of Catholics, Jews, Protestants and especially, Lord help me, Southern Baptists? Why should I worry about incurring the wrath of Apaches when I could upset extremists and fundamentalists who believe it's their supreme duty to lynch heretics or anyone who disagrees with their infallible beliefs?"

"Exactly," Joe said.

Henrietta bit her lip. "I think you need to work on your salesmanship."

"Listen, I understand your fears," he said. "But seeking the Great Spirit's truth and writing about that journey are not acts of heresy."

Intellectually, she agreed with him. But despite her willingness to keep a journal of her soul retrieval experience, it was still a private thing, an attempt to somehow process her awful situation and get in better touch with her real self and thoughts and break through her writer's block.

"You already see the value of the soul retrieval. It's part of the bear medicine," Joe said.

"I'm starting to, but participating in your healing rituals out here, where no one back home knows what I'm doing, is one thing; writing about them in a public way is quite another," she said. "And even if I agreed to do it, how am I supposed to write about a medicine I know nothing about? I'm just an ordinary white woman from South Carolina. I don't have your native history, your death experience, your spiritual insights or your healing gifts. I don't have Jeff's medical knowledge. It'd be like trying to write a cookbook without knowing what a stove looks like."

"Not to worry. Bear has called Altie and me to mentor you, if you're willing, that is. And, by the way, you're anything but ordinary."

The wraithlike cat stood up and stretched its back seductively into the shape of an upside-down "U" before gliding over Joe's folded legs. After leaving a trail of her translucent white fur on his baggy black pants, she ran over to caress Henrietta's calf. Henrietta scratched her silky white head.

"Joe, to be honest, I'm not sure I'm ready to get sidetracked with all this wordsmith stuff." She had been hoping for just a concrete soul-healing experience rather than being sucked into the abstract world of a man who was friend to both spirit bears and albino felines.

"Of course; please forgive me. There's a season and a time for everything. So for now, let's return to your healing and the talking medicine."

She exhaled, feeling a reprieve of sorts, but was quickly reminded of the heavy burdens she carried. "I still have these horrible dark secrets to deal with."

"You are allowing them to block your full healing," he said. "And your freedom."

"I think I need to get them out in the open, and out of my system, so to speak."

"Good idea. Darkness has no power in the presence of light. In fact, it can no longer exist."

"Hmm. I've never thought about it like that."

Joe stood up and stretched like the cat had before limping over to the open bay window. She promptly left Henrietta's side to join him. With the slightest gesture, he directed the phantom-like cat toward the sill, and she slipped out of the window, disappearing into the afternoon as suddenly as she had arrived.

"Joe, I believe I'm finally ready to tell," Henrietta said. She realized that as she spoke she felt a surge of unexpected energy. "Wow, it feels good just to be able to say those words without fear."

"Then don't delay. Give your dark secrets to the light and let your soul be like the great eagle. Fly to your freedom, Henrietta," he said, jumping. "Holy karma!" In his excitement, he tripped over the piano bench and fell to the floor, but there was no thud. He'd somehow caught himself with his arms like a gymnast, and it was perhaps the most graceful fall she'd ever seen.

"Are you all right?" Henrietta asked anyway as she rushed over to help him.

"Perfect," he said. He was looking up and giving her one of his diamond-radiant grins.

Chapter 15

"Please continue," Joe said. He was now sitting on the piano bench that had just tripped him, perhaps, Henrietta thought, to gain some mastery over it.

"Well, after the first and second missions here, Jeff went back to working with Dr. Kepple. But we both decided it was time to leave the Clayborn mansion and move into a house of our own that was closer to Jeff's office and the hospital. Fortunately, we were able to make arrangements to buy something before Dr. Colonel could intervene. We bought directly from the seller to avoid his good-ole-boy network."

"Good-ole-boy network?" he asked. "That doesn't sound that good."

"It isn't," Henrietta said. "It's a strange southern irony. In any case, the sale went through on a nice house in downtown Aiken—all our own. I was so relieved at that point. Hey, the word 'Aiken.' Could that be the *aching* word symbol from your spirit journey?"

"*Ha'aa*, very good!"

"The town we moved to is spelled A-I-K-E-N. The other aching would come later."

Joe made a sound like a hum and moved, returning to his cross-legged position on the floor.

"So we lived in the Aiken house for a while, but then Jeff started talking about resuming his research on the reservation again, which meant Dr. Colonel was soon back to his old ways of meddling in our lives. He'd show up on our doorstep without notice and stay through dinner without being invited. It became a pattern with him. Soon he started leaving behind personal items like his handkerchief, which reeked of his cologne; I think he did it as a reminder that he was omnipotent and always watching. His behavior grew increasingly disturbing."

"Ha'aa."

"But it wasn't just him. I'd also see Jenks, his foreman, lurking around in the yard when Jeff wasn't home. One night, that pig, oh, he's the swine!" she said, again referring back to Joe's journey of symbols. "Yes, Jenks looked and acted like a pig. Anyway, one night, Jenks pressed his face against my bedroom window. So I called the police on him."

"Did your father fire him for peeping at you?"

"You know, even before all of this started, I once asked my father why they kept a reprobate like Jenks on the payroll, and he'd grumbled something about not having a choice. Apparently Jenks had been some sort of good-ole-boy payback, and Dr. Colonel had ordered my father to keep him on a year-round basis—no ifs, ands or buts."

"The good-ole-boy network is no good," Joe said.

"But to answer your question, no. That time, I didn't give him the option. I was afraid my father would get hurt or be fired himself if I told him about Jenks's peeping. So I kept it to myself."

"Another dangerous secret."

"True." She sighed and rubbed off the tear sliding down her face.

"Please know that I'm not judging you in any of this," Joe said. "Getting these things out in the light is a healthy choice now. But it must be your free will choice."

"Yes. I do want to get it all out." She shook her hands, got up and started pacing the room. "Oh boy, here goes." Her heart was racing wildly. "I'm going to tell you … everything."

"You can do it." Joe leaned forward with his elbows on his knees.

She sighed heavily and sat back down. "A couple of nights later, Jeff had to go all the way to the Augusta Hospital, that's twenty-five miles away, for a medical emergency with one of his patients. I'd already put the girls down for the night and was watching TV in my robe when there was a knock on the door. It was that repugnant Jenks again. I made the mistake of cracking the door open to tell him to get lost, but he shoved his way into the living room," she said, and continued on with the story.

"Why'd you have to go and call the police on me?" Jenks had whined. "I wasn't hurting nobody. They said I don't get no more chances."

"Get out of here, Jenks," Henrietta said, frightened by the feral expression in his eyes. She was rushing toward the phone next to the fireplace.

He yanked her wrist before she could grab the receiver. "Wait. I was just doing what—" Jenks started.

Before he could finish, Henrietta seized a handful of pens that were by the phone and stabbed Jenks in the shoulder. As he let go of her wrist, she picked up the fire poker and hit him on the head with it.

Jenks ran for the door, and Henrietta followed him armed with her poker and pens. After slamming and locking the door behind him, she glimpsed Dr. Colonel standing just beyond the porch, smoking a cigar. For a split second, she was relieved to see him.

Chapter 16

"I'm calling the police on that pig," Henrietta said to Dr. Colonel, letting him in without thinking. "But as soon as my father finds out how he broke in here and attacked me, he'll probably kill him," Henrietta said, walking toward the phone after putting the poker away.

"Hampton Smyth will do no such thing, because you're not going to tell him."

"What do you mean? Of course I'm going to tell him. But I'm sure you and Jeff will want to get rid of Jenks even before my father gets at him," Henrietta said as she picked up the receiver.

"I sent Jenks over here to survey the situation before my arrival, and you should know that he always does what I tell him to do." He was speaking in a low, calm tone.

"You? But why would you do that?" *Oh, dear God!* Without waiting for an answer, she tried to dial zero for the operator.

"Not so fast, my dear," he said. He rushed up next to her, grabbing the phone.

"You'd better leave now, Dr. Colonel," she said. She was shaking and could barely speak.

"Let me tell you somethin', girly." He pointed his finger in her face. "I'm not leaving here until I make good on the promise I made you, remember?" His eyes narrowed, and he spoke through gritted teeth. "I told you I was going to hold you directly responsible if Jeff decided to go back to that goddamn Indian reservation. And I let it go once three years ago but guess what he told me today?"

Henrietta stood aghast, shaking her head. *Please don't tell me.* Recoiling, she stepped backward, trying in vain to reach again for the fireplace equipment, but instead bumped her head into the mantel. She felt like the wind was being sucked out of her and up the chimney.

"That y'all are moving back to Medichero, not just for another mission, but permanently."

His bone-chilling look immobilized her, like being stopped cold by the deadly stare of a coiled rattlesnake.

Run! Run! Scream! Grab the poker! But her arms and legs went numb, her voice was gone. *What's wrong with me?*

"You've completely failed, missy," he said. His voice was a hiss. "You only had to do one little goddamn thing: talk Jeff out of moving there, to the one place on earth I don't want him to go."

He squeezed her arms harshly, pinching them. She tried to scream, shout, anything, but nothing came out.

Dr. Colonel ripped her robe open and pulled the sleeves down over her arms in one swift movement so that she was restrained, effectively turning her robe into the symbolic fleecy ropes. "It's time to teach you a little lesson," he said. He was whispering in her ear with his hot slimy breath.

He shoved, then dragged her toward the bedroom.

"No! The children. My babies!" She tried to scream, but her voice was only a whisper.

"From my little interlude outside, I happen to know they're asleep and down the hall," he whispered. Still holding her squirming body, he locked the bedroom door then threw her to the bed. He was on top pushing her down before she could react. While her father-in-law held her mouth closed with one hand, he unfastened his pants and ripped off her nightgown with the other. The force of his weight was suffocating, and she felt herself being squeezed to death.

As he slithered over and in her, Henrietta, immobile and dazed, wondered how long the agony would last. Because she could now move her head, she turned it sideways, away from his vile panting. Her skin was ripping, her mind shattering.

"Why? Why? How could he have done such a thing to me, Joe?" She was crying hysterically by then—but at least she'd gotten the story out.

"There, there, Henrietta," Joe said. He was patting her arm.

"And all of that viciousness, just as you described in your journey, was near 'innocent babes wrapped in blankets'! Our babies—*his* grandchildren—were asleep in the bedroom right down the hall!"

Joe wiped her tears with a bandana, and patted her back gently, like a mother soothing her child.

"It's strange. Although I think the attack was extremely painful, I don't remember my physical wounds at all," Henrietta said. She stood up to grab a tissue from the box on her desk. "It was like the real me was floating or sitting on some invisible shelf attached to the ceiling, observing the violence." She blew her nose.

"Your soul was fragmenting. Pieces of your soul chose to separate out from this experience. That's why you could see it from that perspective."

"Oh, my gosh, yes," she said. "I can remember watching that monster's back heaving up and down on my body, which was as motionless as a corpse. And I've felt like roadkill ever since."

"It's a violation of every law of nature," Joe said. He walked over to an upholstered chair and sat down. He assumed a listening position, like a psychiatrist might do, placing his right forefinger under his chin. "Please continue."

"I thought there must've been some kind of demons possessing Dr. Colonel. I felt unclean, shamed and degraded beyond reason and logic. I hated myself for being so powerless. But what could I possibly do? Nothing! Who could I tell? No one! It seemed I had no recourse, other than trying to forget it. Deny it into nonexistence. Run away from it."

"You've learned this is a mistake," Joe said. He tilted his chin down.

"What I learned is a raped woman can't forget it, deny it or talk about something like that without causing terrible damage to the ones she loves. Without the freedom to object and express our outrage, we begin to shrivel up inside. We transform into these empty mannequin-like creatures that look real but have no emotions, normal instincts or even the ability to think rationally because parts of our soul have been ripped from our bodies," Henrietta said.

"No, that's not the lesson in this," Joe said. "We'll work on that. But for the moment, let's agree you've learned something of the Great Spirit's medicine, that the soul retrieval can begin the process of renewing self-power and healing the fragmented soul caused by this kind of traumatic experience."

"Well," she said. She paused to gauge her feelings. "I guess I can acknowledge that," Henrietta said. "Because even though it's awful to revisit this, I'm actually feeling a little better and stronger in the telling of it. I'm encouraged that the soul retrieval offers a hope for healing from this sort of thing when there was none before."

"There's our young brave," Joe said. "However, please know the soul retrieval is but one tool, one step in an ongoing inner journey of healing and growth that we're meant to take toward the idea that we are already in wholeness with the Great Spirit."

"Yes, I sort of get that," Henrietta said. "But, Joe, you have to understand something. It's still a profound shame to be raped, particularly by a family member. And it puts you in what feels like an impossible situation. On one hand, you want to broadcast it to the world, but on the other hand, you're terrified of hurting yourself further and destroying your family. I couldn't help feeling like a powerless victim."

"*Ha'aa*, yes. The dark spirits capitalize on situations like this as well as your fear to intentionally give you a false sense of who you are, so that you'll never discover your true identity as a spiritual being connected to the Great Spirit. Don't let them trick you into believing their lies," Joe said.

"You mean this is all some sort of dark scheme to trick me?" Henrietta said. "To cause me to buy into a big fat lie about myself? To hate myself?"

"Yes, in a matter of speaking, and why would you want to do that?" Joe asked.

"Hmm. I don't know; it doesn't make sense now that I know more."

"Then reclaim your true self. Be who you truly are," he said.

"I'd like to. But how do I go about learning to do that?"

"You need to first admit to and learn from your mistake in letting this experience alter your sense of identity and cause you to not love yourself," Joe said. "There're also tools and rituals we use to help facilitate a higher understanding of who we really are, while helping to dislodge the blocks in our minds and bodies," Joe said.

"The things that make us blockheads?" she asked, feeling like one.

"No, the false ideas that interfere with the Great Spirit's love flow within you."

"What tools and rituals are you talking about?"

"We use the sweat lodge, vision quests, fasting, prayer, the *Kopave* and, of course, the soul retrieval to name a few. You'd be wise to put any or all of these tools to your good use as needed," Joe said.

"I still don't understand why or how the man could've raped me."

"It was about trying to control you and Jeff, in an attempt to feel better himself. It seems his primary intent was to control Jeff, but you were the one who had more influence over Jeff's heart. You were passion itself, and you were a part of Jeff's. By controlling you and stealing your passion, he could kill two birds with one stone."

"He nearly succeeded. I believe he's the devil."

"Henrietta, Dr. Colonel isn't the devil. He has simply allowed himself to be manipulated by dark spirits that have attached to him through his own pain and enlarged ego."

"Ha! That's a good one! I'd love to see the expression on Dr. Colonel's face if he ever realized he's the one being controlled," Henrietta said.

"Once you fully understand that his behavior is rooted in pain and fear, covering his true identity like an ugly dark mask, it's easier to forgive him for his ignorance, blindness and imperfect decisions. Because of his attempt to steal your gifts, I'd venture to say that he also has a severe case of soul fragmentation."

"I suppose that makes sense," she said, remembering the wisdom of forgiveness, as taught by Jesus. "But, Joe, why couldn't I run? Why couldn't I fight back? This has been so hard for me to accept about myself."

"A turtle's shell cannot move without a life residing inside," Joe said.

Henrietta smiled. "Not knowing about soul loss back then, I couldn't understand my complete paralysis. I didn't understand how I was able to beat off Jenks one minute but turn into a lifeless stone with Dr. Colonel. And I know I'm tough. When I was about twelve years old, I learned I could be strong in dangerous situations."

"I'd like to hear more about this young brave," Joe said.

"It was during the summer just before we moved to the peach plantation," Henrietta began. "I was with a group of friends who decided it'd be great fun and a bit daring to make a human chain to cross the shallow part of the Savannah River's rapids. That's the big river near where I grew up. At that age, a person feels invincible, so a double-dog dare to cross what we thought was a benign current, in a single file and holding hands, was nothing." Henrietta motioned with her hands. "Just as we approached the middle of the river, Darlene, at the tail end, and whose hand I was holding, slipped on a slimy rock and the force of the current took her down. Unfortunately, Darlene hadn't let go of my left hand, and I followed her under. The girl holding my other hand let go. Meanwhile, Darlene's hand was like a metal handcuff, so the two of us were swept down the rapids, headed toward the deeper parts of the river where the current was more powerful and dangerous. Darlene panicked, and while still clenching my hand, she climbed my body like it was a small ladder to reach the air, pushing me into the undertow."

"How did you survive it?"

"You know what? I didn't freeze. I didn't become immobilized by fear, like I did with Dr. Colonel. Instead, I punched Darlene's arm and pinched the hand that held me in a death grip, forcing her to release my hand. I swam to the surface, sucked in some air and grabbed the back of Darlene's shirt keeping her head up, not necessarily to rescue her, but to protect myself from her still clutching hands. The rapids moved us toward a huge boulder, and I climbed out of the water onto the massive rock and pulled Darlene to safety."

"Sweet hero!"

"I wasn't trying to be a hero. I'm just trying to explain that it was a pivotal moment, one that taught me I had the power to take control over my own fate. It wouldn't last. It was an illusion."

"You'll soon learn the mistake of holding on to that thought, that fear."

"I'm not following all this talk about mistakes."

"Henrietta, the important thing to remember about life is not what happens or where you end up, but what you choose to take from your experiences and learn along the way. That is what the Great Spirit wants for us. So there's no need to feel bad about making mistakes and decisions to the best of our abilities at certain points in time, as long as we're willing to learn from them, make better choices and continue forward on the sacred inner path."

"That's a wonderful way of looking at life," Henrietta said.

"Of course, the dark spirits will always try to fool you into focusing on bad thoughts. They do this through deceptions, which may cause you to lose control of yourself, make additional mistakes and take on false ideas about yourself, like thinking you're a victim instead of the powerful creative being you are. The dark ones are very clever. They know exactly what buttons to push, what specific scam to use that'll cause people to fall off the inner path and take on self-pitying thoughts. But this is the only way they can grow and survive—by feeding on the bad thoughts and feelings they encourage you to create."

"Be that as it may, do you see the point I was trying to make about my experience at the rapids?" she said.

"Not exactly."

"My powerful self-defense in response to Darlene at the rapids and even Jenks in Aiken was why I couldn't defend myself to myself for not striking back when Dr. Colonel cornered me. In my mind, I couldn't justify my deer-in-the-headlights response. I've really never forgiven myself for letting it happen."

"Forgiven yourself? Holy karma! Henrietta, don't you see you're creating your own problems? Listen, when we're confronted for the first time by people wearing dark disguises, we're ill-equipped to respond perfectly. What your friend in the rapids did to you wasn't evil; she was obviously frightened and panicked. Your wise soul knew this and acted instinctively by making good choices. With Jenks, I think your soul understood that he was merely a pawn in Dr. Colonel's mind game. You must forgive yourself unconditionally for making a mistake. It's essential to your healing."

Henrietta sucked in a deep breath, wondering if she could ever really do that.

"It's our job, however, to learn from our bad experiences and not take them so personally. Instead, we should always ask ourselves: 'What can I learn from this? What am I holding on to in my mind that the dark spirits are attracted to and can continue to latch on to?' In this way, we can work on letting go of those bad ideas and avoid soul loss and a lot of heartache. We do this by loving and forgiving ourselves and focusing on better, good-feeling thoughts."

"Easier said than done," she said.

"True, but we get better with practice." He smiled. "So what can we learn from your response? What happened immediately after Dr. Colonel raped you?"

"Well, I was naked except for the robe that still held my arms awkwardly beneath me," Henrietta said. She blushed. "After he got off me, I was free to move, but I couldn't. I was disoriented, and I remember wondering if my arms were broken or if he'd actually killed me. I wasn't quite sure. So, I just laid there like a recumbent vegetable, watching Dr. Colonel clean up the bedroom where he'd just raped the wife of his only son."

Joe twisted his mouth, but remained silent.

"Just before he left, Dr. Colonel threw a blanket over my naked body and said, 'You won't be telling anyone what happened here tonight. No one would believe you, anyway.' " Henrietta paused as anger welled up in her. "He laughed when he said it."

"Typical."

"He wasn't finished, adding insult to injury, as he said: 'Now, you get up and dressed. You look terrible. Take a hot bath. Put on some makeup. When Jeff comes home, you tell him you changed your mind. You tell him you don't want to move back to that goddamn reservation. You got that straight?'"

"Did you answer? Did you take a bath and put on makeup?" Joe asked.

"Not just then; I could only stare blankly into space as he continued to threaten me. He said the next time he'd have to teach me a lesson, it would be much worse. At that moment, I didn't see how it could get worse." Henrietta put her forehead in her hands. "But it was like I didn't care. No, that's not it. It was like I was no longer there."

"You were missing parts of your soul."

Henrietta looked up at him with tears in her eyes. "Yes, I can see that now."

"What happened next?" he asked.

Thank God Joe is encouraging me to continue, she thought. It was such a relief to purge some of the evil she'd been carrying around for so long. Strangely, she was starting to feel better.

"After Dr. Colonel left, I crawled to the bathroom, vomited and showered until the hot water ran out. In the days, weeks and months that followed, I had to work hard to act normal when Jeff or my parents were around, masquerading as a woman who hadn't disintegrated," she said. "But it took all of the little strength I had left to pull it off. I was hurt and grieving and on the edge of collapse. To survive, I wanted to withdraw and isolate myself into my writing world, but my stories began to read like obituaries. I was filled with this awful, almost unreachable sense of mourning for something missing in myself. But I didn't understand it. I didn't know what had happened to me, to my soul. So I spent more time sleeping on the couch or just lying in front of the TV in a mindless state. I didn't know what to do with myself," she said. She paused. "Except to buy a new bed and linens without Jeff's noticing. I couldn't stand the thought of sleeping with my beloved husband in the bed where his father had so violently assaulted me."

"I can see why. But all that sounds like you stuck around for a while. I thought Jeff said you were moving back to Medichero immediately and permanently."

"It turned out that Jeff had just said that to his father during a heated argument on that unfortunate day. Ironically, I was the one who ultimately began urging the second mission forward. Despite Dr. Colonel's threats, I made it happen. I wanted out."

"That's fully understandable."

"But truthfully, I wanted not so much to escape, but to forget."

"But if you forget, keeping in the hate and fear, you won't be free to face your mistakes and learn from them."

"Oh, Joe, talk about mistakes. I made another grave error just before we left on that second mission."

At that moment, they both heard the ceremonial drums calling.

"I understand that you have to go now," Henrietta said. "But I need to tell you about what haunts me, at times, even more than the rape," she said.

"Yes, I am needed at the Ceremonies now," Joe said. His voice was gentle. "Hold on, dear Henrietta. We will continue our talking medicine tomorrow," he said. "It will be okay. I promise." And he was gone.

Chapter 17

The next day, Henrietta and Joe were sitting in the multicolored chairs in the Locos' family library, as Henrietta continued her story.

Jeff and Henrietta agreed it would be safer to delay telling Dr. Colonel about their plans for the second mission in Medichero until after everything was set and they were literally walking out the door. However, they were comfortable being up front with Elizabeth and Hampton, particularly as Henrietta wanted to spend as much time with her parents as possible prior to leaving.

One day she and her mother were sitting in rocking chairs on the cabin's front porch, chatting and preparing apples for a cobbler. The seven-year-old twins were riding ponies in the adjacent pasture under their Grandfather Smyth's watchful eye.

Elizabeth was wearing a frilly yellow apron over a white shirtdress, looking fresh and crisp as she peeled and cored her sixth apple with her usual precision.

Henrietta, laboring on her second apple, appeared wilted in a sleeveless brown maternity dress.

"Henrietta, I wish y'all didn't have to go so far away right now," Elizabeth complained. "Especially with the new baby on the way."

"It'll only be for six months," Henrietta said. She kept her eyes fixed on the apple she was peeling.

"I know Jeff wants to do that research and maybe even get away from his father, and I can't blame him for that," Elizabeth went on. "But couldn't you just move to some other Indian reservation that's closer, like one of the Cherokee reservations in South Carolina?"

Henrietta sighed. For the past four months, she'd been on the verge of collapse, trying to keep her dark secrets from leaking out all over the place, although she'd considered confiding in her mother many times. *Tell; don't tell. Ruin everyone's life or suffer in silence. Tell; don't. Ruin or suffer.* The words went round and round in her mind like some pitiful hamster trapped on a squeaky wheel, never going anywhere, never escaping.

"Mama, as you're well aware, Jeff believes the research he can do in Medichero is a unique opportunity to study spontaneous healings and that it'll be in the best interests of science and medicine." She was trying to focus on Jeff's reasons for leaving instead of hers. "And even though his interest in native medicine might confound folks around here, he's always been completely rational and he's usually right about most things. But ..." She sighed heavily. "You're correct about us wanting to get away from Dr. Colonel; the move also conveniently accomplishes that." She nicked her finger on the paring knife. "Ouch," she winced.

"Here, let me, dear." Elizabeth reached over, picked up Henrietta's bag of apples and began to work on them.

Although not beautiful in the traditional sense, Elizabeth was so beguiling and efficient in her manner and dress, she projected an overall attractiveness that far exceeded the sum of her features. Her nose was perhaps a little too long for her delicate face, and her small mouth was a tad on the thin side. But she was as slender and feisty as a saxophone. Despite her petite, five foot two frame, she had an aristocratic carriage, and bobbed golden hair that was fashionable without being fussy. Her large blue eyes were her most outstanding feature though, capable of holding both the fury of thunderbolts and the serenity of a cool summer breeze.

"But, this just doesn't feel right," Elizabeth protested. "I can hardly stand to be so far away from you and the girls and I so wanted to be with you when the baby comes." She paused peeling apples and waved her knife for emphasis. "Plus, I've got to be honest with you, dear. You don't look so well, and you haven't been acting like yourself in a long while now. I think you and the girls should just postpone the trip and stay here."

"I've been having morning sickness, that's all," Henrietta said. She sucked on her bleeding finger and continued to look down, trying to avoid her mother's knowing eyes. "This pregnancy … it's been difficult." It was a half-truth, but she knew she had no choice in telling it: she had to mislead her mother in order to protect her.

"Well, that's all the more reason for not going clear across the country to some remote Indian reservation in the middle of nowhere right now." Elizabeth paused to study her daughter's face more closely. "Now, you just wait a doggone, cotton-picking minute. Henrietta, honey, look at me."

Henrietta knew she couldn't even glance up for a second. With her mother, she'd always been a lousy actor and she'd never been able to lie to her. Up until now, she'd never wanted to.

"I can't." As Henrietta objected, she immediately recognized her mistake.

Elizabeth leaned forward. "Can." The shorthand she used was a clear indication her mother was onto her and wouldn't be letting go. "Spill it."

Henrietta felt like throwing up, but not from morning sickness. "Let's just drop it," she said.

"I think you know me better than that," Elizabeth said.

"I can't tell you because it'll hurt you, okay?" Henrietta said.

Elizabeth put the apples down on a side table and wiped her hands on a damp cloth. She moved to the front of Henrietta's rocker, bent down on her knees and looked up, forcing eye contact. "Honey, you can tell me anything." She touched Henrietta's hands with loving tenderness.

No! I don't want to! Tears poured down Henrietta's face and her shoulders trembled involuntarily. "Oh, Mama, can we go inside?" She didn't want the children to see her like this.

"Of course, dear."

Henrietta turned into a sleepwalker as her mother took her arm and guided her into the family room and onto the couch, where they sat next to one another. Trying to compose herself and regain some sense of self-control, Henrietta looked around the warm room filled with memories, poignant and wistful. Her eyes stung as they floated over special decorative touches, keepsakes and family pictures. She thought about her happy childhood, and the comfort of this home.

"Henrietta, please," her mother urged. She was reaching out and taking Henrietta's hands once more in hers. "Let me help you with whatever is weighing on you so heavily."

Exhaling, Henrietta, with mixed emotions, tried to speak, but her throat tightened and her tongue felt as dry and scratchy as the White Sands Desert. Her lips quivered uncontrollably, as tears ran down her cheeks. "Oh dear God! How can I do it?" Henrietta cried out.

"I can be strong enough for the both of us," Elizabeth said.

"I know, Mama. You've always been that," Henrietta said, sniffing. "But listen: before I can tell you, you have to promise me something."

"Anything." Elizabeth's voice remained unshakable.

"You have to swear to me that you won't tell a soul about what I tell you, or do anything rash, except maybe move out to Medichero with us immediately." She pulled her mother's hands up and laid them across her heart.

"But our life and work are here ..."

"Mama, please promise."

"I promise to do what's best."

Henrietta finally broke down and in spasms revealed how Dr. Colonel had raped her, that she wasn't even sure if the baby she carried was Dr. Colonel's or Jeff's, and how she had suffered in maddening silence, nearly losing her mind.

"Oh, my poor little girl, I'm so sorry," Elizabeth said. She was cradling and rocking her, as she had when Henrietta was a child. "Hush, my baby, Mama's here."

Henrietta breathed deeply through sobs, trying to calm her shaking body, as she basked in the protective circle of her mother's soft, sturdy arms. Then she felt the change and jerked upright to look at the woman who had always given her strength and comfort. Her mother's face had drained of all color. She reached for her mama's hands, now stone cold. Elizabeth's body slumped as the skin around her mouth sagged and turned ashen. Henrietta then heard her mother wailing like an animal caught in a trap. Henrietta sat there helpless, full of sadness and regret.

But soon, Elizabeth's body stiffened, and her mouth became hard. She slowly stood and started to pace back and forth in front of her daughter. The color began to return to her face as she placed her fists on her hips, narrowed her eyes, flared her nostrils and stomped her foot like an enraged bull about to charge. Henrietta was relieved but also terrified.

Elizabeth, though, was calm when she finally spoke as she resumed moving. "We've got to do something to him, and we need a plan. If that doesn't work, I might have to kill him."

"Mama, please, you promised!"

"Now, don't worry. We'll be smart about it," Elizabeth said. She paused pacing long enough to look back at Henrietta with a strange and frightening smile on her face.

Panic-stricken, Henrietta thought, *Dear God! What have I done to her, to my family?*

"We'll get him where it hurts the most. I know! I've got that secret on him, remember, his bastard child secret," Elizabeth said. "Once Julia knows about that, she'll divorce him and throw him out of her house!"

"No, no," Henrietta cried. She was silently cursing her weakness for involving her mother. "Please no! And how could that possibly help us?"

Elizabeth returned to the sofa, bent down and cupped her daughter's face with her hands. "Like I said, we'll be smart about it."

Chapter 18

"Joe, I begged her not to confront Dr. Colonel or tell Julia," Henrietta said. "Even in my damaged state of mind, I knew that hate and revenge wouldn't solve anything, only make things worse. I pleaded with her to bring Daddy out here and visit with us here until she cooled off and we could think of something more rational with clearer heads. We have so much room in the doctor's cottage. And it's so beautiful here in the Sacramento Mountains." Henrietta paused, getting up to peek into Altie's kitchen, where her friend was entertaining Jeffie with an acoustical guitar and some fry bread.

"Ha'aa," Joe agreed. He was still sitting in the twin chair wearing a shirt with red-and-white stripes; his baggy pants were navy blue. He looked like an American flag with two black braided cords hanging on either side.

Relieved her son was occupied and unable to overhear their conversation, she continued. "The best I could do was get my mama to promise not to do anything until we got back from that second mission. But she just couldn't wait … I should have known. My mother actually thought she could outmaneuver Dr. Colonel," Henrietta said. She sighed heavily and plopped back into the chair. She put her head in her hands. "Oh, Joe, this is why raped women are so afraid to tell."

"What do you mean?" He leaned forward.

"Just two weeks after we returned here for that second mission, there was a fire in my parents' cabin and they barely escaped with their lives," she said. She looked up. "Julia wasn't so lucky."

Joe frowned, then nodded for her to proceed.

"Dr. Colonel claimed that Julia had another complication with her diabetes, and though he presumably tried to save her and rushed her to the hospital, it was useless. She died."

"I am so sorry to hear that," Joe said. "I was never clear on the details about your swift departure."

"Thank you," she said. "When we got the news, we left immediately. I didn't see you at all during the brief time we were here."

"I was finishing up in medical school," Joe said.

"Oh, I didn't know. Well, anyway, I never really believed the reason Dr. Colonel gave for Miss Julia's death." She looked straight into Joe's eyes. "In fact, I think Dr. Colonel did something to make her sick."

Joe raised his eyebrows. "He's a doctor."

"Yes, but of course, he'd know exactly how to do something like that with just the right symptoms, don't you think? And there's another strange coincidence that I can't quite get my mind around: Miss Julia died on the very same night that my parents' cabin burned to the ground. What do you think Spirit's trying to tell me with that one?"

"Your mother confronted Dr. Colonel."

"Close, but no. My mama admitted to telling Julia everything." Henrietta gestured with her hands. "I suspect that it was Julia who confronted Dr. Colonel— and look what happened!"

"The police didn't help." It was more a statement than a question.

"The police, like everybody else in our hometown, have always considered Dr. Colonel to be some kind of southern mythological god," Henrietta said. She sighed heavily. "Consequently, they believed every word he uttered."

"And Jenks?"

"Dr. Colonel gave him an alibi for the fire, claiming Jenks was helping him during the crisis with Miss Julia. Meanwhile, the investigators said the fire was an accident caused by the gas stove in the kitchen. Frankly, I didn't believe them either."

"An accident in your mother's kitchen?"

"Honestly, I don't see how anyone who knows my highly efficient and fastidious mother could ever suggest that she might have accidentally left her stove on, not even those dumb good-ole-boy firemen. But that's how they called it, anyway. And what proof did I have? About any of it?" Henrietta exhaled a deep breath. "Nevertheless, I'm very thankful that my parents were able to wake up in time and get out."

Altie came in from the kitchen carrying a tray of lemonade and fry bread. Jeffie waddled in behind her. "I thought I would take Jeffie for a stroll to the playground, if that is okay," Altie said.

"That sounds like fun, doesn't it, Jeffie?" Henrietta asked. After they left, Henrietta stared at the untouched lemonade and thought about things she didn't want to revisit. One involved being cold and aloof with Jeffie after his birth. She was so ashamed of that.

"At least your parents survived."

"Not so well, I'm afraid. With Miss Julia gone, my mother obviously lost her job and she was also grieving over losing her best friend. Knowing her, my mother probably felt partly responsible, too. After Miss Julia's funeral, Dr. Colonel started blaming Daddy for the brown rot growing in the orchards in a more aggressive way, and fired him." She shook her head. "Given the nature of Dr. Colonel's influence with other farmers in South Carolina, my parents had to move two hundred miles south, down to Peach County, Georgia, just so that Daddy could find other work."

"Maybe it's just as well."

"Yes, I agree. I'm actually relieved my father no longer works for Dr. Colonel and they aren't living anywhere near him. They're safer in Georgia."

"Did your mother ever tell your father about the rape and your suspicions about Miss Julia confronting Dr. Colonel?"

"I don't think so."

"You don't sound all that certain."

"She never said one way or the other. But let's just put it this way: if my father had known about the rape or suspected Dr. Colonel of causing Miss Julia's death or the fire, he would've killed Dr. Colonel with his bare hands instead of moving away disgraced."

"Holy karma, your mother's now keeping your secrets."

"Dr. Colonel is so diabolically clever and calculating, a very cool customer. He was able to coerce my mother's silence, like he did mine, with the threat of something much worse. That of losing our husbands."

"I'm not following that."

"If my mother had told my father, he would've killed Dr. Colonel, and my father would be in jail for committing murder. If I'd told my husband, he'd understandably never be able to come near me again. Dr. Colonel had us both in checkmate."

"At least you and your mother had the talking medicine." Joe's eyes held both concern and a strange sort of cheerfulness.

"Not really. After the fire, she was too busy trying to survive and relocate. Miss Julia's death gave her, both of us really, a scare. And I was too busy having a nervous breakdown."

"Come now." Joe frowned and looked upward.

"Given all that happened—Julia's death, having a stressful pregnancy, to say the least, and then watching helplessly as my parents were victimized and forced into moving away—it was more than I could handle. My misery was compounded by the realization that these horrible events, and the secrets behind them, continued to protect Dr. Colonel and cause problems with Jeff and me."

"*Ha'aa.*" He nodded.

"I was living life in a straitjacket. I was literally immobilized with this awful sense of powerlessness. At times, I could hardly pull myself out of bed, spending most of my pregnancy there."

"The same house?"

"No, thank God," she answered. "Because of the baby, we'd moved into a bigger house, but still in Aiken. After the fire, I'd also hoped my parents could just live with us there for a while."

"Didn't Jeff think your tiredness was uncharacteristic?"

"I led him to believe that my pregnancy was more troublesome than the previous one, and he knew how sad I was about Miss Julia and my parents leaving. But he wasn't himself either. He was in mourning for his beloved mother, and he had a lot of guilt for being so far away when she died. It didn't help that his father actually blamed Miss Julia's death on Jeff being in Medichero. He kept saying that this caused her to die of a broken heart. Jeff was also terribly frustrated about not being able to stop what was happening to my parents although he tried to intervene on their behalf."

"Did Jeff ever suspect his father in any of what happened?"

"He may have, but we never discussed it. He responded to all the tragedy by throwing himself into his medical practice with Dr. Kepple, and as it grew, he became even more absorbed. But his drive for research was still in him, and one day he announced that he wanted to break the cycle of sadness in our household. Almost two years had passed since our short-lived second mission, and he thought it was time to give Medichero another try. I didn't have the energy to object or consider any possible consequences of a third mission. Even if I had, I didn't think there was much else Dr. Colonel could do to me or my parents, except maybe kill us."

"And you've been here now for about a month, right?" He sat up straight in the chair and placed his feet on the floor. His palms were on the arms of the chair, and he gazed out the window intensely, in a way that suggested the prescience of a wolf sensing a coming danger.

"Well, not quite a month. Joe, what is it?"

"This isn't good. Bad medicine." He shook his head.

"Look, I'm not planning to ever go near Dr. Colonel again," Henrietta said.

"Would it be possible for Dr. Colonel to travel to this place?"

"It's funny you'd ask that; he did once. He was a physician in the army and was actually stationed at the Alamogordo base years ago, then after his service ended, he stayed a little longer traveling the area before returning to South Carolina, meeting and marrying Miss Julia soon thereafter. That was a long time ago, but Jeff never understood why his father didn't want him here, especially since Dr. Colonel had admitted to being fascinated with the White Sands Desert himself. In fact, he has lots of photographs of it hanging in his study. It's probably why Jeff had gotten interested in exploring New Mexico initially; he loved looking at those old pictures."

"If he's been here before, he knows the way then," Joe said.

Their eyes locked. A chill ran down her spine.

"I don't even want to think about it." Henrietta's voice squeaked. Her fears returned in full force.

"Perhaps you should. But take heed. And recall the words of Master Jesus the Christ who said: 'Be as harmless as doves, but wise as serpents.' "

"What does that mean?"

"You must prepare yourself with the cunning and shrewdness of snakes, while maintaining the peace and harmlessness of a dove. And you must tell Jeff your secrets, for your protection as well as his own."

"But, Joe, this is so hard!" Even as she spoke, Henrietta knew he was right. She would have to tell Jeff. But it was such an unlucky, bitter pill to swallow.

"If you don't choose the right path, you automatically walk the wrong road," Joe said.

"But, Joe! How am I supposed to tell my husband something like this? 'Oh, Jeff, by the way, your father raped me, and because of that, your mother is dead and the son you thought was yours just might be your father's, which would also make him your half-brother.' "

"Ultimately, the answers to life's most difficult questions will come not from your fears, but from the love of the Great Spirit inside yourself. And the only way to receive those sacred answers is to make room for them in your soul—in the way you define yourself in your thoughts and emotions."

"How do I do that?"

"With bear medicine and the *Kopave*."

"The what?"

"Listen. You must let go of your fears for a time, call to the Great Spirit within for guidance. To do that, you must still yourself, your mind and emotions, and then, you must listen and feel your way to feeling better." He touched his forehead with his fingertips, crossed his palms over his chest and then cupped his hands around his ears in one swift and unified movement. "This is the *Kopave*, the divine silence, the way to get answers from within."

"Could you make this a little easier for me to follow?" She was getting weary and more puzzled than before.

"For a better understanding, the sweat lodge is a useful next step. It also feels pretty good."

"How soon can we start?"

Bears Repeating smiled broadly, his eyes danced like mountain spirits.

Chapter 19

Over the next few days, after filling a journal about her soul retrieval and the initial stages of the talking medicine, Henrietta began feeling as if she were finally awakening from delirium. There was still some heaviness from continuing to conceal her burdensome secrets from Jeff, but she also had a renewed sense of hope that she would soon be able to tell Jeff everything. Before she did tell him, however, she wanted to be fully prepared in every way possible.

So she had agreed to take part in "bear medicine training." This meant she'd be committing herself to a spiritual exploration of sweat before hiking and camping in the alpine wilderness for a couple of days with Joe and Altie. They would start tomorrow. She figured she was one of few, if any, white women from South Carolina ever to consider, much less experience, such an adventure with a full-blooded Apache Indian and a half-breed mystic. But she no longer had any qualms about it, and decided that she didn't care what anyone else would think, not even the

U.S. Department of the Interior, which had prohibited participation in such Indian rituals. Jeff, of course, was enthusiastically supportive, even though he was unaware of her real motives.

As she hung clothes out on the line to dry, Henrietta thought about how her opinions of Indians and reservations had changed over the past couple of years. Before experiencing a life in Medichero, Henrietta had assumed Indians were to be feared, ignored or pitied, and that reservations were dreary, depressing places like prisons. And perhaps some of them were; she really didn't know about other reservations. She could only respond to what she'd witnessed at Medichero: a confederacy of Apache sub-tribes as well as individuals who lived and worked harmoniously in a variety of enterprises. She marveled at how the Medichero people, once so brutalized and disassembled, had seemingly transcended their tragic history.

"Greetings," Joe said. He was walking in from the side yard, carrying a paper sack. "I thought I'd take my lunch break here in the sun with you, if that meets with your approval."

"Of course; good to see you," she said.

Joe sat down on the grass cross-legged next to the clothesline. He was wearing a purple shirt with yellow piping and had light-green baggy pants on. He looked like a wild Elvis-iris popping out of the ground.

With closed eyes, Joe positioned himself to absorb as much sun as possible, and said a quiet prayer over his lunch.

"You know, I was just thinking of something," Henrietta said when he began eating, "I'm surprised that I haven't seen much of a victim mentality here." She felt foolish after saying it because she was the one who had felt victimized.

"It's a testament to our people's spiritual maturity," he said. His lids were shut again.

"Most everyone I've met here seems to be so cheerful and, I don't know … I guess the word I'm searching for is … normal," Henrietta said, as though she were talking to herself. "I had never heard about this positive side. It was always about all the Indians' problems and challenges."

"*Ha'aa.* Truth is understood better when it's experienced."

Altie came out of the screened-in porch door, which was propped open, with little Jeffie toddling in her wake. She led Jeffie over to her husband before helping with the laundry. Joe encircled the boy in his arms then allowed him to climb on his back and pull on his braids like horse reins.

After a few moments, Joe smiled at Henrietta. "Will you be ready to start the bear training tomorrow morning?"

"Yes, and you probably already know that Jeff's very encouraging about it," Henrietta said. "He's convinced me he can handle everything while I'm gone. Still, I'm relieved Altie's mother will be able to help out."

"Excellent," Joe said. "We'll start in the sweat lodge. After that, we'll go up into the mountain and find our sacred power place for a vision quest. You should be dressed for warmth in the day and coolness in the night; layers of clothing work well. Altie and I will bring blankets and other gear."

"Remind me again what a vision quest is?"

"As my people have always known, there's a quest that's built into us, and it's the drive for wholeness with the Great Spirit. This ritual helps us find the medicine within ourselves to learn more about who we are, so that we can be that."

"I see," Henrietta said. But she didn't understand at all what he'd just said. "Um, Joe?"

He raised his eyebrows.

"Before we go on with this, um, bear training, I want to make sure you're okay with something." Joe nodded for her to proceed as he handed a box of raisins from his bag to Jeffie.

"I'm going to ask a lot of 'why' questions."

"Oh, about that." Joe looked sheepish. "I may have exaggerated that point before, and I've been meaning to clarify," he said. "As I said, most Apaches and especially the elders consider asking direct questions bad manners, but Altie and I have taken a different view. We've come to believe that there is nothing in the world that is beyond questioning, that it is essential to understanding who we are and, therefore, should be encouraged."

"Well, you could've told me that sooner," Henrietta said. "But I must say that I'm relieved. You have no idea how hard that's been for me. Okay, first question. Tell me again why we're doing this? Are you trying to turn me into some kind of medicine woman? Or teach me how to become an Apache writer?"

"That's three questions. No, I'm not trying to turn you into anything. You need to discover who you are and what your divine mission is," he said. "But it's all up to you." He stood up. "I'd better get back to the hospital."

"How will this, um, bear training help with that?" Henrietta asked.

Joe turned back around to face her. "Henrietta, it's not possible for me or anyone to simply say to you that you're a spiritual being with great power, and already in and a part of the Great Oneness," he said. "You have to experience and learn these truths for yourself."

"So I assume the bear training helps to facilitate that."

"*Ha'aa*, facilitate. That's a good word for these rituals, which are, let us say, physically challenging, among other things. First we sweat."

"You do not have anything to lose to try it out," Altie said. She was bouncing Jeffie up and down on her hip.

"Maybe a little weight?" Henrietta teased. She watched as Joe began walking toward the path that led up to the hospital.

"That reminds me," Altie said. "Do not eat any breakfast in the morning. Just have water before coming to the sweat lodge. Tomorrow, we also fast."

"Okay, definitely a few pounds," Henrietta said. She smiled.

The next day after Altie's mother, Naomi Birdsong, arrived to help out at the doctor's cottage, Henrietta headed for the sweat lodge. She had donned what she thought would be the most comfortable and adaptable clothes for a trek in the backcountry: her dungarees, a plaid blouse and white sneakers. In a tote bag, she brought a heavy sweater, a change of underwear and thick wool socks, Jeff's corduroy jacket, her toothbrush and paste, a canteen of water, toilet paper and, just in case she couldn't hold out on that proposed fast, a few peanut butter and jelly sandwiches.

The sweat lodge was supposed to be in an open, secluded place, next to the Apache River, and surrounded by lush indigenous evergreen vegetation and gigantic boulders. As she came to the end of the path, she could see that it was just as described. Altie and Joe were waiting for her near a rounded tent structure that she assumed was the sweat lodge. It was about ten feet in diameter and covered over with blankets and tarps. A campfire roared fifteen feet away.

Altie wore her traditional fringed-leather dress, while Joe was dressed in his usual casual-Elvis attire: a blue-and-white panel shirt, embroidered with a guitar; rolled-up blue jeans; and the ubiquitous blue-suede moccasins.

"Ya-ta-say," Henrietta said, using the Apache word for hello. "How are you, my beautiful friends, on this fine morning?"

"You're in a good mood," Joe said.

"Yes, I am." In fact, Henrietta was feeling greatly improved and even optimistic for the first time in more than two years. "So, how do we do this sweat lodge thing?"

"Men and women do not sweat together," Joe said.

Henrietta exhaled dramatically. "Well, there's a relief."

"You'll go into the sacred sweat lodge with Altie while I go help Jeff with something and make preparations for our vision quest," Joe said. "But before I go, we'll explain the good in sweat."

Henrietta smiled.

"Before you enter this sacred sweat lodge, it's helpful to acknowledge and let go of the spiritual mistakes you've made and hold within."

"Spiritual mistakes?"

"These are violations you may have made against *All of Our Relations in Nature,* which includes yourself," Altie said. "Here, I wrote out this list for your reference."

"Think of the list as part of a *Beginner's Manual* for young braves in bear training," Joe added, his eyes twinkling. "There are others, but it's a good place to start."

Henrietta looked down at the piece of paper Altie handed her.

"Father O'Reilly would say this ritual is like the Catholic confessions of sin," Joe said. "Well, maybe he wouldn't. But that's how you might compare it to something in the white man's world."

"Violations? Against all of my relations in nature? What does that mean?"

"Everything you see and feel is connected to everything else and the Great Spirit," Joe said. "So when you do something that hurts the Great Spirit's creations, you are in truth, hurting yourself. And vice versa."

"Okay, assuming I can remember and name all the mistakes I've made against all of my relations in nature, please help me understand why that is useful," Henrietta said.

"Only when spiritual mistakes are identified and acknowledged can they be corrected and cleared out," Joe said. "If we don't clear them out of our souls, they can create blockages that prevent the Great Spirit from flowing through us. These blocks act like magnets for bad thoughts, which beget bad feelings, which beget bad health, both mental and physical, and so on. That's why it's best to clear them out."

"I've heard Jeff talk about something similar to that theory, about how negative thoughts and emotions can actually cause disease."

Joe nodded. "But kindly take notice: the good in this ritual will be in direct proportion to the purity of heart of the person who's performing it."

"Are you saying that I must sweat with a pure heart? Is it me or does that sound kind of funny?"

"It's gloriously funny," Joe agreed with a bright smile.

"I may need to have my head examined," Henrietta said. "But, yes, I think I'm going into this sweat lodge ceremony with pure intentions. If I do this, will my sins be forgiven?"

"We're not talking about scary sins," he said. He made a ghoulish gesture with his fingers. "We're simply talking about learning how to correct the spiritual mistakes we make on this journey called life. Also, to be more mindful of *All of Our Relations in Nature*."

"Oh." Henrietta wondered what she'd be like today if the religion of her childhood had focused on this loving notion of correcting mistakes rather than evoking fear about sins.

"After identifying our mistakes, we go into the sweat lodge and surrender them into Spirit, which helps us feel better for a variety of reasons."

"Like what?"

"It's a good first step toward balancing our karma," Joe said.

She raised her eyebrows and frowned. There he went again with a phantasmagorical mix of religious concepts.

"The word karma perfectly expresses how our universe acts as a just mirror ... how we reap what we sow," Joe said. "If you think about and hold in fear, for example, it'll inevitably be drawn into your experience in some way. It's universal law."

"Hmm. So what's the point of the sweat lodge?"

"It has tremendous health benefits."

"Like what?"

"If I tell you, you won't find out for yourself."

"That's not fair. I'm new to all this spirit bear medicine stuff."

"Okay, I'll give you a hint. It's really very simple: all you have to do is this."

She raised her eyebrows.

"Be still and quiet and let the Great Spirit fill you in."

"Well, okay." She smiled. "Hey, Joe, do all Apaches practice the sweat lodge ritual like this?" Henrietta asked.

"Actually, Altie and I have formed our own sweat lodge ritual from a combination of Apache, Catholic and, uh-um, our own good ideas," he said. He looked over at Altie and smiled.

"Won't your elders get a little ticked off at you for changing the Apache ritual?"

"Nah."

Altie shot Joe a dirty glance, and rolled her eyes.

"We like to think of our version as a bit more progressive, keeping up with the times, so to speak," Joe said. "It helps us to be more mindful of the Great Spirit's laws of life."

"I see," she said.

"Now, here's the first item on our list," Joe said. "Humans must not molest, kill or experiment upon animals, birds, reptiles, bugs, trees, plants and fish for no good reason. Or without restoring balance."

"I don't have a problem with that one," Henrietta said. "But I'm curious, don't Indians kill animals for food and wear their skins as clothing? And how about all those feathers y'all use?"

"At this time, it's perfectly acceptable to the animals and plants themselves for humans to take their physical bodies for food, shelter and clothing, as long as we bless them, ask their permission first and thank them, as our people indeed do," Joe said.

"Hmm."

"We also must try to make restitution. That is, we must work to help restore and maintain a natural balance for the resources we use. If we treat nature properly, with respect and gratefulness, living creatures actually will lovingly offer themselves to us. But kindly take note: it is of the utmost importance to treat their gift of life as compassionately as possible. I personally appreciate how kosher Jews bless animals before killing them for food in a way that's the most painless, holy and humane. It is called *shechitah*."

"Joe, did you just say the word kosher? And *shechitah*? No offense, but your bear medicine is a melting pot of religious teachings and rituals. Don't you think you're confusing things a bit?"

"Melting, schmelting."

Henrietta laughed. "You're truly an enigma, Joe Loco," she said, shaking her head.

"Truth transcends the religion of men and their man-made dogmas."

She was astonished that she agreed. After they reviewed the entire list together, Henrietta summarized it through her admissions: "Well, I've never asked my food for permission to kill or eat it. Guilty. Judging others, yes. No to witchcraft, but certainly a lot of hateful thoughts about Dr. Colonel. I'm usually respectful of myself in regard to being clean and tidy. But I'm culpable of wasting my gifts with self-pity and having a victim mentality many times. I've been known to gossip and tell a fib now and then. I've been idle and selfish. No to really unusual sex acts and no to pornography, but sex in nature? Guilty. I don't have any idea what my mind blocks might be or who I am spiritually. Oh dear. It looks like I've committed, um, one, two, three, four, five, six, seven, eight violations, at least. No wonder I feel so out of whack!"

"We will now plead on your behalf to the Nature Spirits and the mighty and glorious Great Spirit for your purification," Joe said. He raised his opened hands in prayer and began singing, with Altie joining him. After a few minutes, they both blew air on Henrietta's face and said in unison, "Your mistakes are blown away."

"Can you do that?" Henrietta was skeptical as she remembered her Christian upbringing. All of a sudden she felt like a child about to get caught with her hand in the cookie jar.

"No, of course not; that power is within you," Joe said.

"I'm confused," Henrietta said.

"We're merely facilitating," Joe said with a grin, "and trying to demonstrate a way for you to learn how to self-correct mistakes now and in the future. You still must let them go and forgive yourself unconditionally."

"Well, okay then, thanks for facilitating," Henrietta said. She felt a little better.

Joe smiled, and his teeth were so white against his tan skin that they seemed to hold a clear beam of morning sunlight.

"Please allow me to seal you with a smudge of burning sage," Altie said. When Henrietta nodded,

Altie stuck an herb bundle into the campfire and fanned its fumes over Henrietta with a large eagle feather as she sang something in her native language.

"I've noticed you always have some of that stuff on you," Henrietta said, referring to the sage.

"In this application, the smudge medicine will further cleanse and protect you spiritually. Good spirits like the smell. Bad spirits do not," Altie said.

She closed her eyes, letting Altie cover her with the purifying herbal fragrance.

"Now we sweat," Altie said after finishing.

Joe turned and limped away. "*Ka-dish-day—*farewell, for now."

"Hey, Joe, did you say you had to help Jeff with something? What is it?" Henrietta asked.

Joe stopped and turned back. "It's with Big Eagle Feathers, Victor Two Feathers and another brother, Danny Running Feathers," he said, using the native names for Ray Santana and his brothers.

"They're making trouble again?" Henrietta asked.

"Nah, not really."

"Joe, I thought you said fibbing was a violation against *All of Our Relations in Nature*," Henrietta crossed her arms.

"Ah, very good; you're a most astute student," Joe said. He smiled and for a second, there was merriment in his eyes. "As you know, Big Eagle and his brothers have expressed some displeasure about Jeff's interest in our spirit medicine and the old ways. Also, Little Eagle Feathers is not improving as quickly as we'd all like. But don't worry. I go to bring them peace and release." He turned and disappeared into the woods.

"I'll pray you can do that," Henrietta whispered, turning back toward the sweat lodge. "Altie, I'm already sweating."

"Do not be troubled, Henrietta. Joe can be quite persuasive," Altie said. "Let us give our attention to you in the sweat lodge. Remember, now that you have identified some of your spiritual mistakes, in here you can surrender them to the Great Spirit. You also can surrender your fears about Jeff and everything. Let it all go."

"Good idea."

"We prefer to sweat naked, stripped of all our clothes, jewelry, symbols, status, wealth and other covering which might hide our true nature," Altie said, slipping off her leather dress. She was now standing before Henrietta completely and unabashedly nude. "We can hide nothing from the Great Spirit, anyway."

"Well, okay," Henrietta said. But she blushed while removing her clothes and looked around nervously. She laid her clothes on a rock.

"Follow this way." Altie walked toward the sweat lodge entrance.

They made a slight duck under the low-set doorway, which was only about four feet high and

covered with a blanket-style door. The infrastructure
was made of willow and pine tree branches.

"We will be like infants in the womb of our
Mother Earth," Altie said. "Afterward, we will come
out more pure, innocent and prepared for nurturing."

"I'm ready for that." Henrietta straightened and
was surprised to see another woman already inside.

"Henrietta, this is Madia," Altie said. "She will
be tending to the sacred fire outside and bringing in the
rocks as needed for sweat."

With the blanket door still open, Henrietta saw
that Madia wore nothing except four leather necklaces.
She looked as though she might be a hundred years old.
Her face was dark, dry and rough like her leather
necklaces. Her thin black and gray hair hung straight
without braids. She tucked it behind ears that were too
large for her small head. Her breasts were long
cylinders and swayed left and right as she moved.

"How do you do?" Henrietta said to Madia
before Altie flapped the door shut. Henrietta blushed
again, realizing how silly her formal comment sounded.
The three women were naked and huddled closely
together in a little darkened dome.

"*Doo ansi,*" Madia said.

"She doesn't speak English," Altie said.

"What did she say?"

"She said, 'I am fine.' "

"How'd she know what I said if she doesn't
speak English?"

"She can understand it; she just doesn't want to speak it."

Madia grinned and continued her work. From the outside fire, she brought scalding-hot stones, the size of baseballs, in a hammock-style basket made of cornhusks, reeds, sticks and blanket strips. She dumped the rocks into a small dirt pit and arranged them in a neat pile with a stick before going out again.

"I thought you said we're supposed to remove all of our clothing and jewelry. What about her necklaces?" Henrietta whispered to Altie.

"Some among us remain stubborn, like with the English. But she makes a great sweat lodge, I am sure you would agree." Altie ladled water onto the mound of sizzling rocks with a large wooden spoon, producing billowy clouds of soothing steam.

Henrietta flinched at the sharp brightness of sunlight pouring through the flap door as Madia returned.

Seemingly satisfied with her work, Madia gave a native farewell and shut the blanket door for the last time, turning the interior of the curved structure into warm, embryonic tranquility. The only illumination came from the bloodred glow of Madia's fiery lava rocks and a few tiny holes in the tarpaulin ceiling, reminding Henrietta of the clear but humid starry nights in South Carolina.

"Now, Henrietta, let us still our minds, surrender our mistakes to Spirit and into the flame of forgiveness to be consumed," Altie said. She used the wooden spoon again. "And if you are so inclined, please ask and allow the Great Spirit to fill you in."

As they sat in the misty warmth, Henrietta said silent prayers to God and Jesus, asking to be released from her acknowledged mistakes that she gladly surrendered, she vowed to be more mindful of her actions in the future. She prayed to be purified and cut free from the dark spirits Dr. Colonel might have injected into her. And finally, with all the self-discipline she could muster, she prayed to be free of her hatred and fear of Dr. Colonel and to come to the point where she might forgive him for the ugly and manipulative masks he wore. It was the best she could do at this point.

Meanwhile, Altie sang Indian hymns and occasionally ladled more water upon sizzling stones. After what seemed like about thirty minutes, the two women's bodies were completely drenched and Altie indicated they should leave. They emerged from the sweat lodge and wiped themselves with thick, unbleached cotton towels provided by Madia, who had already added a blue cotton skirt and blouse to her leather necklaces. As Altie and Henrietta dressed in silence, Madia poured ice-cold mountain spring water into wooden cups.

"Oh, this tastes sooo good," Henrietta said, gulping it. "Um, how do I say thank you?"

"*Ná'ahénsih*, I thank you, Madia," Altie said.

"*Ná'ahénsih*, Madia," Henrietta parroted.

"We will now go to the mountain and quest for a sacred vision," Altie said. "Let us go find Joe."

Altie began to walk toward the trail with Henrietta following like a baby duck imprinted on its mother. As they neared the Locos' house, Henrietta could see Joe standing next to three sturdy Appaloosa horses with Western-style saddles.

"We're all set to go," Joe said. He gave the horses a final check.

"Does that mean everything's okay with Jeff, little Billy and those feathered brothers?" Henrietta asked.

"*Ha'aa*. The boy has stabilized, which means they are all good for now. It's an excellent time to seek the wisdom of the Mountain Spirits."

Chapter 20

By lunchtime, with Henrietta on a native pilgrimage and Billy Santana under the careful watch of Dr. Belzer, Jeff decided to spend some special time with his sweet-faced children.

"Hello, my little peaches," Jeff said as he opened the front door to the doctor's cottage.

"Daddy!" The twins and also little Jeffie ran into his arms, and as he returned their hugs and kisses, Jeff's heart warmed at their touch. How lucky he was to have them here. They stabilized him, giving a soothing shape and balance to everything he was and did in Medichero. His work and research were still as exciting as ever. He adored his wife, and she not only supported his radical interests in native medicine, but also was participating in it. And all three of these golden-haired beauties were healthy and well adjusted. His only regret was his father's opposition to his work. Even though he was a thousand miles away, Jeff could still feel the heaviness of his father's disapproval.

Jeff shook his head, trying to shed hurtful memories. "Wow, something smells really wonderful in here," he said. He stood up with Jeffie in his arms.

"Miss Naomi's making lunch," Frannie said.

"Well, let's go see if we can try it out," Jeff said. They headed for the kitchen.

After Henrietta had left that morning, Naomi Songbird had been busy in the kitchen, making a traditional Apache acorn stew with dumplings for the kids' lunch. She was singing and watching over them, all the while. Acorn stew was both a comfort food and a soft luxury, a happy marriage of sweetness and spiciness.

What a blessing Altie and her mother are, Jeff thought. He put his brown-leather medicine bag on the washstand by the kitchen door.

In addition to being an excellent cook, Naomi also had a knack for creating music, as her surname suggested. She was often heard whistling or singing out loud with joyful abandon. She was as petite as her daughter and usually as flowery in dress as her son-in-law. Today, she wore a cheerful and colorful cotton day dress patterned with a vine of bright-red strawberries entwined on a blue trellis. Crisp-white crocheted trim rimmed the bodice, front pockets and sleeves of the loose-fitting design and flattered her full figure.

After thanking the songstress for lunch, Jeff suggested that she take off the rest of the afternoon, with full pay, of course.

"I would not feel comfortable leaving you with a kitchen in need of cleaning," Naomi said. Her accented pronunciations were somewhat stilted, but exuded a casual warmth.

"It would be an honor and a blessing if you let us do it," Jeff said. "And we'll be fine later; Henrietta left some dinners in the icebox for us."

"Very well. If you change your mind or need me for any reason, please do not hesitate to call me," Naomi offered.

"I've got your phone number, but I'll only call if there's an emergency at the hospital and I'm needed there. So, *ná'ahénsih,* I thank you, Naomi," he said. He was trying to use proper Apache diction.

"Ah, *nzhoo,* very good." She nodded. *"Ná'ahénsih."*

Jeff smiled. "We'll see you in the morning, then." He made a motion for Frannie and Annie to join him. "Come on, girls, if y'all help me clean up lunch, there'll be a special surprise in it for you."

Frannie's and Annie's eyebrows shot up and their mouths formed a silent "oh" before they jumped up to gather the dirty dishes.

After cleaning up the rest of the lunch things, Jeff smiled at his children. "Now, since you did such a terrific job, follow me for your reward." When he reached the sofa, he bent down on his knees, lifted the skirt and revealed three gift-wrapped presents. "Ta-da!"

"Oh, Daddy!" Frannie and Annie cried in unison. Jeff pulled out two small square gift boxes wrapped in paper with pink blooms, then a third gift, which was long and skinny, in light-blue paper, and obviously for Jeffie. But the little guy was still transfixed on the narrow cave-like space under the sofa as if he'd been shown the main vein of Santa's secret gold mine.

"I've been saving these surprises for a special occasion," Jeff said. "And I think our sharing extra time together while your mama is away qualifies, don't you?" The girls squealed in agreement and unwrapped their gifts with delight.

"Oh, thank you so much, Daddy," Frannie said, holding up a turquoise necklace. "I love it."

"Thank you, thank you, thank you," Annie added, fingering her own necklace. They both kissed him.

"And this, my son, is for you," Jeff said, shaking an elongated-shaped gift, which made a curious rattling noise. At that, little Jeffie looked up bright-eyed and smiling, ready to help his dad unwrap the package. It contained a ceremonial Indian rattle. Jeffie's squeals and the girls' kisses and hugs made Jeff so happy he could barely speak. He had to clear his throat to say anything.

"These remind me of something fascinating about how the Apache view bears and our friend Bears Repeating," Jeff said. He was pointing at the bear motif on each of the gifts. The necklaces showcased a bear-shaped stone in the middle of a strand of rounded, pearl-sized turquoise stones. The leathered head of Jeffie's rattle also formed a bear's body. "The Apache actually have a very high regard and great reverence for bears," Jeff said. His voice took on a storytelling quality. "But here's the funny thing about it: they will not refer to the bear directly by his name. Instead, they call him grandfather or uncle. They do this out of respect."

"So why isn't Joe's native name Grandfathers Repeating, Daddy?" Frannie asked.

"Or Uncles Repeating?" Annie added.

"Ha! My beautiful daughters are also little geniuses," Jeff said. He rubbed their heads. "It's because the bear presented itself to Joe in a most unusual and direct way. And the Apache pay close attention to things like that. Do you remember me telling you that after a grizzly bear attacked Joe, he had a spiritual experience that transformed him into a great healer?" The kids nodded. "Well, because of that amazing, miraculous event, the Medichero elders decided to give Joe a special allowance and agreed to let him use the sacred bear name."

The children became busy with their gifts, and while they did, Jeff's thoughts turned to his wife's sudden interest and participation in spirit medicine with Bears Repeating and the sage Altie, something he wouldn't have expected from her. But, in truth, he was so relieved. He'd been troubled and bewildered by the changes in Henrietta since her pregnancy with Jeffie.

He prayed that the vision quest and Joe's healing techniques would somehow rejuvenate her and that she would return to him as she had been before. And quite selfishly, he also hoped that she'd come back with a greater sense of understanding and fluency so that maybe, with her writer's mind and talent, she could help him to translate and distill the mystical aspects of native medicine into something more credible and coherent for his scientific papers.

A knock on the front door interrupted his wandering thoughts.

Jeff opened the door to Craig Mackenzie, local representative of the U.S. Bureau of Indian Affairs. "Hello, Craig. I hope you don't mind; I'm taking the afternoon off while Henrietta is, um, out."

"Not at all; you've earned a break," Craig said. The agency superintendent, about thirty-five years old, had a solid build, deep dimples and sandy blond hair. "Gosh, I'm sorry I missed Henrietta; she's always such a delight."

"Yes, well, thank you. I'm sure she'll be disappointed she missed your visit, too," Jeff said. He was surprised that he had a sudden, uncharacteristic stab of jealousy. But Craig was still single and sometimes a little too friendly around Henrietta—at least to Jeff's mind. "Say, what brings you by?"

"Probably for the same reason you needed a break: the influenza epidemic," Craig said.

"What do you mean?"

"The government requires an official report about such things. Sorry to bother, but I need you to look over and sign some paperwork." Craig held up a file folder.

"No problem. Go on ahead into the kitchen, while I get the kids occupied." Jeff walked into the living room before calling back to Craig. "There should be some coffee on the counter; help yourself." Jeff turned on the TV to the only station that came through on the reservation. Channel seven was airing what looked like a soap opera. "Oh shucks, I guess it's too late for *Captain Kangaroo*. Hey, girls, will you play with Jeffie here while I take care of some business with Mr. Mackenzie in the kitchen?"

"Sure, Daddy," Frannie said. She and her sister ran into the corner to collect Jeffie's Tonka toy trucks.

Jeff looked back at his daughters and smiled. Although they still carried Carolina accents, they had adapted well to the dry, rocky landscape of the Southwest. And he thought them beautiful. *My God, they're little carbon copies of Henrietta.*

As he walked toward the kitchen, Jeff wiped a tear from his eye, then joined Craig, already at the table with a cup of coffee with cream. *Making himself at home,* he thought. Jeff put his fingers on his forehead, unsure of why he was responding to Craig in a jealous-husband sort of way. *I must be more tired than I realized.*

"I wanted to make sure I got the facts straight about the cause and state of the epidemic we experienced," Craig said. He made a nervous chuckle sound. "You know, a few of the Indians believe you were the cause. Of course, I know that's utter nonsense."

Jeff was growing more irritated at Craig. He pulled on his collar with a finger. "Well, there's not much a doctor could do to cause influenza, unless he had it himself, which I clearly didn't have when I arrived, nor have I contracted it since, thankfully."

"Yeah, I'm thankful about not getting it, too," Craig said amiably. "It swept through the reservation though."

"Major outbreaks usually occur when there's an antigenic shift, meaning when the flu virus changes and evolves into a different, more powerful strain," Jeff said. "That's why, even if the Indians had contracted the flu before and developed some form of resistance to it, they wouldn't be immune to a new, and perhaps, more deadly strain." Jeff exhaled, grateful that he could rely on his medical knowledge to dispel his annoyance and project the appropriate level of professional detachment.

"Why do you suppose some of them think you're the cause? Just curious."

Calm down; he's just doing his job. "Well, I guess there's the timing: my arrival about a month ago just happened to coincide with the start of the epidemic. And you know how superstitious some of them are about coincidences," Jeff said. He was trying hard to speak calmly and without emotion. "In addition, none of the white people got it, and unfortunately we had Apache deaths. Four to be exact. The number four has special meaning for these people; it's considered sacred. I'm afraid all of that fed into some sort of suspicion of me, but it's a view held only by a small minority, so I'm not overly concerned about it."

"Agreed. Can you confirm that this epidemic is officially over?"

"I can say the worst of it is. Half a dozen cases still remain, but they're not life threatening, and, actually I expect all of them to go home from the hospital within the week, except for one, Billy Santana. But he's had other complications."

"Could you review the steps you took to contain it? The epidemic, I mean."

"We acted quickly, quarantining those infected in the east wing of the hospital in what we call the flu unit. We were, and still are, strict about protocol, meaning we continually sterilize ourselves and everything we touch. And we're consistent about wearing gauze masks and rubber gloves when in the flu unit. Also, early on, as soon as I sensed the seriousness of the outbreak, I sent messengers to the army hospital at the base in Alamogordo for extra supplies and antiviral medications, while ensuring our lab was fully stocked with the requisite fluid replacements."

"I don't believe anyone could've handled it better." Craig smiled.

"Thanks." Jeff released his clenched fists under the table, relieved that he'd successfully handled a bewildering emotional undertone. Perhaps in his enthusiastic support for Henrietta's vision quest, he'd selfishly dismissed the potential dangers of her being out in the wilderness.

Craig leveled his papers on the table. "It looks like I got the facts straight in the report," he said. "If you'll just look over this document, which summarizes everything, and sign here, I'll get out of your hair." Craig flipped to the back page and made an X on a line.

While Jeff reviewed the report, Craig got up and peeped around the hall corner. "Where did you say Henrietta was?"

Jeff looked up. He had no intention of telling Craig that his wife was participating in the taboo: Indian rituals were officially prohibited by the U.S. Department of the Interior.

"She just needed to um, run some, um ..." Jeff started, the words catching in his throat.

"Errands? Is she shopping?"

"Yes, you could say that," Jeff said. *Yeah, she's out shopping for a spiritual vision with a couple of our Indians.*

Chapter 21

"That's it?" Henrietta had said earlier that morning to Joe and Altie, looking up at two rolled-up Indian blankets and a saddlebag on each of three Appaloosa horses. "We're going to camp up in the mountains for a couple of days and that's all we're bringing? Where're we going to sleep?" Henrietta asked, getting nervous. "What about black bears? Mountain lions? Snakes? Bugs? Hello? Is anyone worried about wild animals?"

"There is no need to worry, Henrietta," Altie said in her calm, confident way.

"You will be safe in the hands of Medichero Apaches in the land of good spirits," Joe added.

Henrietta nodded because deep down she knew Joe and Altie would somehow keep her well protected. They mounted and rode the Appaloosas up the path that led past the white hospital buildings in the direction of the northern Ponderosa pine forest, where they picked up a well-worn mountain trail leading toward a higher plane. On the other side of the woodland, a peaceful nation of cattle and elk grazed along the sloping grasslands, and a couple of rare bighorn sheep watched their progress from a massive scalloped rock. Jackrabbits and rock mice jumped out of their path. The crickets sang to no particular rhythm.

Henrietta was exhilarated as they traveled on the steep, scabrous trail, and she remembered how much she loved riding. But this ride was more extraordinary than those she'd been on before, perhaps because of the stunning panorama, crisp mountain air and the sacred visions they sought. After riding all day, they finally came to a clearing with a half-circle grouping of giant boulders on one side and an ascendant view of the Sacramento Mountains and Sierra Blanca on the other.

"Spectacular," Henrietta said. She was transfixed by a sunset of liquid gold, oranges and reds against a range of snowcapped mountains. She inhaled deeply and closed her eyes, wanting to capture the moment in her memory forever. It was the ultimate big-top attraction, a vivid multicolored extravaganza full of showy vistas and breathtaking scents, and she thought of them as her tickets to a grand adventure of self, where she could feel a part of the Great Spirit and the all-ness of everything. There were no fears of a darkened past in this place. They couldn't exist here, not in this holy light.

"There's much value in looking at things from a higher perspective, *ha'aa*?" Joe said. It was like he had preordained this divine manifestation for one of his bear secrets.

"Yes," Henrietta said. She continued to gaze out at the leavened mounds of earth floating in waves of clouds. "I can see why you call them sky islands," she said.

"In earlier times, young Medichero boys would come to our sacred sky islands when they were old enough to begin their training as braves," Joe said. "They'd come here to be alone, fast and pray for their visions. They were seeking wisdom from the Great Spirit because, in the old ways of the Apache world, revealed spiritual knowledge from within is the highest form one can gain. This is a truth that lives on through us and we continue to seek it."

Joe and Altie dismounted and led their horses over to an unexpected mountain spring, concealed behind an outgrowth of pinion junipers and tall grasses. Henrietta followed their example before stretching and shaking her legs after the long ride.

"If the young braves meditated and were pure of heart, they were honored by the presence of spirit guides who appeared before them," Joe said. He dipped a metal cup into the highest part of the spring, away from where the horses drank downstream. He gave the full cup to Henrietta before pulling out two more cups from one of the saddlebags and filling them for Altie and himself. "Some of these spiritual beings came in the form of an elder or an animal, bird, plant or tree," he said. He took a long sip of cool spring water. "Whatever appeared in the vision became the young brave's medicine. Afterward, he'd carry something representative of the spirit guides in a small leather pouch, which he would call his 'medicine bag.' "

"A medicine bag. Hmm," she started.

Joe held up a palm. "Kindly, please listen." He sat his now empty cup down on a rock and moved without speaking or making noise, unfastening his horse's saddle and hanging it on the trunk of a fallen tree.

After a few moments, Henrietta had to ask: "Listen to what?"

"This is a sacred place with much to say. If you'll but open yourself and your mind to it," Joe said. "Listen for the Great Spirit, whose mighty presence is here and everywhere." He began removing the next saddle.

"Joe, how do you really know that the Great Spirit is here?"

After softly placing her saddle on the trunk next to his, Joe stood motionless except for his right hand, which moved over his heart. "Our dear young brave, we know the Great Spirit is here because we are here."

Henrietta tried to understand what he'd said as he limped back to attend to Altie's horse. "But what exactly does that mean, Joe?"

He turned to face her. "Henrietta, if you're looking for the Great Spirit outside of yourself, you won't find what you think you're looking for."

"That's not what I learned in Sunday school at church," Henrietta said.

Joe eyed her with a gentle intensity. "Ah, but remember, 'the kingdom of God is within you.' " It was all he said as he carried two of the saddlebags over to the secluded area, protected by the half-ring of boulders.

Henrietta stared at him with her mouth open, knowing full well that he'd just quoted Jesus.

"Hey now, the firewood and rocks want to be found," he said, changing the subject.

"We hide firewood in the woods for safekeeping," Altie said. "But sometimes, a little too well. We must consult the elementals to locate it." Altie began to sing an Indian hymn as they walked around and in between the trees and boulders.

Watching Joe and Altie pray to the woods, pick up stray branches and pre-cut logs from obscure places and talk to rocks they gathered for a fire-pit, Henrietta's mind turned: *What am I doing here?* She felt an unexpected rush of confusion as old fears of the forbidden came shooting to the surface.

"Henrietta, we must talk about your spiritual protection," Joe said. He had gotten the fire started.

"My what?"

"Your spiritual protection," he repeated. "Now that your soul's on the mend and you're beginning to walk on the sacred inner path of oneness, the dark spirits will be at you as never before, hounding you and nipping at your heels, trying to throw you back off balance and derail your healing progress with fears, doubts and other delusions."

"Oh, dear!" *Had he somehow picked up on her negative thoughts a second ago?*

"Not to worry. When they come, just remember to tell them this," Joe said. He stood up from the fire with a stick in his hand. Using it like a microphone, Joe broke out into a remarkably good, albeit intentionally revised, rendition of one of Elvis's smash hits. "You ain't nothin' but a hound dog ... Cryin' all the time ...You ain't nothin' but a dark, dark dog ... Cryin' all the time ... Well, you ain't never gonna get me, 'Cause you ain't no friend of mine."

"Very impressive," Henrietta said. She was laughing and clapping.

"Ah, but you'll never forget this teaching," said Bears Repeating.

"How to impersonate Elvis?"

"Ho, ha! Our young brave in training, that's a good one. No! It's this: When your thoughts turn dark, stop! Listen! Call to the Great Spirit for protection. Picture yourself surrounded by a circle of light in the shape of my soul-catcher, while saying: 'Be gone you hound dogs of darkness! You have no power in me! Be gone and never come back!' " He paused. "Then, turn your thoughts to feel-good ones. This will protect you spiritually," he said.

"I wish I had known about that before."

"We learn as we go."

Henrietta smiled. Thanks to Joe's good humor, she began to relax and feel secure even as she once again was wonderstruck by Joe's inimitable capacity for translating and simplifying the confusing jargon of shamans into unobjectionable quips and amusing impersonations.

As the mountain air moved softly with an increasing coolness, Joe and Altie sat down next to the roaring fire, cross-legged on blankets. Henrietta joined them, and, together, they listened in silence to the sounds of nature all about them. "Feel the fire and wind's love on your face, trust the inner voice."

"I have to admit something," Henrietta said. "Sometimes the inner voice sends me dark and disturbing messages. What does that mean?"

"That you must not confuse the inner voice with the mind games and negative babble of the ego's voice. It's our responsibility to learn how to discern the difference between the two."

"How can we do that?"

"The true inner voice is a comforter of wisdom, unconditional love and a dissolver of all hound-dog fears and anxieties. It's intuitive and comes from oneness with the Great Spirit. This is something the ego cannot experience or understand and therefore tries to, let us say, spoil and muddle up. The ego voice is far away from that of your true self, which is why these thoughts always feel bad."

"Hmm." Henrietta pondered Joe's words as she stared into the fire, wishing she had brought a notebook. But she would have to rely on her memory and hope it would serve her well later.

The flames finally produced a red-glowing bed of coals. Altie burned sage under a pot of water she positioned on a small, foldable grill held in place with rocks. "May this sacred sage help purify our minds and thoughts about who we are, our feelings and our bodies," she said. She began to chant something in her native Athabascan language while looking up toward a silvery full moon. After the mantras, she withdrew a small bundle of unidentified dried plants from a cotton bag.

Henrietta refrained from asking questions, wanting instead to be the silent observer. But it was sometimes difficult as Altie's pot of water was slow to boil.

"This is a blessed Indian herbal mix," Altie said at last. She placed the bundle into the readied hot water. After a few minutes, she used a stick to scoop out the string and discard it into the fire before extracting most of the boiled leaves and dividing them evenly into three green-colored bandanas. "This expression of the Great Spirit aids us in achieving spiritual sight," she said. She then demonstrated the procedure for tying on an herbal headband.

Henrietta donned her headband in polite silence, while Altie poured some of the remaining liquid, steeped in Indian herbs, into their three metal cups.

As the tea cooled, Joe added wild native tobacco to the fire. "Henrietta, are you willing to know who you truly are?"

"Yes, I want to know who I truly am."

Joe closed his eyes and raised his hands above his head, palms cupped and pointing to the sky.

Henrietta felt a strange flutter in the middle of her chest.

"Oh Infinite, Mighty I AM THAT I AM, Magnificent Creator, Healer and One Writer of the Universe ... Beloved Great Spirit, we come before You, our Father and Mother Light reflected in the Radiant Grandmother Moon, Mother Earth and each of us ... to seek Your wisdom and give prayers of thanksgiving," Joe said. He was speaking loudly. "We bring our purified bodies, open minds and this sacred tobacco as tokens of appreciation and ask that You shine Your divine intelligence into us and charge our herbal tea with your eternal love, peace and harmony. Speak to us, oh Great I AM THAT I AM, in a way that we can see, hear and understand. Awaken the inner memory of the I AM Presence in each of us. Show us who we truly are and what we are here to do."

Altie whispered to Henrietta: "We are making the call—the quest—tonight. Tomorrow, after fasting and meditating in the *Kopave,* we may receive our visions."

"Why does Joe use the words I am that I am?" Henrietta asked, addressing Altie.

"It is the name the Great Spirit gave to Moses. You know, in the Old Testament."

"Oh, yeah, you're right," Henrietta said. And she was again pleased and surprised.

"If you wish, in your personal prayers," Joe said to Henrietta, "you also may want to go ahead and ask the Great Spirit directly: 'Who am I? Who am I, really, Great Spirit? What is my divine purpose for this life?' "

Henrietta listened and tried to internalize Joe's words and guidance. Presently, she took in a big breath of freshly brewed aromatic herbs and burning tobacco commingling in the cool mountain air. Closing her eyes and feeling the fire's warmth on her face, Henrietta prayed as hard as she could and as never before to the Great I AM THAT I AM.

And it happened, as quick as a camera flash, she saw through Joe's lameness and strangeness and understood that Bears Repeating was a being of great power, truth and purity, but he covered it in a mask of entertaining human paradox, like the silly *Libayé* character he had played in the Sunrise Ceremonies.

As the night unfolded, Altie would occasionally beat a small drum and sing with words foreign to

Henrietta's ears. Joe sat like a native Buddhist most of
the time, getting up only to add logs to the fire, check
on the horses or relieve himself in the woods. He'd
make a cryptic remark every now and then such as:
"When we're quiet on the outside, joy sounds loud on
the inside."

The next day, the three campers continued to
spend most of their time around the fire and in the
Kopave silence. The experience to this point was more
interesting and fulfilling than Henrietta had ever
imagined. Before coming to this place, she'd been
skeptical about meditating and fasting, presuming both
to be painfully tedious and that she would be starving.
But as she sat for hours with her cup of herbal tea,
trying to mimic Joe's and Altie's continual prayers, and
to hum along with their chants, peacefulness came to
her, although she chuckled at the idea that the tea
tasted vaguely of sweaty T-shirts.

By the second day, Henrietta was more
introspective about her traumas and personal suffering,
not understanding the reasons for the devastating hurts
in her life. In the evening, though, after hours of
communing with nature and being in the *Kopave*,
Henrietta began to see how suffering could be a way to
learn and grow into something better. As a mother she
had felt that paradox with the strange ecstasy of
pushing a baby out of one's body in a bloody mess.
Through the pain, the experience is transformed into
something holy. Could personal trauma be viewed in a

similar contradictory way? Perhaps learning from karma and hard knocks was required for waking up the stubborn amongst us to the spiritual truth behind all of life and for making better choices. And what about death? Could it also be a creative rite of passage into a transcendent new form? She thought of Miss Julia, now in a heavenly place. These reflections and feelings stayed with her for a while until she began to get weary, and she snuggled between two blankets feeling no sorrow or worries in the world. Her mental anguish was rising up and away from her, disappearing into the air like steam from a boiling pot on a medicine woman's campfire.

Much later, Henrietta awoke to the sound and vibration of horse hooves. Opening her eyes, Henrietta was startled and frightened to see a gigantic chocolate-colored horse with a white mane and tail towering before her. Henrietta quickly estimated the large mare's height to be more than sixteen hands.

In the moonlight, its coat shone like a glassy lake, broken only by a small star-shaped white patch on its forehead. A red-tailed hawk perched casually on her thick white mane. A court of perhaps a dozen comely palominos, much smaller, followed. They walked in deliberate, gracefully measured steps until they encircled the three campers.

After gasping for air, Henrietta half-shouted, "Joe, Altie, wake up! The horses! Look at all the horses! Hey, wake up, look!" They were sitting up cross-legged, but remained still with their eyes shut, the fire's shadows dancing on their angelic faces. They seemed to be in some sort of trance.

The chocolate horse began to speak. "My name is Hildegard. I have come to offer guidance."

"Okay, I'm dreaming, I've flipped," Henrietta said. Her fears were mounting. "What were in these herbs, anyway?" she said to herself, thinking they must be hallucinogenic and that she should have questioned Joe better before drinking them. Her heart thumped rapidly.

"Fear not, little mother. We come not to frighten you, but rather to give you medicine and the writing answers to the Mystery of Mysteries for which you quest," the horse said. "Hawk and spider offer the gift of spiritual sight. Frog's talent is one of healing."

"Medicine and writing answers?" Henrietta repeated. "With hawks and spiders and frogs?"

Hildegard moved her sculptured head up and down and snorted as the hawk screeched and flew up and overhead. The bird's talons transformed into tiny sparklers, but when they landed on Henrietta's shoulder, they were surprisingly cool and diaphanous. A frog jumped from behind the mare's ears, croaking loudly before landing onto the peach-fuzz softness of Hildegard's brown muzzle.

Boring down on her, the great horse's eyes were so intense, it felt like she was able to peer deep within Henrietta's soul and see through all of the brokenness, pretenses and masks she wore. Unnerved, Henrietta was about to duck under the blankets. But in the next instant, she was sitting bareback on Hildegard, with the hawk still riding on her shoulder. But she now felt fearless, as if the great animal had graciously transmitted some of her immense power to Henrietta.

They began to travel, but Henrietta was apprehensive about leaving Joe and Altie, who continued to sit in their trance-like states by the slow-burning campfire. *Joe! Altie!*

"Be not afraid for your friends; they are safe and in receipt of their own inner medicine," Hildegard said, as if reading her mind. "We journey to find yours."

As Henrietta calmed down she noticed the spider guide. It had woven a shimmering web between the horse's ears. The sun was beginning to rise, illuminating a winding path that paralleled a sparkling creek. The trail led them through a green thicket and eventually up to a mountain lodge seamlessly built into the dramatic limestone escarpments, cliffs and spires.

Massive boulders formed the lodge's foundation, which supported an amazing labyrinthine structure. The main room was round, maybe twenty-five square feet in diameter, and featured a massive stone fireplace as well as an expansive pillowed sitting area. It connected to twelve guest cottages via walkways positioned in a semicircular pattern, like spokes of a half-wheel. The other half was open to accommodate a gargantuan deck that overlooked a waterfall, canyon stream and alpine meadow. Throughout the interiors, smaller rocks were used, with turquoise and other gemstones, to create mosaic designs on walls and floors. Hand-carved cedar and pine furniture, rock fireplaces, stone baths with turquoise finishes, wall trellises and branch-like banisters adorned surrounding cottages.

In the next blink, Henrietta saw herself in one of the cottages, confirming she was in dreamtime. Yet everything she witnessed seemed so intensely alive and substantial. She could have sworn she was awake, in ordinary time and space.

Like a child peering into a dollhouse, she watched a miniature version of herself at a desk, composing happily on a typewriter, while people she did not know mingled with Indians she did know in the lodge's dining room. Colorfully clad Medichero women collected fresh vegetables from a large native garden nearby.

All appeared joyful, while hummingbirds and songbirds danced about. A grizzly bear, walking upright on his hind legs, was bringing in more chairs before acting like an attentive waiter. After the guests retired to their individual cottages for the evening, the sunrise soon brought them back out. All rode on the palominos, with Henrietta on Hildegard, through forests teeming with other friendly wildlife.

At the end of the day, the horses returned them to the lodge so they could pack for their final departure, and Henrietta could see there were new visitors arriving in the lodge's main room. But this new group was markedly different than the first. Men and women clothed in tatters were covered in an ash-like powder with tears leaving tracks on their faces. Strange-moving, baseball-sized black dots of indeterminable origin were orbiting around each guest like personal dark moons.

"What's wrong with these people?" Henrietta asked Hildegard, who was now standing next to her. "And why are they here?

"They are beautiful spiritual beings, but they are not aware of this truth. They have been dirtied and shattered by something in this world, but there is hope for them. They are the ones who want to learn how to heal from their soul wounds. They are like you."

"Like me?" Henrietta gasped and jerked awake. She was covered in sweat despite the chill of the early morning. Her head ached something fierce. Her back, neck, arms and legs were all stiff and sore.

The campfire smoldered, having completed its purpose, while Joe and Altie sat cross-legged with eyes open. They appeared lucid and awake. But were they really?

"I had some very unusual dreams," Henrietta said as a test. She was breathing hard while her eyes adjusted uneasily to the bright morning light.

"Ha'aa," Joe said. He was smiling.

"Did you, by chance, see any horses last night?"

Joe shook his head. "Nope."

"Was it just me?"

Both Joe and Altie nodded. "Yes."

"Well, did y'all have any dreams at all?"

"Bear showed me plans for a healing lodge I'm supposed to build in and among the trees and rocks up on that mountain over there," Joe said, pointing.

"The grackles came to me," Altie said. She described them as the greenish black birds that travel in colonies. "They showed me how to train our people to become waiters, gardeners and innkeepers."

"You're kidding!" Henrietta recounted her dream to Joe and Altie, realizing the similarities. "Holy cow! Just like our dreams, we are unique and separate, but also directly connected to each other." *Could it be that I actually made contact with the strange inner world of the mystics? And of shamans, clairvoyants and native healers?*

"What an amazing coincidence!" was all she could say aloud.

At that, the three of them exchanged a look of collective understanding. Grins brought forth giggles, which turned into hearty laughter, which grew into a deep and cathartic release that held until tears fell from their eyes.

"We've been blessed with a sacred vision and given a glimpse of life's oneness," Joe said, after settling down. "You now see what can be seen."

"Joe, I'm worried."

"I guess it's my turn to ask why," he said.

"I'm starting to get this stuff."

"Ah, *nzhoo,* very good." Joe bent over on his knees and gave a prayer of gratitude to the Great Spirit. Altie and Henrietta followed his example. He laid out another offering of fresh tobacco not intended for burning and covered the fire-pit with dirt.

Later, the three Appaloosas carried them back home. The air felt electric and smelled of a spicy freshness. Henrietta felt euphoric as she thought about what her little medicine bag should contain and how the visions and experiences she'd had might play out in the life to which she was returning. *Dear God! How grateful I am to really know and understand the meaning and nature of that elusive feeling of oneness Joe has so often spoke about.* She also realized with astonishment that she no longer feared telling Jeff her secrets. Instead, she was actually looking forward to the relief that revealed truth would bring. Hildegard, the horse, had been right: she did want to heal from her soul wounds. And she also couldn't wait to get back to her writing desk to begin recording the bizarre and blessed visions she'd been given. Even though she had doubts about being able to do it, she wanted to give it a try.

While mulling over a potential approach, the pain of her empty stomach interrupted, and the image of a steamy hot sweet potato with melted butter crossed her mind. She wanted nothing more than to get home, even for a carrot or piece of celery. But crunchy vegetables were hard to come by on the reservation, requiring a twenty-five mile drive to Tularosa, and most of the time, they weren't that fresh. *Oh! Maybe I could create a garden in the side yard of the doctor's cottage. And maybe Joe and Altie could help me.*

"Hey, y'all, guess what?" she blurted out. Joe and Altie halted their horses and turned to look at her.

"This might sound strange, but I suddenly have an incredible urge to plant a vegetable garden, but I'm not sure how to go about it," Henrietta said. "What do you think that means?"

Joe and Altie gave each other a knowing look.

"What?" Henrietta said. "What do you know that I don't?"

"How to build a native garden," Altie said.

Chapter 22

Standing in his undershorts, socks and a white dress shirt, Dr. Colonel watched the deaf Brodie Thompson, who now worked as his personal assistant, grapple with what should've been an easy zipper on a special-delivery garment bag.

"Goddammit, Brodie, hurry it up," Dr. Colonel said. He had crossed his arms and was tapping a foot.

"Ahh!" Brodie uttered. After finally opening it, he turned toward Dr. Colonel with a wide grin. The silky black cloth bag contained three new Italian-made suits delivered by courier from Culling's, the most exclusive men's store in their immediate two-state area. It was now lying flat and open on a fancy French-style table centered between two walls lined with perfectly organized men's suits in the spacious dressing room.

"Hand over the one on top, boy," Dr. Colonel said. He extended his right arm.

"Yus, suh," Brodie croaked after reading Dr. Colonel's lips. As amenable as always, Brodie had grown into a lanky eighteen-year-old. His black curly hair was cropped short and smelled of Ivory soap, which Dr. Colonel had come to appreciate.

Brodie withdrew a luxurious light blue-gray Brioni suit made in a year-round weight, comfortable even in the South's warm summers. The second suit was a navy blue, while the third was a charcoal pinstripe.

"Let me tell you somethin', Brodie," Dr. Colonel said. He donned the pants before slipping his arms into the sleeves of the three-button jacket Brodie held open for him. "Everything requires discipline, and I mean everything." He was speaking more to himself than to Brodie. "Otherwise, you get chaos and insubordination, and I simply won't tolerate either one."

Brodie was skilled at reading lips and nodded as if he understood, although Dr. Colonel was never sure if he ever actually did. But Dr. Colonel didn't really care at that moment. He put on an alligator belt, a pair of Italian-leather shoes and a red silk tie to complete his ensemble. "You've just got to know how to control things, which, of course, I do." He paused to appraise himself in the six-foot gilded mirror. "Excellent! Culling's followed my instructions precisely." He buttoned the jacket. "How refreshing."

"Yus, suh, look good, Dota," Brodie said.

"Yes, siree, I am looking fine too-day," Dr. Colonel said. He turned to admire himself in the mirror. Along with his ever-present smile and impeccable attitude, he thought of himself as having the classic good looks of a Southern-style Cary Grant. Pausing briefly, he gave a final pat down to the small mound of expensive brown hair, which blended seamlessly with the slight graying at his temples. Satisfied and supremely confident, he walked with precision from the bedroom toward the grand circular staircase.

"You simply have to let people know who's in charge," Dr. Colonel said. He descended the stairs. "And you can't allow people to disrespect you in any way, shape or form and especially not the goddamn help in your own goddamn kitchen." He was referring to what he'd deemed an appalling domestic incident with Cook and the housemaid the previous morning. He had caught Regina and Cook copulating on the kitchen table.

"Goddamn fucking Cook," he muttered to Brodie as they entered the dining room.

There was no mouthwatering smell of bacon on the sideboard. No eggs. No grits. And no buttery-good biscuits. Because, of course, there was no Cook. "Hey, Brodie, you'll have to fix breakfast this morning." Dr. Colonel signed and spoke the words at the same time. "But bring in coffee first."

"Yus, suh," Brodie said. He scurried off into the kitchen.

Brodie had come to live in the Clayborn mansion from Julia's orphanage under a foster-like arrangement because Brodie had been so needy and, as most everyone knew, his wife simply adored the boy. They made an odd pair; he deaf and she blind. And though Brodie had learned to speak a little and Miss Julia had some ability to hear, they usually communicated with their hands, using the tactile sign language pioneered by Helen Keller, which was taught in Julia's school. Dr. Colonel thought Brodie was nice enough and easy to have around the house, but Julia hadn't been satisfied with that. She'd wanted to officially adopt the kid, feverishly so, especially after Jeff had gone off to college.

But that was never going to happen, thought Dr. Colonel. Adopting a part Negro, part Cherokee into the Clayborn family's bloodline was simply unthinkable. Hell, if he'd wanted to raise half-breeds or bastard children, he wouldn't have gone to all the trouble of maintaining appearances for all these many years. It had been one of only two times that Dr. Colonel had ever refused his Julia anything. *But goddammit! If I had let her, she would've brought home every one of those goddamn orphans like they were a bunch of ratty stray kittens.*

Unfortunately, Julia had persisted with her maddening desire of wanting to adopt Brodie, and their heated arguments about it had regrettably continued up until the day she died.

All that's dead and gone now, he thought. Still, Dr. Colonel had wanted to ease his conscience a little about his Julia, and so, in loving memory of his honorable wife, he let it be known that he'd made an extra-kind gesture toward Brodie, letting him stay on and live in the Clayborn mansion. Not as an adopted son, nor merely a domestic, but as something he thought more important: he would be Dr. Colonel's personal assistant, though in reality Brodie was more of a glorified gofer.

"Cook and Regina are gone, outta here," Dr. Colonel said. He motioned as if he were swinging a golf club. "But we don't need their goddamn dirty hands on our food anyway. Let's just say I didn't like the way Cook beat Regina's eggs on my goddamn kitchen table." He chuckled out loud.

As he continued to wait for Brodie to bring in coffee, Dr. Colonel's face grew redder just thinking about Cook. "No one in this town would blame me for firing his goddamn white-trash, niggra-fucking ass," Dr. Colonel said to no one. "Had to fuck right there on my kitchen table. Couldn't wait to get home to his own goddamn kitchen table. Good Lord," he said. He was shaking his head in disgust. "Looked like a bunch of goddamn fucking rabbits."

Brodie finally returned, looking ridiculous in Cook's extra-large white chef jacket, which hung loosely on his skinny six-foot frame. He was carrying a five-piece silver coffee and water service, while a crisply ironed cotton towel draped over his right forearm.

"Now you put that down right here before you drop it, boy. Right here. That's it. Right here," Dr. Colonel said, indicating the head of the large table.

After Brodie set the service down, he nodded again, reminding Dr. Colonel of the bobblehead toy soldier he'd put on the dashboard of his Cadillac. *At least Brodie tries to be obedient.*

Dr. Colonel finally started to calm down as he took his usual seat at the head of the twelve-foot, highly polished mahogany table where Brodie had neatly laid a stack of mail and the morning newspaper, dated Monday, July 13, 1959. "Oh yes. I was so busy this weekend with my peach business and trying to replace the kitchen help, I completely forgot about the mail." It was stacked next to a proper place setting of Waterford fine bone china, crystal and Christofle silver, just as Dr. Colonel had instructed.

Brodie's bony fingers trembled slightly as he picked up the silver pitcher, dripping with a cold sweat, and poured ice water in and slightly over the sides of a crystalline goblet. But Dr. Colonel paid no mind to Brodie's usual fumbling; his focus was centered on an envelope postmarked Tularosa, New Mexico, addressed in a familiar hand.

After successfully pouring the coffee without spilling it, Brodie sighed and stood quietly next to Dr. Colonel, a blank expression on his face.

"Goddammit, Brodie, don't just stand there like some kind of dodo bird ... go make some breakfast, like I said." Dr. Colonel waved his hand in front of Brodie's glassy eyes.

Clasping his hands over his deaf ears, Brodie said, "Sorry, no catch, Dota. No catch."

"Okay, looky here," Dr. Colonel said. He used sign language and mouthed the words slowly so his lips could be more easily read. "Broodeeee, goooo maaake some eggs or grits or something. Bacon. Toast. Anything. Now go!" Dr. Colonel pointed. Brodie darted away.

Dr. Colonel picked up the letter and ripped open the envelope. It read:

July 3, 1959

Dear Father,

I've decided to stay on for a longer period of time in Medichero, beyond the usual six months, so that I can continue my research without interruption and be of service to others in a way that most interests me. Also, the timing is critical right now: an influenza epidemic has swept through the reservation, and the Medichero people, of whom there are approximately three thousand men, women and children, are in need of any and all healthcare that can be afforded them.

I've accepted the position of head physician and medical researcher at the Medichero Indian Hospital and am planning to serve in that capacity for at least the next year. It's an official appointment through the U.S. Department of the Interior, so there's nothing you can do to reverse it. I pray that you don't even attempt it, but instead come to share in my excitement about having the opportunity to study spontaneous remissions and learn from an extraordinarily gifted native healer, named Joe Loco, who's also become an inspiration as well as a terrific medical assistant to me in the clinic. He's only about two years older than I am, and surprisingly, we have more in common than one might think at first glance.

When I was a child, you often told me how you were once stationed in this area of the Southwest and lived briefly in this spectacular scenery. Do you not remember that you also held a passion for this place, the passion so evident in your photographs? Please try keeping that in mind and be happy for me, if that is possible. I'm dead-sure Mother would be agreeable, and that she would have blessed my decision to serve others in need of quality medical care.

I'm not certain when we'll be able to come back home, but I'll write or call you as our plans for a visit develop.

Yours respectfully,
Jefferson

As he stared at his son's signature, Dr. Colonel took out a silver Zippo from his pocket and ignited the bottom right corner of the paper. The flame traveled upward, devouring the correspondence. As it burned, fury filled Dr. Colonel's chest and moved toward his throat, like molten lava erupting from the depths of hell.

Chapter 23

"Brodie!" Dr. Colonel shouted. He dropped the burning letter onto his empty plate. "Get our bags packed!" *Oh, damnation, that stone-deaf boy can't hear a cotton-picking word I'm saying.* With venom shooting through his veins, Dr. Colonel stomped into the kitchen where Brodie was tossing a chunk of fatback into a frying pan.

"Brodie!" Dr. Colonel screamed again as though he might be heard better. "I know you didn't hear me, but I said to get our bags packed. We're leaving, and I mean today, goddammit!"

An expression of bewilderment and fear crossed over Brodie's light-brown face. "No catch!" he cried. "No catch!"

Dr. Colonel's chest expanded and his shoulders dropped as he exhaled and began using sign language. "We've got to go get my son and bring him home."

Then Dr. Colonel began shouting again, pounding his fists on the table and forgetting to sign or speak slowly for Brodie's benefit. "I will not tolerate my son living on some goddamn, dirty, foul, godforsaken Indian reservation. And working for goddamn no-good sub-human slime!" He grabbed a long sharp knife from the butcher block and waved it up and down like a pointer stick at Brodie, who backed up into the stove. "And nobody, not no heathen goddamn Loco-crazy Indian, not no white-trash bitch he calls a wife, not even the U.S. Department of the goddamn Interior is going to stand in my way." At that, he jabbed the knife into the table's wooden surface.

Brodie's eyes shot wide open and he stood frozen until the scalding liquefied fat popped out of the fry pan. "Argh," he howled. He rubbed the back of his right arm and stepped away.

Ignoring Brodie's pain, Dr. Colonel marched back into the dining room, snatching up his jacket. Seconds later, he headed for the garage with the gathering resolve of an impending storm.

Brodie turned the stove off before running after Dr. Colonel, holding his hands to his ears, and crying, "Dota, no catch, no catch."

Breathing easier finally, Dr. Colonel stopped and used sign language, while slowly mouthing the words to Brodie. "That letter was from Jeff. It said he's not coming home ... which means we have to go out there to change his mind."

Dr. Colonel figured it would take about five days to get there by Friday night. "We'll leave as soon as I get back from town, in about an hour."

Brodie signed back, asking if Dr. Colonel still wanted breakfast.

"No, forget it. I'll pick something up at Lindsey's. While I'm gone, get our bags packed and fill a cooler with Cokes, water jugs and sandwiches. And take our pillows and sleeping blankets, too," he said, remembering how there wouldn't be any proper lodging out in the middle of goddamn nowhere.

"Yes, sir. But, maybe I should stay here and watch the house?" Brodie signed.

"The goddamn house don't need watching, boy," Dr. Colonel said while signing back. "You're going to help me with this messy business of bringing Jeff back home."

Brodie fell still.

Dr. Colonel could see that Brodie was overwhelmed and probably didn't want to go on the long drive with him to New Mexico, but he didn't care. "Let me tell you somethin'. As my personal assistant, you're coming to help me, and that's that," Dr. Colonel said, signing. "So start moving on what I told you to pack. Now!" Dr. Colonel grabbed a felt hat off an ornate hall tree and walked out, slamming the door behind him.

The influenza epidemic Jeff mentioned in the letter had given Dr. Colonel a workable idea for a new plan, and he'd already made a mental list of what he'd need to successfully execute it. While mulling over his scheme, he drove his jet-black Cadillac sedan into town.

Although to outsiders it seemed to be a small and insignificant southern farm community, Greenfield, South Carolina, could boast of having more governors, more Revolutionary War heroes and more peaches per capita than anywhere else in the world. So unlike the outskirts of Spartanburg, where he'd grown up the son of a lower-class millworker in a meager household, where he'd always felt like a stranger; Greenfield was a special slice of heaven. Dr. Colonel had never felt so connected and a part of a place as he did here. He loved and treasured everything about it, but especially the fact that he'd become one of its most celebrated residents, having been named Citizen of the Year five times, which was more than anyone else, even those who'd been born there.

After parking in front of Lindsey's Pharmacy, he approached the glass entry doors and noticed the most prominent member of the Greenfield Baptist Church choir about to exit. Dr. Colonel became all smiles.

"Well, hey, Ida Jean, how you doing, little darlin'?" Dr. Colonel said. He held the door and made a gallant gesture with his felt hat for Greenfield's most notorious and beloved gossip.

Middle-aged, pleasantly plump, yet impeccably clothed in a smart tailored tea-colored day dress with matching gloves, Ida Jean Middleton giggled like a schoolgirl. Dr. Colonel didn't mind. She, like most Greenfield citizens, was obviously bewitched by his charm and venerable social standing. "I'm fine, just fine. And you?" she asked.

"I was just okay, 'til seeing you," Dr. Colonel said. "Now, I'm feeling real good! And my, oh my, don't you look lovely this morning?" he added, placing his hat over his heart.

"Oh, Dr. Colonel, how kind you are," Ida Jean said. Her voice was slightly seductive and just loud enough for everyone in and out of the drugstore to hear clearly.

Dr. Colonel didn't mind that either.

She giggled again as she sashayed through the door. "Now what brings you into town from that wonderful plantation of yours?" Ida Jean asked, lingering. "Or are you on the way to Columbia, for one of your very important engagements with the gov'nor?"

"Well, ma'am, after seeing you, I plumb forgot." He gave her his signature wink. "Now you'd best be on your way, so I can remember what I need to do today, you hear, little darlin'?" He reached again for the door handle.

"Ohhh, of course," she said, about to turn away.

"Now you have a good day, Ida Jean, and tell ole Harold that I said hey . . . now wait a minute," he said, realizing he might need a cover for being away. "Why don't y'all come out for some peach ice cream in, um, a couple of weeks or so?" *I'll be back by then, and with Jeff,* he thought. "Our red globes will be mighty good for ice cream by that time; I'd say just about perfect."

"Oh, my, yes. You know we have always loved visiting at the Pridgen Planta—I mean, the Clayborn Plantation," she said, hurrying to correct her mistake. "And I just adore your peaches. They're simply the best, much better than anyone else's. Why you just say when, and we'll be there, you sweet man, you."

"I'll give y'all a call, little darlin', but only when the peaches are absolutely perfect for ice cream and someone as perfectly sweet as you." He flashed his best smile. "You give Harold my best! And we'll see y'all in a couple of weeks, you hear, Ida Jean?"

"Oh, yes, ah do. Toodle-doo, Dr. Colonel." She walked down the sidewalk, grinning from ear to ear, looking as though she had just been crowned prom queen.

Dr. Colonel walked over to the soda fountain counter and sat down on one of the round padded seats. *It's just as well Cook and Regina are gone; there'll be less witnesses to the fact I'll be gone for a while.* "Hey, Lucille, how you doing, little darlin'?"

"Well, hey, Dr. Colonel, what brings you in this early on a weekday?" Lucille pulled out a pencil from her netted bleach-blond permed hair and a pad from the pocket of her pink-and-white waitress uniform.

"Why, one of your famous breakfasts, little darlin'."

"Oh, yeah, I heard about … umhum … about your kitchen help, sugar," Lucille said. She was whispering and chuckling at the same time. Her dimples and busty hourglass figure made the forty-year-old mother in standard waitress garb look sensual.

"Can you believe it? Let me tell you somethin'," Dr. Colonel said. "They should've known better than to butter their toast where I butter mine." He winked and gave her a flirtatious smile, causing Lucille to laugh again, a little too loudly.

"Oh, Dr. Colonel, you're killing me. What can I get for you, sugar?"

"Why I'd like The Lucille Special, of course."

"And that would be what, sugar?"

"Eggs sunny-side up, naturally, the best grits in Greenfield County, bacon and biscuits with that heavenly gravy of yours. Mmmmm," he said. He raised his eyebrows and gave her a slightly suggestive grin. *Good God, this woman's a spicy dish.* He felt a raw lust stirring, and he shifted himself on the padded seat.

"You got it, sugar," she said.

After breakfast, Dr. Colonel, never wanting to appear parsimonious in any way, made an exaggerated gesture of overpaying the fifty-cent check by slapping a one-dollar bill on the counter. "Thank you, little darlin', de-lish!" He blew Lucille a kiss, gave her another wink then strode briskly to the back of the store toward the pharmacy counter and walked boldly through the swinging partition and behind the counter.

"Hey, Branden." Dr. Colonel looked around. "Now where's that ole rascal of a boss of yours?" he said. He feigned a one-two punch on Branden's arm.

"I'm afraid he's not feeling too well today, sir," Branden said as he simulated the guarded stance of a heavyweight boxer, pretending to block Dr. Colonel's air punches. "See you got breakfast this morning. Nothing like Mama's cooking."

"Hey, let me tell you somethin'. Your mama's not only the best-looking, she's also the best cook in the whole state of South Carolina, Georgia, too, probably in the entire Southeast. But back to your daddy: maybe I should run over there and see about him?" His tone held the greatest of concern. "Be happy to dash over there right now. Don't mind a bit!"

"Thank you, sir, but I don't think it's too serious. Daddy's just miserable. Bad cold, I suspect. Didn't want to infect any customers."

"Guess he's right to stay home. Hey, Branden, I need to do some compounding for, uh, a patient," Dr. Colonel said. He was lying, but it didn't matter. "And since the old man isn't here, well, you know he usually lets me help myself even when he's around, don't you, son?" He smiled broadly.

"No problem, Dr. Colonel, go right ahead," Branden said. "Fortunately, we're not too busy. I'm just doing some stocking and hanging around in case there's an emergency. Just leave a note about what you use and I'll put it on your tab." Branden made the offer casually, as though it weren't at all unusual for a customer to manufacture and fill his own prescriptions at Lindsey's Pharmacy in Greenfield, South Carolina.

"Good man. I won't be but a few minutes," Dr. Colonel said. He headed back to the small lab located behind massive shelves of drugs and supplies.

Dr. Colonel grabbed a jar of gel base and a bottle of benzyl alcohol and triturated them in a clean mortar and pestle. Blending in diphenhydramine, hydrocortisone and pramoxine powders, the mix became a blue-colored ointment. Next, with the economical precision of an experienced surgeon, he sliced open a box containing ointment jars and removed one for his mixture. Pausing just long enough to pinpoint Branden's exact location, he seized what he had actually come into the pharmacy for: five one-dram amber glass vials. He took them from a box already cut open for his unscrupulous plundering. Deftly concealing the small vials in the pocket of his pants, he began transferring the compound from the mortar into the empty ointment jar just as the floorboards squeaked out a warning.

"Say, who you compounding for, anyway? I thought you were supposed to be retired these days," Branden said. He was carrying in another large box of containers to stock.

"Well, son, I try to stay retired and look after my beloved Julia's peach business, but sometimes I just can't help myself, especially since Jeff's had to be away." *Goddamn Indians.* "Anyway, you know I can't stand to see someone in pain or discomfort of any kind, especially if I can be of service."

"Yes, sir."

"This here's for Brodie," Dr. Colonel said. He was easily improvising. "He's got that arm rash he gets now and then. My special compound's the only thing that clears it right up," Dr. Colonel said. "I gotta be quick though; Brodie's fixing to scratch himself to death."

"You ought to market that stuff," Branden said. He was moving the ointment jars from the opened box onto a shelf.

"Maybe I should, but I probably won't. Hey, just like politics. Everybody says I should've gone into politics. But I just like to stay behind the scenes, be a patron, that's it. I like to contribute that way. Besides, I prefer leaving all the politics to Strom and the other good ole boys," he said, chuckling. " 'Course I was hoping Jeff might get into politics one day." *Goddamn Indians.* "Anyway, maybe I'll show you how to mix up this little concoction of mine so you can market it," he said. He labeled the ointment jar. "You could switch your major from pharmacy to marketing and make a million." Dr. Colonel laughed. "Happy to do it!"

Branden smiled as he bent down to unpack the box with the one-dram amber vials.

"I know your daddy wouldn't mind you making a million," Dr. Colonel repeated. He was trying to divert Branden's attention from the box he'd just pillaged.

"You're right about that," Branden said as the telephone rang. "Excuse me, sir." He left to answer it.

"Hey, I'll just give you a hand with your stocking," Dr. Colonel said. He offered in a loud voice before quickly unpacking the box of small amber vials as well as the one with ointment jars. Thinking he better ensure an adequate supply of weapons, just in case things got out of hand in Medichero, he grabbed five more of the small vials, adding them to the others in his pocket. *Goddamn Indians.* He then went back to the table, cleaned up and wrote out a list of items and the amounts he had used for the ointment on a sheet from his own personal prescription pad, tucking the list under the mortar. There was no mention of ten missing one-dram amber vials.

"I got everything taken care of. Thank you, son," Dr. Colonel said. "Oh, and I stocked the vials and the last of your jars for you. My list is on the table back there. Put everything on my tab. And hey, now you tell your boss I said to feel better, you hear? And that's an order from Dr. Colonel." He used his hat to cover the bulge of vials in his pocket.

"Yes, sir, I sure will. Thanks for coming in," Branden said. He went over to the soda fountain to give his mother the telephone message he had received. "Daddy said he's feeling better and will probably come in this afternoon."

"Ain't he a great guy?" Dr. Colonel overheard Lucille say to her son as he lingered a moment at the front of the store, pretending to tie his shoe.

"Daddy?" Branden said.

"You bet, sugar, but I was talking about our Dr. Colonel."

"Oh, yeah, right, Mama. Can you believe he did some stocking for me?"

"I still feel so sad about Miss Julia's passing, even though it's been, what? Almost two years now? And Jeff moving way out to New Mexico and all," Lucille said.

"What a shame," Dr. Colonel heard her say.

Dr. Colonel dropped his head. The old ache was still there, that excruciating shame of his childhood, and it was flying up to the surface right now, forceful and stinging like the brutal slaps to the face he had regularly endured. Dr. Colonel's shoulders sagged as he remembered one cursed day in particular, the one that should have been the best day of young Jules Beaufort Clayborn's life, especially after his mother had left. It was when Jules was eleven years old and in the sixth grade. He'd earned straight A's for the first time with absolutely no help from his papa and while working seven days a week as a paperboy. After school, he'd rushed home proud and eager to show his good works to his papa, who was usually there since he'd lost his job at the mill. But on that afternoon, his father was nowhere to be found. So, Jules went out and toward town in search of him, holding the report card up with pure pleasure all the while. He found his papa lying on a park bench, passed out. From the smell of him, he'd been drinking all day. Jules tried to revive and help his papa sit up, and as he was doing so, his perfect report card blew away, caught in an unexpected gust of air. He was about to run after it just as the immaculately tailored mayor walked by.

Mayor Maynard was the kind of man who exuded charisma from his top-quality felt hat down to the shine of his well-polished shoes, and he was also known as a pillar and fount of great wisdom. In Jules's young mind, Mayor Maynard was the very personification of success and genteel society. And the good mayor always seemed to have a nice word for everyone, including him.

But when the mayor saw the elder Clayborn lying recumbent on the bench like a common bum despite Jules's desperate attempts to stir him, Mayor Maynard shook his head and muttered to his companion, "What a shame. The Clayborns are nothing but poor white trash. Always have been, always will be. What a shame," he repeated.

Jules overheard him and in that instant he was disgusted with the mayor and his critical gaze, looking down on them as if they were the decaying remains of vermin. Then he noticed other people staring: Mr. Barns, the postman, various shopkeepers and their patrons; they were all gaping in his direction. Did they also know about his mama and secret shame?

If she hadn't been neglecting him, his mama was poking him. And hard. It sometimes left bruises, but he hid them from others at school. He didn't want to even think about how she'd burned him with her cigarettes when she was bored or mad. Or how confused he'd felt when she called him to her bed, even after he knew she'd been with a man who was not his papa. When she finally ran off with one of those other men, Jules was both enraged and relieved. It was good riddance! After that, it was just the two of them, him and Papa. Jules loved his father, even though he was drunk most of the time and slapped him around every once in a while. But now, as if a blinding dust had fallen from his eyes, Jules saw his papa for what he was—the way others had always seen him. He'd never noticed before that his papa's face was dirty and unshaven. They both wore tattered, unwashed clothes, and they reeked of body odor. It dawned on him that his papa was so weak and unsuccessful in life that he may not have been man enough for his mother. But at the same time, he hated her for what she was, for what she'd done to them, and for leaving.

With everyone still staring, Jules was seized with a sudden and overwhelming humiliation, nearly suffocating him in its assault. He wanted to cry. Scream. Explode with anger. Run away. But in that pivotal moment, and with the faultless report card lost to the four winds, Jules Beaufort Clayborn simply stood up straight and made a solemn vow: he would do whatever it took in this life to never feel that way again.

Chapter 24

Dr. Colonel straightened his spine and walked out of the pharmacy and across the tiny court square, past the landmark obelisk that was engraved with all of Greenfield's governors, war heroes and Citizens of the Year. He was heading to Henderson's Feed & Seed. *I have to take care of this embarrassment now, before folks start thinking my Jefferson's defective somehow, that he's not good or smart enough to be a real physician, here, in the civilized world!* Dr. Colonel pulled on the glass door and walked into the store. *That's it!*

Surveying the interior, devoid of customers at this hour, Dr. Colonel detected some movement through the open windows of an upstairs office that overlooked aisles of livestock feed, hardware, garden implements and other farming products. The place smelled of the usual wood pulp, assorted dry feed and the acrid odor of fertilizers. But Dr. Colonel was already so lost in thought, he barely noticed. He'd put up with Jeff's first mission to New Mexico, chalking it up to youthful indiscretion; then he'd tried to get his fool daughter-in-law to keep her man home before that second trip, but she was goddamn useless. So now he'd do it the right way. Dr. Colonel smiled. *Jeff's coming back home and staying put once and for all. Because this time, I've got a better plan.*

"Hey, JimBo, how's it going up there, big guy?" Dr. Colonel shouted happily while waving at the proprietor.

"Morning, Dr. Colonel. I'll be off the phone in just a minute," Jim Henderson shouted down. He was covering the mouthpiece with his hand.

"Hey, don't trouble yourself," Dr. Colonel said. "I can help myself and leave you the right amount of cash up front."

Henderson signed an okay with his forefinger and thumb.

"Thanks, JimBo." Dr. Colonel's smile broadened. *I'm at least ten paces ahead of the goddamn fools in this town.*

In Dr. Colonel's opinion, his new plan was not only the best means of achieving his goal of getting Jeff back home, it was also inspired: if necessary, Indians would start getting sick from what appeared to be a new wave of influenza. They wouldn't have to die; he was confident that he wouldn't need to take it that far. But even if they did, their autopsies would reveal nothing more than death caused by acute inflammation of the liver, the disease of alcoholics.

"I'm goddamn genius," Dr. Colonel muttered out loud. He was walking toward the end of the aisle where farming pesticides were stocked.

Chapter 25

After falling asleep in the comfort of their bed, cuddled in the warmth of Jeff's arms, Henrietta dreamed again about Hildegard and the healing retreat built into the mountains. At about three a.m., she shot straight up in bed, turned on the bedside lamp and began writing hurriedly in a notebook, which she kept by her bed.

"What're you doing, Peaches?" Jeff asked, squinting from the sharpness of the lamp.

"Oh, I just had a dream about the healing retreat, and it was so full of good ideas, I wanted to jot them down before I forgot them," she said. She was almost beside herself with awe and excitement.

"A treat? Full of goodies? What treat?" Jeff said.

"A re-treat, you know the healing lodge that I told you about yesterday. Oh, honey, I'm sorry I woke you up," she added. She felt bad about that because she knew that Jeff had recently lost many a night's sleep over the care of his flu patients, not to mention Billy

Santana. "I'll just go to the kitchen to finish." She kissed him on the cheek and slid out of bed.

He was snoring before she put on her robe and tiptoed from the bedroom.

Henrietta worked steadily until six a.m., when she finally took a break to stretch in the new day's sun, then make some coffee and reflect on what she'd written. Actually, it was more like what she'd transcribed. Henrietta realized she'd simply recorded on paper what had appeared in her mind, and it not only made sense, it made beautiful sense. She wondered if the Great Spirit was the source of this burst of creativity. *Of course it was!*

She had covered twenty pages with copious notes for feature articles, the beginnings of a brochure, an outline for a book and lots and lots of lists. *Whew!* Her morning had been so prolific, she wanted to sing out loud, wishing for some kind of special song for writers in times like this.

"Morning, Peaches!" Jeff said. "Now, what do we have here?"

"Oh, Jeff! That vision quest has somehow inspired all of this." Henrietta gestured, spreading her arms over the numerous papers covering the kitchen table. "I've had so many ideas for that healing lodge and I've even started writing about it. Isn't that amazing?"

"It is and it isn't," he said, biting into a piece of leftover apple pie. "But it's really great that you're finally over the writer's block." His mouth was full, but he continued, "Hey, maybe now, you'll also be able to help me with my research papers." He raised his eyebrows and gave her a silly grin.

"Maybe," she said. "Speaking of your research, how's it going?"

"We've completed part one and are moving into part two," he said. His face brightened even more as he poured himself a cup of coffee. "We only have some initial data so far, but just like your new connection with spirit medicine, I'm really excited about it."

"Where are you with it? Right now, I mean?"

"I might've mentioned that we started with bacteria and cells." He took a sip from his cup.

"Yes, I remember."

"Well, now we're actually seeing the positive effect of spirit medicine on the healing rate of knife cuts, the production of goat milk, even the growth of chicken eggs. I could go on but I've got to run to the hospital." He picked up his brown medicine bag from the washstand.

"Hey, how about bringing home some of those spirit eggs?"

"I'll try." He chuckled before kissing her good-bye.

"Jeff, what time do you think you'll be home today?"

"I'm not sure, why?"

"Oh, I was planning to make your favorite dinner tonight." She spoke nonchalantly, but really she was trying to anticipate the possible timing of her dreaded task.

"I'm afraid I won't be able to take off as early as I usually do on Fridays. Everything's hinging on the Santana boy and a few others stabilizing. But maybe I can get out by seven. I'll call you. Okay?"

"Okay." She was planning to tell him everything.

"Love you," Jeff said. He blew her a kiss as he walked toward the front door.

"Love you more," she said. But he was already gone.

Henrietta was in her chair, looking at the paper-strewn kitchen table when Altie knocked on the door.

"Hey, Altie, thanks for helping with the kids today so I can go shopping." She got up to put out some coffee cake. "But they're still upstairs sleeping."

"It is a pleasure to be here." Altie said. She gestured with her chin, pointing it toward the table. "It looks like you have been busy this morning." She hung a cloth handbag on the back of a chair.

"I think it was the vision quest. Ideas are just pouring out of me."

"Spirit guides can be very helpful. Do not forget to thank them."

"Oh yeah," Henrietta said. Remembering how Joe had used wild tobacco as a token of appreciation to the Great Spirit, she walked over to her kitchen cabinet and pulled out her freshest and most prized herbs and spices. After mixing her favorites in a bowl, she waved over to Altie to join her outside. Once they were in the backyard, Henrietta scattered her dried libations into the wind and shouted: "Oh, thank you, Great Spirit, for helping me to heal, learn and create. In the name of the Father, Son and Holy Ghost. Amen."

"It is wise to thank the Great Spirit's feminine side, too," Altie said.

"Oh, and, Great Spirit? I also want to thank you for Mother Earth and all of your good mother light and nurturing, too."

"*Nzhoo.*"

Henrietta breathed in and said, "That felt so great!"

"*Ha'aa.*"

As they stood looking at each other, a young Indian woman known as Ora approached them in the yard and came to a standstill in front of Altie. Ora cradled a whimpering child whom Henrietta guessed to be Ora's daughter and about the same age as Jeffie. The child's body was mostly wrapped in a white cotton sheet, but oozing burn-like sores could be seen on her face and neck. The hideous wounds might have been the result of a grease fire, chicken pox or, for all Henrietta knew, something as aberrant as leprosy. But even as Henrietta mentally cataloged the list of heinous possibilities, Altie opened her arms without hesitation and received the injured girl before carrying her through the screened porch and into the kitchen. On the way to the living room, Altie hooked the strap of her cloth bag in her fingers as Ora and Henrietta followed.

In one graceful movement, Altie lowered herself to the sofa without further disturbing the poor girl who now rested in her lap. Altie extracted some herbs and a bottle of oil from her bag and made a salve in the palm of her left hand before applying it tenderly onto the child's sores with her right. All of this transpired without any words or explanations. The only sound came from the wounded child who continued to cry softly.

Withdrawing a white cloth from her bag, Altie wiped her hands clean before holding the girl close to her ample breasts. She kissed the child's black hair and began rocking while singing a song in her native language. The girl relaxed and fell asleep while her mother sat cross-legged on the floor with a stiff back, her eyes transfixed on the bundle in Altie's arms.

Without knowing how to help or what else to do, Henrietta went to the piano bench and sat down to watch. After about fifteen minutes, the girl looked up at Altie with a sweet smile through cracked lips, showing brown dimples on her tear-streaked face. Ora began to weep, and Henrietta did, too, moved by the scene and the mother's bounteous tears of relief.

"I have been able to offer only temporary aid," Altie said. "She will be fine, but you must take her to Dr. Clayborn now."

Henrietta was alarmed when a look of fear and panic returned to Ora's face. She spoke to Altie in her native tongue, shaking her head back and forth.

"Fear not; it is okay," Altie said in English. "Dr. Clayborn's medicine can be trusted and it is needed to prevent infection." Her voice was calm, but her gaze was firm on the young mother.

At that, Ora stood up and said in English: "All right." She picked up her daughter while saying, "*Ná'ahénsih*, I thank you." Turning toward Henrietta, she repeated her thanks. Ora departed the doctor's cottage with a slight smile on her lips.

Once they returned to the kitchen, Altie washed her hands.

"Here you go," Henrietta said, handing her a clean towel. Henrietta's admiration for Altie grew even more, and she was moved again to tears as she realized how much she missed her own mother. "You are truly an amazing woman," Henrietta said. She pulled Altie's clean hands into hers and kissed them. "And I'm so thankful that you are my friend and that you are here."

Altie looked down, her cheeks flushed pink. It was the first time Henrietta had ever seen her like that.

"Why don't we sit a moment at the table before I go to town," Henrietta said. She wanted to change the subject to something less emotional. "I'd like to get your opinion about my shopping list for our native garden."

After scanning it, Altie used Henrietta's pencil to make a few additions.

"You also might want to look over these pages for the Medichero Healing Center," Henrietta said. She picked up her stack of papers.

"You have a name."

"It's just a working name, until we come up with a better one. Any suggestions are welcomed, of course."

"It is a good one," Altie said.

"Um, Altie," Henrietta said. She paused before blurting out: "I'm planning to make Jeff's favorite dinner tonight."

Altie remained silent, but she looked at Henrietta as if she had a question to ask.

"It's sort of a good excuse to get him to sit down after work so I can tell him, you know," she said.

"Ah, *nzhoo*."

"Thanks again for helping and being here when the kids wake up." Henrietta picked up her purse and walked toward the kitchen door. *"Nish'ii."*

"You just said, 'I see you,' " Altie said.

"I meant to say 'I'll see you later.' How about this, then? *Ka-dish-day*."

"Ha'aa, ka-dish-day, farewell. *Nzhoo*."

Pleased she'd used and pronounced an Apache word correctly, Henrietta headed toward their government-issued Ford truck with a light step.

Later that afternoon, with the shopping done, Henrietta returned to the doctor's cottage. Altie had filled the kitchen with the sweet aromas of Indian fry bread.

"*Ya-ta-say*, Altie," Henrietta said.

"Jeffie is napping, and the girls are teaching hula-hooping to Mary Little Thunder in the front yard."

Henrietta thought it would be a good time to have Altie teach her how to make fry bread. "May I watch how you make it for a moment?"

"It is very easy. You need honey, oil, salt, hot water, dry yeast, flour and baking powder. Plus, lots of lard," Altie said. She pointed to the container of fat on the counter.

"Lard. I should've known. The root of all failed attempts to reduce."

"I have already combined the ingredients and allowed the dough to rise in here," Altie said. She lifted a damp cloth up a little from a ceramic bowl. "This one's ready. Now we mold."

While she made small balls with the dough, Altie heated some more lard in an iron skillet. When the fat sizzled, Altie flattened the dough balls with her palms until they were about five inches in diameter and then carefully dropped them in, one at a time. She fried the bread for about a minute and a half on each side until each turned a light golden color. She laid them on a towel to drain and cool with the others she'd made earlier. Before handing Henrietta a still-warm one, she sprinkled a little powdered sugar on it.

"Oh, Altie, thank you. This is heavenly."

"You also can dip it in this honey, yum-yum, *nzhoo*," Altie said, taking a bite.

Henrietta helped herself to another piece, with honey this time, as the girls came galloping into the kitchen.

"Hey, I wanted the first one," Annie said, followed by a "me, too" from Frannie and Mary Little Thunder.

"Well, here's the deal: fry bread will be a reward only to those who help me bring in the rest of the groceries and supplies," Henrietta said.

The three girls dashed out of the kitchen door.

Chapter 26

"It's after eleven, and I'm getting nervous," Henrietta said to Altie. She sat at her writing desk while Altie was on the sofa applying colorful beads to a sash. "They're still not answering the phone."

"I am also sensing something out of balance; something is not right," Altie said, looking up from her work.

"Little Eagle Feathers is obviously still sick. They're short-staffed, and it's a lousy, rainy night," Henrietta said. She got up and started pacing the living room.

"It is something more."

Henrietta stopped in her tracks, having learned to trust Altie's fine-tuned intuition.

"I must go to the hospital to offer my help." Altie started gathering her beadwork into her cloth bag.

"Maybe we should both go," Henrietta said.

"I will get the children, then," Altie said.

Henrietta sighed heavily. "What am I thinking? No, I don't want to do that. They're sleeping and I'm not about to wake them up. You'll have to go without me." She sighed again. "It's just that I hate to wait and be useless. It drives me nuts."

"Still your mind. Relax. Do not give power to thoughts of dark nuts," Altie said without trying to sound funny. "It may be that Jeff can still come home tonight, so you can get your secret out and over with."

"You know, I'm thinking it's too late now anyway, and I'm suddenly feeling way too tired and … kind of nauseated."

"You have held this darkness in too long. It is understandable that you are feeling ill at ease. You must pray for spiritual protection, think better feeling thoughts and hold on to your power."

"Don't worry; I'm still committed to telling Jeff as soon as I can."

"Ah, *nzhoo*. Until then, let your creative mind flow with light and beautiful words," Altie said.

"Here, take my umbrella," Henrietta offered.

Altie stuck her nose out of the front door to evaluate the air like a small feline. "No need," she said. She held up the palm of her right hand. "The storm is taking a rest for now, and I will be able to run up the hill faster without it."

Henrietta nodded, knowing that Altie could probably outrun a bobcat. "If you can, please let me know what's going on."

"*Ha'aa.*"

Henrietta bent down and embraced her friend. "Thanks for being here and keeping me company for as long as you did, even if it didn't work out as we planned. If you hadn't been here, I might've lost my courage forever or even fallen apart . . . again."

"Not true," Altie said. She grinned. *"Ka-dish-day."*

"Ka-dish-day." Closing the door behind her friend, Henrietta thought, for a split second that she had seen someone staring in through the bay window behind the piano. Cautiously she approached the bays and stared out blindly into the darkness, her heart beating wildly. She saw nothing, and pulled taut the cords of the venetian blinds as an unexpected dizziness whipped through her. She might have fainted if she hadn't jumped from the sharp crash of falling metal blinds.

Chapter 27

Altie had been gone less than a half hour when Henrietta jerked her hands up from the piano keys and, without thinking, started praying: *Please, God, please help me forget. Let me forget, so I don't have to tell Jeff.*

With her eyes squeezed tight, one clammy hand clasped over the other, Henrietta watched, like one who dreams, as her closed field of vision became alive with flashing white-bright dots and dashes. She waited, gritting her teeth, and strained to see or hear something snap, anything that would cause amnesia.

A sudden thunderclap caused her to jump and come back to her senses. *What am I doing?* It seemed the only things she'd forgotten were the words of Bears Repeating and her earlier resolve. Pondering the mystic's teachings, Henrietta played a soft tune on the baby grand until the grandfather clock in the foyer bonged out twelve long, maddeningly off-key chimes.

I've got to find out what's going on. Henrietta leapt up from the piano bench, ran over to the telephone and dialed. *Maybe someone will answer this time.*

"Medichero Injun Hospital."

"Hello? Nurse Burke?" *Oh, thank goodness.* "It's Mrs. Clayborn. Have you seen Jeff, I mean, Dr. Clayborn?"

"Sorry, Mizzus Clayborn, not lately. He had surgery."

"What?"

"It was for dhat Lit'l Eagle Feadhers, I mean," said Nurse Burke, who sounded as though she had removed her dentures.

"Again? Oh! What happened?"

" 'Fraid dhat boy got himself more of dhat bad 'nfection. Had to get it removed."

"Well, I just knew something wasn't right."

"I'll shay. Phew! What da night!" Nurse Burke slurred. "Sorry, but I'm not sure where the doc's gone off to this minute. Got 'udder 'mergencies keeping us gals in ER a hoppin'. Plus, a couple more Injuns just come in here with violent c'vulsions. Strange ones, too. Da symptoms, dhat is. Looks like it might be a nudder fu epidemic. And all dhis been keeping our hands full 'til Doc can see to it. Phew! Been ah long night."

"Is there anything I can do to help?"

"My gracious, no! What in heaven's name? I'm comin'!" Nurse Burke shouted to someone off the phone. "Mizzus Clayborn, gotta go, 'nudder 'mergency comin' in, and it don't look good." She hung up.

There was a click and a buzz as a clash of thunder rolled while lightning continued to rend the sky. The lamps in the living room flashed off and on. And then off again. The phone went dead.

Henrietta found one of her candles for such cases, lit it, and trudged back to the piano, attempting to continue the melancholy song, but, soon, she was overwhelmed by an eerie loneliness. Tears fell again as she looked down at her hands on the piano keys by candlelight. Her fingers no longer looked graceful and slender, but ashen and skeletal. *No! I can't tell him; it'll destroy us. It'll kill me!* She shook her head. *Stop! Dear God, how the dark spirits can play tricks. I should just go to bed and forget it until tomorrow.* But she wasn't at all sleepy.

She continued playing until she heard a loud crash in the kitchen.

"Jeff? Is that you?" Henrietta shouted, jumping up from the piano bench.

No sound.

With the candle in hand, Henrietta hurried toward the kitchen; Jeff usually came in through the back when it was muddy out.

Wham! She jumped. The candle blew out.

"Jeff?" she called out again, struggling to relight the candle. In the newly flickering candlelight Henrietta could see the screened-in porch door, usually left open, had banged shut. "Who's there?"

No one answered but she heard someone splashing through puddles of water as the candle blew out a second time.

Henrietta ran out to latch the hook of the screened-in porch door. "Altie? Is that you?" she squeaked. She went back inside and locked the kitchen door as well. Something crunched under her feet, and Henrietta looked down, but couldn't see anything. Blindly feeling her way to the washstand drawer, she found some matches and again relit the candle. Her porcelain pitcher had fallen to the floor, presumably from the wind, and she bent over to pick up the broken pieces. In the next moment, there was a shuffling noise behind her, and she whipped around. "Oh, it's you." Henrietta exhaled with relief after seeing one of her daughters. "You startled me, pumpkin. What're you doing up out of bed?"

"Mama!" Annie started to run toward her.

"Wait!" Henrietta moved quickly, picking up her daughter before her bare feet reached the porcelain shards. "We need to be careful. A pitcher just broke and there are sharp pieces on the floor."

"I couldn't turn on the lights, and I'm scared," Annie cried.

"Oh, honey, there's no need to be afraid. It's just a bad storm. It knocked out the electricity. And blew the doors open. But everything's okay."

"Where's Daddy?"

"There was another emergency up at the hospital with your friend Little Eagle Feathers."

"Is he going to be okay, Mama?" Frannie asked, peeping around the corner.

"Hey now," Henrietta said, putting Annie down on the clean part of the floor and motioning to Frannie to join them in a group hug. "I'm sure Daddy will make things right and hopefully, Little Eagle Feathers will be back home with his family and your daddy will be back home with us real soon. Come on, pumpkins, let's go back to bed."

After Frannie and Annie were back to sleep, Henrietta tiptoed out of their bedroom and checked in on little Jeffie. He was still sleeping soundly. She walked quietly down the stairs and turned into the kitchen. There on the sideboard sat Jeff's favorite dinner, starting to spoil. She moved to put it away. *I'll just have to tell Jeff first thing in the morning. I sure can't hold it in much longer.*

Chapter 28

Dr. Colonel had parked behind an old abandoned barn and watched a cumulonimbus cloud hurl jagged lightning bolts across the bruise-colored sky, illuminating the vast Sacramento mountain range. It was an arresting image, one he had photographed many years before. Another flash revealed the Indians' acreage, and in that split second, Dr. Colonel's quick mind absorbed the lay of the land.

This parking location will do just fine. It was far enough away from the Indian housing to avoid detection, but only a short walk to the hospital, which he had circled several times after seeing Jeff through its windows. The angle of his position also provided an indirect view of what was obviously the doctor's cottage with its conspicuous Victorian-style architecture.

Dr. Colonel hesitated a moment before turning off the engine. He wanted to listen to the end of "Come Rain or Come Shine" by Billie Holiday who had sadly died earlier that day. It was July 17, 1959, and she had been only forty-four years of age. The local Tularosa radio station was playing a Billie Holiday marathon this evening in her memory. *At least someone in this godforsaken state has some good taste,* he thought.

He'd always been in love with the woman's sensual voice, and felt an almost tangible sorrow when he'd heard of her passing on the radio earlier because it reminded him of a loss almost too great to bear. His eyes welled up, as he became nostalgic, remembering how he and Miss Julia had often danced to "The Very Thought of You." They had similar jazz tunes played by the orchestras at both their engagement ball and wedding reception. When his beloved had gotten pregnant soon thereafter, he'd doted on her something fierce. And then there was the birth of their perfect boy: Jefferson Pridgen Clayborn had been his pride and joy. The son and heir he'd always known was necessary to secure his legacy.

In the darkness, Dr. Colonel turned his head away from Brodie and toward the window to wipe his eyes dry. *Goddammit, I don't have time for any emotion, and it'll only get in my way.* He had to regain his self-discipline. He shook his head and looked around, allowing calm to again come over him.

No one was outside, so Dr. Colonel turned on the interior car light for the purpose of communicating to Brodie. "I'll need you to watch some Indians for me in a little while," he said. He was exaggerating the words with his mouth while signing. "But first, I have to test something out and maybe say hello to my daughter-in-law."

"I want to say hello to Henrietta, too," Brodie signed.

"No! Not yet," Dr. Colonel shouted and signed. "I want you to guard this right now." He pointed to an old cigar box that held the ten amber vials. "But don't touch it. It's full of poison." He turned off the car's interior light before grabbing a flashlight out of the glove compartment. Carefully removing one of the vials from the box and transferring it into his London Fog raincoat pocket, he shined the flashlight beam on his face so he could mouth some final words to Brodie. "Now, you stay put until I get back."

With a tap on his felt hat he left, trekking down the steep path that went past the doctor's cottage toward the Indian housing. On the way, he eyed several outside fires covered with various types of canopies, enabling the flames to survive in the rain, should it start up again. At one of the more isolated houses, two old women were sitting by a fire under a tarp, drinking and rolling cigarettes. They didn't look like they would be budging any time in the near future, so he decided to investigate another yard, one with a smoky fire-pit. From behind some bushes, he examined its potential, seeing a half dozen people inside a small house. An Indian woman came out with some fresh wood. After re-igniting the fire, she went back inside.

Dr. Colonel saw his chance and ran quickly toward the newly stoked flames, then, while holding his breath and covering his mouth and nose with a handkerchief, lightly sprinkled some heptachlor granules from the vial onto the campfire. He smiled as he crept away.

Heptachlor was a common insecticide used by Greenfield farmers to destroy cotton parasites and other pests, and, as a dry powder, it was relatively harmless to humans. But when exposed to fire, it became invisible, odorless and highly toxic.

As the son of a peach farmer, Jeff was well aware of this. Dr. Colonel had often lectured his son about how an accidental dusting upon a fire could produce symptoms that mimicked a violent flu-like episode, often within a half hour of exposure. Large doses of burning heptachlor could cause death to anyone unfortunate enough to inhale its undetectable fumes, especially during its initial phase of transformation. As a doctor, Jeff was also well aware that heptachlor left no traces of itself within the body. They both had witnessed autopsies of people who'd died from heptachlor poisoning, which ultimately translated into severe deterioration of the liver—also commonly seen in the bodies of alcoholic Indians.

It was the perfect blackmail tool for Jeff.

But Dr. Colonel already knew the situation wouldn't require autopsies or anything close to that. Of course, he wasn't planning to take it that far, it wasn't necessary. All he had to do was just make a few Indians temporarily sick and Jeff would cave in faster than an imploding mine. Everything would eventually settle down, everyone would recover. No one would get hurt, at least not too bad.

Back again behind the bushes a safe distance away, Dr. Colonel hovered as two Indian men stumbled out of the targeted house as though they'd had a little too much *tiswin,* their homemade Indian beer. Heading straight for the contaminated fire, they sat down under the canopy and began roasting some kind of meat on a stick. Next, the woman who'd toted wood came back out. She stopped and pivoted, talking to the others who were still indoors, then went back in.

Excellent! There'd be at least two "flu" victims, maybe more, and a few other Indians to take them all to the hospital in very short order.

Confident his plan was unfolding as easily as he'd imagined, Dr. Colonel strode back up the hill toward the doctor's cottage. Once on the back porch just in the shadows, he took a moment to contemplate how to approach Henrietta while he waited for his test subjects to help validate the threat he'd soon be making to Jeff. He saw the venetian blinds close just before the lights in the doctor's cottage went out. He stepped quietly to the bay window to investigate.

There she is. He was able to see through cracks in the blinds after Henrietta lit a candle. He continued to watch as she returned to the piano. In the light of the candle, her tear-streaked face glowed with a belle-like innocence and gentility he'd never noticed before, and he felt a strange stab of regret for what he'd had to do to her and how he'd sent her parents away. If only she'd been able to keep Jeff in South Carolina none of it would have been necessary. Still, he'd handle everything now and afterward, they could let all the unpleasantness fade into the past.

He moved away from the bay window and headed toward the back door. When he got to the screened-in porch, he knocked, but Henrietta's piano play coupled with the rain pelting on the roof prevented her from hearing him. The screen and kitchen doors were both unlocked, so he went ahead and ventured in, keeping his flashlight low to the floor so as to not alert her prematurely to his approach. He was about to call out her name when he caught sight of something that stopped him dead in his tracks: there was the fine, handmade black-leather medicine bag he'd given to Jeff, just sitting on a low shelf of a washstand, gathering dust.

His heart tightened with misery as he quietly reached down and picked it up. What another painful disappointment it was. All he'd ever wanted was for Jeff to be the great success he knew he could be and for them all to live together as a wonderful close-knit family. *Didn't every father want that?*

With his sleeve, Dr. Colonel rubbed off the dust from the clearly unused, empty bag, barely catching himself from sneezing. Where had he gone wrong? Why didn't Jeff want the life he had worked so hard to provide for him?

He took in a deep breath, sighed and remembered as he often did the shame caused by his parents and mortifying childhood and how the hometown's much-loved Mayor Maynard had called them poor white trash. Even now, it felt like a knife twisting in his heart. He'd spent years reinventing himself, building a life that raggedy little boy could never have dreamed of. And when he'd tried to hand this golden existence to his son on a silver platter, the ungrateful boy had run off to the very goddamn part of the world Dr. Colonel himself had left behind to make it possible.

In his growing rage, he decided to take the black medicine bag with him. Jeff would be using it when he returned. Dr. Colonel tucked it under his arm and started to turn back to the door, but feeling the need to sneeze again, he accidentally bumped the bag into the washstand's porcelain pitcher, which sent it crashing to the floor. He bolted from the kitchen, leaving the doors hanging wide open and his daughter-in-law probably frightened. But he didn't care. As he ran up the hill in the pouring rain, his only thought was: *Get Jeff back home where he belongs, and now.*

After peeking through the hospital's front doors, Dr. Colonel entered them when he remembered that Brodie was still in the car. *Damn!* He'd meant to go back and send Brodie to monitor his test subjects while he was in with Jeff. *Oh, well, the boy can wait. He'd probably screw it up, anyway, and get himself poisoned in the process.*

The main entrance was deserted, but at least the lights were still on. Dr. Colonel was soon able to find a small storage room with an ample supply of towels in it. He dried himself off. After hanging up his coat and hat on a hook, he snuck out carrying the black bag. In search of Jeff, he began prowling down a hallway in stealth, examining each patient room until he came across one containing a cluttered desk with a weathered brown medicine bag sitting on top.

It looked like Jeff's office; that certainly looked like Dr. Kepple's ratty hand-me-down bag. But Jeff was nowhere to be seen. Dr. Colonel continued down the hall, moving past a half-dozen more rooms before he finally came to where his son was working.

Jeff was wearing a standard-issue white surgical suit and cap, but minus the apron, which was the part that got the bloodiest. He was obviously fresh out of the operating room, and checking in on the patient: a frail Indian boy who looked to be about ten years old. Two petite women stood near the foot of the bed, arms around each other. A huge Indian man was sitting in a side chair, with a queer-looking skinny man standing behind him. *That goddamn Indian actually has his bangs gelled and puffed up into a pompadour.* After checking the boy's vitals and the fluids that dripped into his patient's thin light-brown arm, Jeff began to speak in low tones to the one with the weird hairdo.

Over their whispers, Dr. Colonel heard hospital doors slamming shut followed by the muffled sounds of wet moccasins sliding across wooden floors. Ducking out of sight, he spied two more sizable Indian men going into the room where Jeff was still tending to his young patient. One had to duck to enter the door, but the feathers adorning his head still brushed the lintel.

With so many others around, Dr. Colonel thought it best to return to Jeff's office. He took a different route back, went inside and closed the door. He looked at his watch and decided he could wait another fifteen minutes before interrupting. Hopefully, Jeff would be done with the young patient and the family by then.

What a mess, Dr. Colonel thought. He felt another wave of disappointment; Jeff's office was as disorganized as his life. Papers and files were all over the desk. Books were turned upside down. Drawers were hanging open. He hadn't even bothered to have the bed removed, instead shoving it into a corner. And there again was that blasted brown-leather bag, the one that had belonged to Dr. Kepple. *I'll just remedy that little problem right now.* Dr. Colonel sat down at the desk and was busy filling the superb black bag with the contents of the shabby brown one when his son opened the door.

"What the hell?" Jeff half-shouted.

Dr. Colonel looked up casually from his task. "Well, hey, is that any way to greet your father? And me coming all this way to see you and all. Where're your manners, Jefferson?"

"Sorry, you just startled me," Jeff said. He pulled off the white cap. "Hello, Father. And I suppose a welcome is in order." He offered a handshake and hug that was both tentative and slightly awkward. After backing up, Jeff added: "I was just coming in for a quick call to Henrietta."

"Good idea. It's pretty late." Dr. Colonel's voice was subdued as he sat back down. Despite the brief embrace, it felt like a warm homecoming to him. He also felt the urgent need to get Jeff out of this hellhole as soon as possible.

Jeff removed the surgical suit, which covered his plain clothes. "You're right it is, which begs a few questions: What in the world are you doing here, and at this late hour? And where did you get that?" Jeff pointed to the black bag.

"Oh, Henrietta let me borrow it," Dr. Colonel said. He was keeping his eyes on his task. He would let neither his face nor words betray his desperation.

"I see. *Why* are you doing that?" Jeff continued. He nodded toward the bag switching while wadding up the surgical suit into a ball. He tossed it into a corner hamper like a basketball shot and looked expectantly at his father.

"I saw you with a sick kid and his family and didn't want to disturb you, so I was just passing the time."

"Until?" Jeff put his hands on his hips and knitted his brow in consternation.

"Until I could get the chance to tell you something important. Look, I made the long trip out here because I felt like I needed to talk to you in person."

"What's so important?"

Dr. Colonel set the bags aside to give Jeff his full attention and his most loving facial expression. "I wanted to tell you … you're needed at home, son, now more than ever before."

"I doubt that," Jeff said. He slipped on a white lab coat and washed his hands in the sink.

Dr. Colonel tried again. "The peach business and orphanage are really too much for just one man to run and without your help, and your mother being gone and all . . ."

"Oh, good grief," Jeff said. He exhaled loudly. "You can handle anything and everything, and more efficiently than most people."

"Please, son. I'm asking you, in the most profound way I know, to come home because you're needed there. I need you. Our whole town needs you." He tilted his chin down and looked up, trying hard for something that resembled puppy eyes, but he'd never been more serious about anything in his whole life.

"Father, I told you I want to be here for the research opportunity. It's unique and it's not forever. And . . . I'm needed here, too."

Dr. Colonel's face was growing hotter by the second and he nearly choked trying to contain his rage. *Goddammit, why does this boy have to be so goddamn stubborn?* "You're needed here, huh? Well, I guess that's true enough. The ER is probably already full." Dr. Colonel looked down at his wristwatch. "Or it's about to be."

"What's that supposed to mean?"

"Let me tell you somethin'. I've tried to be patient and reasonable. But you've left me no choice," Dr. Colonel said. He felt himself clenching his teeth.

"What're you talking about?" Jeff said, his voice escalating.

"A new wave of influenza is about to hit your ER, if it hasn't already," Dr. Colonel said as he again took up the bags and finished his task.

"But, how would you . . . "

"If you come home right now for good and without a fuss, no one else has to get sick. If you stay? Well, I'd hate to see anyone else get the flu or perhaps even die from something as peculiar and mysterious as, say, heptachlor poisoning. You know how lethal and untraceable it can be." He snapped shut the emptied brown bag and mashed down the sides of it.

"I'm not doing what you want, so you're blackmailing me?" Jeff said in a strained whisper. He turned around and slammed his office door shut. "With people's lives? Dear God, you can't be serious!" He was shaking his head violently and shouting now. "Please tell me that you're joking!"

"No, but I will tell you this: whatever ends up happening to these Indians is completely in your hands, Jeff," Dr. Colonel said. He remained unflappable in his resolve. "Come home now, and everyone will be just fine and dandy."

"I can't just drop everything in the middle of the night," Jeff shouted. "I have a critical case in there. And I'm in the middle of some very important research!"

"I know. Listen," Dr. Colonel said. "I'll be fair about this and give you some time to think about your options and wrap things up. How does two days sound? You can turn in your resignation on Monday. I've got some old army buddies to look up in Alamogordo, anyway."

"How can you be so cavalier about poisoning innocent people? You're a doctor, for God's sake. You've gone mad! You're still clinging to some crazy idea about me living up to some ridiculous fantasy of yours, to the point of insanity!"

"No, I just want my son to come home where he belongs. Where he's truly needed more than anywhere else in the world. Let someone else take care of these Indians."

Jeff grabbed his hair with both hands. "Dear God! This can't be happening!"

For an excruciatingly long second, they simply stared at one another, Jeff's face registering a disgust that bordered on hatred. But Dr. Colonel knew it wouldn't last. *He'll see the light and be back to his old self once we're all living together again on the plantation.*

"Well, son, since you're going to be needed in the emergency room in very short order, I'll leave you now," Dr. Colonel said. He stood up and walked in front of the desk. "Remember, you've only got two days to decide if these goddamn Indians live or die, but keep this in mind: if they have what looks like another deadly flu epidemic, it'll definitely be all your fault!"

Jeff's mouth fell open, but nothing came out. Suddenly, he grabbed the black bag from the desk, threw it down on the floor and kicked it like a football. It flew under the bed.

Dr. Colonel had a treacherous urge to strike him, but restrained himself. "You'll be sorry you did that," he said calmly, shaking his head.

Dr. Colonel turned and exited with the crumpled brown bag tucked under his arm. Jeff followed him into the hall, making wild gestures with his arms and sputtering fragmented sentences in an attempt to dissuade him from his plan. But Dr. Colonel already knew what his son obviously didn't. This was an argument Jefferson would never win.

Chapter 29

With more courage than he believed he possessed, Brodie had removed the cigar box of poison-filled vials from the car and buried the whole thing in the woods behind the hospital. He couldn't let Dr. Colonel hurt anybody. But Brodie felt like crying when he thought how mad and abusive Dr. Colonel would become once he found out that Brodie had disobeyed him. Which meant that Brodie wouldn't be able to return to his employer tonight or possibly ever. He had to hide from Dr. Colonel, and his best bet was finding Jeff or his wife, Henrietta. But if that didn't work, he might have to hide out in the Medichero forests for a while. For that reason, he was glad he'd also thought to take Dr. Colonel's rifle out of the car. He carried it with him now.

Still muddy from digging in the dirt with his bare hands, Brodie navigated the hospital's perimeter through trackless puddles, examining the interior of various first-floor rooms like a kid peering into the exotic fish tanks of a pet shop. If he spotted Jeff, he would run in and warn him, mud and all, then he'd beg Jeff to take him in.

But it was too late. There was Dr. Colonel, already coming into a room that also served as someone's office. Brodie froze as Dr. Colonel sat down at the desk, his back to the window, inches from where Brodie stood. Gazing in from the pouring darkness, letting the rain cleanse his hands and clothes, Brodie watched as Dr. Colonel began doing something peculiar even for him: he was moving the contents of one medicine bag into another.

Jeff walked in, and Brodie jerked back into the shadows. Then, slowly edging his eyes around the window again, Brodie witnessed father and son arguing, but he couldn't quite make out what they were saying. He wondered if it had something to do with the bags. With wider eyes yet, he leaned in closer, and learned that it wasn't.

God, how I hate Dr. Colonel. And how he resented being pressed into another one of Dr. Colonel's unspeakable schemes. Brodie may have been deprived of hearing and his birth parents, but that didn't mean he was deficient of brains or feelings about folks who'd been good and kind to him. He just wanted to scream out: I'm deaf, not dumb!

Brodie had been able to read lips fluently long before Dr. Colonel realized it, but it wasn't until he became Dr. Colonel's assistant that he figured out what was really going on: the old man's hunger for attention and control, especially over Jeff, was as insatiable and unstoppable as the kudzu vines consuming Greenfield's roadside trees. And Brodie was perhaps the only one who knew how desperate and sadistic Dr. Colonel had become in recent years. Without Miss Julia's soft power and sedate influence, Dr. Colonel was like a self-created Frankenstein, finally awakened and on the loose.

Brodie was scared to death of Dr. Colonel and had been for a while. Most times, he felt weak and powerless around him, and he knew he'd been an inadequate defender for those poor souls caught in Dr. Colonel's cruel gun sights. But what could he or anyone have done to stop Dr. Colonel from sending Jenks to the Smyths' cabin on that terrible night? And what could Brodie have done to prevent that ugly bull from charging through the peach fields to complete his destructive assignment?

With Dr. Colonel glued to Miss Julia's sickbed all that night, preventing anyone else's approach, Brodie decided he'd better follow after Jenks. He watched in terror as Dr. Colonel's giant lackey causally entered the cabin door with the key Dr. Colonel had given him and turned on Miss Elizabeth's gas stove. But Jenks didn't start the deadly fire: the smoldering embers in the fireplace did that for him.

Brodie had failed to save his beloved Miss Julia or the Smyths' cabin. But at least he'd been able to pull Miss Elizabeth and Mr. Hampton away from the fumes and flames, and that made him feel better. They'd

always been so decent and nice to him. And he loved
Henrietta almost as much as Miss Julia.

Because of the gas, the Smyths had been
unconscious when he'd finally gotten to them. He was
able to carry Miss Elizabeth out, but had to drag Mr.
Hampton, on account of his bigness, and maybe he got
him a little bruised and cut on the way. But Brodie
suspected he wouldn't mind so much if he knew. The
Smyths didn't understand how they'd arrived in the side
yard that terrible night, waking up in the grass a safe
distance away from their burning home, before the fire
trucks had even arrived. Brodie later learned they
believed their mysterious escape had been the result of
divine intervention. But it was Brodie, just trying hard
to do what he thought Miss Julia would have wanted
him to do.

And now, with Dr. Colonel blackmailing poor
Jeff and planning to hurt these innocent Indians—
didn't someone once say he had Cherokee in him?—
Brodie could just imagine Miss Julia crying and signing
to him, "Stop him, Brodie! Do something, Brodie!"

Maybe I should just shoot him, Brodie thought. *But
no.* Miss Julia wouldn't want Brodie to do that. She
would want him to protect Dr. Colonel from himself
and others from Dr. Colonel; just like she'd always
done. Brodie had stuck around only to fulfill what he
thought would be her best wishes.

Brodie looked up and saw Dr. Colonel and Jeff
continuing to argue, even as they left the room and

went out into the hall. Then, Jeff came back in alone and sat down. He looked more than defeated.

Only two days! Think, Brodie! He hit himself in the head with his fist. *What can I do to help?* His body was shaking, but not from the cool rain.

Catching a movement in his peripheral vision, Brodie looked back into the office. *What is he doing? Oh no!* Brodie was seeing something even more frightening than what he'd witnessed just minutes before. *Help, Miss Julia!*

Chapter 30

It wasn't unusual for Jeff to work all night, but this particular morning, Henrietta could hardly stand it. She hated that her bed had felt so empty and cold, and she hated that Jeff hadn't called and she was still waiting.

The oven timer buzzed, and she looked up at the kitchen wall clock. *Dadgummit!* It was nearly eight a.m.

Up at the crack of dawn after tossing and turning for a few hours, Henrietta could only stare at a blank page in the typewriter once again. She had paced, fretted and turned the TV on and off. As a last resort, she'd started making buttermilk biscuits and cheese omelets. At least she could feed her family well.

She opened the oven and burned her forearm removing a baking sheet of steamy biscuits. Cursing under her breath, she put in a final batch before padding out onto the screened-in porch, thinking the cool air would ease the burn on her arm and restore her courage. The winds, still whipped up from last night's storm, bristled over the sides of mountains, straining through the screens with an eerie nasal-like hiss.

On a lower plateau, she could see Joe half-running toward the front yard of a small house, where a group of men were already gathered. She leaned over to get a better look as a red-tailed hawk whizzed by her head like a bullet. It gave off a high-pitched screech. Her eyes followed. Cutting up and easily through the damp gales, the hawk circled gracefully overhead for a few moments before making a swift dive to the ground. Henrietta braced herself for a grisly scene, some poor creature squirming painfully in the curve of long, sharp talons. But when the hawk came up empty, she felt a surprising pity for the bird of prey and its missed breakfast.

Henrietta ran back inside and into the living room, urgently trying to repress a growing sense of foreboding. She picked up the phone and dialed with shaky fingers; her stomach once again felt like it was trying to digest rocks. The call rang once before she heard little Jeffie screaming out for her. She banged the phone down and raced upstairs.

Jeffie's forehead and body were too warm and his nose was all gooey. As he continued to cry, she changed his diaper and hurried him into the kitchen in search of the thermometer and the Johnson's baby aspirin. Once the medicine had kicked in and she got Jeffie's nose cleaned up and his body settled down in the high chair with some apple juice and a cooled biscuit, she tried dialing again. But then the oven buzzer went off and upset Jeffie all over again.

After pulling out the final baking sheet, Henrietta turned off the oven, replenished Jeffie's juice cup and tried to make the call yet again.

"Medichero Injun Hospital."

Finally, success. "Nurse Burke?"

"Yes, Mrs. Clayborn?" Nurse Burke sounded as though her dentures were back in place.

"Have you seen Jeff, I mean Dr. Clayborn? I think he's been there all night. Could you please ask him to come home now?" Her own nagging voice made her cringe a little.

"I'm sorry, Mrs. Clayborn, no can do."

"Why's that, Nurse Burke?"

"When the doc's office door's shut and locked, and the phone's off the hook, that means he's getting some shut-eye and doesn't want to be disturbed."

"He's sleeping, then. Good."

"I'll bet Doc Clayborn was up all night with that Little Eagle Feathers and these here other sick Injuns. No doubt he's exhausted. I just walked into the flu unit, but haven't finished making my rounds yet, so to be honest, I can't say exactly for sure if he's still sleeping or not."

"Since he missed his supper last night, he needs a good breakfast," Henrietta said. She was thinking about putting ham and maybe some scrambled eggs into a few biscuits for him. "I can bring something up now."

"Mrs. Clayborn, with all due respect, if I was you, I'd just let him sleep right there in that office 'til he wakes up. He'll need his energy for later."

"Well, he won't be good to anyone if he doesn't get some proper nourishment, for heaven's sake," she said. She turned. Jeffie was banging his juice cup loudly on his table.

"Mama!" he called out before crying again.

"I'll be right there, honey," Henrietta said to Jeffie. "Nurse Burke," she said, turning back to the phone and speaking quickly. "Our baby's also sick this morning, so it'd be better if I could send the girls up with Jeff's breakfast. Do you think it'd be safe for them to go straight to his office and back?"

"Oh, good God!"

"What? What is it?"

"Not more of them! Judy, hon, how many? Three? What'd you say? Mrs. Clayborn, we got more emergencies coming in."

"What's going on?"

"Mama!"

"Good God," the nurse repeated. "They're vomiting all over the place. Listen, Mrs. Clayborn, just be sure the girls stay far away from the ER and this here flu unit. Should be okay way down on Doc's end. Gotta go." She hung up.

Henrietta ran back to Jeffie and cleaned up the juice that had spilled onto the floor. Then she carried him with her into the girls' bedroom. "Annie, Frannie, wake up, my sweeties."

They moved and stretched, then popped up almost simultaneously.

"Hey, after your breakfast, I need y'all to help me with something." She put Jeffie down on the floor between the girls' beds.

"What is it, Mama?" Annie said. She was rubbing the sleep from her eyes. "Hey, little Jeffie, crawl on up here, baby."

"No, better not. He's got a fever, and I don't want y'all getting too close." She picked him up again. "Since I can't take Jeffie out, I'd like you two to deliver breakfast to your daddy's office at the hospital and maybe ask him to come home for a little break. Could you do that for me?" She started laying out the girls' white dresses and sweaters on the ends of their beds.

"Sure, Mama."

Feeling a little unsteady herself, Henrietta sat down on Frannie's bed. Was she getting a fever, too?

"Do you think it's okay for us to go up there now?" Frannie asked.

"Yes, but you must stay far away from Nurse Burke's area in the east wing, you know, where the emergency room is," she said. She put the back of her hand to her own forehead, but it was cool. Perhaps she was just tired from not sleeping well and running all over the house this morning. "Nurse Burke's tending to some new patients who came in last night and this morning with something that didn't sound too great. So please don't go anywhere near her area. But you shouldn't have to, since it's on the opposite end of the building from where Daddy's office is."

"You don't have to worry about that, Mama. We don't like going near Nurse Burke anyway," Frannie said, picking up the dress her mother had laid out. "We'll definitely stay far away from her."

"Yeah, she's kind of mean," Annie said, wrinkling her freckled nose.

"You think we can get Daddy to come home?" Frannie asked.

"Well, if anyone can get him to do her bidding, it's you and you," Henrietta said, rubbing the white-blond hair of each girl. "But, if he can't get away, and it's more than likely he won't be able to, just leave him with the breakfast."

While she waited for the girls to finish getting ready and come downstairs, Henrietta put Jeffie back in his high chair with some toys, more juice and another biscuit. Then she fixed the girls some breakfast and went out onto the screened-in porch again, feeling a little better and confident that the girls would be able to at least remind Jeff to take a break at home. She left the door open to half-listen to Jeffie, who seemed occupied and happy for the moment.

The noisy stirrings of the girls eating breakfast soon caught her attention, and she hurried back into the kitchen. She poured coffee and fresh cream into a Thermos and filled a brown-paper lunch sack with ham-and-egg biscuits as well as some plain ones.

"Here, give these to Daddy to tide him over until he can get home," Henrietta said after the girls had finished. They were headed toward the front door.

"Can I have another one?" Annie said. She raised her eyebrows and smiled.

"I guess so, if you're still hungry. There are plenty in there," Henrietta replied.

"That's okay, Daddy needs them more than us," Frannie said, elbowing her sister hard.

"Hey, speak for yourself," Annie said as she pulled one of the plain biscuits from the bag. She took a huge bite out of it before shoving the remains back in the bag.

"Now, Annie, you aren't going to give your sweet and starving daddy a bunch of half-eaten, crumbled-up biscuits, are you?" Henrietta quizzed with arms crossed.

"No, ma'am." Annie grinned, grabbing out the half-eaten biscuit and stuffing it in her mouth. "Let's go," she said, sending out a spray of baked dough. "Oh, sorry, Mama." Then she giggled.

"Here, before you go, let me replace the one you just ate," Henrietta said, retrieving another biscuit from the sideboard and putting it in the bag. "Now, out you go," Henrietta said as they walked into the foyer. She was clapping her hands and shepherding them out the front door. "But remember, be quick about it. Straight to Daddy's office and back. Stay far away from the other end. I don't want you picking up any stray germs."

Through the sidelights, Henrietta watched her towheaded girls pick up their hula hoops from the front yard before skipping toward the adjacent path. Jeffie waddled in and tugged on her full skirt, starting to scream again for attention.

"Now, now, Jeffie, I know you don't feel well, but I need to clean up the kitchen before Daddy gets home. How about we see if *Captain Kangaroo*'s on TV?" Henrietta picked him up to soothe his cries, and carried him into the living room.

Chapter 31

With a hula hoop in one hand and part of their daddy's breakfast in the other, Annie and Frannie followed the steep path to the Medichero Indian Hospital, careful not to soil their white dresses and sweaters. They liked dressing all in white to go to their father's hospital office because they knew he would say, "Look who's here, my beautiful little nurses."

After their ten-minute journey, the twins pushed through the hospital's heavy double doors, and skipped toward a deserted hall. With the uninhibited clatter of white patent leather shoes and pink plastic hoops on wooden floors, they attracted the disapproving attention of Nurse Burke, who'd just walked up to the pharmacy counter near the front entrance.

Nurse Burke raised an arthritic-looking forefinger to wrinkled lips. "Shhh!" she said in a loud whisper. "We have a bunch of sick Injuns in here. You better hurry with your business and get on back home 'fore you catch something bad. But 'til you do, shhh!"

Complying immediately, the girls tiptoed until they turned the corner. Then they scuttled, skipped and hopped down the hallway toward their father's office like two rambunctious colts.

"Nurse Burke looks like this," Frannie said. She scrunched up her face just as she arrived at their father's door.

"No, she looks more like this," Annie whispered. She crossed her eyes and stuck out her tongue. "And if you look directly into her eyes, you'll turn into the scary Black Painted Woman," Annie said, trying to remember an old Apache story Altie had told them.

Frannie turned the doorknob to the left.

Click.

Then to the right.

Click.

"No, dummy, it's the White Painted Woman. And she was a beautiful Apache goddess," Frannie corrected.

"Was not."

"Was, too."

"Was not."

"Be quiet now," Frannie whispered. "He's probably still sleeping." She knocked lightly on the door. "Daddy?"

No answer.

Because the glass door was opaque, Frannie peered through the keyhole, but her hair kept falling in the way. "Here, hold these." Frannie shoved her hula hoop and the Thermos into her sister's arms.

Tucking her hair behind her ears, Frannie peeked again.

"Hey, let me see," Annie said.

"Stop pushing on me," Frannie whined. "I can't see with you on me like that. It's hard to tell, but it looks like Daddy's still asleep on the bed."

Frannie gripped Annie's forearm about the same time she started frantically rattling the doorknob.

"Hey, you're hurting me," Annie cried. "What's the matter?"

"Go get help!" Frannie shouted. Pounding on the door, she shouted, "Daddy! Please wake up!" As tears flowed she screamed into her sister's face: "Don't just stand there. Go! Run! Find Nurse Burke! Move!"

But in the end it was Frannie, who had promised to stay clear of Nurse Burke, who ran down the hall screaming for her or anyone else as if her life depended upon it.

Left standing there, Annie looked through the keyhole as Frannie had done. Tears began to blur her vision. She wanted to scream, as her sister had, or run, anything. But she could not move. Seconds, perhaps minutes, passed.

"Oh Lord, what should I do?" Annie said to herself. "Oh my Lord Jesus, what should I do? Please tell me what to do."

She stared in again at her father. *Why is my daddy lying there on the bed like that? Why?*

She knew her daddy worked too much, too hard, especially lately because of all the flu and her friend Little Eagle Feathers being so sick. Her daddy had often slept in his office after working long hours. And they'd awakened him many times before. Only this time it was different. He was lying on the low bed, but it looked like there was blood on her daddy's face and neck. Her daddy's eyes were not the warm-loving ones she had known her whole life. They were half open and lifeless.

Chapter 32

Father John O'Reilly was walking through the front doors of the Medichero Indian Hospital to make his morning rounds when he heard a child screaming for help. He lurched toward the echoing shrieks, holding up the front of his black robe as he ran. But the Clayborn girl had already made it out into the lobby, and she was running straight toward him.

Because he was over six feet tall, Father O'Reilly bent down. She rushed into the waves of his long black sleeves, crying and shouting at the same time.

"Help! Help, Father!"

"What is it? Slow down now. Take your time and tell me what's happened." He wasn't sure which twin girl it was.

"I can't! It's Daddy, it looks like ... he's ... he's hurt, I think," she said, crying and gasping. "But his door, it's locked. Annie's still back there!"

"Okay, Frannie, hold on." Father O'Reilly's head darted left then right. Seeing Nurse Burke down the opposite hallway pushing a cart, he yelled: "Nurse, nurse, come quickly. And bring the key to Dr. Clayborn's office. Hurry! It looks like an emergency!"

"Not a 'nudder one!" Nurse Burke shouted. She sprinted toward them on her skinny, rickety legs.

Once there, it seemed to take forever for Nurse Burke to pull out her large ring and find the right key. But as soon as she had it in and turned, Father O'Reilly and the girls exploded through the door, shooting past her and heading straight for Jeff, lying supine and motionless on the low corner bed.

"Daddy, Daddy, please wake up, get up," Frannie cried, pulling on his lab coat.

Annie joined her, then she began moving as if she were having a seizure of silent wails.

"Dear merciful God, what's happened here? Jeff?" Father O'Reilly tried looking at Nurse Burke who was checking Jeff's throat for a pulse.

Jeff's cheeks, neck and clothing were inked in dried, brick-colored blood. His face was discolored blue and swollen hideously. Nurse Burke shook her head as she found no pulse.

Father O'Reilly turned toward the girls and gently tugged on their arms. "My poor little lambs. Let's go find your mother. Where is she?"

"She's ... she's ... she sent us ... we were supposed to fetch Daddy ... and ... bring him home," Frannie managed between sobs.

"Nurse Burke, perhaps you should call the sheriff and Mr. Mackenzie at the Agency," Father O'Reilly said. "I'll take care of the children."

"Of course, Father." But she hesitated, shutting Jeff's half-opened eyes with one hand and wiping away her own tears with the other before stepping out of the room.

Father O'Reilly tried again to pull the girls away. "Come, we should find your mother."

"No, I won't leave Daddy!" Annie screamed.

With a great sigh, Father O'Reilly finally saw the futility of trying to coax them away. "Very well, let us pray," he said. "Saints of God, come to the aid of Jefferson Clayborn, beloved earthly father of Frannie, Annie and Jefferson Junior, and beloved husband of Henrietta. Come to meet him, angels of the Lord! Receive his soul and present him to God, the Most High. May Christ, who called you, take you to Himself; may angels lead you to Abraham's side. Oh Lord, give him eternal rest, and may Your light shine on him forever."

As Father O'Reilly continued, the girls hung on tightly to Jeff's bloodstained lab coat, the sides of their blond heads on his chest, perhaps seeking the thump of a heartbeat that would never come again. After his second round of prayers, their cries began to fade into whimpers, their hands at last went limp and they were now lying pitifully still, as silent as withered roses.

Finally, Frannie lifted her head and her blue eyes glistened through her tears and unarmed innocence. "I want to go to Mama now."

"Me, too," Annie sniffed.

Without pause, Father O'Reilly scooped up both girls easily, carried them out and started down the hill. Their trembling bodies were light and their small bones felt as fragile and vulnerable as two baby robins fallen from the nest. He continued to whisper soft prayers in their ears, as tears poured down his cheeks. *Oh, merciful God, please give them strength. Give us all strength.*

Chapter 33

Henrietta heard the front door open as she scoured off dishes in the kitchen sink. "Are y'all back already?" she asked.

Hearing the door slam and the sobs of her daughters, she whipped around.

"Henrietta, I'm so, so sorry," said Father O'Reilly, entering the kitchen and unfurling the anguished girls, who ran to Henrietta, nearly knocking her over.

"What ... what in the world?" Henrietta shouted. She saw the dirt-colored smears on her daughters' faces and white dresses. Both were crying. "What happened? Did you fall into the mud? Are you hurt? Please tell me what's happened," she said, looking desperately to Father O'Reilly for answers. His large face was red and stained from tears, and Henrietta knew something had gone horribly wrong.

"Where's Jeff?" Her eyes were wide, her mouth already trembling.

"Oh, Mama, Daddy is ... Da-Daddy's ..." Frannie stuttered. Both girls were crying and shaking uncontrollably.

"Daddy's what?" Henrietta rubbed what looked like dirt from their faces. "Father, what is this? Where's Jeff? I don't understand," she said. She was crying too without knowing why.

"Henrietta, I think it might be best if we first get the children settled down, perhaps into bed."

"But, Mama, I don't want to go to bed," cried Frannie. "Daddy's dead, and I don't want to leave you!"

"What? No! Father, please tell me this isn't so!" Henrietta gasped. She felt like the wind had been knocked out of her. Time stood still even as it shattered. "No! No! I don't believe it. I won't believe it. No! Never!"

"Mama!" Annie was crying hysterically. "Mama, please don't leave us!"

"Oh, Frannie, Annie." Henrietta cradled them. Jeffie toddled into the room and screamed along with them.

"Oh, my babies, I'm right here," Henrietta said. Blinded by tears, she clung to them, holding them close to her heart. "I'm not going to leave you ... but I need to go see about this ... oh, no, this can't be ... oh, my poor babies ... we must get you cleaned up ... come."

While Father O'Reilly held Jeffie, Henrietta somehow was able to put the girls, limp and crying, back into the nighties they'd worn only an hour ago, before their world had been ripped apart. She wiped the dried blood from their hands and faces and returned them and Jeffie to their beds and lay with them there, holding them and praying with Father O'Reilly who joined them.

After a while, all three of the children passed out, exhausted by grief. Afterward, in the kitchen, Father O'Reilly filled in the details of how they had found Jeff.

"Oh, Father, I must go to him right away. Can you stay here while the children sleep? I'll try to get back before they wake up."

"Of course, dear. But before you go, let's first pray for your strength, for your children and for Jeff's soul. Oh, merciful God," he went on without waiting for Henrietta to agree.

She didn't want to listen or feign praying, but out of respect for Jeff, she walked over to the kitchen table, sat on the hard surface of a wooden chair and tried to sit perfectly still. Her eyes were open as she twisted her wedding rings, rubbing red lines onto her skin.

Maybe this wouldn't have happened if she'd not been so totally absorbed in her own pain, her own damn secret. Perhaps all of those mournful and sick feelings in the pit of her stomach last night were premonitions, warnings. Her little voice had been giving her a forewarning about Jeff being in danger, and she'd ignored it!

Oh, my God! Henrietta gasped with the shock of this terrible insight.

"In the name of the Father, Son and Holy Ghost, Amen," Father O'Reilly said, and looked over at Henrietta, seeing her staring moon-eyed at the window. "Henrietta, Amen."

"Yes, of course, Father. Amen."

Joe and Altie opened the kitchen door without knocking and rushed in and over to Henrietta.

"Henrietta, dear friend, we are so shocked to learn of Jeff's passing," Altie said. She and Joe opened their sturdy brown arms to Henrietta who fell into them and let go of another waterfall of tears.

"Joe, Altie, thank—" Henrietta choked, nearly drowning from her ceaseless tears. She was about to tell them that she just realized she'd gotten an intuitive warning last night about Jeff being in danger.

But before she could get it out, Joe stepped back with an alarmed expression on his face. "Little Eagle Feathers also passed to the other side last night," Joe said. "It was after Jeff left his room."

"No!" Henrietta shouted.

"How do you know that?" Father O'Reilly asked.

As though ignoring the priest's question, Joe continued to face Henrietta. "Jeff thought he'd stabilized Little Eagle Feathers and decided it'd be a good time to call you."

"But he didn't," Henrietta cried. "He didn't call me!"

"When he didn't immediately return, we thought maybe he went to the ER or finally left for the evening," Joe continued.

"He didn't," Henrietta repeated. "Joe, what do you think happened?"

"Honestly," Joe said, "I don't know."

"But you were both there," she said.

"After Jeff left the room, Altie and I sensed we should stay there with Little Eagle Feathers and his parents, Big Eagle Feathers and Lily. Two Feathers and Danny Running Feathers were also present. After a while, without warning, the boy gave up his spirit, and I was unable to resuscitate him. The boy went quickly."

"Why didn't you try to get Jeff back or go find him?" Henrietta cried.

"There was no time. Once we realized Little Eagle's passing was meant to be, Altie and I opened the window and performed bear medicine to help his spirit pass to the Light. We stayed with Lily even though Big Eagle Feathers and his brothers stormed out of the room. I don't know where they went. Later, Altie and I chose to walk Lily home so that we could continue the bear medicine for her," Joe said. "We've not seen Big Eagle Feathers, his brothers, or even Jeff, since last night."

Father O'Reilly's eyes met Henrietta's, exchanging the same fear and suspicion of Big Eagle Feathers and his hostile brothers.

Henrietta turned to Joe. "Would Big Eagle Feathers have murdered Jeff for not being able to heal his son?"

"I really don't think so," Joe said, shaking his head. "I got the feeling he left the hospital just to be by himself and get out of that place of death. But, admittedly, there have been some bad feelings among the elders and Big Eagle's brothers about Jeff. They blamed him for the flu epidemic, and they didn't like Jeff's interest in our sacred native medicine. Some think he wasn't paying enough attention to his own white medicine. I suppose it's possible that some might blame Jeff for not being there to save Little Eagle Feathers."

"That's ridiculous!" Father O'Reilly roared.

"What about you, Joe? Do they blame you for not saving Little Eagle Feathers?" Henrietta snapped, unable to withhold her frustration.

A heavy silence fell on the kitchen.

Joe raised his eyebrows. "I agree that would be ridiculous. It was simply the little one's time to pass into Spirit. Altie and I were there to help him pass over peacefully. That was our privilege. Big Eagle Feathers and the brothers also know, very well, that it was the little one's time, even though they may not want to face their own negative karma, self-pity and other imperfect thoughts right now. They'll see the light, eventually."

"Joe, what's this talk about karma? What do you know about karma?" Father O'Reilly asked questions that went unanswered.

"Sometimes it's not in our power to heal when the Great Spirit calls us home," Joe said, paying no attention to Father O'Reilly. "But, of course, when we're in the position to heal and bring wholeness and peace, we must do so. It's our duty. It's why the Great Spirit gave us many good medicines like the inner science."

"Karma! Inner science? Joe, I demand some answers! What're you talking about?" Father O'Reilly shouted.

Henrietta broke down. "Oh, Joe, how am I going to handle all of this? I feel like a part of me has died, too, and I'm so alone here."

"Not true," Altie said. She picked up a wet cloth from the sink to wipe off the browned blood residue on Henrietta's cheek. "We are here for you, Henrietta."

"The Church is here for you," Father O'Reilly said.

"Henrietta, for your sake and the children's, we must journey and seek wisdom in the *Kopave*," Joe said.

Henrietta was frozen, unable to think.

"Joe, Henrietta can't go on a journey in a cave right now," Father O'Reilly said. "Is he talking about one of those vision quest things again?" He looked over to Altie with a confused expression on his face.

Altie shrugged her shoulders.

"Would somebody please answer a simple question around here for me?" Father O'Reilly asked, exasperated.

"Joe is trying to remind Henrietta that prayer and inner communion with our Heavenly Father and the Christ are needed at this time," Altie said.

"Prayer! Communion with Jesus Christ! Yes, well, why didn't he just say so? Let us turn in the Prayer Book to page 115 and I'll read aloud," Father O'Reilly said after pulling out his personal copy from his robe pocket. Henrietta, even in her stupor thought the priest was acting strangely, as if they'd all been transported to the St. Paul's Mission Catholic Church. It only added to the surrealism of the devastating situation.

As Father O'Reilly became engrossed in his readings, Henrietta's eyes wandered to one of her husband's rumpled jackets hanging limp on a peg by the door. *Please, God, please don't let this be true.* From the jacket, her gaze fell onto the walnut washstand where Jeff typically placed his unpretentious brown medicine bag, ready for an emergency or a "teepee call" in the camps. Some of the Medichero called it *beena'izee*, the bag of the white man who makes medicine. His spare medicine bag, the black one his father had given him, always sat on the lower shelf. It was this bag-placing ritual that reminded him he was doing the right thing with his life. It suddenly hit her that the black bag was missing. She was about to consider what might have happened to the missing black bag when Father O'Reilly interrupted her thoughts.

"Henrietta, my dear, since Joe and Altie are here with you now," he said, getting up, "I think it might be wise for me to go see Lily Santana and determine what's going on there with her and her husband. Do you think you'll be all right for a while?" He kissed her on the forehead and patted her shoulders.

"I don't know. But you're right. Joe and Altie are here, and I should go to the hospital now anyway." But she just sat there after Father O'Reilly left, unable to move her arms and legs. *What was I thinking about before?* She couldn't remember now.

"The fire's burning, but no one's in your teepee," Joe said from the kitchen table.

"What?"

"Henrietta, you're feeling disconnected. Once again, part of your soul's no longer in residence. Am I right?"

Henrietta nodded and sighed. "I don't feel like my old self or my new self. I feel like I'm living in another nightmare I can't wake up from. I don't know how I'm going to handle all of this … I don't know what we're going to do, where we're going to live or how we're going to survive. I don't even know what happened to my husband."

"You'll handle it, but it must be all of you. You must be whole and in the right frame of mind to make good decisions that will produce good karma for yourself and your children. You must allow me to journey in Spirit for you, and you also must reach for the comfort and healing power of the Great Spirit within yourself."

"Joe, I'm sure you're right, but it'll have to wait until I see Jeff."

"We will revisit this after your visit."

"Would you and Altie be able to stay with the children while I... take care of ..." She was crying again. "If you could help them, soothe them somehow."

"I will go sit with them now," Altie said, moving toward the staircase. Bears Repeating followed, leading Henrietta by the arm.

Chapter 34

As she prepared to force herself to face the horror lying in wait at the hospital, Henrietta was reminded of another dreaded task: telling Dr. Colonel about Jeff. *Dear God, how can I do it?*

"Joe, Altie," she whispered, "I'm going up to the hospital now." Tears were again falling down her flushed cheeks. They nodded in unison. *Thank you, dear God, for sending Joe and Altie to help us.* She knew her children would be in good hands. Jeffie was contentedly asleep in Altie's loving arms, thankfully oblivious to the events that had just shattered their world.

She turned and walked down the stairs. Before she could open the front door, there was a knock. Looking through the sidelights, Henrietta saw two white men standing there. Sighing, she opened the door.

"I was just on my way to the hospital," Henrietta said. Her voice was hoarse, her eyes swollen, wet and red.

"You already know about your husband, then," said the one in uniform.

"Yes, the girls . . . and Father O'Reilly."

"I'm Sheriff Andrews, from Tularosa. I assume you already know the Superintendent of Indian Affairs, Craig Mackenzie."

She nodded.

"Henrietta, we're so sorry about Jeff," Craig said, moving in close to give her a kiss on the cheek and wrap one of her hands in his. "He was a good man. Listen, if you need anything at all, please call on me."

"Thank you," she said, idly noticing the bandage on Craig's left hand.

"Mrs. Clayborn, I hate to bother you right now, but if you don't mind, ma'am, we need to ask a few questions," began the sheriff.

"Sheriff, I've just settled the children down and haven't been able to get to the hospital yet to see my husband," she said. She was nearly choking on the words. "I was on my way to do that, so, if y'all will just excuse me, we can talk afterward." Henrietta threw her sweater around her shoulders, ready to leave.

"Sorry, Mrs. Clayborn, but I'm afraid the medical examiner's there right now," Sheriff Andrews said. He angled himself in the doorway to block her passage. "We'll need to give him and his team ample time to complete their initial examination, as required by law. We might as well chat in the meantime, ma'am."

"Henrietta," said Craig, "I know how difficult this is, but the medical examiner just needs a little more time, and then we'll walk up with you. It'll be better if you're not alone, anyway, don't you think?"

"I guess so," Henrietta said. She led them back into the kitchen. She went through the motions of getting coffee for them without asking if they wanted any. The men sipped in silence for a few moments; Henrietta sat at the table, tapping her fingernails on its surface.

"Well? Let's get on with this. I need to go," she said. She was staring at them, not caring if she sounded rude. "I feel like everyone keeps delaying me and I can't seem to get there as fast as I want, to see my poor Jeff," she said. She was crying again into the handkerchief.

Craig got up and patted her shoulders. "We'll go with you in a few minutes."

"Now," the sheriff said, looking down at his notes. "Is there anything you can tell me about someone known as Big Eagle Feathers?"

"He was unhappy about Jeff's, um…" She looked at Craig with a guilty expression. She was still in the habit of being discreet and protective about Jeff's research. "Big Eagle Feathers made it clear that he wanted Jeff to focus less on the research and more on his son."

"There are some Indians who say Jeff may be to blame for the death of his son, uh, Little Eagle Feathers," Sheriff Andrews said, looking down again. "And the flu epidemic."

"Well," she said, looking down into her handkerchief. "I've heard that. Sheriff, do you think Big Eagle Feathers might have killed Jeff?"

"It's possible, but we'll have to let the evidence lead us to the truth. But I have to be honest with you: so far the evidence—what little we have at this point—doesn't immediately point to Big Eagle Feathers, at least not directly."

"What do you mean?" she asked. "What happened to my husband?"

"From first glance, Jeff was covered with blood. But on closer inspection, it looked like the cause of death was strangulation, and the blood came from another source."

"How would you know?"

"There were petechiae, tiny, ruptured blood vessels, on Jeff's face and eyelids."

"Peta-chi?"

"The presence of petechiae usually means death by asphyxiation, suffocation or strangulation."

"Oh, dear God. But I don't understand: wouldn't that point to a large man like Big Eagle?"

"There were no obvious incisions on his skin."

"I still don't understand."

"Because there weren't any bleeding wounds on Jeff's face, neck or hands, the blood most likely came from the killer who cut his hands on the broken window glass. The window had been smashed. One of the nurses said that she may have overheard Jeff arguing with someone in the hall about that time, but she wasn't sure because she was attending to patients. In any event, it looks like our suspect probably came in through the window and will no doubt have sliced-up hands."

The sheriff looked pleased with himself and his theory. But with a sudden realization, he and Henrietta both looked at Craig's bandaged left hand.

Craig squirmed, visibly uncomfortable. "Hey, wait a minute. You know I'm a bachelor. I just cut my hand making dinner last night. I got carried away cutting up carrots for a stew. I would never hurt Jeff or anyone."

"Don't worry, I'm not accusing you," said the sheriff.

"Strange coincidence though," Henrietta said. But she didn't really think Craig could be capable of such violence either. "Do you think we could go now, Sheriff?"

He looked at his watch and nodded. "Yep, let's go."

As they were walking out the front door, Henrietta saw Big Eagle Feathers standing on the incline between the doctor's cottage and the reservation's hospital, looking as though he had walked out of a photograph taken by the legendary Edward S. Curtis. He was dressed in his ritual ocher-colored leather pants and shirt, although the Sunrise Ceremonies had ended two weeks ago. And she noticed that he'd cut off the ends of his hair, as was the Medichero custom when a family member died.

Even from the distance, Henrietta could tell that the oversized Apache had been crying. But he just stood there staring at her, his accusatory, frightening black eyes taking away Henrietta's breath. She returned his hard gaze, but could only hold it briefly, fighting the urge to vomit.

She turned when she heard Altie coming down the steps behind her. "Oh, Altie, the sheriff and Craig detained me a bit. We're just now leaving."

"We will take good care of your babies, no need to rush," Altie said. "It is important to say *ka-dish-day*, farewell, this way now, and in another way later."

"Thank you, Altie," she said. She was crying again but infinitely grateful for Altie's presence. Henrietta turned back toward the path that led to the hospital, but when she looked up, Big Eagle Feathers and his furious dark eyes had vanished. Perhaps he'd been a figment of her imagination, created by her grief and a growing fear she could no longer contain.

Henrietta shut the front door with trembling hands. "You know, I'm glad you're coming with me, after all," she said to Craig and Sheriff Andrews.

Chapter 35

After she saw Jeff's ruined body still lying on the low narrow bed, Henrietta felt like her soul had shattered again, leaving only a brittle shell of a woman to deal with overwhelming pain and misery.

Jeff's office felt cold and almost wet, as though the room itself had been crying. She hugged Jeff's spiritless body trying to will him back to life. But it was no use. Like the dried blood on his face and clothes, her husband was stiff and smelled sour.

"Oh, Jeff," Henrietta sobbed. "I can't stand to be here without you. Come back, please!"

"Mrs. Clayborn, I'll take good care of the doc," Nurse Burke said in a surprisingly gentle tone. "We'll clean him up real good. You should go on back with the children now. Go ahead. They need you now more than he does."

"Yes, the children need me," Henrietta said, almost in a whisper, and she kissed Jeff's cold lips. She put her head on his chest. *Oh, dear God, I don't want to believe this.* She felt like she was sleepwalking and that this was all just a horrible dream or some sick joke. Perhaps if she could just remember something good, they'd both wake up and laugh uproariously at the absurdity of it all. But it was too hard to think of anything good in that awful moment. It was too much to bear.

She sat up, shaking her head.

"Henrietta?" Craig said.

"The blood. I don't want to touch it anymore," she said, rubbing it off on her skirt, the finality of their life together all at once hitting her.

"We can go then," he said.

But she didn't want to leave, knowing it would be the last time she'd ever see him. "Oh, Jeff, I loved you so, so much, more than anything or anyone," she whispered, speaking to his closed eyes. "Good-bye and good night, my love, until we meet again in Spirit." She kissed his hair, which was the only thing that still looked and felt normal, and slowly left his side.

"Now, now, Henrietta, you go ahead and let it out," Craig said, offering his shoulder for her to cry on.

And she did.

"Come, I'll walk you home."

"No, I need to call my parents first," she said. "Let's go to the lab; there's a phone there."

Afterward, in the doctor's cottage, she wobbled and would have collapsed onto the floor if Craig had not been there to catch her. He swept her up effortlessly. He carried her upstairs to her bedroom and placed her in the bed, where she and Jeff had made love only two nights ago. She grabbed part of the sheet and held it to her face, breathing in Jeff's smell that still lingered.

Craig took off her shoes and started to unbutton the top of her blouse, startling her.

But he stopped after the first button. "Try to rest awhile, Henrietta," Craig said. He tucked her under the covers, fully dressed. "I'll make sure Joe and Altie are with the children and that everything's secure," he said. He went into the bathroom, getting a washcloth to wipe off the dried remnants of the killer's blood from her lips, cheeks and hands.

As he did that, she noticed his bandage again.

"I'll come back to check on you in a little while," Craig said.

Henrietta suddenly realized he was in the bedroom she'd shared with her husband and wanted him to leave in that instant. "Thanks, but that's not necessary. I'd like to sleep now. Joe and Altie are here."

"Well, if you need anything or if you decide you want me to stay in the doctor's cottage with you, just give me a ring, okay? I'll either be at the hospital or in my office at the Agency."

She didn't awaken until the next morning when she heard some Indians talking in the front yard. Grief and paranoia ripped through her, and she feared for her children. Not knowing where they were, she leaped from the bed and ran down the hall, checking first in

Jeffie's room. Relief came on the other side of the door. "Oh, thank you, dear Lord," she whispered. Joe's and Altie's personal items were lying on the extra bed that was next to Jeffie's crib. And that meant they were with the children.

Henrietta returned to her bed just as she remembered she still needed to contact Jeff's father. She pulled the covers over her head. *I can't do it! I can't tell him.*

She steeled herself and dialed the number at Clayborn Plantation.

No answer. She opened the side table drawer and pulled out a little orange address book. She dialed Lindsey's Pharmacy and then the Clayborn Orphanage & School.

No luck. But she did find out that there was talk in town about Dr. Colonel firing his household help. His whereabouts, as well as Brodie's, were unknown. Despite her growing anxiety, coupled with a frayed state of mind, she forced herself to get up, moving slowly toward the stairs. She heard her children in the kitchen.

Chapter 36

"Mama!" cried Frannie. She jumped out of Altie's lap and ran over to Henrietta. "What took you so long to wake up?" Her daughter's face was pale and her eyes lusterless.

"I'm so sorry; I'm here now," Henrietta said. She hugged a shaking Frannie with one arm while gesturing out with the other for Annie to join them. "I don't know how I slept that long." Yes, she did. She hadn't wanted to wake up and face a living nightmare.

In their huddle, Annie rubbed her nose on the thick collar of Henrietta's terry-cloth robe. "What's going to happen to us, Mama?" she asked. Her voice was barely there.

Seeing her daughters' suffering, Henrietta felt as if she were splitting apart at the seams again. *No! I have to hold it together; I have to be strong for them.*

"We'll be the ones deciding that," Henrietta said. She straightened her spine with a show of maternal grit for their benefit. "Come; let's sit down at the table and talk about it."

"Do you think Daddy's in Heaven with Grandma Clayborn?" asked Annie. In the harsh morning sunlight, she appeared even more anemic than her sister.

"I sure do," Henrietta said, despite not being sure of anything. In the silence, Altie brought over a cup of coffee and a plate of scrambled eggs with the last of the biscuits Henrietta had made just yesterday morning, but after only a sip and a few small bites, Henrietta pushed the food aside. "Listen," she said. "We need to make some decisions about Daddy and our lives, and y'all can help with that." Her voice was hoarse and uneven.

"What kind of decisions?" Frannie asked.

"I think it's important for all of us to have a say," she said. Water was filling her eyes. "The first thing to decide is where to bury your father. Do you think he'd want to be here in Medichero? Or in South Carolina?"

"I think next to his mama back home would be best," Frannie said. She spoke with a self-assuredness that was both solemn and sweet. "Yes, next to Grandma Clayborn. I think he would like that."

"I think so, too," Annie said, closing her swollen eyes.

"Then I think so, too," Henrietta said. Her voice was nearly a whisper but she was relieved and moved by their sensitive and level-headed suggestion.

Frannie and Annie nodded slowly in unison with their eyes cast down, tears spilling on their nightgowns.

"It's just that we have to find, um, your Grandfather Clayborn first, and tell him about all of this. Of course, we would have to do that anyway." Henrietta paused, realizing how strange her comment sounded. She took in a deep breath to steady herself. "What I'm trying to say is that I've been unable to get in touch with your grandfather by phone. And I've called all over Greenfield; no one's seen him or Brodie for a while."

"Where do you think they are?" Annie asked, rubbing her eyes.

"I don't know," Henrietta said. She grabbed her forehead, feeling the onset of a headache.

She downed two aspirin tablets and stared out of the window, where she'd so often found solace, observing the softness of Medichero mornings. But as she tried to center herself on the camps below, all she seemed to see was an impoverished hodgepodge of Apache Indians moving around on the uneven plateaus like drone bees, searching for their sacred pollen in the flowerless dank earth. Sharp rocks poking out of the mountain looked like decaying bones. Thunderclouds were gathering like small-town southern gossips on flat-topped summits, readying themselves to pound her with rumor and innuendo. Ponderosa pines looked like armies of plastic green soldiers and reminded her of the

Carolina pines that grew near her parents' cabin, the ones that had stood useless as an angry fire ravaged their blessed home and turned it into ruined acreage.

A slam of the screened-in porch door and a knock on the kitchen door interrupted her escalating fears, but before anyone could answer it, the door burst open and banged onto the washstand.

"O-oh, sweet karma," Joe called out after catching his lame leg on the threshold. It sent him sprawling onto the floor. "Don't get up. I'm okay, I'm good."

Without turning around, Altie said, "Nice to have you here, husband."

"I had to check on the new flu patients at the hospital this morning. But they are already better," he said. His voice held a strange sort of astonishment. Instead of popping up from the fall, as he usually did, Joe shut the door with a foot and began crawling on his hands and knees toward Altie. But he abruptly stopped short, jerking up his right hand as if he'd caught a splinter in it. "*Ch'iin*, be gone, devil!"

"What's the matter?" Henrietta asked.

"There's something sharp on the floor, or rather, in my skin now," he said. He didn't sound angry. He simply plucked out whatever it was from his palm.

"Oh," Henrietta said, remembering. "A porcelain pitcher fell and broke on the floor the other night; it was during the storm when I was waiting for

Jeff. Sorry, I thought I'd gotten up all the pieces," Henrietta said.

She bent her head down and pinched the bridge of her nose. The aspirin had been useless. When she looked up, Joe had the handle of the pitcher in one hand and was holding up a small part of the spout in the other.

"These broken-off fragments are often difficult to find, but a full repair can't be achieved without retrieving all of them and putting them back in their proper place," he said.

He gave Henrietta an intense and serious look, and even through her rising grief, she understood what Bears Repeating was saying: he was speaking in shaman code, trying to hint about the healing advantages of another soul retrieval for her.

"But we have so much to do today," Henrietta started, her voice slightly defensive.

"*Ch'ün!* Found another one," he said, pulling it out of his pinky finger.

"Listen, I don't need that pitcher, and to be honest, right now, I don't care one hoot about putting it or anything else back together!" she snapped. "All I can think about is Jeff, and what we need to do for him today," Henrietta said. "But I can't seem to think clearly. My head is pounding. And I haven't been able to get ahold of Jeff's father. He doesn't even know yet." She threw up her hands, trudged back to the kitchen table and dropped herself onto a chair.

"Dr. Colonel?" Joe asked.

"Yep, you got it." She connected with his knowing gaze, and they exchanged a silent glance of grave concern. "He doesn't answer the phone, and no one back home has seen him for days."

"Uh-oh," Joe said almost inaudibly before speaking clearly. "You and the children must be protected with bear medicine." Still on the floor, he crossed his legs, closed his eyes and began singing in his native language.

"What does he mean, Mama?" Frannie whispered with some alarm.

"I think Mr. Joe wants to say some Apache prayers for us," Henrietta said. She didn't want to even consider the implications of Dr. Colonel's unknown whereabouts right now. She had way too many other things to do and think about today.

"We can stay with the children while you do what is needed," Altie said. "Or they could come to our place for the day. *Shimaa*, my mother, is there making Apache toys and foodstuffs for a charity craft fair."

"But, I hate the thought of having them go out today," Henrietta said. Her voice was filled with apprehension and worry. "I don't want to leave them."

"It's okay, Mama," Frannie said. "We can go with Miss Altie. You need to get things done for Daddy."

"Annie, would you be all right with that, too?" Henrietta asked. She touched her daughter's chin. "So that I can go to Tularosa and see about moving your daddy back home next to his mama, like we talked about?"

"Yes, Mama," Annie said. Her voice was almost a whisper. "I guess as long as we're with Miss Altie and Miss Naomi, it'll be okay."

"Oh, my sweeties," she said. She was hugging her daughters and letting go of another waterfall of tears. "I don't want to leave you, but you'll be safe with them. And I'll feel better about going to town."

"Don't cry, Mama," Frannie said. "It's all right."

Henrietta hugged them even tighter. "I know y'all will be my brave girls until then."

"We can do the cooking tonight," Altie said. "You will need to rest."

Henrietta shook her head. "You know, this may sound strange, but I'd rather do it. I need time to think and plan our future. And I do some of my best thinking when I'm cooking. Let's just meet back here about, say, seven o'clock. That should give me enough time."

"Sounds good. I will get Jeffie ready," Altie said, and left the room. After a few minutes, she came back with the toddler and her Apache-style backpack.

Joe stood up, and Henrietta thought she sensed a question from him.

"Listen, Joe," Henrietta said before he could talk. "If there's time for some more, um, bear prayers with you after I get back and before I need to make supper, I'll come down to your place. Okay?"

She realized she was still trying to be discreet about her participation in spirit medicine in front of her children when it dawned on her: Why shouldn't she tell them about something that had so profoundly helped her? And she wondered if she could become a mother shaman for her children's hurt souls. She decided she would tell them about her spiritual dealings with Bears Repeating and their father's research, but would wait for the right time.

"Bye-bye, my babies ... I'll see you tonight," Henrietta called out from the front door. Joe, Altie and the girls waved, turned and started down the hill as Craig came trotting up.

"Henrietta, I hate to bother you right now, but I have some paperwork for you to sign. May I come in?"

Seeing his still-bandaged hand, Henrietta hesitated. "Sorry, but I need to get ready to go to town," she decided to say, pulling her robe tighter around her.

"It'll only take two seconds," he said, holding up a file folder. "I promise." He cracked a smile, revealing his deep dimples.

"Well, okay." With some reluctance, she waved him in.

"How are you doing, Henrietta?" he asked as they entered the kitchen. His voice was soft.

"I suppose as well as can be expected." She poured a cup of coffee for him, wishing he wouldn't sit down.

"So, Joe and Altie are looking after the kids today?" he asked, taking a chair at the table.

"Yes, so that I can work on Jeff's... funeral arrangements and start thinking about where we'll need to... move," she said, her voice cracking. *Dadgummit.* She didn't want to get emotional in front of him again. "I assume you'll need this house for another doc . . . "

"Henrietta, listen, please know that you can stay in the doctor's cottage for as long as you need," he said and smiled warmly. "Besides, my office has already contacted a couple of part-time doctors from the army base, and they'll be commuting, as needed."

"Oh, thank goodness," she said. She was relieved she would have time to get battle-ready for Dr. Colonel and not have to move out right away.

"As I mentioned, I wouldn't bother you right now, but I've started the process for you to get the insurance money, which is why I brought this," he said. He pulled out a form from the file folder. "If you'll just sign this paper, I'll get out of your hair." He gave her a pen from the inner pocket of his suit jacket. "Unless you'd like some help today." He grinned and didn't seem threatening, as he had the night before.

Without a reply, she accepted the pen and paper, sat down and stared blankly at the document, unable to decipher the words. "I'm sorry, but I've got a terrible headache."

"Clearly understandable."

"Can we do this later?" She put her head down on top of her hands and the table.

"Of course, but . . ."

She lifted herself back up only to find Craig's ice-blue eyes transfixed on hers. Unexpectedly, he reached out and gently covered her hands with his unbandaged one, and she felt something like a light charge pass from his fingers to hers.

What is he doing? My husband just died! She yanked her hands under the table and diverted her eyes.

"Oh, I didn't mean to offend ... I'm sorry," he said.

She felt herself blushing and desperate to get back to something impersonal. "About the policy, then." Her voice was gravelly.

"Of course! It's a good one, about $25,000, but we really should get the ball rolling on it right away, which is why I'm here about it this morning."

"Well, at least we'll be able to buy our own home with that," she said. She hurriedly signed her name where he had marked an X.

"I assume you'll be moving back to South Carolina?"

"I haven't decided yet."

"You mean there's a chance you might stay around here?" he asked, leaning forward.

His voice, enthusiastic, made her uncomfortable. She walked over to the sink. "No, I'm considering Georgia, where my parents are living now." She filled a glass and swallowed more aspirin.

"I see," he said, slumping back in the chair.

"Honestly, I can't think about that right now. I feel like I need to get going today on those arrangements for Jeff, even though I haven't been able to get in touch with Jeff's father. Apparently no one's seen him in several days."

"That's strange. Why not?"

"I don't know exactly, maybe he's just off somewhere for the weekend, but I don't see how I can wait to find him. Craig, where's Jeff now?"

"He's at the morgue in Tularosa."

"That's what I figured. I don't want my Jeff lying on some cold slab. I want to get him into a funeral home in Tularosa as soon as possible. I'm hoping they can help me move Jeff to a funeral home in South Carolina. We've decided to bury him in the family cemetery."

"Of course," Craig said, pausing. "Hey, I just thought of something: maybe the funeral home in South Carolina could also help you with locating Jeff's father and notifying him."

"Yes, that would be of great help; I hope you're right," she said.

"Cal Nation runs the best funeral home in Tularosa, and he's a personal friend of mine," Craig said. "I could take you there and help out, if you'd like."

"That's really not …" she started. Craig was being so nice and helpful, and she could really use some support right now. "Yes, if you don't mind, I'd really appreciate that."

"Do you want to go now?"

"Just give me a few minutes to get dressed," she said. Henrietta started toward the stairs, but stopped. "Perhaps we should call first?"

"How about I do that while you're getting ready?" Craig offered.

Less than an hour later, in her black suit dress and twisting her white cotton gloves in her hands, Henrietta sat at a highly polished table in the Tularosa Funeral Home conference room with Craig.

"I just spoke with Mr. Bailey from the Greenfield Funeral Home," said Cal. He was coming back into the room. Cal was a large, heavyset man with Indian facial features, but he had graying short hair and an all-white beard. He looked like a native Santa Claus, as he clasped her hands in his. "You don't have to worry, Mrs. Clayborn," he said. "We're able to coordinate the moving logistics with the morgue here and with Mr. Bailey in South Carolina. Everything will be taken care of as you wish and with the utmost respect." He placed her hands down softly before pulling up a chair next to hers.

If she hadn't felt so overwhelmed and sad, Henrietta would've smiled at this sweet, jolly-looking funeral director. Instead, all she could do was nod her head.

"Mr. Bailey also wanted me to express his deepest and sincerest condolences and to assure you that he'd handle all the details on his end."

"Will he be able to help with finding and notifying Jeff's father?" Craig asked.

"Given the circumstances, he thought it best to contact the local police about that," Cal said.

"I think that's a good idea, too, don't you, Henrietta?" Craig asked.

"Yes," she said. Her voice was almost a whisper. *At least I won't have to be the one to tell him.*

"They'll be able to find him, I'm sure," Craig added.

"Craig, I can't thank you enough for going with me today," Henrietta said later. They had arrived back at the doctor's cottage and were standing in the foyer.

"I was happy to help and be with you," he said. "Listen, I don't mean to be rude, but you look tired, Henrietta. If you want to take a nap, I can hang around so you can rest without worry."

"I am tired. But I've got two things left to do today. First, I need to go to Joe and Altie's place to check in with the children and, um," she said, ending vaguely, not wanting to divulge that she intended to seek Joe's medicine. "After that, I'm going to make us some comfort food tonight for supper. I already have everything needed and might as well use it before it spoils, anyway."

"That sounds a bit ambitious after the day you've had. Maybe you should rest instead. The gals at the office and I can pull together a meal, even though I'm not too good at it," he said. He held up his still-bandaged left hand.

"Thanks, but you know what? I need to keep moving. I need to do something ordinary and normal, like cooking. It'll also give me time alone to think about what I need to do for Jeff … and my children's futures," she said. She was tearing up. "Besides, I'm sure you've got things to do. But why don't you join us for supper tonight?"

"I'd be honored. What time would you like us here?"

"How about seven-ish?"

Chapter 37

Once again inside the Locos' ceremonial teepee, Henrietta sat cross-legged on the blanket edged with repeating bear motifs. She began to cry.

"Oh, Joe, I've been trying so hard to be strong for the children and to just get done with Jeff's funeral arrangements," she said in between sobs. She covered her face with her hands. "But I don't know how I can possibly hold up much longer. I can't live without Jeff. I don't have the will or the energy. Why in the world did I think I could make dinner for everyone tonight? I must be insane." She rubbed her watery eyes. "I just want to give up and die."

Not even Joe's healing gifts can pull me through this one, she thought. But as she looked at him, she heard drumbeats from somewhere down the hill. With firelight dancing on the shadowed canvas, Joe's face seemed to shape-shift into something strange and unexpected. He looked like some oversized owl with large round eyes, high-arching eyebrows and a feathered heart-sculpted head.

At first, the bird-like Joe said nothing. He simply returned her stare with his huge unblinking eyes. After a shake of her head, he transformed again, returning to his usual form seconds before he finally began to speak.

"Just when you think things couldn't get any worse, just when you doubt everything and are completely confused," Joe said, "that's the time when you can make the most spiritual progress, if you can do just one thing. If you can surrender …" He spoke softly.

"Hey, wait a minute." She wasn't quite ready to embrace his customary ministering, even though she had come to him for that very purpose. "Whatever that one thing is, how could I possibly do it? I've lost the love of my life. I've lost the father of my children, my home and even my childhood home. Didn't you hear what I said? I'm broken. I can't surrender anything. I want to give up."

The unflinching big-eyed stare was back.

"If we return to Jeff's ancestral home, assuming we'd be allowed back in, I wouldn't survive," she said. "It'd be impossible to live in Greenfield and fight off the cruel gossip, the malicious whispers, the mean stares and the constant blame thrown at me. Especially without my parents there anymore." She sighed deeply, letting her head fall again into her hands.

"Gossip? That doesn't sound right. Blame? For what?"

"For the unforgivable sin of taking away Greenfield's most favored and adored son," she said.

She raised her head back up. "Jefferson Pridgen Clayborn was born to carry out the traditions and old ways of his ancestors. Sound familiar? He was revered almost like a mythological god, southern style. I will be blamed for his absence, for his death, regardless of who actually killed him—Dr. Colonel will ensure it. It will be a subtle form of punishment, but it will be felt with great force nonetheless."

"Don't you think you're being a tad melodramatic?" He turned to light a large beeswax candle on the altar table.

"I know you don't understand what I'm talking about. But Dr. Colonel will see to my continual torment; I'll be in small-southern-town hell," she said.

"Only if you see it that way. Only if you feel that way," Joe said. He spoke calmly in the flickering light, moving his attention to the arrangement of his rattles and other sacred objects on the altar table, preparing for the soul retrieval. "You'll become what you're feeling and stuffing into that mind of yours right now, even if it's false information."

"I'm not stuffing anything. I'm suffering and I'm afraid."

"Let me ask you something: Why are you so hell-bent on making negative life forms all around you with your miserable-feeling, indecisive thoughts? You don't get that you're using poison pins to stick bad mental notes on your life's bulletin board."

"I'm stuck all right. I don't want to be here. I don't want to go back to Greenfield and live anywhere near a madman. I don't want to move to some little run-down place in Georgia, where my parents had to move in disgrace. I don't want to go anywhere. I just want to give up and die, and be with Jeff in Heaven." She was weeping again.

Joe shook his head. "Now's not the time to give up, but to surrender up." He handed her a tissue from a box on the altar table.

"You've got to be kidding! She grabbed the tissue and blew her nose. "I've nothing left! Tell me what I must surrender?"

His eyes narrowed, his mouth twisted. "For starters, your selfish disregard for your children and your attachment to this ridiculous victimhood." His tone was stern.

Henrietta dropped her mouth open and jerked her shoulders back, blindsided by this unexpected slap of words.

Joe stood up and actually started wagging his finger at her. "It's time to surrender up this self-pity and step into your power. Now!" he said.

"Why, why … you've got some nerve. Don't you think, after all the violence I've endured, after getting raped, after losing the only man I've ever loved, that I have the right to a little self-pity?" She felt the resentment she held for Dr. Colonel rising.

"No, not at all," he said. He continued to challenge her. "Not even Jeff's passing gives you the excuse of letting in the darkness without care or thought. This blocks your ability to feel good and make good decisions."

Tilting her head up, she scowled at him. He no longer had the guise of a wise bird. He was more like an annoying squirrel scolding her from a limb for stealing his hidden nuts.

"Henrietta, there comes a point in time when every being has to make a monumental choice about life and death. This is one of those times," Joe said. His voice was again calm. He picked up the turtle-shell ashtray with dried sage. After lighting it, he began to gently massage the sage smoke with a prayer feather, navigating it in a clockwise direction.

"But I don't want to choose." She realized she sounded like a petulant little brat, but she didn't care. Maybe it had been a bad idea to come here while she was so grief-stricken. She thought about going back to the doctor's cottage, but because she was also tired, she got up and moved next to the altar table instead. Bending down, she touched the wooden statue of Mother Mary before raising it to her heart. *How in the world did you survive your son's death?*

"Regardless of what's happened, you can decide to be who you are, and live," Joe said, continuing with the sage-smudging ritual. "Or you can opt to do nothing, which is the same thing as choosing the alternative. Henrietta, what do you want for yourself and your children? Do you want life or death?" He stopped to face her.

"I don't know. I'm at a loss." Tears were rolling down her face. She lowered her head, still sensing his eyes on her. She felt exposed and a shame that made her tremble, as if Jesus were looking upon her in person.

She put down the statue, but was startled to clearly hear an inner answer to what she'd thought had been a rhetorical question to Mother Mary: *You will learn, beloved. And choose. This is why you are here.*

"Listen, the Great Spirit has given you free will for the very purpose of making this all-important choice," Joe said. He added more sage to the shell before re-lighting it. "Think about it. The Great Spirit didn't have to do it. He could've simply forced you to do whatever He wanted. But He didn't. Why? Because the Great Spirit's nature is to love, create and grow in pure freedom. Because we're made in His image, it's our true nature to want to love, create and grow in pure freedom, though there's much in us that might obscure this truth."

"But," she started, as he laid the turtle shell down on the altar table.

"Please, no more buts," he said. He held up a palm. He limped away from the altar table and sat down. "You can choose to live or die right now! The Great Spirit's not going to force you to make the preferred choice. And neither am I. But kindly take

notice"—he pointed the prayer feather toward her—
"there are consequences to each. It helps when you
know what they are."

She went back to the bears repeating blanket
and plopped down. "If I choose to die?"

He looked down at his knees and tilted his head
as if to turn his ear toward the voice of some invisible
presence. "The dark spirits win, and inevitably you'll
have to learn your life lessons in another, perhaps more
difficult way."

"Lovely," she said. She stared into the fire.

"Did you know that sarcasm and a self-pitying
victim mentality actually give more power to the dark
spirits and attract more of the bad stuff you say you
don't want?" His eyebrows arched and his mouth
tensed. "That's how and why they quickly learn exactly
how to play you, to break you, to cause you to give up.
That is what they need to survive." Still holding the
smoldering sage, he made a swift wafting motion
toward his face with the prayer feather, as if to ward off
the dark spirits she had allowed in. "They actually live
off the negative choices, emotions and reactions you're
making. You're like a feeding trough for them right
now."

"How grotesque," she said. She was becoming
disgusted by all this talk of dark spirits. "And if I choose
life?"

He gestured with the feather as if he was
conducting an orchestra and his tenor became

singsongy. "You'll see and be the reality of who you truly are."

She sighed deeply. "Is that baffling statement supposed to inspire me? I'm hanging at the end of my rope here. Come on; give me something I can understand."

"If you can do this right now, that is, if you can choose life at this critical point, which means surrendering your self-pity and false beliefs about yourself, and start choosing better feeling thoughts, you'll be making tremendous progress on the sacred inner path."

"Tell me why I should care."

"You'll win in oneness!" He moved the feather to make a giant exclamation mark.

"What are you talking about?" She shook her head and threw up her hands, growing sick and tired of his mystical mumbo jumbo.

"Your reward will be an ascending spiritual joy that'll transcend your suffering and other human limitations, but, alas, cannot be effectively expressed very well with my poor, limited vocabulary."

"That couldn't possibly be self-pity I hear?" She realized she was being sarcastic again.

"I'm simply trying to say that words alone cannot adequately convey the ecstatic, bubbling joy of knowing oneness with the Great Spirit within yourself. That is where all the things you want are already alive."

He kneeled in front of her, fanning the sage fumes toward her face.

"I don't understand," she said, squinting. Eventually, she hoped she would think back to this time and see the wisdom Bears Repeating was giving her. But, right now, her mind was too balled up; her heart was still tight-fisted with grief and anger.

"You just have to open yourself to experience it." He put the turtle shell down on the blanket to gently pat the top of her shoulders, perhaps for emphasis or to redirect her thinking, and she noticed his sage-fragrant hands were beautifully shaped, like Jeff's.

"How can I do that?" she asked.

"First you have to make a life decision," he said. He gave her a final pat. "That means you must choose to live life by being who you are." He got up and returned to his seat next to the altar. "To be who you are, you must understand who you are. You do that by developing your inner life with ongoing, daily meditation in the *Kopave* with the Great Spirit in you. Through this process of walking the sacred inner path, of seeking first the kingdom within, you'll eventually learn how this life is simply designed to lead you to understand what the ancients knew, what Jesus's true teachings were about, what shamans explore."

"And what is that?"

"That we're all spiritual beings going with the flow of the Great Spirit. We live, we create, we experience, and we learn, we grow, we feel good. We change into something better. Physical death is but another change."

She repeated what he'd said silently in her mind.

"And once you get that, you'll begin experiencing freedom from the darkness and a sense of wholeness more beautiful than you ever imagined. It's the ultimate soul retrieval; it is the retrieval of feeling good and having clarity, of remembering the love, wisdom and power of who you really are."

She exhaled, at last trying to accept his counsel and allow it penetrate into the marrow of her deep sadness. She searched her memory for good-feeling thoughts.

Joe lit the three remaining ceremonial candles that stood on the altar table and the two smaller ones on the table next to the drum. She noticed his attire for the first time since arriving. He was wearing pink Catholic rosary beads like a necklace over his short-sleeved purple and white panel shirt. She smiled.

"It's possible you also could start developing other spiritual gifts," he said. "You might learn how to, for example, heal others or connect with your loved ones on the other side, even while you're still residing in this human body."

"Really? I could learn how to communicate with Jeff? While I'm still here?" Her heart skipped a beat. It was the first genuinely positive and feel-good sensation of hope she'd had since Jeff died. "Okay, Joe, you're

finally making a real dent in the ole thick noggin here."
She knocked gently on her head with a fist. "I'd do or
learn anything to stay connected to Jeff forever. I'll even
try to make the right choice."

"Not exactly the motivation I was looking for,
but let's go with it. Are you choosing life, then?"

"Yeah, I think so."

"You were so enthusiastic and all, I couldn't
tell," he said.

"Sorry. It's just that I'm still so bone tired," she
said. She sighed and touched her temples with her
fingers. "I think I need a spiritual transfusion."

"*Ha'aa*. It takes a lot of energy to carry around
grief and so much anger."

"Yes, apparently." She pursed her lips.

"Try to let go of all that weighs you down.
Now's the time to surrender it up," Joe said.

"Okay, um." She paused to gather her thoughts.
"You know, there is something I want to surrender, or
at least get off my chest before we begin."

"Ah, very good."

"It still really bothers me that I don't know who
Jeffie's biological father is. And maybe it doesn't matter,
especially now that Jeff is . . . not here. It's just, well …"
She remembered Altie telling her how Joe's father had
been a magazine photographer who had never returned
after getting his mother pregnant. "Haven't you ever
wondered about your own father's identity?"

Joe nodded.

"I wish I knew for sure," she said.

"I'll seek answers in Spirit."

"You can find out something like that? By journeying within?"

"If Spirit wills it, and you're clear enough to hear it."

"Wow, I didn't know you could do that," she said. "Did you do that, for your own father?"

Again Joe nodded.

"Okay, here's something else I'd like to know." She leaned forward. "Is Jeff … is he okay?"

"I can see if he's gone to the Light, if you'd like."

"You can do that, too?"

"Ha'aa," Joe said, nodding a third time.

"That's so great! The Light. Joe, is that Heaven?"

"We only know that Spirit wants us to go toward it once we leave Mother Earth. And it is wonderful."

As he answered, Altie came into the teepee, wearing her ceremonial leather dress. "The children fell asleep," she said. She sat behind her drum. "So did *Shimaa*, my mother, but they are with her. They are safe."

"Are you ready to choose life, Henrietta?" Joe asked again.

"I think so."

"We are what we think. Do you want to be the uncertainty you're expressing?"

"No. I want to be positive and feel good."

"Then be and live it by believing it!"

She smiled because she knew in her heart that life was what God and Jeff wanted for her, even though she was in mourning and would be for a long time.

"Now, let's try again. Are you ready to choose life?"

"Yes, I am." And she heard the inner voice again: *You wanted to learn, beloved. This is why you're here.*

"Let's begin," Joe said. He began summoning the wisdom and healing power of the Great Spirit from the four sacred directions of the universe. He shook his rattle in unison with Altie's drumming. Sage fumes performed their cleansing dance upon the air. And the teepee was again enlightened with more than just firelight and ceremonial candles.

As in the first soul retrieval, after Joe rose from his supine position, he blew the sweet-scented mist over Henrietta's face and chest. Only this time, he did so in three distinct sprays before helping her sit up.

Henrietta noticed immediately how different she felt from her first soul retrieval experience. She was anything but giddy. She felt calm and still curious about what Joe would say, but not overly anxious.

As she was trying to form her first question, Joe began offering a travelogue of his inner journey.

"Symbolically, I traveled in a canoe to an island in the middle of a great pond," Joe said. "When I arrived, an old Indian woman came out of a small forest and greeted me with a quartz crystal about the size and length of my soul-catcher," he said, holding it up. "She explained that this crystal contained the piece of your soul that fled because it couldn't face a horrible secret."

Joe's voice became animated as he continued his storytelling: "I thanked the old woman for safeguarding your soul part in the crystal and asked if I could place it in my soul-catcher as a way to carry it back to you, which the old woman agreed to. That was the first soul part I blew into you."

"After I placed the crystal in my soul-catcher," Joe continued, "and it fit nicely in there, the great chocolate-colored horse from your vision quest trotted up next to me and offered me a ride to a field in the middle of the island."

"You mean Hildegard?"

He nodded. "In the field was a massive fruit tree, with some kind of exotic fruit I've never seen before. And it had a house-like structure built into its trunk. That's where I found your second lost soul fragment. She was hiding in the trunk house behind a wall that she'd built out of the tree's fruit.

"She'd gone into the tree trunk looking for Jeff, but, of course, he wasn't there. She waited because she hoped he'd eventually come back to rescue her. But deep down she knew it was a false hope, because she believed he was gone forever. Your soul fragment did not want to confront those fears and contradictory thoughts. So she built the fruited wall around herself and refused to leave her own self-limiting refuge, even for the sake of the children."

"Oh, it sounds so awful when you say it like that," Henrietta said. "I wish I could change the way I've reacted to things in this life. I wish I could've been stronger."

"Ah, but like all writers, you always have the option of revision. Of correcting the mistakes you've made in the first draft."

Henrietta smiled.

"So what happened after I built the fruit wall?"

"I reminded your soul part that she was needed for you to realize a full healing and be able to make good life decisions. I asked her to come back with me. But she was, at first, being stubborn."

Henrietta rolled her eyes.

"Fortunately, your horse friend, Hildegard, was there to trigger an inner memory. And the mare suggested to your soul part that she tear down the wall and put the fruit in a basket for use as medicine as well as nourishment for the journey home."

"That sounds like a practical idea."

"Your soul part thought so too, and agreed to come with us," Joe said. "Hildegard took us, me and your two soul parts, across the pond and up to the mountain healing lodge. There, Bear and another power animal welcomed us and joined us in the main gathering room. They came to answer our questions."

"And what did we ask them?" Henrietta felt her old curiosity stirring and growing stronger.

"Through them, Spirit spoke of Jeffie being the son of both Jeff and Dr. Colonel."

"Oh! That would mean he's Jeff's," she said. Henrietta realized, of course, Joe's affirmation offered no tangible or scientific proof. But she wanted to believe it. "Oh, thank you, dear Lord."

"Yes, but that message came with a warning," Joe added.

"A warning?" Her smile vanished.

"As I said before, there comes a time when everyone must make an important choice in life. Because he's the son of Jeff and Dr. Colonel, little Jeffie is predisposed to, let's say, extreme journeys of will. There will be a critical point in his life, when he'll have to choose to be either more like his father or more like his grandfather. It may appear that he has no choice in the matter, but that will be an illusion."

"How do you know that?"

"I know because free will is an immutable law of the Great Spirit. We are in charge of making our choices. We all are the authors of our own lives."

"Can we help Jeffie make the best choice?"

"Yes, of course. Jeffie will have lots of help. From you, from me, from your spirit guardians and from his own. Also from your new power animal."

"My new one?"

"*Ha'aa.* Your new power animal is the blue jay."

"The blue jay!" Henrietta said.

"It's a bird that only passes through these parts. But he's often a permanent resident in South Carolina and Georgia. There's a message in that as well."

"What kind of message?"

"Hold on," Joe said. "I'll happily give you the medicine of the blue jay, but first, you'll want to know the rest of this inner story."

"Oh, yes, of course!"

"Right before the journey ended, I was told Jeff has indeed gone to the Light. And actually, he's become something of a spirit guide for you. So even though it's perfectly understandable that you are in mourning for his physical presence and will be for as long as you need to be, you can take comfort in knowing that Jeff is still with you. You can continue to have a relationship with him, although it will require a new frame of mind on your part. I'll show you how to achieve a higher understanding of this in the days to come, but it's a gradual learning process, as we open our minds and hearts to such possibilities."

"Joe, you've made me feel a lot better about Jeff, my life and the future. I'll look forward to learning more about how to stay in touch with him by myself." Henrietta paused. "But you blew three times... What was the third part?"

"The medicine of the blue jay. As I said, he's a new power animal who will function not only for you, but also for your little J," Joe said. He had a perplexing wide grin on his face.

"I thought blue jays were bully birds and nest thieves. They sound like a better power animal for Dr. Colonel," Henrietta said.

"It's true that blue jays can have those tendencies," Joe said. "But they also bring good qualities. The jay can show us how to use our power in the right way so that we achieve our highest potential by living in the present and creating good by focusing on the good. He reminds us not to obsess about the past or future. He shows us how to let go, to live in the present, to be aligned with who we truly are."

"Hmm. I wish I had known about that kind of power before," she said. She was thinking back to Dr. Colonel and the way he continuously tried to control her with threats and attacks.

"There's more to know about the jay, just as there's more to you now than before."

"I'd love to learn more about what that more is, but I can't right now." She looked down at her wristwatch. "It's already three o'clock."

Joe raised his eyebrows.

"Sorry, but if I'm going to make that supper, I must go now." She was feeling so much better she almost smiled.

Chapter 38

After changing into a blue shirtdress and donning a frilly yellow apron her mother had made for her, Henrietta started dinner.

She would be making Jeff's most-loved dish as well as Miss Julia's and her parents' favorites. In memory of Jeff, she'd already placed a pot roast surrounded by vegetables from Joe and Altie's garden in the oven. In honor of her mother, she'd made Elizabeth's famous cracklin' cornbread recipe in two Lodge iron skillets. The baked cornbread was already cooling on the sideboard. As a tribute to her father, she was in the process of preparing a couple of cinnamon apple pies, a dessert he loved so much he would often eat his slice before the meal. And in remembrance of Julia, sweet Miss Julia, Henrietta would serve the butterscotch fudge bars her mother-in-law had adored.

As always, the smell of roasting beef, the bacon bits of cracklin' cornbread and cinnamon-coated apples invoked wonderful childhood memories, feelings of love and laughter. And she desperately needed those happy memories, now more than ever.

Yes, this feels right, she thought as tears reemerged and fell down her cheeks. *Tonight, with this warm meal, we honor the angels we've been blessed to know. And tomorrow, we go home to face the devil.* Thank God, she had arranged for her parents to meet them at the airport.

She wondered if the Greenfield police would be able to find Dr. Colonel. Hoping so, she switched on the transistor radio she kept in the kitchen. It was playing Bobby Darin's hit song, "Dream Lover." "That's what you are now, Jeff, my dream lover. If you can hear me . . . I love you! Please come to me in my dreams." She spoke out loud, removing some chilled dough from the refrigerator. "And help guide me to know what's right for our children." Tears rolled down her cheeks.

Henrietta was rolling the dough for a piecrust, deep in thought, when she barely heard from behind her the sound of the kitchen door opening. "Are y'all back already? Sorry, it's not quite ready yet."

There was no answer, so she turned around to look. The kitchen door was hanging wide open.

She rinsed the flour off her hands and walked over to the open door. "Altie? Is anyone there?" *Must've been the wind again,* she thought. She closed the door, thinking she should ask someone to check the latch. Remembering what the sheriff had said about her not being safe alone, she backtracked, and turned the dead bolt.

She resumed rolling the dough, imagining Jeff being there. After attaching the flattened dough over the two apple pies, she turned on the faucet and placed her used bowls under running water.

"Just when exactly were you going to tell me about my son, bitch?" Dr. Colonel hissed. His voice came hurling out of the shadows, like a dagger being thrown.

Henrietta jumped, sucked in air and whipped around, sending the rolling pin and a tin of white flour flying into the air.

Shocked by his sudden and frightening appearance, Henrietta's whole body began to shake. Every nerve shouted terror. "Wh ... wh ... what are you ... h ... h... how did you?" she stuttered.

The faucet was still running. Elvis was belting out "Jailhouse Rock" over the transistor radio.

"I said, just when were you going to tell me about killing my son, you white-trash bitch?" Dr. Colonel yelled, rushing at her. He grabbed a fist of her hair at the scalp, making it impossible for her to move.

"I tr... tr... tried to call ... I called ... but you weren't ... Hey, wait. How did you find out ... and get here so quickly? Stop! Ouch! Stop, let go of my hair!"

"You're the reason he's dead, you miserable piece of shit," he said. He was spraying saliva on her face.

"No, no, I'm not!" she cried.

"But, look at you, you cold bitch, making a lovely pie, as though Jeff doesn't matter!" While he held her hair with one hand, he unfastened and jerked off her apron with the other. "You're the one who should've died." He wrapped the apron ties around her neck like a leash before letting go of her hair. He pulled out a surgical knife and held it up to her eyes. "You're the one who should be cut."

She closed her eyes, feeling like a field mouse corned by a nighthawk. But instead of slashing her throat, he moved the knife to her chest. He sliced through the buttons at the top of her dress and cut her bra in two, nicking her between the breasts. She cried out as her blood dripped down her waist and onto the floor.

"If you had just done your part, you evil, worthless woman."

"But you're the one cutting and strangling me. Oh my God!" she gasped. It suddenly hit her that Dr. Colonel must have been here all along; he must have been the one who had argued with Jeff in the hall and strangled him. "You! You did it! Let me see your hands!"

"What are you talking about?" Dr. Colonel shouted, as he unexpectedly let go of the apron ties, shoving her away.

"The sheriff said that Jeff's killer most likely had cut-up hands." She pulled the ties off her bruised neck as she looked down.

His hand was bleeding. "There! You're cut! I knew it. You're a murderer!" She pointed at his hands. "You killed your own son!"

"You don't know what you're talking about. I just cut myself on this knife, right now, goddammit."

She shook her head.

"I would never have done anything to hurt Jeff," he said, waving the knife up and down. "I loved him more than anyone, anything, even Julia. I had everything perfectly arranged for Jeff and me on our beautiful plantation, everything was perfect until you ruined it!" Unexpectedly, Dr. Colonel began to cry uncontrollably.

"Do you expect me to feel sorry for you? You wanted to control Jeff like some kind of human puppet, so much so, you were willing to do anything to achieve it, no matter how foul or evil," she screamed. "That's why you're here. But once again, he refused you, didn't he?"

Dr. Colonel continued to sob.

"Jeff's life and motives were pure and noble. He didn't want to live in your selfish superficial world. It felt like a prison to him. So he came out here to escape, to find his calling and to serve mankind. But you just couldn't live with that, could you? So you murdered him."

"I told you I didn't kill him, goddammit!"

"Of course you didn't. Jeff found out you were here, so he strangled himself just so he could get away from you forever!"

For a full second, they held each other in a hostile gaze, tears in both their eyes. But in the next instant, Dr. Colonel was in front of her and slapped her hard across the face. Henrietta fell back against the apple pies, sending them and her onto the floor.

"I ought to cut your fucking throat for saying that."

The faucet was still running, squealing; Elvis still crooned.

"But I'd rather teach you another lesson." He grabbed her hair at the scalp again while she sat stunned on the floor and jerked her to her knees. "You're going to pay now, and all of those goddamn Indians you love so much are going to pay in short order," he said. He was leaning against her; his breath foul in her face.

"What do you mean?"

"I've already placed heptachlor poison on several campfires."

Because of her father's frequent warnings about burning heptachlor, it took only an instant for her to understand the deadly implications of what he'd done. "No! You can't," she screamed.

"There's nothing you can do about it." He cut open the rest of her dress with the knife and pressed the blade against her cheek.

"Dear God, take command," Henrietta said. She was praying with a fervent calm, finally understanding she had to somehow step into her inner power and transcend the madness.

"Let me tell you somethin', you goddamn white-trash bitch. I'm the one in command," Dr. Colonel said. He pushed her backward and released her hair.

No longer reacting to him or even hearing him, Henrietta willed herself to surrender all traces of fear and hatred. "Oh, Divine Father, Mother Mary, I am here; I am ready to be who I am. I surrender my fear," Henrietta prayed in whispers, concentrating on breathing in and out, focusing on staying in the present, but in calm control of her being, of her emotions. She didn't feel the sharp edge pressed against her cheek. Nor did she feel the rip of her remaining clothes or his cold flesh on her bare legs. She filled her mind and heart with God's golden light and an image. Of running and laughing with Jeff in a heavenly row of peach trees, hand in hand, and free forever. She reached up. She was ready to go there. *I am that I am. I am here.*

Without warning, glass shattered; shards flew across the kitchen. Dr. Colonel sprang to his feet and jerked up his pants. Though she could barely lift her head, she turned toward the crash. There was a rifle barrel poking through the window of the locked kitchen door. Dr. Colonel moved toward the door. Henrietta rolled under the table.

"Stooooop," Brodie shouted. He fired. The bullet skidded across the top of Dr. Colonel's right shoulder. It knocked him back a few feet.

"Why, you goddamn traitor, what do you think you're doing?" Dr. Colonel shouted. Quickly regaining his footing, Dr. Colonel rushed the door and pushed the rifle up just before it discharged again.

"Argh!" Brodie was panicked.

Dr. Colonel grabbed the rifle out of the Brodie's grasp, turning it back on him. "How dare you? There's nothing I hate worse than a goddamn turncoat. Now you're going to pay just like the rest of them."

Henrietta jumped up and brought one of the hot iron skillets down onto Dr. Colonel's head, sending him and freshly baked cornbread onto the floor in a steaming heap.

"Oh, Brodie," Henrietta said. She grabbed the rifle from an unconscious Dr. Colonel before unlocking the door to let Brodie in. "Thank God you're here," she said and hugged him.

"I'm soooorrryyyy, Hen-etta," he said, crying and signing at the same time as he pulled away from her. "I tried to stop him."

"Oh, Brodie, I'm grateful that you came when you did."

"I'm soorryyy," Brodie said again. He looked at her semi-nakedness and began backing up from her.

Henrietta immediately covered herself with the bloody apron and the remains of her dress. "Please don't be embarrassed, Brodie. You saved my life, and I'm grateful." She spoke slowly, looking at him so he could read her lips. "Here, hold this on him while I get something else on," Henrietta signed after giving him the rifle. "Don't let him take it from you again. I'll be right back," she said and ran up the stairs.

When she returned in her bathrobe, Brodie was crying like a wailing dog. The rifle was bobbing pitifully up and down in his arms.

"Please, Brodie," she said, signing. "Hold the gun steady on Dr. Colonel so I can call for help." She turned off the faucet, oven and radio.

"I'm soorryyy," he kept saying, oblivious to the stirrings of the man on the floor.

Before Henrietta could take another step toward the phone, Dr. Colonel roared: "You goddamn turncoats!" He hurled himself at Brodie, tackling him to the floor.

Henrietta reached for the other skillet of cornbread, but in a blink of an eye, the kitchen was packed with pureblood Apache Indians. They were dressed in full-feathered ceremonial regalia.

It was Big Eagle Feathers who moved first, hurling himself toward the three of them with the speed and accuracy of a well-thrown tomahawk. In reflex, Henrietta pulled the skillet up to her face as though it might somehow deflect a fatal body blow. But the impact didn't come. Instead, time seemed to shift and fill with a strange mix of simultaneous, slow-moving commotion.

Chairs snapped like toothpicks. Feathers flew. Indians were making shrill war noises. Brown-skinned bodies moved as one in a whirling blur. Big Eagle's oversized hands were on expensive Italian lapels. Dr. Colonel was hoisted in the air and hurled across the room. Then for a split second, every movement ceased, every eye focused on the enemy, now crumpled in the corner like a sack of potatoes.

Undeterred, Dr. Colonel somehow rebounded, shouting, "You goddamn Indians are going to die." Pulling a pistol out of his jacket, he shot Big Eagle Feathers, who toppled like a sequoia. "Now the rest of y'all better stay put, or I'll blow your fucking heads off." Dr. Colonel inched himself to standing by pressing against the wall.

"Holy karma! I am here! I bring peace! I bring love!" It was Joe, running into the ruined kitchen toward Big Eagle Feathers just as another shot rang out.

Dr. Colonel was propelled backward, hitting the plastered wall with a thud. Clutching his heart, he slid back down to the floor. His eyes remained open and defiant, transfixed on the one who had just shot him. Smoke rose from the rifle. It was no longer bobbing up and down in Brodie's arms.

Chapter 39

"Henrietta, Henrietta, are you all right?" Craig shouted. He was banging on the front door of the doctor's cottage. "Stand back." He motioned for Father O'Reilly, who had joined up with them, Altie and the children to gather behind him. The twins were screaming, clinging to Altie's skirt. Just as Craig was about to break the door in, Henrietta unlocked and opened it.

"Henrietta, we heard gunfire. Are you all right? What's happening in there?" Craig said. He pointed toward the kitchen.

"Mama!" Annie cried, running to her mother. "Please don't die, Mama!"

"What's on your face, Mama? Why're you in your bathrobe?" Frannie asked, grabbing her mother's waist. "Ooh, it's dirty," she said, leaning back to hold up sticky hands.

"I'm okay, don't worry. But you can't come in here right now," she said. She looked over at Altie, panicked. "Father and Craig can come in and help, though."

As Altie held Jeffie in her arms, she exchanged a glance with Craig and the priest; it was not necessary to say that something was terribly wrong. The house reeked of death and ruin.

"Henrietta, of course, I will take the children back to our place where they will be safe," Altie offered. "Come with me, girls. Let these men help your mother."

"No, Mama!" the girls screamed. "You're hurt!"

"I'm all right, I promise," she said calmly. She wiped her neck and chest wounds with her hands. "Please, it's best if you go back with Altie. We must take care of an emergency here, and I'll join you there as soon as I can. I promise. But you must let Altie take care of you right now. You'll be safe with her. Please trust me on this."

"Well, okay, Mama, but don't be too long. I'm scared," Frannie said.

"I promise to come as soon as I can, my babies. I love you," she said. She turned toward Altie, reaching for her arm. "Before you go, please listen to me carefully about something important: it's possible that poison has been put on the campfires throughout the reservation. This poison can be deadly. Don't go anywhere near a campfire, avoid all flame like the plague. Do not breathe in the fumes. Warn everyone you see of this."

Altie nodded, turned and led the crying children back toward the refuge of her home.

"I'll call the sheriff," Craig said. He bolted toward the telephone in the living room. "We'll get some men out there to put out those fires safely and spread the word."

"Yes, that'll be best," Henrietta said. "Make sure they do not inhale the fumes! Father, I'm glad you're here. Please come with me, we need your help."

"We?" said Father O'Reilly, following Henrietta. He stopped when he saw the bloody scene in the kitchen. "Oh merciful God." He crossed himself and started to pray.

"Where's Ray, the big one who was shot?" Henrietta asked, signing to Brodie.

"The Indians took him away. I think he's still alive," Brodie said with his hands as Henrietta noticed for the first time all the Indians had left the room.

"Ray Santana was shot trying to save us, Father," Henrietta said.

"Save you? From what? And who's that?" Father O'Reilly asked, pointing to Dr. Colonel, dead on the floor, his pants and eyes grotesquely still open.

"Father, this is Dr. Jules Beaufort Clayborn, also known as Dr. Colonel, Jeff's father, highly respected doctor, good ole boy, and let us not forget, outstanding pillar of the community."

"Henrietta!" Father O'Reilly looked at her, aghast.

But she didn't care that she was speaking of the dead with blasphemous sarcasm in a robe covered in blood, cornbread and apple pie.

"Oh merciful God, come to the aid of um ... Dr. Colonel," Father O'Reilly finally said, after throwing a dishtowel over Dr. Colonel's exposed groin. "Henrietta, what'd you say Dr. Colonel's real name was?"

"Don't worry, Father. I'm sure God knows," Henrietta said. "If you want to stay here and pray, go ahead. But please also pray that Ray's still alive." Then she ran toward the front door, not bothering to bandage her own wounds or change out of her dirty robe.

Chapter 40

Big Eagle Feathers was lying on a bloody floor mat in the main room of his house, where he had been placed for emergency care. Joe and Lily tended to him and were able to stop the bleeding while they waited for Dr. Belzer to arrive. After the doctor came to treat Big Eagle Feathers, the rest of them sat in the kitchen, where Henrietta bandaged her cuts. After a while, Dr. Belzer came out, reporting that he was able to remove the bullet from the upper right side of Big Eagle's abdomen. The lung had been saved from damage. He would live and be fine.

"How are you, Ray?" Henrietta whispered after Dr. Belzer left and Joe took off to check on Altie and the kids. She intended to join them as soon as possible.

He grunted as a way of communicating that he was okay, but his eyes had softened at her approach. So she sat down next to him, noting that his oversized hands held no fresh cuts or scars. But of course it had been Dr. Colonel who'd killed Jeff, despite his denials.

Brodie sat down behind her on the floor, clutching the back hem of her soiled robe like an insecure boy of eight instead of the young man of eighteen he was. Noticeably traumatized, Brodie would no doubt benefit from Joe's bear medicine, and Henrietta made a mental note to line up the two of them before leaving Medichero.

"Ray," she repeated his English name, "you saved me and Brodie here, and even while you were grieving for your own son. I want to thank you."

Lily brought over a fresh blanket and gently placed it over her husband.

"I also wanted to express to you and Lily how much we loved Little Eagle Feathers. We feel your loss and pain. And I'm sorry you got hurt tonight," she said. "Is there anything we can do for you?"

Lily remained quiet while Big Eagle Feathers shook his head. After a few moments, he spoke. "When you give help, it helps you heal," he said. Tears began falling down his cheeks.

She almost couldn't believe it. *He had wanted to help her!* This big hulk of an Indian, who looked and often acted in so frightening a way, had revealed a softer side. Looking at him with new eyes, Henrietta could now see that he was traumatized and surprisingly vulnerable, and she wondered if he, too, would at some point seek Joe's medicine.

"Yes, you know, that's what Jeff was trying to do," Henrietta said. The tears pricked her eyes. "He was trying to heal himself by helping others. He wasn't always successful at it, but he was trying to help."

When Big Eagle nodded, Henrietta was again taken aback.

Sheriff Andrews knocked on the door and walked briskly into the room. Craig and Danny Running Feathers, one of Ray's brothers, followed behind him.

"Sorry to barge in like this, folks, but it can't wait. We've just consulted with Dr. Belzer out there," the sheriff said.

"He says you'll heal up with no problem, Big Eagle," Craig said.

Big Eagle Feathers grunted, but his eyes had cooled and were now unreadable.

"Mr., um, Santana, I'm afraid we must go over a few things before we can let you get some rest," Sheriff Andrews said. "Sorry about that." He cleared his throat. "Danny tells me that you and your other brother overheard Dr. Clayborn and his father, known as Dr. Colonel, arguing on Friday night."

Big Eagle Feathers nodded.

Henrietta gasped. "I knew it."

"Let's see," the sheriff said, glancing down at his notes. "Apparently Dr. Colonel said to Dr. Jefferson Clayborn, and I quote, 'You've only got two days to decide if these goddamn Indians live or die.' After that, Dr. Colonel left the building for the night, and Danny followed him to Tularosa?"

"What?" Henrietta asked, stunned. She was so sure that Dr. Colonel had been responsible for Jeff's death. "Are you saying that Jeff was still alive when Dr. Colonel left?"

"Ha'aa," Danny said, answering for his brother. "We decided that I should trail that Dr. Colonel to make sure he couldn't follow through on his threat of hurting the tribe," Danny explained. "I tracked him to the Tularosa Hotel. He stayed in town for a day before taking off to Alamogordo; I kept watch, tracking him the whole time. Two Feathers was supposed to keep an eye on Jeff."

Brodie squeezed Henrietta's arm before making agitated hand gestures and indecipherable croaking sounds. Finally he signed: "It was a man with two feathers who strangled Jeff!"

"What?" Henrietta said. "Oh dear God. Brodie, why didn't you come and tell me before now?"

"What did he say, Mrs. Clayborn?" Sheriff Andrews asked.

"I don't understand," Henrietta said. "Brodie said that it was a man with two feathers who strangled Jeff!" She was half shouting, half crying.

Danny fell onto his knees, his hands over his face. Big Eagle shook his head and closed his eyes.

"Mrs. Clayborn, who is this young man?" the sheriff asked, pointing to Brodie. "And what's his involvement here?"

"Sheriff, this is Brodie Thompson," Henrietta said. "I've known him since he was a toddler, and I can vouch for him being an honest, good person." She explained about his background and recently going to work as Dr. Colonel's personal assistant. "He's deaf, but he's very good at reading lips," she added. She turned to face Brodie before signing and saying: "Brodie, we need an explanation. Tell us exactly what you saw."

Brodie answered as Henrietta interpreted his sign language: "Brodie says that Dr. Colonel made him come out here to bring Jeff back, and when he realized Dr. Colonel was once again up to no good, Brodie wanted nothing more to do with him. In fact, he was trying to get away from Dr. Colonel, and that's when he found what he thought would be a good spot to hide behind the hospital, just under Jeff's first-floor office window. Brodie says he planned on begging Jeff to take him in, so he wouldn't have to go back with Dr. Colonel."

"So he witnessed Jeff's murder," the sheriff said.

After watching Brodie's hands, Henrietta nodded. "He says it's true about Dr. Colonel blackmailing Jeff with the lives of the entire tribe," she said, turning to face Sheriff Andrews.

"Brodie says that Dr. Colonel had put some of the heptachlor poison on one of the Indian campfires as a way of making sure Jeff took his blackmail threat seriously." Henrietta sighed. She paused to explain to Sheriff Andrews: "Heptachlor is a farming pesticide, but it can cause flu-like symptoms and even death if turned into fumes by fire."

"I suppose that's why those Indians got violently sick last night," Craig said.

"Yes," Henrietta said after watching Brodie's hand movements. She thought of Miss Julia's convenient death and how Dr. Colonel knew how to make people sick, and decided to quiz Brodie later about her suspicions.

"What was the blackmail about?" the sheriff asked.

"It was about giving Jeff an ultimatum," Brodie signed to Henrietta who spoke the words for him. "If Jeff came home permanently without a fight, no one else on the reservation would get sick. But if Jeff refused to leave, Dr. Colonel would make good on his promise to poison the entire tribe."

"Why would a doctor do such a thing?" Craig asked.

"I can answer that," Henrietta offered. "Dr. Colonel hated, and I mean hated with every fiber of his being, that Jeff chose to work here in Medichero instead of his hometown in South Carolina. Brodie knew that, too, didn't you, dear?" She reached out and tenderly touched his arm.

He nodded and continued signing as Henrietta spoke out loud for him. "He says, after Dr. Colonel left, I think Jeff was stunned. He was just sitting at his desk with his head in his hands, and I was asking myself what could I do to help Jeff? What could I do to stop Dr. Colonel? He's crazy and must be stopped."

"I was thinking the same thing," Danny said.

"Jeff looked so tired and worried," Brodie signed. "Then, this big stocky Indian, with two feathers stuck in a headband, came into Jeff's office and slammed the door behind him. They argued about something, I couldn't tell what, but then, the Indian with the two feathers went nuts and started choking Jeff."

"What did you do?" the sheriff asked, looking directly at Brodie and then to Henrietta.

"At first, I thought Jeff would be able to defend himself, but I soon realized that the Indian was going to kill him if I didn't do something fast. I struggled with the window, but it was stuck, maybe in old paint, and I couldn't get it to open," he signed. "I started to pound on the window and shout out as best as I could. The Indian with two feathers looked over at me, and when he saw me, he let go of Jeff, who fell onto the floor. I smashed the window open with the rifle, but the Indian ran out of the office before I could stop him."

"What'd you do after that, Brodie?" Craig asked.

"I crawled through the broken window. Even though I cut my face and wrist on the window glass and was bleeding all over the place, I did everything I could to revive Jeff, honest I did. I gave him mouth-to-mouth resuscitation on the floor, like I learned to do at the orphanage. I picked him up and put him on the bed and tried again. But it was no use. He was dead."

"That explains the blood on Jeff's face and clothing. It came from your attempts to resuscitate him. I see the fresh wound on your cheek," the sheriff said. "But your hands look uninjured."

Brodie pulled up his long sleeve to reveal a large gash on his right wrist.

"Are you sure he was already dead?" Henrietta asked timidly. Tears were pouring from her eyes.

"Mrs. Clayborn, the medical examiner confirmed the cause of death as strangulation," the sheriff interjected before turning back to Brodie. "Why didn't you seek help from the hospital staff?"

"I could see that Jeff was already dead," Brodie signed as he cried. "And I was scared they'd blame me. I was confused. For a while, I stayed there, just trying to figure out what I should do about it. Then I remembered Dr. Colonel and what he would do when he found out about Jeff being dead, and I started to panic. So I locked the door, took the phone off the hook and began praying. First to Jesus, then to Miss Julia. I prayed Miss Julia would tell me what I should do, like she always does. That's when Miss Julia came into the room …." He smiled as if he were remembering something that pleased him.

Henrietta gently reached for Brodie's hands to still them. "But, Brodie, Miss Julia is dead," Henrietta said. "Sheriff . . . "

Brodie pulled away and slapped the top of his legs. "Noooo! Henrietta, please listen!"

"Okay, tell me, Brodie," Henrietta said, signing. "I'm listening."

"You've got to believe me! Miss Julia really does come to me and she tells me what to do. All the time. And I can hear her talking with my own ears."

"Okay, Brodie. I believe you," she signed in silence before asking out loud: "Tell me what Miss Julia said."

Brodie looked at her face, perhaps searching it for ridicule.

Henrietta smiled and touched his hands. "It's okay, Brodie. I'm here."

He nodded and continued with Henrietta translating. "Miss Julia thanked me for hiding all the poison, except for what Dr. Colonel was carrying with him, but said that I should stick around to guard, um, he said me," Henrietta said pointing to herself. "He says that Miss Julia told him to wait in the woods, keep the rifle loaded and watch for Dr. Colonel's return."

"He may be delusional, but at least he was able to help save you, Henrietta," Craig said.

"Shush!" Henrietta scolded Craig, and Brodie smiled. She signed and said: "That's good, Brodie. Thank you."

"Weren't you concerned about Two Feathers coming back, Brodie?" the sheriff asked.

"More scared of dota," Brodie said out loud.

"How did you leave the room?" the sheriff asked.

"I crawled back out the window," Brodie signed with Henrietta speaking for him. "I hid in the woods after borrowing some food and blankets from the hospital," he said. "Don't worry; I plan to pay them back," he added.

"It's okay, Brodie," Craig offered and Brodie sighed with relief.

"What did you do when you realized Dr. Colonel had returned tonight?" the sheriff asked.

"All afternoon I sat on a boulder, where I could see who came and went from the hospital," signed Brodie. "I saw Dr. Colonel come back a little after six o'clock. I also saw that Indian following him." Brodie pointed to Danny.

"That's Danny, Brodie," Henrietta said.

"Danny didn't go back to the hospital. He took off. I was really nervous then because I knew something terrible was about to happen," Brodie signed.

Turning to Danny, the sheriff asked, "Where'd you go after Dr. Colonel returned to the hospital?"

"To gather some men. I figured I would need help to take care of that doctor devil," Danny said. "I'm sorry, Mrs. Clayborn. I didn't know about Jeff yet."

"But Dr. Colonel was about to find out," Craig said. "After learning about Jeff's death at the hospital, I'm guessing he went straight to the doctor's cottage."

"Let's don't put words in his mouth. Brodie should continue his eyewitness account," the sheriff said.

"He's right," Brodie signed. "Dr. Colonel came out of the hospital and headed straight for the doctor's cottage."

"Mrs. Clayborn, now would be a good time to explain what happened from your perspective," the sheriff said.

"I was in the kitchen, making dinner for my family and friends, who were supposed to all come back at about seven. I had told everyone that I needed time alone to think about what we needed to do, which is why I was by myself. But somehow Dr. Colonel got in and started to assault me," Henrietta said. "He wanted vengeance for his son's death, starting with me."

"Why'd Dr. Colonel want to take revenge on you, Henrietta? You clearly had nothing to do with Jeff's death," Craig asked.

Henrietta briefly explained her history with the Clayborn family, how Dr. Colonel blamed her for Jeff's move here and even his death, and his plans for her punishment. She suggested that Dr. Colonel would've succeeded in raping and possibly killing her if Brodie hadn't come when he did. She described the struggle that ensued before Big Eagle, Danny and some of the others came, just in time. "In helping us, they also saved the tribe," she said.

Silence fell on the room.

"Obviously there was another struggle. How did you get shot?" the sheriff inquired, turning toward Big Eagle Feathers.

"I did not see it," the large man said. "Just felt a hot bite that threw me onto my back."

"Dr. Colonel must have had a pistol in his coat pocket, because, out of nowhere, there was a shot," Henrietta explained. "Big Eagle fell. And then . . ."

"I shot the bastard dead!" Brodie shouted out in a startling, crystal-clear voice.

"You certainly did," Henrietta said. "Brodie shot Dr. Colonel with the rifle."

"But, obviously, in self-defense," Craig added.

"Does anyone know where Two Feathers is now?" the sheriff asked, redirecting their attention back to Jeff's real murderer.

"I'll find him," Danny said, heading for the door.

"Just a minute, Danny," Sheriff Andrews said. "You have to stay here and let the legal system handle your brother."

"Sheriff, we can take care of our own," Big Eagle Feathers said. "But it probably doesn't matter. If I know Two Feathers, we'll never see him again in this lifetime."

"That may be, but let's finish here first," the sheriff said.

Danny lumbered back in and sat cross-legged on the floor.

"Do you have any idea why Two Feathers would've wanted to kill Dr. Clayborn?" asked Sheriff Andrews.

Danny looked to the ground, refusing to answer.

"Sheriff, I'm sure Danny won't want to implicate his own brother," Craig said. "But I know firsthand Two Feathers was furious about Jeff wanting to mix conventional medicine with the Medichero's native medicine."

"You knew about that?" Henrietta asked. She was stunned Craig was aware of Jeff's secret obsession. "But weren't you supposed to ... discourage that?"

"Yeah, but Jeff was such a great doctor, his interest in it didn't bother me," Craig said. He shrugged his shoulders. "Of course, my superiors might have thought otherwise."

"Jeff was practicing native medicine?" the sheriff asked.

"Not practicing, researching it, as it relates to spontaneous healings," Henrietta said.

"That explains why Two Feathers might've resented him," the sheriff said. "And I happen to know from personal experience that Two Feathers has an explosive temper, especially when he's been drinking. We've had to throw him into jail several times for drunkenness and disorderly conduct down in Tularosa."

"Knowing Two Feathers is both resentful and volatile, my guess is after he overheard how Dr. Colonel intended to destroy the whole tribe and how Jeff would be the one deciding whether he did or not, he just lost control," Craig said.

"Two Feathers had Jeff all wrong," Henrietta said, addressing Big Eagle Feathers. "Jeff did everything in his power to help your people and save your son." Tears were falling down her cheeks.

The big man nodded. "And what Two Feathers did was wrong. As I said, he'll realize the mistake himself at some point, if not already."

Henrietta felt a strange sort of comfort from Big Eagle's words.

"My men will find Two Feathers," the sheriff said. He stood up, indicating that he was wrapping up the inquest. "Danny, you'll need to come with me. I've got a few more questions for you."

"Ray," Henrietta said. She paused, not really sure what else could be said, but ended with this: "Again, thank you so much for saving us and I'm so sorry for your loss. I'll pray for you."

"We're both sorry for our losses," Big Eagle said. "I'm truly sorry about Jeff."

She patted him gently on the arm, turned and headed to the door with Brodie following her like a shadow. Craig walked over swiftly and took her arm. "Henrietta, if you want, I can speak to Cal for you about, um, Dr. Colonel's remains, which you'll be relieved to know have already been taken to the morgue," Craig said.

"Well, at least I don't have to think any more about that right now, I'm exhausted," Henrietta said. Tears filled her eyes again. "Craig, would you mind walking me and Brodie over to Joe and Altie's place? The kids are there, and we're all going to stay together with them tonight. As you can imagine, we can't go back to the doctor's cottage even with Dr. Colonel no longer there."

The next morning, Craig returned. "Hello, Altie," he said. "I hope you don't mind, but there are some things I need to go over with Mrs. Clayborn." Altie let him in. "Is Joe around?"

"He's in the teepee, if you need him."

"That's okay," Craig said. "I just wondered."

"I'll get Henrietta," Altie said. But she was already walking in from the kitchen, dressed in a bathrobe borrowed from Altie. It was about five inches too short.

"I hate to bother you now or bring this up again, Henrietta," Craig said. "But being that you were the only next of kin to Dr. Colonel, you have to decide what to do with his body. The sheriff asked if I would come talk to you about it."

"I know, but I really don't feel like it yet," Henrietta said. She sighed deeply and clutched her robe tighter around her neck. "I'll try to make myself."

"Actually, and I hope you won't think me too presumptuous, I took the liberty of consulting with Cal and asked him to put a hold on Jeff's body until you decide about Dr. Colonel. Might as well send them back on the same plane, right?"

"Yes, that makes sense," she said. "I should probably go ahead and tell the sheriff to send Dr. Colonel to the Tularosa Funeral Home."

Craig blushed. "Already done. I hope you don't mind."

"Of course not. I appreciate it and the clear thinking on my behalf," Henrietta said. She was genuinely grateful.

Craig smiled with a look of relief. "I'm happy to help you with anything, Henrietta."

She was quiet a moment, listening to the children trying to sing an Apache hymn with Altie in the kitchen, pitifully off-key. "Actually, there is something else you may be able to help me with."

"Name it."

In a low calm voice, Henrietta explained that she'd never been quite sure about the paternity of Jefferson Junior, that Dr. Colonel had succeeded in raping her once before, about the same time as her son's conception.

"Do you think it'd be possible to get blood from me, Jeffie, Jeff and Dr. Colonel, while their bodies are at Cal's, and get a ... some sort of test done?"

"Are you sure you want to know?"

"Not really, but I think it'll be my only chance to find out from a clinical standpoint. And I wouldn't want to get a test like that done in South Carolina." She got up to stare out of the Locos' back window. Hearing the distinctive call of the blue jay, she looked in the direction from which it came, surprised to see not just one but four, maybe five, blue jays hopping around on the branches of an adjacent pine tree.

"From what I understand, all they can do is rule out someone as the father," Craig said. "So I'm not sure about cases involving a father and son. But, I'll see what can be done, if anything."

"Thanks," she said, turning to face him. "I'd really appreciate that." She returned her gaze to the jays in the tree, only to see a flurry of sapphire flapping away. "I hope you don't think me rude, but I just remembered something I need to do."

"Do you need help moving back to the doctor's cottage?"

"Thanks, but no." She went on to explain that because the Locos had offered, she'd decided to move her family in with them for two reasons. She had adopted a Medichero philosophy that suggested a dwelling should be vacated after a death, especially a violent one. She also was worried about the whereabouts of Victor Two Feathers, but knew that Joe and Altie would keep them safe until she could finalize everything that needed to be done before going back to South Carolina.

"So what else do you need to do?" Craig asked.

She looked again at where the blue jays had gathered. "I need to see Joe about something. But it's kind of a long strange story about why."

"No need to explain. Call me if you need me."

Chapter 41

Fifteen minutes later, Henrietta was sitting cross-legged in Joe's teepee. She had changed into her dungarees and a plaid shirt. "I've been thinking about the blue jay and how you said its power relates to both me and little Jeffie," Henrietta said. "There were lots of them in your yard this morning. Maybe they've been around before. It could be I'm just noticing them now."

"What a lovely coincidence," Joe said. There was a touch of humor on his lips.

"Could you tell me more?"

"The blue jay symbolizes the ability to link our minds to the heavens to give us greater power on Earth. If the blue jay shows up in your life, you should be aware that something extraordinary is about to happen."

"Joe, no offense, but I don't think I could take much more," Henrietta said. She sighed.

"Sweet karma, there's no need to worry," Joe said. He smiled broadly. "This is a good sign for you, Henrietta. The blue jay reflects the mastering of your own state of mind through the power that comes from your inner connection to the Great Spirit."

"Okay."

"But as I said before, the jay also serves as a warning. We must remember that the jay doesn't care if you choose to accept or reject the laws of the Great Spirit. He doesn't care if you choose life or death. He'll help facilitate your thoughts so they can fly in the direction of your choice. In this respect, the jay is like the creative power found within, in our subconscious minds."

It was a great abstraction, but Henrietta sensed that it could somehow apply directly to her life. She intended to find out how. She wanted to understand. "Go on."

"Whatever you hold, give or allow into your conscious mind as well as the rich depths of your subconscious mind, good or false, that is what you will bring into your physical world. This is the final lesson of the blue jay; he's here to remind us of this universal law."

"Which is?"

"Our thoughts and beliefs create what we experience, as I've said many times before. So isn't it better to focus on the positive things we want instead of fear or what we don't want?"

"Yes, of course," she said. Her voice was a whisper, for in that breathless moment, she thought back to her final confrontation with Dr. Colonel, just before Brodie and the Indians saved her. Was it her absolute surrender to peaceful thoughts and unconditional love that had really saved her, that had attracted the rescue? She smiled at Joe. *Think about what I want. It seems so simple.*

Joe raised his eyebrows as if asking what else she wanted to know.

But she wasn't quite ready to ask Joe those questions, sensing the answers would come from further pondering and introspection. So instead, she asked: "What do you think I should do with Dr. Colonel's body? I hesitate to bury him on the land back home for fear of contaminating the orchards."

Joe chuckled, taking her statement as a joke, even though she'd been halfway serious.

"Your concerns are groundless," he said. "Although Spirit might offer some practicality. Seek answers within, and you will know for yourself the right action to take."

"Can we do that together? And compare notes?"

Bears Repeating nodded as he began to sing in his native language and shake a bear-claw rattle. Henrietta closed her eyes, concentrating on her heart and praying silently.

After a few minutes, Joe became still just before exclaiming: "Thank you, Great Spirit, oh mighty I AM THAT I AM, many, many thanks." Joe opened his eyes and smiled at Henrietta.

"Well, what did Spirit say to you?" she asked.

"Nothing."

"Nothing?"

"Nothing," said Bears Repeating.

"I don't understand."

"Bear said that you'd know what to do with nothing."

"How would I know that?"

"Henrietta, if I were to give you all of the answers all of the time, you wouldn't learn the lesson of flying solo. Even though I'm happy to journey for you now, while you're on the mend, my help must, out of necessity, be temporary. We're all meant to learn the inner science for ourselves," he said.

"Don't get me wrong. I'm grateful for all that you've done to help me," she said, smiling. "But, honestly, what am I supposed to do with nothing?" She motioned with her hands.

"Listen to your inner guidance, and let the Great Spirit fill you in."

"Believe it or not, as you shook your rattle, I was trying to do just that," she said. "Maybe I did get my answer."

"Ah, very good."

"I was thinking the kids and I are the only ones left of the Clayborn family, which means we're the ones inheriting the power that goes with being the legitimate owners of the Clayborns' massive peach business. That got me thinking about what you said about the blue jays' power."

"Ah, very good," he repeated.

"We should use our peach power and financial resources to help others heal by continuing to fund the orphanage and helping you to build your healing center. Do you think that's what the basket of fruit meant in my last soul retrieval?" Henrietta said, talking fast. "Anyway, it also started to dawn on me ... we can use the jays' power to have Dr. Colonel's remains cremated and scattered over the White Sands Desert down there," she said, pointing down the mountain.

"There's an interesting idea."

"I actually heard Dr. Colonel say once that when he was at the Alamogordo army base thirty or so years ago, he'd been fascinated by that pure white sand phenomenon down there in the Tularosa Basin."

"Dr. Colonel was here about thirty years ago, huh?" Joe asked. He looked down as if thinking what that meant.

"Yes, so I think it's a fitting place for him, don't you? The sandy ashes of his remains will appear as *nothing* out there, and maybe they'll even be cleansed in the pure white heat of the desert."

"Bear was on the mark once again: you knew exactly what to do with nothing," Joe said.

Epilogue

"Mama, isn't Mr. Craig supposed to be coming here for a visit today?" Frannie asked. She was gulping down a glass of sweet tea Henrietta had placed on their picnic blanket.

"Yes, ma'am. Good memory," her mother said. She put down the notebook in which she was writing.

"I think he'll be surprised it's so hot here in Greenfield," said Frannie. Her red face glistened with sweat in the bright sunlight. "Being that he's used to a cold November in the Sacramento Mountains."

"I'm sure you're right. It's nearly ninety degrees today," Henrietta said.

"When's he going to get here?"

"I sent Cook to the Columbia Airport to fetch him a couple of hours ago. So they should be here any time now."

"Do you think he'll be able to find us way out here next to the horse pasture?" Frannie asked. "Hey, I think my Bridget's reins are coming loose."

"I'm sure Regina will show him where we are," Henrietta said. But Frannie was already running back to the pony she had sloppily tied to the gate.

Smiling, Henrietta resumed recording some of her thoughts in a notebook.

And the young woman truly felt a sense of wholeness in her heart and soul for the first time in a long while. "Wow, I feel so much better," she said. Tears of relief flowed from her eyes. "Thank you for healing me."

"It's the Great Spirit within you that did the healing," said Bears Repeating. "And it's been there all along."

"Yes. I used to think healing from trauma like mine was impossible. Now I know souls can be mended and healed. I know more than before."

"You have learned well, my friend. It's good to learn and feel good. Don't ever stop," he said. Turning, the medicine man limped toward a thatched cottage in step with the beat of a drum floating on air perfumed with the sweetness of peach cobbler and the piquancy of medicinal herbs simmering over the glowing embers of a medicine woman's campfire.

Henrietta smiled as she waved to Frannie and Annie who were riding their brindle ponies in a figure-eight pattern. After they waved back, she placed her pencil back down on the paper and simply wrote *The End* before closing the notebook, which contained an outline and first-draft promise of a story longing to be told.

Though she was an accidental correspondent, she intended to write about the wonders and secrets she'd witnessed, even while knowing many people would find them strange and offensive. She was like Jeff in that. But she'd learned that one man's heresy could be another man's search for divine truth. There was no shame in searching for God's truth.

She looked up again toward the girls before glancing over at her little JJ, the name she now called her son. JJ was amusing himself in a sandbox, built by his sweet grandfather, Hampton. Her parents were temporarily residing in the mansion while she arranged for construction of a new cabin for them. She had been thrilled that her father wanted to come back as general manager of the orchards, and happy that he wouldn't have to fire Jenks, who was already gone when they'd returned. No one had seen or heard from him for months now, and that suited Henrietta just fine. Brodie never moved out, and at Henrietta's urging, he was enrolled in Augusta College while working part-time with her mother at the Clayborn Orphanage & School for the Deaf and Blind.

All at once, she felt a reverence for her loving family and friends, the ordinary pleasures of life, of just being herself with her children and watching them at play. Though she'd suffered great loss, she also had experienced the extraordinary and gained something in wisdom and inner strength, indomitable gifts that could never be taken away. Her soul was riding high and without the reins of Bears Repeating, so she breathed a silent prayer of thanks for his and Altie's examples.

"Hello, Henrietta!" Craig called out, interrupting her thoughts as he strode across the field with Regina who went over to keep an eye on JJ.

"About time you got here," Henrietta said. She stood up and greeted Craig.

"Henrietta, you look beautiful. I trust you've been getting better and feeling good?" he said, holding her at arm's length.

"Thanks. By God's grace, I believe we're all mending. It's great to see you."

"Hey there," Craig called out in the direction of the girls, waving to JJ who didn't glance up from his sand project. Seeing the children occupied, Craig lowered his voice to a whisper. "Henrietta, I know you're anxious to hear this, and I want to tell you straightaway before the kids come over."

"What?"

"I've got it," he said. He pulled out an envelope from his pocket and handed it to her.

"What's this?"

"The results from the paternity test. I was able to get the medical examiner to get them done; he owed me a favor."

She opened the envelope and looked at the papers.

"He's Jeff's," Craig blurted out before she could comprehend the data. "Or at least, the test was able to exclude Dr. Colonel as a possible father after all. That's all you wanted to know anyway, right?"

"Thanks, it's a tremendous relief," Henrietta said. "But you want to know something really strange? Truly, I already knew."

"What? But how? I thought … "

"Bears Repeating might be unorthodox, but he's usually right," she said. "Joe said Spirit told him that, but you've just confirmed it."

"Wow, I'm happy for you. I'm sure you're relieved," Craig said. "And honestly, come on, aren't you glad to know, from a solid scientific perspective?"

"Yeah, I am. Thanks, Craig." She smiled and squeezed his arm, tucking the results into her pocket.

"Speaking of Joe, I decided to go with your hunch about Dr. Colonel being the anonymous *National Geographic* photographer who had passed through Medichero on his way to the White Sands area thirty years ago. Funny, but Joe didn't seem to be surprised by your theory and freely gave his blood for testing."

"Everything about Joe is funny," Henrietta said, chuckling.

"Well, I think Joe's paternity test results are shocking. According to these tests, Dr. Colonel could not be ruled out, which means, for all intents and purposes, Dr. Colonel is Joe's biological father. It's hard to believe."

"I knew it," Henrietta said. "My inner voice was right!"

"No wonder Jeff and Joe seemed so much like brothers," Craig said.

"They were true blood brothers," she added.

"Joe said almost exactly the same thing just before he told me to tell you something rather cryptic, even for Bears Repeating," Craig said.

"What's that?"

"Joe said to tell you, and I quote, 'nothing' ... whatever that means."

"Believe it or not, nothing actually makes a funny kind of sense." She laughed again before turning serious. "Did they ever catch Two Feathers? I haven't heard anything yet."

"Yeah, they finally found him. Or I should say that Danny found him, up in the mountains. But he was dead. He'd shot himself in the head."

"Oh, dear. I don't know what to say about that," she said. She felt both relief and sadness. "But, I guess there's some closure in that, too."

"Were you able to find out the cause of your mother-in-law's death?" Craig asked. His voice was sympathetic.

"I had Julia's body exhumed and autopsied. And it was just as I suspected." She bit her lips.

"Dr. Colonel murdered her?"

"She had traces of cyanide in her system, but I'm not sure. It's possible he was just using it to manipulate her bouts of illness for the purpose of controlling Jeff. I think it might have been an accident."

"That's pretty charitable of you. Why do you say that?"

"The man may have been a psychopath and his tactics were frightening to say the least, but in his own demented way, I think he truly loved Miss Julia. In a lot of respects, they had a good marriage; they were happy together," Henrietta said.

"I think you're the one who deserves to be happy, Henrietta," Craig said. He gently touched her arm.

"Thanks, Craig. Hey, let's talk about something else, like what we'll do while you're here on vacation," she said. She was determined not to become emotional.

"Okay, I'm game."

"I want to show you the Clayborn mansion and our lands. We have a really full house right now, but we also have a nice private guest room made up for you. Oh, and I want you to taste the best peaches in the world. Of course, the girls want to show you the Clayborn Orphanage & School."

"I'm honored that you want to share it all with me." He picked up her hand and kissed it. "I hope you'll return the favor and come visit me in Medichero someday."

"Of course we'll visit," she said. She let him hold her hand. "We need to visit you, Altie and Joe, and the healing center as it's developed. I'm sure we'll have many adventures there. And Bears Repeating is, um, an ongoing study."

"Is there any chance your visits might turn into something more permanent?"

At that moment, a blue jay flew by, landed on a peach tree limb, and called out with its familiar, one-syllable power song.

She had to smile. "Craig, we'll always be a part of Medichero, and since my healings there, I believe our spiritual lives are intimately connected with our native friends, Jeff's half-brother and that sacred place they live in. I know we'll visit often. Journeying there will help remind me that I'm whole and connected to something bigger than myself. I need to do that. It'll be like a ritual that'll help sustain me while I learn to live in this world without Jeff.

"But what about ... I mean, is there any chance for you and me?" All at once, his light eyes were both expectant and puppy-like.

"Craig, I hope you and I will always be the good friends we've become. And who knows? Maybe one day, we might even be more than that. All I know is ... this is where my children belong right now, which means this is where I belong right now." She gestured with her hands to the panorama that surrounded them.

"I understand, Henrietta," he said, his puppy face now pitiful looking.

"But, Craig, I'm so grateful to you for all you've done for me. For your friendship. Getting the tests done. And your visit. All of it means so much to me."

"It's my pleasure."

"Well, it's my pleasure to show you our peach business and the orphanage," she said, trying to remain light. "As you tour it, you'll learn we employ up to a hundred temporary workers during the year for the production and harvest of more than thirty peach varieties. My daddy could probably use someone with your superb management skills. Know anyone like that who might be interested in being assistant general manager of orchard floor management?"

Craig blushed as his huge dimples caused the surface of his cheeks to nearly disappear. "Well, I might know someone," he said, extending his forearm to her.

"Why don't we get started on your tour?" She patted her growing tummy, expectant with a new baby, and took Craig's offered arm. They turned and walked on a path toward a home imbued with enough beauty, character and power to transcend the fragmented disguise of one of its own inhabitants. And in that slow travel, Henrietta held in her mended soul the hope of a destiny being fulfilled, the covenant of an ongoing spiritual journey within and the sweet anticipation of telling secrets: the secrets of Bears Repeating.

The End

Acknowledgements

To create and launch something as massive and ambitious as a 400+ page novel, it takes an incredible team of loving and supporting people. And I'm so in love with and grateful for mine. First and foremost, I want to thank my husband, Paul Jarvie, for believing in me as a writer and for giving me the opportunity and freedom to pursue my writing dreams. I also want to thank my sons, Dane and Luke, just for being the beautiful, brilliant, loving and creative guys you are and for enriching my life like no other.

Waves of appreciation go to my editor, Rita Robinson, a terrific writer and the author of many books, including *Exploring Native American Wisdom*. Rita, thank you for sharing your editing wisdom and excellence with me. I also had the best beta readers, and I raise my glass to toast and thank these smart, articulate women (listed in alphabetical order): Allison Contris, Leigh W. Everett, Genevieve Hogan, Connie Jarvie, Susan Jarvie and Margaret McKibben Key. I'm so grateful for your constructive feedback and encouragement on this sometimes arduous writing journey; your perspectives helped me make the novel better and I love you all. Maureen Pasley, you are a great designer, and I give you kudos for really nailing the character illustrations as well as the cover design, which I absolutely love. I also want to acknowledge my writing friend, Barbara Claypole White, author of *The Unfinished Garden* and *In-Between Hour*. Barbara, thank you for your friendship, counsel, inspiration and for giving me an authentic glimpse into the published world. And last but not least, I want to thank my brilliant copyeditor, Madeline Hopkins. Madeline, your keen insights, eagle eyes and copyediting skill have given my novel the professional polish it needed to shine brighter. And I thank you with all of my heart!

I'm a lucky child of great parents, Jack and Jerrie Weibel, who planted the seed in me that I could do anything if I put my mind to it and believed it. They are in Spirit now, but I continue to feel their love and support. I'm so thankful for them as well as my grandmother Henrietta, who inspired this fictional adventure and my love for Native Americans.

And finally, I thank YOU for reading *The Soul Retrieval.* My wish and prayer is that you have been entertained and found something useful and inspiring within ... yourself.

Interview with the Author

Ann W. Jarvie

In a nutshell, what is your novel about?

The Soul Retrieval is a suspenseful novel of love, loss and healing centering on a traumatized southern woman, her spiritual journey, the Native American mystic who guides her, and the murder mystery that ultimately threatens to unravel her.

What was the inspiration for this novel?

My maternal grandmother, Henrietta, inspired the story. She lived on the Mescalero Indian Reservation with her physician husband until he mysteriously died there in 1919. I am a product of my grandmother's second marriage, so by the time I became interested in this family mystery, most of those involved had already passed away. My mother was able to tell me a few stories about her mother's positive relationships with Native Americans, but no one could answer the questions I had about her first husband's mysterious and premature death. So I decided to make up a story about it. *The Soul Retrieval* is the result.

How closely does this novel parallel your grandmother's real-life story?

The only things the real and fictional Henriettas share are their first names, physician husbands working on Indian reservations in the Southwest, and the Victorian-style doctor's cottages they both shared with their husbands and children while on the reservations. Most everything else about Henrietta Clayborn's life and all of the other characters and events in the novel are pure fiction, including all of her family members and the towns of Medichero, New Mexico, and Greenfield, South Carolina, where the story takes place.

Why did you choose to set the novel in the 1950s?

I chose an era when both Native Americans and women were seriously limited by the social norms of the day; I wanted it to be at a time that enabled me to believe the Native Americans were still practicing their spirit medicine, but in secret. I also wanted my main Apache character, Joe Loco, to be not only spiritually wise, but also amusing and quirky with an Elvis fetish and a '50s fashion-forward sense of style—just for fun. In addition, it was a time in the U.S. when women were greatly limited by society's expectations and therefore far more powerless than they are today. And it is this transition, from feeling powerless to being self-empowered, that I wanted to address as one of the novel's main themes. Henrietta's spiritual journey is about healing from trauma by overcoming her sense of powerlessness and her fears of the so-called forbidden in order to find the "Kingdom of God within."

What is your background?

I have a B.A. in journalism and more than twenty-five years' experience as an award-winning writer in advertising and public relations agencies, both in South Carolina and Chicago. I now live near Phoenix, Arizona, where I spend part of my time as a freelance copywriter and the rest writing fiction.

Your novel contains spiritual insights and mystical secrets. How did this come about?

I grew up in South Carolina and was raised in a traditional Christian culture. But I have always been intensely curious about and drawn to spiritual subjects and ancient mystical secrets outside of those conventions. I consider myself a truth seeker, which may sound ironic since I am a fiction writer. Even so, I enjoy doing research and asking questions (which may be why getting a journalism degree appealed to me in the first place). At the same time, I have always believed there's an answer for everything, even if I haven't found it yet.

As a child, I asked my mother endless questions about religious teachings and practically drove her crazy with it all. My curiosity was only sated when I started finding answers that resonated with truth through what some might consider unconventional spiritual paths, including Ascended Masters' teachings, ancient wisdom teachings, Native American spirituality and the Law of Attraction. I began to see how the teachings of Christ were in alignment with some of these other "religions" and schools of thought. This insight was inspirational to me. The more I learned and resonated with, the more I wanted to incorporate into my novel.

Your novel presents Apaches accurately and respectfully. What kind of research was involved in writing it?

I very much wanted to present the Apache characters in my novel with as much authenticity as I could because I respect, honor and value all Native Americans, their culture and their inherent goodness and spirituality. I spent years researching the Apache culture and the Mescalero Indian Reservation in particular. On a visit with my mother, we actually found the doctor's cottage—an unexpectedly large Victorian-style house—

where my grandmother, her husband and her children lived while he served as a physician for the U.S. Department of the Interior in 1919. The timing was fortuitous, because the doctor's cottage was torn down the year following our visit.

Who are your favorite authors?

My favorite author of all time is Pat Conroy: *The Prince of Tides* is beyond brilliant. It's one of those rare jewels that never fails to inspire me as a storyteller and lover of words. I've probably read it a dozen times. There are too many other authors to name here, but a few who have positively influenced and inspired me (in no particular order) are Daphne du Maurier, Charles Dickens, Anne Rivers Siddons, Kurt Vonnegut, Paulo Coelho, Stephen King, Patricia Cornwell, Michael Connelly, Anita Diamant, Dan Brown, Barbara Taylor Bradford, Thomas Wolfe … I could go on.

Are you working on other novels?

Yes, I'm currently working on the next adventure of Henrietta, which also explores the secrets of Bears Repeating. Stay tuned.

www.annwjarvie.com

Made in the USA
Lexington, KY
01 April 2015